THE GREAT SPHINX

OF AMUN-RA

Herbert L. Smith

Contents

FOREWORD

The Great Sphinx Of Amun-Ra is a novel based in infinite history; a collection of stories that are tied together by compelling forces, stretching from circa 5500 B C to the present day; a panoply of 7500 years. Inter-connected through various themes, the stories gradually unfold to create a cohesive whole. The Egyptian creator-god, Amun-Ra, and his remarkable staff (which might be called magical in another setting) are two primary elements which make the novel a fantasy, but there are no virulently evil bogeymen or other powers that threaten humans, although these were sometimes invented by priests or pharaohs to provide explanations for evils that were done. Malicious people were the source of disputes and difficulties in each conflicting situation.

The Great Sphinx, often called by its ancient name, Hor-em-akhet, the Giza pyramids, the Nile River, and the Sahara desert are brought into the chronicle and are a constant presence, providing man-made and natural wonders. There are wars and intrigues that follow the timeline of history, and there is always a parade of fictional characters as well as pharaohs and kings who are well known from the past.

Spirituality is a major component of the novel. How could it be otherwise? The people of the Nile Valley have consistently maintained fundamental religions, and their belief in "the god," as they refer to Allah (or the gods of the ancients), has always ordered their lives. No story of any part of Egyptian history could be accurate or complete without an understanding of how important religion was and is.

These narratives and the chronological order in which they appear are especially intended for readers who want to take an intimate look at ancient times - the allure of the earliest Egyptian social order - and for those who appreciate a thoughtful, well-constructed storyline that offers entertainment and fascination for people who are interested in travel, history, spirituality, Egyptology, or archaeological anthropology.

Herbert L. Smith

Eugene, Oregon, April, 2012

PROLOGUE

The creation act of Amun-Ra runs profoundly throughout the history of ancient Kmet, which eventually became known as Egypt to the wider world. His story is similar to other early accounts of creator-gods from diverse cultures and nations, but it is also dissimilar, and the distinctions make Amun-Ra's encounters unique. In the Kmetian story the creator-god stood upon an island in the midst of the stars and called forth all the world as it was known to the ancients. He first made the land, the light, and the water, but the next thing he made was a tree, a thing of noble beauty and harmony, with strong branches of dark wood that glowed in the new light of the new day. Soft green leaves hung suspended from its branches, translucent in the light, and he was delighted with the tree and the water that flowed around the island where he placed it.

Amun-Ra gazed and pondered for a time, then gently pulled a single, slender branch from the mother-tree, cleaned it of leaves and its soft bark with his hands, and wrote words upon it with his finger, starting from the top down to the handclasp he indented at its center. The words could not be understood except by the god himself, for he wrote in his own language: 'Felm Ketirah Heb'i' - 'It Will Be Forever.'

He did not mean the branch, which became a staff, nor did he mean the tree. He did not mean the creation of the water, or the land, or the light, or even the living creatures; he meant his labor in the creation of all things, and he himself, his own presence, was the foremost part of his signification. His work would never cease, although it might be changed in some way through the ages, warped by misuse, or even considered inconsequential, but it would always be looked upon by countless millions of humankind, regardless of their understanding or belief. It would be the continuous thread that held everything together, the never-ending Life of all things, whether they were considered animate or inanimate. He would always be there to watch it change and grow and to tend it, as he had the tree, and it would forever prosper in the place where he set it.

Chapter One

Circa 5500 B C

Gan was small, but wiry and strong for his age. His warm brown skin was colored with a reddish glow, the product of recent hours under the full brilliance of Ahm, as his tribe called the sun god. He waited, calm on the outside but bursting within, for the last words of the rules to be spoken, the words that would send him out into the Bab. He had heard the words before, when other boys stood in his place at dawn as the whole village gathered around to see them off. Only this time the words were for him. He stood, looking small and humble, with his father and the elders near a watchfire on the rising side of the mud and stone wall that surrounded their village. The empty lands stretched far away from the tiny thorp; the Bab was a desert with steep, rocky hills that were covered with tawny sand the color of a lion. It surrounded them as far as anyone could imagine. But there was a small bluish-green lake in their valley, which made it possible for human habitation to exist at Nomo.

Palm trees grew near the lake, widely scattered across the sand and parts of the swamp land that lay close to the deeper water. The trees bore wonderful sweet-crisp dates that the tribe liked to eat, giving them energy and strength for life in the hot, deserted lands. There were also crops; rows of grain in short strips near the water, planted and cultivated by the women and children. The grain produced the flour that they used to make whole meal bread. And there were fish in the water and small animals and birds that darted along the ground or through the air, and *kadg* - crocodiles - who lived in the swamp and the lake, creating an ever present danger, but also proving useful at times. Life was a balance; there was just enough plant and animal life to sustain the village, but in some years when something upset that balance, circumstances were difficult. The clan stored as much as they could of everything - it was their key to survival.

Max, the chief elder, a short and somewhat stout little man whose hairless head glowed in the morning light, was dressed in the skin of a leopard he had killed many years before. He intoned the rules. "You are to walk across the Bab to the Great Hill, gather as much *bik* as you can carry, and bring it to us. You will be followed by three men, and they will observe your going and returning so that we will all know where you found the stones. They will remain at a distance and will not help you in your task, but will rescue you if you can't complete the work."

Those words stung. At eleven full seasons, Gan was the youngest boy anyone knew to become a man through the ritual trials, and he knew that many of the watching tribe thought he was incapable of completing the task. It was a long way to the Great Hill of Bik, the stones of glass later to be called obsidian, and it would be very hot. He had little food, but was allowed to carry all the water he needed, and would walk for the entire time it took Ahm to travel across the sky-way. Then he would complete his return after the dark had covered the land in its shroud. No one was allowed outside during the dark time except for unusual circumstances like the test,

1

and it was dangerous to be out even in the full light of Ahm. The tribe believed there were evil specters in the Bab who could tear Gan's spirit from his body if he walked alone.

Bik was used every day in the village. It was chiseled and used for spear points to kill the varied creatures of the oasis for food, and to cut the skins from the bodies of the small beasts the hunters brought home. It was used in the working of skins into garments and bags and warm coverings for the cold time, as well as to chop and grind the roots and grains the tribe ate. Bik was an important tool, but the problem was that it often splintered or gradually wore away completely, so there was constant need of a new supply.

Gan had already completed two trials. The first was the killing of a kadg, one of the group that inhabited the pond, and bringing its body back to the outer wall so the elders could measure it. He selected one that was smaller, according to his own size, and had done the job with quick dispatch, using a small but lethal bik knife. The tribe was impressed. His second task was much harder; offering himself to Ahm in a ritual that would have taken his life had the great god accepted him. He went into the Bab very near the village as three observers watched, and placed his naked body on the sand while Ahm passed over him, ever so slowly. He was to lie there, still and apparently calm, until the elders came out to say that it was time enough. He had fallen into a nearly unconscious state and his skin was afire with the flames of Ahm when he was released and brought back to the village where he sat in a vat of water for several hours. For days after that he felt sick and was troubled and stayed out of the brightness of Ahm, but eventually recovered enough to go on with the trials. There had been boys who were received by Ahm during their hours of trial in his full light and strength, who were now walking in the sky-fields above the oasis. But Ahm did not choose to take him; had denied him the honor of an early passage into the beyond. Gan was secretly pleased that he had not been given that honor.

The boy wore a simple kilt of animal skins that was held together with strong leather strips, and his rich mahogany skin was now almost impervious to the heat of Ahm unless he was exposed for many hours without water. He wore no head covering, but his short, crimped hair was thick and added an element of protection from the intensity of Ahm's gaze.

Everything was ready, but the elders waited. Set, the tribal shaman, had not yet completed his morning circuit of the village, and no official business could be conducted until that was done. At last Set approached, said the closing prayers, and placed an amulet of glinting bik in Gan's hand. It lay there, smooth and radiant in the early morning light. Then Max and the elders released him and he walked through the open gate into the Bab.

The walk was not unpleasant in the early part of the day; Gan felt free and daring as he climbed the hills of the Bab. He kept the Great Hill, which rose higher than the others, straight ahead, and walked at a steady pace. He had no fear. Ahm was above, watching out for him, and would intimidate any evil spirits. Trouble, if it came, would be in the dark when Ahm was resting at his home. The greatness of the Bab surrounded the boy. It was a beautiful place, and he looked across it in wonder as he walked. The colors and the light were always extraordinary, but on this day they gleamed with special significance. He had been included in the group of explorers, the young men who would travel to find the Great Water that lay far beyond Nomo, although he was a year short of the usual time when a boy became a man. His inclusion brought the number of explorers to two-hands, as they referred to ten, a lucky number according to the shaman and the elders. If he failed, there would be no one who could take his place, and the young men would have to travel with one-and-a-split hands. That was not lucky, and he knew that the success of the entire venture might depend on what he could do that day and night as he walked alone. Cautiously, he glanced backward to see where the observers were, but there was a long hill of sand he had come over, and his friends were hidden somewhere beyond it. He felt very alone, as was the intention of this task. He needed to be able to accomplish difficult things without support, surrounded by loneliness and fear, alone in the Bab as he would always be in life. "Everyone lives alone and dies alone," was a saying of the tribe, and he believed it.

After many hours spent gathering bik; after stars and a thin crescent moon lighted the hills and valleys, Gan moved quickly toward home, following the star-path to Nomo that he had learned in his earliest years as a safeguard for this very moment. At times he ran along the path for the sheer exuberance of the joy he felt. He was nearly done! His place was secure - almost. Shreds of doubt hung on the edges of his mind, but he cleared them away as soon as they began and watched the shadows of the land without fear. He was a conqueror!

During the final and darkest hour of the night, after the moon had gone, he came to Nomo. The waterside watchfire was burning cheerfully as he approached, but the watcher only nodded slightly as Gan passed through the gate. Gan didn't speak to him. Watchers were not to be disturbed for anything less than an emergency during their hours of duty. The boy, now a man, sat on the ground and waited, sipping from his waterskin. He had to wait for a long time before he saw the observers approaching just as the eastern sky was lighting with the coming of Ahm, and he moved quickly away toward his own hut to sleep for a short time before the village was called together to witness the manhood ceremony that was now his due. He felt a little smug as he thought of the naysayers who hadn't believed in him, but he was happy, and he resolved to live up to his new status as well as he could over the days and years that stretched ahead.

The men of the tribe of Nomo all carried spears of various size and appearance; whatever kind suited individual arms and throwing styles. Some of the explorers carried an additional spear on this trip, in the event that one was lost or broken, but each guarded his own hand-crafted weapon carefully. His life and that of the others could depend upon it. They also carried a leather bag suspended from one shoulder that contained a waterskin, a small supply of dates to be eaten one each day, an ever-dwindling measure of flour that started out as enough to make bread for five hands, or twenty-five Ahms, from the grain the women ground at the oasis, and a little salt. The only other thing in the bag was a bit of carefully wrapped fat rendered from the animals the hunters killed. It was added a little at a time to the bread meal. That was all.

The ten explorers walked for several days across the stark and empty hills of sand and rock of the Bab that flowed all around them and had been their only world all their lives, as well as the lives of their father's fathers for unknown generations. Not one of the walkers had been anywhere or seen anything else, but had lived in their remote oasis by the rhythm of the Bab, Ahm shining down on them endlessly. The daily presence of his heat and light were the only realm they had ever known. The elders told them that the Great Water lay somewhere toward the place where Ahm rose each morning, and by moving steadily in that direction, the elders said they would one day find the huge waterway that many in the village thought only a fable and a false hope. Two of the elders, very old and too feeble for the journey, said they had seen the Great Water in their youth, and they revered it almost as much as they honored Ahm, as the source of all life.

There was a strong resemblance among all the explorers. Mur, their captain, was the tallest at about five feet and three fingers. All the others measured two to four fingers less. They were dark skinned with bright black eyes and shiny hair, muscular and intelligent, and capable of good humor or serious thinking as the need required. They all loved good times and idle talk, but their current business was serious, and their current situation a struggle between life and death. They had no real idea as to where they were going, but they went anyway, for the survival of their tribe and life as they knew it. They were true adventurers.

The Bab was a place of wonder and beauty, although it did not seem so to the young men who walked across it on that journey. From a distance everything looked brownish-yellow with sand covering the monochromatic rocks and hills, but on a closer view there were staggering differences that a discerning eye could distinguish. Some of the sand was almost silver; the rocks held various colors that could be seen in the bright light of the fullness of Ahm, and many sparkled with minerals. There were deep valleys and tall hills of gravelly sand that surrounded them, and many of the valleys still held water near the surface, although it wasn't evident with a hasty look. The scent of water was often present, tantalizing the thirsty walkers who could see no indication of its presence. They didn't know they had only to dig into the valley floor a few feet to find it. At other places there were lakes or ponds that formed an oasis, although many had dried completely on the surface, and there were far fewer than had been there even fifty years before. The oases were green and bright with reeds and other plants and flowers, lying amidst the domes of sand that threatened to swallow them up. Animals lived there too, just as in Nomo. There were plentiful birds and small creatures of many kinds, and an occasional family of crocodiles was still existent along the shores of the larger lakes.

The Bab was rapidly expanding as well, growing southward into the continent, filling some good and arable lands with sand as it moved. It would finally cover more than half again the land it had in the past, reaching the plains of Africa that were the northern boundaries of tropical jungles no one in the great Bab could even imagine. These wet and fruitful lands survived only in the center of the continent.

The enormous Bab lay across the northern end of the entire east-to-west span of Africa, although no one who lived there knew that fact, either. The Bab was simply home, and the clan of Nomo all supposed that it was the whole world because it was the only one they knew. They had no way of comprehending the size and scope of an entire planet that was ever-changing but always seeming to remain the same. The Bab, later to become known as the great Sahara Desert, had just completed a time when it had been a massive semi-arid savannah, filled with grass and trees and lakes and the life, including human habitation, which accompanied such a terrain. That period had been relatively short in its long history. It had been a desert about three and a half thousand years before, and was in the final steps of returning to its dry condition. Where there had been gentle rainfall and enough water for rudimentary cultivation there was now only deep, dry, shifting sand that stung the eyes when the wind came up, and was unforgiving to anyone who dared to travel into it during the heat of the day.

The walkers went into the Bab seeking a new home for their tribe. The two men who had once been across the Bab toward the rising had gone there in their youth, during a time when the climate was slightly more favorable for travel. They had seen the Great Water, the magnificent Nile River as it came to be called, with their own eyes.

"Ah, yes, you'll come right up to it if you keep going toward Ahm's rising. You can't miss it," Fut, an old man with thin white hair and shaky hands said. "We saw it, way back then, didn't we, Ram?"

"It's there, all right. Just like he said. You'll get there if you're lucky," the other man responded. "But don't go beyond the Water, even if you can find a way. You could make Ahm angry and he might not come to us anymore. Go carefully."

Ahm was walking high overhead, flaming fiercely on the group of young men as they worked their way slowly across the gritty sand, traveling from one oasis to another, if an oasis could be found, setting up a camp that was as much as possible like the circular village of Nomo they had left, and always straining to look toward Ahm's rising place in the hope of finding the elusive waterway they pursued. But as the days passed and they had little to eat or drink, they faltered. On the fifth night out from Nomo the three appointed leaders of the group held a formal discussion that followed all the tribal rules for decision making. Each of the three stated his own case, and then their head elder, Mur, would make a final judgment and decision.

"They told us it was only four or five days," Eno stated simply. "I don't think they gave us the right directions. We should probably be going toward the top or the bottom of the Bab."

"They seemed to know what they were saying," Mur replied. "And both men said the same thing."

"We haven't seen any water but those little ponds yet," Eno continued. "If they were right about the direction they must have forgotten the number of Ahms it took to get there."

"And everything seems to be getting drier. Not like we're anywhere near water. Nobody has even gotten a smell of it for the last couple of days." Ket added in a doleful voice. "They must have been wrong."

"What can we do now?" Mur asked them. "If we go another way we'll get lost and could die out here. We have a better chance if we go on toward Ahm's rising."

Despite the fear of dehydration and death, the leaders all decided to continue trusting the information and instructions the elders had given them and move on toward the rising place. Mur was spared the necessity of a decision.

The nights were fearful for some, due to the possibility that evil spirits could come upon them, alone and far from home, but for most of the explorers the dark took on a new enchantment. The stars, which also glowed above Nomo, seemed brighter and nearer than they had ever known, and the deep dark of the sky was filled with their fiery twinkling. It was a thing of such beauty that Gan found it difficult to sleep at first, but after a few nights his increasingly tired body needed rest, so he dropped off into sleep as soon as he lay down on the soft and compliant sand. The Bab became much cooler at night, and everyone was soon covering with the sand to keep warm.

The long, hot Ahms stretched out. They hadn't found an oasis for three nights after the elders' decision to move forward, so their waterskins held almost nothing, and there was no food except for the ground meal they carried in their bags. They were almost defeated. Their pace slowed as even the leaders were all but overwhelmed by heat and thirst. Golden Ahm, who had begun to look like the red god of war instead of the gentle, kind god he was known to be, glowered at them from his sky-trail as they struggled up the sand hills - very steep hills whose tops looked as if they had been sculpted with a knife. They had all experienced thirst before on occasional forays into the Bab, but with the exception of their manhood trials, had never craved water so desperately. On the final morning, the day of the discovery, they began to smell water as they plodded along, and their courage as well as their stride quickened. The first three explorers who arrived at the top of a long hill of sand and rock stopped suddenly, staring into the east, and as the others reached the pinnacle they all gazed ahead with unbelieving eyes. It was no mirage. Below them lay a broad, brilliantly green valley of trees and plants and vines, running from the lower Bab toward the upper, and in its midst was the amazing and beautiful blue-green water that sparkled in the light as it flowed slowly around a curve in its bed. The immense supply of water, far greater than anything they had expected to see, flowed endlessly past the hills and rocks below them as it moved languidly away and disappeared into the vastness of the green sward that was surrounded by the Bab.

On the second morning of encampment along the water, Gan awoke at dawn, before Ahm climbed above the eastern cliffs that towered over the Great Water valley. He watched the pale morning sky for a little while, allowing the sense of peace that settled over him to reach far into his mind and vision. He had no concept of places where there was rain or cold. Wind he knew, but most of the time, except during the period of sandstorms, the wind was only a gentle breeze that was hot or cool according to the season. He looked carefully at the sky, reading the signs he knew well, knowing that another hot day was upon them.

The explorers had arrived at the camp two days before, ravished with thirst and hunger but giddy with joy at the end of the long day in which they had found the Great Water and drunk from its fountains, first kneeling on the bank, then soaking their bodies in its flow despite the threat of the great number of kadg in the area; and had rested and eaten well of the fish they caught there. On this second morning at the waterside, the fires on both ends of the circle were burning low, and only one watcher, Eno, who was known for his physical strength, remained since the light had come. He sat upright and alert, looking across the sand toward the green valley along the River, watching the reeds that were closest to their encampment with caution. Gan approached him, and the watcher turned a confident face.

"They already left at first light," Eno said, "to go down to the Water to fish." The evil creatures and demons of the dark were forgotten, now that Ahm had come. During the long night the fires, feeble reflections of Ahm that flared all through the dim hours, were the main thing that kept them safe.

"I'll wait until Hab and Luk are up and go with them," Gan spoke quietly. "Did you see anything last night?"

"Nothing dangerous. Just some of the lions from up there," the watcher gestured toward a large rock that lay in the sand a distance toward the south. "They didn't pay any attention to us. They stood on that high place above us for a while. Must have wanted to come down to get water."

There was a call from the riverbank, and soon they saw three boys climbing the sandy slope between the reeds.

"Fish! Loads of fish!" one of them exclaimed, holding up his bag full of fish that glinted silvery-gray in the growing light. Two other bags of fish were in their hands as they climbed joyously up through the sand. Everybody on the ground awakened to the shouts. They all ate the raw fish eagerly.

As Ahm's disk appeared above the horizon, Ket, the son of Set, the village shaman, who should eventually take the role his father and all his fathers before him had fulfilled, conducted the rising ceremony for the group. He walked the stone circle twice to symbolize the movement of Ahm across the sky, chanting the ritual words as he went. No one paid much attention to him, as they never paid attention to his father or the others who had conducted the daily invocation of Ahm, but they understood his importance. After Ket had completed the rite they finished eating the fish, along with some of the bread they had made on the hot rocks the night before, and then sat on the sandy earth waiting for Mur to decide what they would do that day.

"We have walked for eight full Ahms," Mur declared in his best formal style. "We have come a lot farther than we ever thought we would. This is a place of good water with plenty of food, so we will stay here for a few more Ahms while we go out to find the best place to settle near the Great Water. Do you all agree?"

They all agreed. The long trip had been hard for everyone, and all but the strongest were still tired despite the fact they were used to working in the full strength of Ahm, and everybody was burned. They had rested as long as they could, and as the time passed they increasingly marveled at the immensity of the size and flow of the grey-green Water as it tumbled along, foaming and spraying over rocks and deep places on its way toward the immense sea that some of the elders who knew the lore of the land, said existed toward the boundless upper regions of the Bab. They had never before seen such a sight. When the dark approached on the day of discovery they had to set up camp in that spot, close to the Great Water, but in the familiar sand above the green belt that spread along its bank. The hastily arranged stone circle was small but adequate for their needs at the moment, and was enlarged the next day. There were only two watch-fires instead of the usual four; one on the water side toward the east, and the other at the opposite side that led toward the Bab. Four watchers were appointed, and all the rest slept until it was their turn to keep the vigil through the hours of the night. The circle was protected by small amulets Ket placed at the four 'points' that enclosed them, and they felt secure after that was done. Nothing, except for the appearance of the lions, had happened during the first two nights.

"We will start our exploration today," Mur said importantly. "We will go in three groups, one up, one down, and one into the Bab. Don't go too far. Start back at a little more than half-Ahm. We should all be here again before dark."

They stirred and watched with eager consideration as the little stones they had placed into a bag were drawn, and each was assigned his place in the groups that were led by the three elders. Gan's stone was drawn for Mur's group. After the draw, Ket walked around them again, offering his prayers to Ahm who was glowing in the eastern sky. He gave each of the groups another small amulet just before departure time.

As his group walked north along the edge of the green vegetation line, Gan thought about the possibilities of living there. They all knew the reasons they had come and the things they were looking for, but not many of the explorers had thought much about life as it would develop along the Great Water. What if they found something really new and totally unexpected? He was enthralled with the prospect.

They walked slowly, not wanting to miss anything that could be interesting along their way. They wandered into the dry edge of the Bab and back to the very brink of the Great Water, examining the wet bank for footprints and other evidence of animals, or maybe even men; searching the tangled vines and trees for nests and the eggs they could contain. They looked for familiar edible plants and flowers and berries, and anything else that could possibly be foraged for food. They searched the palms for dates, and found them in abundance. Everything was unspoiled, untouched by humanity as far as they could see, but the gray-green and unending flow of moving water was something they would have to get used to, and although the sand was familiar and seemed more home-like, they were always drawn down to the Water's edge.

"I could live here," Gan declared as they stood beside a particularly wide sweep of sand that coursed right into the River. It was actually from a wadi that had washed into the water during recent drenching rains, but no one knew.

"I don't think that would be very wise, my friend," said Mur with a smile. "We don't want to live in constant guard against the kadg."

"Well, maybe a little higher then, up there above the line of trees. In the Bab, but close to our water, like we do at Nomo."

Mur smiled with a little superiority. To him Gan was still a child even though he had passed all the trials. "It is a good place," he agreed. "Keep your eyes open, this is all new to us and we never know what may be nearby." That was a sobering thought, so they drew together and moved ahead, voices quieter, tall Mur leading the way.

It was Ket's group, however, that found the best advantage for a new village. A good-sized lake, just past the top of the rock where the lions lived, and only a short distance from their camp, lay between green banks set into the yellow-brown sand. There were scrubby trees, also lots of reeds and plants of various kinds, some of which they recognized from their own pond that was shrinking at Nomo. They dreaded the presence of crocodiles more than anything else because it was so close to the Great Water, but saw none as they skirted the banks of the pond and looked carefully among the reeds.

"It's a big supply," someone said about the shining pond. "So close to the Great Water. Maybe it's just a part that hasn't dried up yet."

"I don't think so," Ket responded, "The Great Water is a lot lower than this pond. I think it comes from underground." Their pond at Nomo had an underground source.

"Then why isn't it shrinking?" Hob asked.

"I don't know," was Ket's answer, a response that was to become common during the exploration. "I don't know."

"The big problem is kadg," Sim, another explorer, declared. "If they're here they're well hidden, and that could be a danger."

"Or maybe it's the lions. Their rock is just behind that dune. That's the top of it sticking up above the ridge of sand. Hab had better watch out or he'll get too close."

Hab, a grandson of Max, the head elder of Nomo, was short and squat but without any of the extra weight his grandfather carried. He was standing in the deep sand above the pond, a little too close to the lion rock that rose behind him as he noticed when he turned around. There were no lions to be seen on top of the rock. Its base was hidden by the dune.

Eno's group went south, retracing the steps they had taken as they came up along the Waterside on their last day of the march. They looked into the Bab this time instead of watching the water as intently as they had before. They found only sand and rock and a few rock-shaded places that looked as though they were homes for animals; bones and pieces of skins and other debris lay scattered in the sand near the base of the larger rocks. "Nocturnal animals, maybe hyenas, live here," Eno guessed, but they were nowhere to be seen in the morning light. "They must be sleeping in dens beneath the rocks," he told his group, and they pushed out of the area quickly. They walked for the half-Ahm without finding anything of significance, then headed back just before they would have entered a low-lying swampy area along the bank of the Great Water that was filled with strange new plants, a large grove of date palm trees, and an old stump of a tree that was hollow and filled with bees and honey.

The explorers converged at the stone circle when there was little light left in the day. No one talked much; they were all weary. "We'll talk at dark while we eat," Mur told them. "Now is the time to fill the waterskins and get some fish." Gan and Eno took Hab with them as they went to the Water for the drinking supply. Another group of four were fishing close by; two were attempting to catch fish while the others watched the water for kadg or other dangers. Crocodiles, one of the most subtle and treacherous perils people faced, were almost always part of the scene wherever a decent supply of water was found. The boys had learned from their earliest days to recognize the presence of that fearful beast and how to escape should they come near. Eno and Gan were watching while Hab filled the skins when Eno suddenly raised his spear and sent it down with a smashing thrust. The large form of an adult kadg suddenly appeared near the surface of the water. "Go!" Eno shouted. Gan turned to run up the long, sandy bank with Hab beside him and Eno at their heels. There was a heavy splashing-thrashing of the water. Gan turned his head for a moment. The kadg that had tried to take Hab was twisting and flailing his long tail, and the waters all around roiled with other crocodiles, called by the blood spouting into the river from the heavy blow Eno had planted. There was pandemonium among the beasts, and none of them seemed to notice the fleeing boys. They were all intent on getting their own share of the dying kadg. The four fishermen fled the River at the same time, running through the narrow band of reeds that stood along the water, caring no more about the possibility of snakes or scorpions lurking there. Escaping from crocodiles was one of the major lessons that everyone learned at a very early age.

The reports brought little of interest except for the pond that lay behind the lion rock. "Is it really that big?" Eno wanted to know. "If it is, and if it has an underground source, then a village between the pond and the Great River would be a big benefit."

"Unless there are kadg in it," Hab noted.

"There may be some, but there weren't any to be seen yesterday," Ket replied. "It looked like a place where the lions would go to drink."

"That could be a danger, too," Mur said aloud, although he had been unusually silent throughout the discussion. "Lions are not our friends, although these don't seem to be mean."

"And there were lots of reeds. They'd be easier to harvest if there weren't any kadg." The tribe had special uses for the reeds that grew near their pond at Nomo. They wove them into mats and baskets, and pounded the reeds to soften them before they made coverings they used on cooler nights.

"Were there any fish?" Sim asked. "Would they be good to eat or taste like the fish in Nomo?" The fish they knew at home tasted muddy. The Great Water fish were sleek and fresh and delicious.

"There is always the Water for fish, and lots of them!" Ket pointed out. "The pond would be best for drinking water, though."

They all agreed. The river had far too many crocodiles, and water was a necessity. Fish were not, although they were a part of their regular food. In this new place there had to be more animals they could hunt than in Nomo.

Mur stood at last. "When Ahm comes we will go and look at the pond beyond the rock," he said, pointing toward the place in the distant shadows. "If it's a safe place, and the water has a good source, that will be important for us to think about. The lions are not the problem, but we don't want them agitated, either. We will go there soon after the rising." He was done, and gave the sign for the ending of the meeting.

The watchers took their places for the first shift while the others lay down on the sandy ground to sleep, covering themselves with reeds and leaves and grasses because the night had a bit of a chill. They had no way of gauging time precisely, but experience had taught them how to judge the passing of the hours, so the watchers awakened four others to take their place after the moon, which they called Ta, had passed through his first third of the night sky. Gan was new to watching. His teachers had stressed how vital the watch was, so he took his place very seriously in front of the fire nearest the Great Water, and watched in the opposite direction, across the stone circle and up the hill toward the ridge that was the opening to the Bab. He kept his attention on the ridgeline and swept his eyes around all the surrounding landscape in a pattern he had been learning from the experienced watchers. This was his third night to guard in that place, and he was already acquainted with all the features of the hills and the sand that swept upward in front of him. The other watchers also peered across the stone circle, looking into the darkness as far as they could, eyes always sweeping near and far to catch any unusual movement or action that might represent a new danger.

After a little more than an hour into his vigil, Gan saw two lions step up onto the distant ridge, their sinewy bodies outlined against the sky. He knew at once what they were. They stood, almost like sentinels who wished to be seen, watching with him. He called softly and the other watchmen turned to where he pointed. "Lions," he said in a single word. They looked for a moment but turned again to survey their own area of responsibility. "Tell us if they move," another watcher said, and silence fell on the camp once more.

The lions did not move. They stood on the ridge, patient and still, apparently watching past the camp toward the Great Water for their own purposes. When it was time to change to the third shift, Gan pointed the lions out to his replacement and then allowed his eyes to close. Sleep came quickly.

In the last hour of the night, one of the watchers called out to all the camp. "Someone is coming up the bank from the River!" Mur jumped up, and all the others followed immediately.

"Men?" Mur asked.

"Yes, but only one," the watcher hissed.

Gan looked toward the River expecting to see the leader of a group of many men, perhaps there to fight them off, or possibly evil spirits to be dealt with in some way. Ket was on the alert for that as well. He pulled an amulet out of his bag and held it up toward the approaching unknown. Mur looked at the fire, which was burning low, and commanded more sticks and wood to be thrown into it. Soon, however, it was obvious that only one solitary figure approached. Even in the darkness he seemed old by the way he was walking, slowly, with a limp, and his shoulders were stooped. He carried what looked like a long spear, but had nothing else with him. They all stared into the night, ready for anything, as he approached. The old man stopped just outside the stone circle and they saw him clearly in the firelight as he stood looking at them with black, rheumy eyes. A long, stained gray beard flowed from his chin, and his lengthy hair was pulled back and tied with a vine of some sort. He was dirty, and his kilt was ragged from wear. He had no spear; the object he carried was only a tall staff. By the light from the fire they could see that it was marked with a line of symbols that began at the top and worked down the rod to the place where his hand gripped the shaft. The old man did not speak, but gestured with his free hand, apparently to ask them where they had come from. Most of the explorers were gripped with fear that he might be an evil spirit.

"We come from the great Bab, from that way," Mur told him slowly, keeping his eyes on the man and his staff that held the symbols. "Are you alone?"

The old man still did not speak. He looked them over carefully, and then stepped deliberately inside the circle. They all drew back as Eno held out his new spear - the replacement for the one he had lost when he killed the croc - but Mur intervened. "No. Not yet," he said. Then he spoke to the stranger again. "Who are you, Father?" he asked in a voice tinged with respect. "Why are you alone?"

At last the old man spoke, but they didn't understand what he said. They had never imagined that anyone they met might speak a different language to their own. They had never even thought such a thing as another language existed. He said a few words and looked at them closely, realizing they hadn't understood. Then he pointed to himself. "Gan!" he said distinctly. "Gan." It was his name. The boys all looked at him, and some even looked at their own Gan for a moment, but the three elders watched the old man intently. "Gan?" Mur asked.

"Ond," he said. "Ond. Gan."

Gan the watcher stood beside Hab, who poked him, but everyone else was too fascinated by the stranger to notice. They had never seen anyone from a different tribe. They lived so far out in the Bab that their lore had only two stories about travelers who had come to their oasis many long seasons ago, and none of the explorers had been outside Nomo before their recent trek.

Mur motioned to the leaders, Ket and Eno, who came up beside him. They studied the old man together.

"Where could he come from?" Ket was the first to ask. "We haven't seen any sign that people live near here. And he's alone."

"Or he seems to be," Eno held his spear tightly. Everyone knew he was very skillful with it.

"I haven't any idea where he came from," Mur said with caution. "But he is alone. He must be."

"Do you think he's a demon?" Ket asked with a little tremor of excitement in his voice. To his knowledge no one from Nomo had ever encountered a demon. It would be a first, and he would be forever credited if he could destroy an evil spirit.

"No, he's a real person. Look at him!" Mur nearly laughed. "He's old and he's weak."

"Maybe it's a disguise."

"I don't think so. Do you really think that?"

"No, but we have to be careful."

"We are - we are. But he's still able to get around on his own." Mur was thinking of the very old in Nomo who needed constant attention from family just to walk or eat.

No one ever walked alone; they had been taught that all their lives, so some of the boys were not convinced that this man could have come by himself. The old man watched them with equal interest, but he seemed to be very tired, and Mur thought he understood. He had come when he saw their fires because he was as curious about them as they were about him.

"Bring him something to eat," Mur commanded suddenly, and they all scrambled for whatever food they could find in their bags.

"For you," Mur said, holding out some bread and two small fish to Old Gan. He accepted it with a smile of appreciation. "Now eat," Mur told him because the old man hesitated. Old Gan smiled again before he started chewing on it. He seemed not to notice the stares of all the explorers as he delved into the food.

11

"He needs water," Gan-the-watcher said, handing his waterskin to Mur. "Yes," Mur gave the old man the skin with a quiet motion. Old Gan drank a little and turned back to the fish, but not without giving a quick look at the watcher. When he had finished eating, Old Gan settled onto the sand and laid down, pulling some of the leaves and reeds that were strewn inside the circle across his shoulders, and closed his eyes. He showed no sign of mistrust or fear. Everyone except the watchers, who were still staring into the last vestiges of night, centered attention on the old man as he stretched out and relaxed his body into a deep sleep. An expression of quiet peace came over his face, which looked waxen and pale as he slept, his features sharp and clear beneath the thin skin that stretched across the bones.

As Ahm stirred from his home and began to light the sky from below the horizon, they were assured that the man was not an evil spirit, for none could remain under the watchful eye of Ahm, who now opened his full face to shine upon them. A few of the boys went down to the Water cautiously, to get fish for breakfast. Once again they brought back an abundance, but no one went for water. They had decided to try the pond in the Bab beyond the lion rock to fill their waterskins that day.

"We will go out today to learn about this water," Mur, who was organizing the activities for the day, said in the firm voice of a leader. At that moment Old Gan awakened as though he had finished a good night's sleep. They had saved some fish and bread, which he ate readily, and then to their surprise, started to speak in his strange language while he was still chewing on the fish. It was a cheerful sounding and very expressive language; Mur made no attempt to stop him. He said a few words that he repeated several times, and pointed to one of the boys to repeat the word that he had spoken. Next he held up his staff and motioned toward Gan. Old Gan used the bottom tip of the staff to mark in the sand, where he drew lines and designs for a little while. He handed the staff to Gan, and stepped away from the drawings so the others could see.

The boy felt his fingers start to tingle, and then the eye of his mind opened on a world that he had never seen. He heard Old Gan explaining the marks, and he understood his words. He knew it was his job to repeat them. He started at the beginning.

"He is from a village about three Ahm's from here," the boy said, "and he wants to lead us there. It is a place of many small streams and trees and lots of fish. There are all kinds of things to hunt, and food from the land as well. Grain and sweet berries and some kinds of leaves that are tasty."

The old man stopped in his narrative to look questioningly at Mur, who was staring at Gan.

"How do you know what he's saying?" he asked the boy.

"I don't. It just seems right to say what I think. Should I stop?"

"No," Mur told him, "go ahead."

"There are good houses available, and more can be built," Gan said. "It's a good life. Now he wants me to ask if you're willing to come along with him."

"It doesn't sound safe to me," Eno declared firmly. "How do we know where he wants to take us? How does Gan know what he's saying? He's not an evil spirit, but he may be in contact with one. How can we trust him?"

"But what if there is such a place and we could have a better life there?" asked Ket. "We wouldn't want to miss that!"

"No, but we don't want to be led into a trap, either. He seems like a good man, but we don't know if he's only being clever and would take us to a slaughter."

12

The debate continued until Mur declared that they couldn't resolve the question immediately. He decided to wait for further discussion and set out to find the pond that the Bab-walkers had discovered the day before. Old Gan went with them, swinging along through the sand with his limping gait. The explorers held back a little to accommodate him. The pond, bigger than most of them expected, was surrounded by small clusters of reeds and plants. They approached it carefully although there was no sign of kadg. Only Old Gan stepped up to the water's edge confidently. He raised his staff above the water and shouted out something incomprehensible in a sing-song chanting voice. After a short wait he turned and smiled as he pronounced "Ba snug!" loudly. He didn't need a translator. He repeated his statement with gestures, arms wide and flailing and as the others came up to the edge of the pond he stepped into the water, using his staff to feel the bottom, and walked across the pond slowly. There were no kadg in the water, which was only waist deep. Although the bottom was impossible to see because of the sand and silt, they were assured that the place was safe. The water was satisfactory. It tasted a little muddy compared to the Great Water, but was a much safer place to drink, and the supply was obviously renewed on a continuing basis. They didn't see any fish, although they may have been hidden by the murky water.

As they left the pond they turned toward the deep desert, but Old Gan urged them to walk the other way, past the lion rock toward the upper Bab. He pointed to a high ridge along the edge of the Bab, and as they walked past it they recognized that it was the place where they had seen the lions during the night. There were no lions there then, but the high point commanded a great view of the tumbling Water flowing along below, and the desert on the other side. They could also see their camp and the line of green growth that followed the River from the south, a clear line that marked the bottom of the slope just beyond the lion rock which was at their feet. One lion stood atop the rock, watching them as they watched him. All the others were settled along the flank of the rock itself, lying close together in the shade. The boys could hear the animals murmuring softly among themselves, a language that only a lion could understand, but to the boys it sounded like contentment. Even the rock outcropping resembled a lion lying on its haunches in the sand, a sharp ledge of rock that were its forefeet extended toward the Great River, watching over all the land that lay below.

"Does it look like home?" Mur asked. He didn't mean Nomo, but the new place they were searching for.

"It could be," Eno replied. "We'll have to get used to the idea, though."

"I think everybody would like to live here," Gan offered. As the youngest he was the least likely to be giving advice or information.

"Do you think you could live here when you have a family; so close to the lions and all?"

"Oh, yes!" Gan replied confidently. "The lions don't scare me, and not even the kadg, if I have Ahm to watch over me." The others were amused at his confidence.

They spent the rest of the day in deliberations, and then lay down to sleep after they had eaten more bread and some oryx meat the hunters brought in. Old Gan slept alongside the group, and in the morning he delivered a surprise that puzzled all of them even more. When they had finished the morning fish and bread, he stood and demanded attention from everyone. He walked around them slowly, in a large circle, talking softly and looking very solemn as he went. Eno feared that the old man was attempting some kind of enchantment that would bend them to his will, and that might have been the case, for at the end of his circumnavigation, he stepped into the center and called on the younger Gan to come stand in front of him. The boy moved obediently to face the old man, but he and all the others were baffled. Old Gan, however, seemed self-assured as he stood looking thoughtfully at the younger. Then he held out his staff.

"Hetu Gan, beffot na wopa, na lulen, na kedme!" he thundered three times as the boy stood, wondering. Then the old man held out the staff and signaled Gan to take it. The boy reached out, but Mur shouted, "no, Gan. Don't touch it!" The hand withdrew.

Old Gan was surprised and looked sharply at Mur. He said again, "Hetu Gan, beffot na wopa, na lulen, na kedme!" But the boy stood as he was, feet planted on the sand, hands at his side. Old Gan simply asked, "Fi?"

"What are you doing, old man?" Mur asked with annoyance in his voice. "We can't take that gift from you!" Then he turned to Gan. "Do you understand what he's saying?"

"No. Not today."

Ket turned with a question on his face. "We saw him use that staff at the pond. He seemed to be talking to the pond with it, or maybe even to the kadg."

"Yes," Mur said more quietly. "We have no idea what magic may be in it!"

All of the boys were quiet, watching the leaders for a signal as to what to do next. Mur rose from his place on the sand and approached Old Gan. "We don't understand, Father," he said in a more respectful tone. "Why do you want to give your staff to Gan? Is it because you have the same name?" He signed and pointed in an attempt to make his question clear.

Old Gan signed and pointed in response, smiling again, despite the fact that he knew they didn't understand him. "I have no need of it now. And I think a boy who bears my name should have it. Gan," he said again, pointing to himself and then the boy.

"You need the staff to get around," Mur said as he signed the words.

Old Gan seemed to understand. "My days are over. I have no needs. He should have it. The staff has chosen him!" Then he turned and sat on the ground again, far on the other side from Mur and young Gan. There was a stir of curious activity, but at last the group turned to face Mur who walked to the water side of the stone circle, ready to give the day's assignments.

The circle developed a lull of quiet after they had eaten the evening meal. No one talked; everyone felt the need for rest. They had worked hard that day, walking in the desert directly west of the camp as far as they could for the half-day. Mur wanted to know what was there, and they all walked together, including Old Gan, who refused to be left behind. Although they were still suspicious of him, he spent the day helping them find the vistas and valleys of the region, climbing high on ridges of sand, and looking as far as he could into the surrounding lands. Old Gan told them about another small oasis pond about half a morning walk from the camp, but Mur refused to go there. They found a few places where there was swampy land and a little grass. These were all good signs; underground water lay close to the surface. As they approached the camp late in the day, the old man knew that the group was still suspect of his motives, but he seemed oblivious to their concerns. He sagged even more as they walked the final slope down into the camp, and settled onto the ground as soon as they had crossed the circle. He didn't eat much that evening.

The night passed uneventfully. The only thing that they had noticed was that the lions had returned to the western ridge and seemed to be keeping watch on *them*. There were several more lions, it looked like the entire pride, who stood high on the horizon, facing toward the great River. The big cats gave no indication of hostility, however, so the watchers remained silent but kept a constant eye on them. The lions left the ridge a little before daybreak, and all was quiet as the world awakened to a new day.

It was a little later in the morning when they discovered that Old Gan had died. His staff lay beside his lifeless body on the sand.

They found a place above the camp where an ancient watercourse had flowed in the days when the Bab had been a savannah covered with grass and dotted with trees, watered with sufficient rain. The burial pit was easier to dig there, in the deep sand, and there were plenty of rocks strewn along the edge of the primitive creek bed. Some of the boys had remained in the camp to prepare the old man's body, and they carried him up to the site on a pallet of branches, which was carefully lowered into the pit. Ket circled the grave, chanting. Just as they started to cover Old Gan with sand, Mur reached down and pulled the staff from beside his body. "For you," he said to Gan-the-watcher. "It fits your hand."

And so it was that Gan of Nomo received the River Staff, as it came to be called, the ages-old branch of the first tree that the Great God Amun-Ra had created on the first land when he made the world. The staff that had passed from the God's own hand into the hands of men.

"Here it is!" Mur informed the small group of elders proudly as he strutted along the panorama that stood above the lion rock. "We think this is the best place for us to settle."

Ket and Eno agreed, watching the faces of the older men as they surveyed the summit and its surroundings. The pond of fresh water lay to the south at a short distance, and the broad green never-ending Water Valley waited down the slope. All was peaceful that morning, the first time the elders with an advance party from the clan had come to the site. The three elders held prominent places at the front of the group. Sun and Jak looked old, with patches of white hair and skinny arms and necks, while Max was smooth and round with heavy jowls and a bald head. He had a reputation for a bad temper and a stubborn mind, but he was the chief of the tribal fathers.

"It is a good place, but have you looked as carefully at other places?" Max asked Mur, watching for the young man's response as he spoke. "Do you know that this is the best?"

Mur was undeterred. "We believe it is," he replied quickly. "We walked for half an Ahm from here in all directions," he gestured toward them, "and this place is the best we've seen. There may be good places toward the upper Bab, but we don't think any would be like this. We did our work!"

"You have done well," Sun, the oldest remaining elder, offered to Mur and the others. "We're pleased to find this home. It has an even better situation than we had at Nomo."

"The fish taste great, uh, fresher, and there are more animals. And we think we could grow things along the Water that would do better than the crops we had in the Bab," Eno eagerly agreed.

"And what do you say, Jak?" Max asked the other elder who stood watching the exchange. "Do you think we could live here so close to the lions?"

"They're watching us now, without any threats or noise," Jak said. "We've had little experience with lions in the Bab, so there is no way of knowing, but these explorers all say that they didn't ever bother them." The lions looked peaceful, even sleepy, as they lay at the base of the rock. There was no sentinel lion that day. They slept and stretched along the rocky edge that was deeply shaded from Ahm.

"We can't decide yet, anyway. It has to be taken up by the whole tribe, not just among us," Mur declared. He wasn't intimidated by Max, who was annoyed by what he considered a lack of respect from the much younger man.

"Come, then," Max moved away toward the Water, avoiding the lion rock that was to his right as they descended. "We should look more closely at the Great Water."

The entire clan had crossed the treacherous Bab, taking only six days because the explorers had worked out an angled trail on their return to the village. It led them from their former home to the oases the young men had found on their first journey of discovery, then turned toward the upper Bab to a newly discovered pond they had found on their return trip. It was obviously drying, but supplied enough water for the group as they proceeded onward. Still lamenting the village of Nomo, and finally arrived, after a lot of complaining, close to the place the boys had found for their resettlement. After they had come to the Great Water the others waited a little further down the Water Valley toward the south as the three explorers led the elders to the spot near the lion rock, the site to be considered for New Nomo. The elders inspected it carefully and Max asked so many questions that Mur thought he was attempting to find some fault that the explorers had never considered. After the tour, they returned to the tribe which was waiting for their report.

That evening, after the meal had been taken, the entire group sat on the sand above the Great Water, surrounded by the stones they had used to build their customary circle, and listened to the explorers and the elders discuss every possible consideration that could impinge upon the security and stability of the place. Although it wasn't their custom, the elders asked for opinions from the women, but none were forthcoming. All the women refused to be a part of the serious debate that was carried on that night.

"We want everyone to be happy in our village," Max told them. "Women have a right to question in such matters." No one spoke, but the men knew that if a wrong choice was made, or a perception that the choice was flawed developed, there would be misery.

Max sighed and turned to the men again. "We have all heard the story of your exploration," he said formally to the young ones who had gone on the first adventure. "Now we must make a decision based on what we've seen as well as what you've told us." He stood beside the watch-fire without speaking for a long time. They all waited in silence. "All of you take a stone from the pile," he indicated the small stones at his feet. "If you believe this choice for New Nomo is right, place the stone beside me here," he pointed to the ground with his right forefinger. "If you think it isn't, then put it over there," he indicated a place on the far side of the fire. "There can be no guesswork in this decision. If the count is less than a hand in difference, the elders, including the three younger men who went on the exploration, will cast a deciding vote." The men, twenty-eight in all, placed the stones solemnly, and when they were finished no one had placed his stone beyond the fire. They had made a firm decision.

Gan was silent during the discussion. He stood apart, holding the staff in his hand, leaning on it, watching events unfold throughout the entire process. At last he spoke, and his words seemed strange to their ears. "It's a good decision, but I warn you that things may not go as planned, and there is danger nearer than you think."

Some of the men laughed. The grave child seemed foolish to speak so ominously, even though he had been chosen to go on the exploration. Gan's father moved away from the fire and stood at a distance watching his son.

"Know this," the boy continued, "there are terrible men nearer than you can imagine who will come one day to eat your hearts and steal your women. They are a great plague on all the folk who live along the path of the Great Water." Then he seemed to become himself again as he walked away from the group. He knew that no one would take him seriously, and even he had difficulty believing the thoughts that filled his mind. No one knew what to say in response to his warning.

There was no celebration that night or the next day. They had too much to do, and needed to do it quickly. The stone walls had to be constructed and their individual huts built before they could be secure. So they slept that night, as they had the night before, between two watch-fires, and teams of watchers looked into the darkness from the sand above the Great Water. There was no moon; they needed alert and steady watchmen on all sides. When Ahm rose the next morning from the cliffs on the far side of the valley, Set, Ket's father, circled the stones and invoked the god for their good fortune that day. Soon the entire clan was on the move again, trudging slowly along the edge of the sand, following the steps of the explorers as the entire tribe moved upward along the Water to begin their settlement at the lion rock.

Only three had died on their long days of walking across the Bab. All were of the older generation and one was especially weak before they had started, but she was in good spirits until the day before she died, walking along, slowly but with dignity, in the midst of the group. Seventy -nine people, the remainder of the tribe, climbed the slope from the Great Water and stood on the panorama above the lion rock that day. No one thought of it as historic, but the story keepers of later times learned the tale from their ancestors, and the legend of the Long Walk and the foundation of the village that came to be known as Karnua quickly became the lore of the people, and they loved to hear it told and retold around the fires in the centuries that followed. Gan, the solitary prophet, figured prominently in the tale.

They set out to build a large stone circle-wall first. Set, a small but powerful man whose body looked as though it was composed of one coiled muscle, conducted all the essential ceremonies as they built the enclosing wall and then the small huts, and whatever religious observations Set may have been unsure about were never a problem. He simply invented a new rite and used it to honor Ahm, the Great One, who shone upon them graciously in their new home and seemed to understand them, so great were his blessings, although the journey had been hard.

The lions watched at night from the ridge above the Great Water, but now they had moved toward the south. The eastern edge of Nomo-Karnua sat on the very place where the animals had conducted their nightly watch in the past, but they paid no more attention to the clan than they had to the group of ten explorers who had camped just below them. The lions rarely made any noise. No one in Karnua knew they could roar.

The village was soon strong. Watchers continued the night shifts as they had for centuries, and were even more vigilant because they didn't yet know the place very well. Gan walked the perimeter of the circle as well as Set, and as he paced, sometimes inside and sometimes out, he watched the green line along the Great Water with caution. He didn't talk to anyone very often, not even his mother, who was anxious about the boy because of the great change he had experienced while he was away on the discovery trip. She watched him from a distance, and the things he felt were dim shadows in her mind as well.

A few days following the onset of building, a child named Tul went fishing and was pulled into the Great Water by a kadg. The watchers weren't blamed, but there was a sense of loss that was different. Although they knew there were large numbers of crocodiles along the banks, no one had thought such a thing would happen. Set was tasked with the ceremony for the dead. There were no remains in this case, so he invented a new rite. People seemed to like the things he usually said at burial time, but there was nothing he had learned from his father that fit the situation. No one was especially saddened by death; it was simply and easily accepted, unless the dead was an infant or the village head elder or someone else of importance. There was generally no weeping, only a strong reminder that everyone who watched the ceremony would have the same said of them when they lay quiet and still in the deep sand-pit. Life was life, and death was death. They were different, but part of the same whole.

"We send Tul into Ahm," he said the new words with a steady voice. "Ahm has guided and guarded us on our way, and now he has taken Tul to be with him on the sky-path." Although these ideas had been part of their belief for generations, they had never been spoken at a burial. No shaman had ever said anything about the god receiving the dead, or Ahm's active role in human life. The words were heard with some hesitation by those who didn't like to change the old ways, but children especially liked the idea, and the next morning they looked up to see Ahm on his path, and believed that Tul was there, waving and smiling at the new village of Karnua and his friends as the boy leaped along the path under the protection and guidance of Ahm. It seemed a very pleasant thing to do.

The weather changed slightly, bringing with it a thin breeze and some cool nights. People liked to sleep more at that time, and used animal skins as well as woven mats to cover themselves during the night. Food was plentiful, and life took on a pattern that was similar to that of Nomo. Women swept out their huts and kept them as clean as possible to avoid infestations of insects and other vermin, and everyone worked at various tasks for the hours of light while Ahm walked across the sky-fields. As the nights grew longer, they rested inside their own huts. Contentment was the norm rather than the exception.

Gan was the only one who seemed troubled, and as the days passed into the cool season he became agitated. He walked alone to the Great Water every day and sat among the reeds, hidden from the water's edge, and looked across to the other shore between the spindly green stems. He seemed to have no fear of the kadg and he was never troubled by them, to everyone's amazement. He was not challenged very often, but even then he refused to listen to the reasons that his father and the elders gave him about keeping the rules. He turned twelve, two hands and a split, at the change of the season, but showed no sign of interest in the life of the village.

"You are assigned to watch for the first round, starting at the dark," he was told one morning by the head watchman.

Gan refused. "I watch every night and all day as well," he said, "and my watching is more than all the others together. I will continue to watch in my own way." The head watchman could see that it was useless to argue, so he told the next man to watch and left Gan to himself.

"He is meant to be alone," Gan's father told anyone who asked. "He has his own ways and concerns, and no one should bother him now." So the villagers left him in his isolation. It was when he started going to the Water after dark that Mur went to him one day to inquire about the lonely sojourns.

"You go out after Ahm has left us, and it is dangerous," he told the boy, concern in his voice and face. "We can help you if you will talk to us."

"I only do what I must do. I don't ask anyone to do it with me," was the response. "Remember old Gan? He came to us in the dark. I think he taught me that I could go out after Ahm has gone and be as safe as I am here."

"Is it his staff?" Mur asked carefully, remembering his decision to give it to the boy. "Is it his staff that makes you want to do this? Is it magic?"

Gan chose words carefully. "No, that's not the purpose of the staff, and I don't think it's magic, at least it's not bad magic. When I hold it I think things that I never would at other times. The staff came from a powerful source, and is a strong connection for me."

"What things do you think about when you have it in your hand?" Mur asked . He decided to be direct. "Does the old man talk to you then?"

"No, there is no voice, just some thoughts that come when I handle it, or even look at it sometimes."

"Do you wish you had never taken it?" Mur asked with the full intention of offering to take it back himself.

"No! No - I want to keep it! It's just that I don't know what to do with all the thoughts yet. I know that someday soon I'll be able to understand the things I think about when I have it. Anyway, it will never leave me now, unless I give it to someone else. Like he gave it to me."

Mur was distressed but tried not to let it show. "You could always take it back to him - over there where he's buried."

"He doesn't want it. I have asked, and he has no need of it now. It is mine."

Gan didn't have long to wait to understand his thoughts. A few nights later, in the moonless black between Ahm's setting and rising, with a cloud obscuring even the starlight, Gan sat on the bank of the River and stared into the darkness. He had been increasingly restless for two days. Then, out of the deep darkness he saw a strange and startling sight. Several coracle-like little boats came bobbing along over the choppy water, silently floating toward the shoreline - his shoreline. He had never seen a boat before and thought they might be evil spirits, but he did not fear them as he had in the past. The boy-man sat low near the edge of the water as he counted the tiny boats - there were at least three-hands count coming toward him on the current - and they seemed to be steered by something that was dipped into the water in a rhythmic motion. As he watched he could see there were men inside each capsule. Although awed by the sight he was witnessing, he slid away as quietly and invisibly as he could. When he was far up the bank toward the village he jumped to full height and ran headlong toward the wall.

"A lot of men are coming! They're coming to fight!" he called in an anguished voice to the watchers, and then ran on.

The watchers piled more wood on the fires and called to the elders who, in turn, called the men who were sleeping to come and take their stand against an invasion. Everybody hoped that Gan was wrong, but they could not take the chance of refusing his warning. They also hoped that the approaching enemy was only men, not demons.

Gan ran on, heading for the rock that lay ahead near the pond. He was panting and breathless when he came close and a lion sprang out to meet him. He stopped in front of the creature, held up his staff, and said, "They have come!" The lion made a low sound, like a call, and immediately many of the other beasts appeared behind him. They seemed to speak with each other through soft growls and body movement, and then they were gone, sliding silently away into the night, gliding over the sand with deadly sinews, claws, and teeth.

Gan ran back across the sand to the village wall, struggling to catch his breath. The battle was about to start. The invaders, men who were still only shadows, kept their distance from the fires as they fanned out around the sides of the new village of Karnua, taking positions that encircled the wall, and when they were in place someone started the assault with a great cry. Men flung well-aimed spears over the wall in both directions, and there were shouts and shrill screams all around. Gan waited, holding the staff in his hand, some distance from the part of the wall that faced the lion rock. The invaders surged past close to him, but did not seem to see him in the gloom, in a place no one would have expected a boy to stand. The shadow men were intent on hurling their weapons toward the men who were illuminated by the fires inside the circle. Gan waited for the lions that had not yet appeared at the battle scene. The invaders were no taller than the members of Gan's clan, but were broader, and strong and cruel. Several gathered along the opposite side of the village and were ready to jump over the wall, spears in hand, when the lions came at last. Gan saw their approach. The tawny beasts crept along the edge of the darkness; five large male lions, sufficient for the work at hand. They sprang with tremendous roaring upon the backs of the men who were about to climb over the wall. As the lions leaped, Gan hoisted himself over the rocks that formed the opposite wall and jumped down into the chaos.

The center of the village was complete turmoil. Men of Karnua were attempting to hold off the invaders, who were a greater number. They slashed with short knives and thrust spears at the strange men who were determined to destroy all they held dear. The invaders heard the lions making quick work of their companions along the wall and realized that something had gone wrong. The men of Karnua also knew that something unusual was happening, for the cries of their own had stopped altogether. Only the terrified screams of the invaders and the roaring of the beasts, which was intended to strike horrendous fear into their foes, could be heard. The fires were still burning brightly, making clear targets of the defenders as well as the invaders, and all were fighting for their lives in the lurid light of the flames.

The lion attack was well-timed. The invaders could not retreat over the wall on the side where the lions were fighting, mauling and tossing the bodies of the evil men as though they were made of straw. When the men of Karnua saw the situation, they grabbed the spears that had been thrown inside and sent them with great accuracy into the enemy who were attempting to climb out of the circle over the opposite wall. Several fell screaming from the barbed points that stuck into their flesh as the lions leaped along the narrow paths of the village to complete their work. A few of the invaders attempted to fight off the beasts, but most turned and ran. Men who were similar to themselves seemed to be a fair exchange in battle, they thought amid the confusion, but lions? Why did the beasts fight against them and for the village? They had never encountered such resistance, and were terrified to find claws and teeth ripping their bodies. Soon all the invaders who still lived were scattered, running blindly toward the water, chased by lions who were angry because one of their own kind had been injured by spears; driving the invaders into the mighty jaws of the kadg who lay in wait along the edge of the Great Water.

The lions disappeared into the night when they had accomplished their purpose, and a short time later they stood in a group on their promontory, gazing out across the green belt of the valley toward the Great Water that rolled along as though nothing had happened at all.

The night was very dark, but the fires were kept at a lower level as Karnua counted its losses. Some of the younger men volunteered to search the area for other ravagers, although Gan assured them that there were no living enemies anywhere nearby. When the lions had withdrawn, they left one of their own dead beside the entrance to the village, and the men eyed its body with both respect and apprehension. Three of the village men had been killed, and five more had wounds. Gan went among them, saying very little, for he had no power to heal and knew it. They laid the bodies of their dead inside the wall, and it was only when he looked closely that Gan recognized Ket. He bowed his head with respect, his throat swelled and his eyes began to sting with tears, but he was not ashamed.

Max, the head elder, made a few comments over the dead, and announced that they would bury them in the following light of Ahm. Set began to prepare a fitting ceremony for his son and the others.

"What about the lion?" Gan asked. "We should bury him, too."

Max stammered a bit about letting the lions take care of their own, but Mur also spoke. "We need to take his body back to the rock at least."

"We will need to take it there and bury it beneath the rock," Gan said with finality.

"That won't be possible," Max responded with a show of indignation. "We can't bury a lion. They would attack us!"

"No, there is no need to fear," Gan told him. "After what you saw tonight you should know it, too." Not one of the men of the tribe of Nomo-Karnua had been touched by a lion.

Max said no more.

"The explorers will take him after we have buried Ket," Mur said calmly. "We owe them much more, of course." Max turned away with a quick step that told everyone he was angry.

There were five bodies of the invading force lying along the village wall, where they had fallen, and four more inside the village among the huts. They were brutish looking men with painted green faces, and two had bodies that were painted as well. No one wanted to touch them. At last, after some debate, they decided to haul the dead enemies to the Water and dump them in. The kadg would take care of the remains. Gan didn't like the plan, but said nothing. There was no need to go against the will of the people in that matter. He had other work to do. The bodies were taken outside the wall where they lay until Ahm's earliest light appeared and all the men helped drag them to the Water. Gan went along, the first of the procession, and stood on the brink with his staff as the men tossed the dead into the swirling water. The bodies sank like stones, but no kadg appeared anywhere near them.

Then the procession turned their attention to the tiny vessels that had brought the enemy across the Great Water. They were astounded that such a thing could be done. No one in the tribe had ever imagined that people could sail on water in a thing that floated. They had no word or concept for boats.

It happened much as Gan and Mur planned. As the village men were buried at the place where Old Gan and young Tul lay, Set spoke with dignity and skill. Then the explorers returned to the thorp where they made a pallet of gigantic size and strength from large branches and reeds bound together with strong vines, and heaved the lion's body onto it. They pulled and pushed it across the sand until they approached the lion rock where two of the fiercest males stood guard. Gan held up his staff and approached them until he was looking into their sad eyes. To the men who watched, the entire exchange seemed absolutely normal. It was only after the work had been done and they had returned home that they understood the truth. Gan bowed, and said, "We have come to bury your brother with our respect. Will you allow us to do that?"

The lions stood for a moment, and then, as one, they stepped aside. Gan approached the outer base of the rock and walked out from the rock for a distance. He paused a couple of times, then turned to the others. "Here is the place. We will bury him here." They began to dig with their hands and some wooden tools and sticks to make the pit. The lions stood atop the rock and looked down at the proceedings. The men did not look up at them until later when they had finished their work, as Gan spoke to the lions again.

"We will place your brother into the sand here and cover him. That is how we do for our own." He motioned, and the young men pulled the pallet up beside the pit. As carefully as they could, they gently slipped the lion into the sand and arranged him on his side. When all was ready, Gan spoke again.

"Set and the elders are coming now. Set will speak to the lions."

So it was that the lions stood atop their rock and heard the voice of a man pay tribute to the beast who had died, and to all the lions for their part in the battle against the invaders. He pronounced his gratitude and that of all the people, and even mentioned that he had lost his own son in the battle. The lions looked on as the men pushed sand over the body of the young lion, smoothed it across the top, and placed protecting rocks on the surface over the pit.

When all was complete, the men retreated slowly; the lions remained on the rock, watching with their sorrowful eyes as the funeral procession crossed over the sand to the little settlement of Karnua.

Chapter Two

Circa 3700 B C

Karnua lay in the deep shadows of night. There was no moon, and a few drops of rain fell from a fretful sky. Some folk thought that rain came when a demon was assaulting one of their gods, although the town shaman was silent on that matter. When it rained, which was rare, people were afraid and drew together inside their huts and houses trying to stay out of the drops that seeped through the poorly thatched roofs which were designed to keep out the scorching heat of Ahm, not water. "It's the tears of a god," they said. But they also took some comfort in knowing that it was not the tears of Ahm, their great god, especially when it fell at night. At that time Ahm was at his home beyond the earth, resting and waiting for his next trek across the sky-fields in much the same manner that they rested from their work every night.

Pan waited near the door of his father's house with a long, shining stick in his hands, ready to strike anyone who tried to get inside without his consent. His mother and two sisters huddled in the back of the large but barely furnished single room in a state of quiet panic. His father, Dopan, lay unconscious, breathing slowly, on the floor. There was no fire.

Karnua had grown. It was no longer the tiny thorp of seventy people, but a minor metropolis of about four hundred, although no one knew the exact count. The place had spread back from the ridge, as well as in both directions toward the upper and lower Bab, but not down toward the Great Water. Kadg were still a problem there, and watchers continued to maintain a vigil every night, their numbers greatly increased since the old days when the entire town felt safe under the keen observation of only four men.

Karnua had never been invaded successfully. The only attempt, in the rare and dim past, had proved deadly to the attackers, and the sages and story keepers had kept the events of that night vivid in the collective mind of the townspeople. Since that ancient time, they said, no one had made an assault on Karnua. It sat proudly on the edge of the Bab above the green line of the River Valley, its larger houses and little huts and market area secure in its strength and position. There was friendly intercourse with neighboring villages and towns as far away as the Wide Riverland that bordered the upper Bab, and trade had been established for at least a millennium. All had been peaceful for many long years as far as negotiations and alliances with neighboring settlements were concerned, but that was not true of all the relationships within the town. There seemed to be constant squabbles between some of the families, creating a sense of disquiet in most quarters.

In the house of Dopan, his family waited in agony as the rain fell. During the light-filled and happy past they had covered their large house with limbs and reeds and daubed them with a thick mud mixed with sand that kept out the sun and some of the infrequent rain. Dopan's wife, Mera, had given birth to two daughters and a son, who was their middle child, a boy of thirteen, in that house. The boy was named Bropan although everyone called him Pan. He was dark skinned and tall, and was still considered young, only a boy, but was very wise for his age, with a disciplined mind and an eye for the beauty of almost everything he saw. His parents and his sisters, Meran and Jonda, were proud of him for his sometimes misunderstood talent of carving and drawing portraits of the creatures that lived in the Great Water Valley and the Bab, and even of people he knew. He could cut wood into fantastic shapes and images, and was working on making some figures from stone that he had searched out for that purpose.

The situation on that night was complicated. Pan's mother, Mera, had come from a lovely green village in the Wide Riverland where the Great Water parted into many channels, some only as large as a small, trickling stream. Pan's father had found Mera there when she was a girl of thirteen and was not yet ready for marriage. Dopan, being seventeen at the time, had worked hard to convince Mera's father that he could care for a wife; that he truly wanted to marry the girl and share life together. He also discovered that Mera's family had come from Karnua in the distant past, which made the negotiations a little easier. Many generations before, the family had moved to Harna, their village in the Wide Riverland, and had continued there from that time. But the family lore had not forgotten Karnua, and all the young ones could recite from memory the fact that their ancestors had come from there, or Nomo-Karnua as they called it. The stories of the lore were interesting, if not factual. They involved lions; how lions had befriended Karnua, and other tales of a man named Gad and his magic stick which helped him conquer other tribes and even vicious animals. Children loved the stories, especially those children with vivid imaginations. Most of the details of the stories had been lost in Karnua itself, but still lived among the small group of people who had removed to Harna.

Dopan left Mera in Harna for the full three cycle of seasons: hot, cool, and wet, so named for the annual flood of the Great Water, with the promise that she should be his bride, but when he returned her father again refused to allow her to go with him to Karnua, so far away and so strangely different. Mera had dreamed of a new life with Dopan for the entire year, and begged her father to keep his word, but he continued to refuse the young man, and sent him away forever, or so he thought. Dopan remained near the town and continued to see Mera when he could. Mera, however, had made a discovery during the year, and determined to use it to change her father's will and allow her to marry Dopan.

One day while helping her mother at the outside cookery, the girl had gone into the dark hut to hunt for a special utensil her mother needed, and as she looked in the open shelves she realized that a voice was speaking to her. Not an audible voice, but one that awakened her mind and filled it with new thoughts and ideas. She searched but could not find the source of the silent urging until she reached onto the floor beneath a table and her fingers touched a smooth stick of some kind. It was stuck there, but she worked it out of its deep hiding place and looked at it in the faint light that came through the central smoke vent in the roof. It was a curious wooden thing, long and dark, and it had something cut into the top of it - some kind of design. Mera went quickly to her bed alcove and slid the stick beneath her straw mat before she returned to the cooking fire to help her mother.

That was the beginning. Soon Mera heard the voice again, late at night in the darkness of her little space, speaking in her mind without a sound, but clearly telling her things that she longed to know. She saw Karnua as it had been long ago, and the Great Water, deeper and stronger in its flow than it was in the Wide Riverland. She watched and listened as the pictures and the story unfolded like a repetition of some of the lore she had learned as a child about Nomo-Karnua.

In the end, it was the stick that told her that she should go to Karnua, and insisted that she should take it with her. She couldn't imagine why, but the stick was adamant, and she was willingly swayed by its influence because her father had refused her suitor. She deftly persuaded Dopan to take her and escape from her father and Harna. They left two days later. Dopan carried the stick that had spoken; for him it was a talisman, not an independent being as Mera thought it to be. They were almost overtaken by the girl's father the morning after they left. He came rushing through the wetlands, following their tracks, shouting and searching, angry and fearful at the same time. But she hid herself and her young man well, peering out of their hiding spot through the leaves and vines as her father passed. She never saw her father again after that day.

It was years later, after she had lived in Karnua and given birth to her first child and participated in the community and all its events, including the daily rituals to Ahm and the yearly festival in his honor, that she told her neighbor Karsha the story of her father and the departure from Harna - and she told her about the stick - that Karsha began calling her a witch. That was a dangerous thing to be accused of; witches were thought to be in league with demons and the enemies of Ahm, so they were almost always drowned in the Great Water when they were discovered. Mera had lived in fear of Karsha since that time, but gradually the fear lessened and she decided that Karsha didn't plan to accuse her of witchery. She decided too soon.

When Pan was thirteen years, he started drawing a portrait of Karsha as a surprise for her. She was his mother's friend, he thought, and she would often talk to him about Mera and the things she liked to do and the things she said. The boy had no idea of any bad feeling between the two. It had happened before he was born, and so he offered his knowledge of his mother freely to their neighbor. He made the picture of Karsha on a flat stone, cutting into it with a sharper blade made from another stone, and then rubbing a compound into the cuts to bring out the features of the portrait. He enjoyed the work, as he always did, and it presented Karsha as a pleasant woman with a strong forehead and chin, and large eyes that stared back at the viewer. It looked very much like her.

When he showed his mother, she thought it a good likeness and commented on the fine lines and character of the face, but when he gave it to Karsha the woman screamed and threw it onto the ground. "How could you? How could you?" she shrieked. "You have enchanted him with your witchcraft and now he has made this - thing - of me, and you will use it to cast spells!"

"Witch! Witch!" she screamed. All the neighborhood could hear.

Mera left the broken stone likeness on the ground, pulled Pan into their house and closed the latch on the door. Karsha could be heard moaning and crying outside her house, and all the people in the neighborhood listened to her shouts and threats and the names and accusations she aimed at Mera and Pan.

Fortunately, no one believed them. They saw the evidence lying broken on the ground, but almost everyone knew that Pan could do such things, so there was no issue with anyone but Karsha. Then the raving woman began talking about the magic stick that Mera had, and how it could talk to her. That was a new element that no one had heard before, so the elders came to see Mera and Dopan early the next morning, to clear things up. Mera and then Dopan denied the story of the stick, and, having no clear evidence to the contrary, the elders left, declaring that Karsha had gone mad.

Pan was curious. He had seen a long stick in the house, behind a table in his mother's cookery, and at times he had thought that someone was speaking to him, speaking clearly in his mind, but not finding anything or anyone, he had gone on with the drawing and thinking that had been his principal occupations since he was a child.

Nothing else happened that day, but on the next day, late in the afternoon, at a time darkened by clouds and rain that flowed in from the Bab, Karsha's husband Lep, a beefy man about the same age as Dopan, burst into their house demanding that Mera come with him to the elders. "She has bewitched my wife!" he shouted in fury. "The woman can't talk of anything but Mera and her witchery, and she has been lying on the floor all day, unable to rise!"

Dopan attempted to calm him, but it was useless. Lep staggered in his wrath and struck Dopan on the side of his head. With that one blow Dopan fell to the floor, and Mera, gasping, fell on her knees beside him. Lep jerked her by the arm and pulled her from the floor, all the while raging and shouting, and Mera's screams added to the melee. Meran and Jonda tried to pull the big man and their mother apart, but Pan took another action. He dove beneath the table and grabbed the long stick; the Staff of Old Gan and Gan the Lion-tamer, the mighty staff made by the Great God Ahmun, and Pan raised it with authority, pointing the shaft at Lep.

Go!" the boy shouted. "Let go of her – get out of here!"

Lep fell back and released Mera as he bent over in apparent pain. He turned, fumbled at the door, and fled into the rain and dark. Mera collapsed onto the floor near her husband. The two girls sat in a daze beside them. They remained there for a short time until Pan called attention to his father, and Mera recovered enough to spread a soft skin over him, then sat beside him weeping. Pan stood close behind his father, panting as though from great exertion, holding the staff that he continued to point toward the door.

All was quiet in the house for a little while. Only the sounds of Mera's sobs and some small whimpering from the girls interrupted the patter of the raindrops until Dopan stirred and spoke. "Mera - - Mera?"

"I am here," Mera sobbed with agitation and relief.

"Has Lep gone?"

"Yes, father," Pan spoke quickly. "He is gone and I don't think he'll come back."

"My son," Dopan answered in a hoarse whisper. Then he looked at Mera. "I'm tired. I need rest. What happened?"

Mera, overjoyed by his sudden questions, told him. "You fell when Lep hit you, husband. That man is a brute!" Her fear spilled out with those words and she began to weep in earnest.

"I'll sleep," was Dopan's response. The weeping Mera covered him with another skin where he lay, and he fell again into sleep. His breathing was soon deep and regular.

The two girls loosened their tight grip on each other, but Pan stood all the while, waiting close beside the door, listening. Eventually, Mera covered herself and lay down beside Dopan. Time moved slowly, but Pan did not change his position.

Some far away sounds began outside, first a few voices in quiet but urgent conversation, then an increase of voices. Finally, sounds of the movement of a large, hushed crowd approached the front of the house, and someone pounded on the door. "The elders are here." a man called in a loud, hoarse voice. "Open the door!" Mera pulled back against the wall as far as she could as the pounding came once again. Pan placed the end of the staff on the floor with a thud and opened the latch. In front of the house was a good-sized crowd of neighbors, with Lep and Karsha in the foreground. They all shouted at Pan when they saw him. "Bring Mera out here!" He stepped through the door and pulled it shut behind him. He didn't speak. No one wanted to approach him, and he suddenly realized that they were afraid. He knew that Lep had told them about the staff. He thumped it on the earth for good measure.

"Pan," the chief elder said as he stepped forward. "Be reasonable. We only want to talk to your mother."

"That man," Pan pointed the staff at Lep, who moved aside quickly, "hit my father and knocked him down. My father did nothing to him. Now he is hurt and I demand that Lep be punished!"

The neighbors looked at Lep. This was getting more interesting all the time.

"Your mother is a witch!" Lep shouted as Karsha encouraged him. "She told you to make that image of Karsha and intended to use it to put an evil spell on my wife!"

"I made the image myself, and no one told me to do it!" Pan shouted back. "I won't let you take her!"

"We can all see that she's bewitched you!" Karsha shouted through the ominous air. "Get out of the way!"

"She's my mother and I won't let you take her!" Pan shouted back.

"Pan," the chief elder soothed with his voice. "We just want to know the truth."

"You can have her only if you can get past me!" Pan shouted again, pounding the staff on the ground again. "They have no proof, nothing."

"You have the stick she told me about!" Karsha wailed. "You attacked my husband with it."

"I'll do it again if you don't go away!" Pan called loudly so that all the crowd could hear his words. He waved the staff over his head and the crowd moved a step backward. "You are a deceitful woman, and I won't allow you or anyone else to touch my mother!"

At that moment the storm decided to unleash its strength on Karnua, especially those who stood there seething in the night. A terrible flash of dazzling light followed immediately by a rolling roar of thunder cracked over their heads, and the crowd cowered in the little street, covering their ears. Most of them had never seen lightning or heard thunder. Those storms were highly unusual in the Bab, and they were dumbfounded. The lightning struck again a few seconds later, and the rabble stood paralyzed with dread. Pan took his opportunity.

"That is the light from the Great God Ahm," he shouted above the storm. "And you have heard his voice. He is angry. He demands that you leave Mera alone, and that you take Lep and Karsha instead. They are the witches!" He struck the staff on the ground as the lightning and thunder rolled across the Bab, near and far, filling the night with flashes of the light and voice of Ahm who had been awakened from his sleep by the brazen people of Karnua, and was angry. They had never heard his voice before.

Someone in the crowd turned and bolted down a path toward his house, and at once all the others did the same. Only two of the elders and Lep stood in their places. Karsha had fled as quickly as she could.

"We see no reason to accuse Lep," an elder started to say, but he was interrupted by another giant flash and a house down the path sputtered into flame before a sudden downpour of rain doused the fire. That was enough. The last three headed toward their own houses, and Pan stood, thoroughly soaked, on the doorstoop alone. He turned then and went inside to a house that dripped with mud flowing from the roof. They all huddled into corners or under the low table to escape the deluge, but no one slept very much that night. The tension that covered them like a flood was still in the air.

Although there were no further charges from anyone, Dopan's family did not forget that long night and its strange events, nor did Lep and Karsha. The families avoided each other, and even if there were no more confrontations, there was no peace. Pan was alone most of the time. The people of the village didn't know how to approach a boy who was in league with the gods. His friends could not or would not talk to him. Some people bowed respectfully as he passed, but most turned aside before he could call some kind of doom down upon them. Pan was obviously aware of his new position, and as a show of authority he always carried the staff. Even his father was in awe of the staff and Pan's status, and kept a watchful distance between himself and the boy. Dopan didn't understand what had happened. He only knew that Pan was powerful, almost a god in the eyes of the Karnuans. The boy's mother was the one person who appreciated what he had done, and soon even Pan himself began to regret his new authority.

Several weeks after the lightning storm his mother decided she should talk to him about the staff. "I found it in my house in Harna and used it myself," she told him. "I don't know how it got there. I know what it is and how to use it, but I don't think I could do the things you've done with it." She didn't believe that the storm was a natural circumstance that Pan had used to his advantage.

Pan was somewhat mollified by those words. "I didn't know what it could do," he told her, "until you were in trouble and then it just happened."

"I am glad. You did very well, my son. But now can you put it away? It makes people nervous when you carry it around."

"I can't, mother. It won't let me. It calls to me as soon as I wake up in the morning and will hardly let me sleep at night."

"Ah, yes," Mera remembered. "It kept me awake too, until I did what it told me to do. What does it want you to do?

"I can't say, not yet. I want to be sure that I understand before I tell you."

"But you understand that I am no witch," Mera gently insisted.

"No more than I am, mother," the boy answered with a sigh.

After that the staff was quiet; no new ideas came into his head for a while, even when it was in his hand. He began drifting outside the village, visiting the now drying pond that had been their source of water for nearly two millennia, and he spent a lot of time at the huge mounded rock that stood near the pond at the lower-Bab end of the village. He walked round and round the rock for several weeks, surveying with his eyes from every angle, and carefully noting its great size from all the vantage points he could find. He went onto the plateau in the edge of the Bab to look down on it, never knowing that it was the very place where his ancestors had watched the lions when they had made their first visit to the pond with old Gan as he carried the staff. The people of Karnua watched the boy from afar, curious and yet afraid of what he might do.

Pan took the staff, which seemed remarkably resistant to time and wear, and measured the rock. The span of the staff was about one and a half times the height of an average man, and he measured the lion rock again and again. It became his obsession. The lines from the end that faced the Bab toward the one that faced the Water were thirty-seven lengths of the staff, its width from side to side measured about five lengths, and he noted the particular dimensions to its very top on the end that overlooked the water as seven lengths upward from the sandy floor of the Bab, but that wasn't tall enough for his purpose. He dug around the base of the rock on all sides, intending to remove part of the sand in order to expose more of the natural rock so he could keep his measurements in proper scale.

The trenches through the sand on all sides were still shallow when Pan hit bedrock. He dug channels in all directions to see how far the rock extended before he realized that he would need to remove the upper layer of the bedrock in every direction in order to get the proportions he needed for the lion. The beast would sit in a pit, surrounded by a flat, rocky floor. It was a serious problem; he would have to excavate. Despite his efforts he could find no other solution. He studied the problem for several weeks, but became increasingly sure that there was nothing else he could do.

Pan spent hours drawing in the sand along the base of the rock, and he saw it in his dreams at night. He looked at other rocks nearby, but there were none of the same scale and size. He knew they wouldn't work. It was then that the staff started to speak directly to him, guiding his thoughts with details, and the information was repeated so many times that he memorized the smallest parts, even how it would look when it was complete. The way he would accomplish it was left almost entirely to him, and he didn't yet have a solution.

When he started his sixteenth year at the beginning of the hot season, he heard the voice of the staff.

"You will need help. Everyone in Karnua should help you," the voice told him.

"Who are you?" Pan asked. It was the first time the voice had been so obvious.

"It does not matter who I am," the voice said gently. "I need you, and you need the people."

"How can I tell them that when I don't know who you are, or if you are really me talking to myself?"

He heard the voice sigh, and then it said: "I am the god of the Water. I made it and all the earth, and all the people on the earth. I am the creator of all you can see. Is that enough for you?"

"Yes, well, almost. What name do I call you?"

The god laughed softly. Pan heard the laughter plainly. "I am called Ahmun, the name I have given myself. You and your people call me Ahm, and some now call me Ra. That will soon be my name that everyone will recognize. Ahmun-Ra."

"Where are you?" Pan asked.

"You do have many questions, Pan." Ahmun-Ra responded. "Hold the staff up toward the sky."

Pan held it up to the light of the sun.

"I am there, and I am also near you, and I am near all living things, and the hills and the rocks, and the water. I am all things, and I am the creator of all things. Is that enough for you?"

Pan dropped the staff and fell down to the ground. He was suddenly ashamed of his thoughts and questions and fears. "I am sorry," he started to say, but the god Ahmun-Ra interrupted.

"You do not need to fear, Pan. I have chosen you to be my voice to the people, and to do the work I want you to do. I will not answer all your questions, for you cannot understand the answers now. One day you will. Just do as I tell you, and all will work out for the best."

"I will, I will," Pan promised. "Whatever you tell me, I will do it."

Then the voice was gone, but images poured out in his head, and he understood what the pictures meant.

He needed the cooperation of everyone in Karnua. There was no other way to get the work done, but he didn't know how to approach the people. He had to create the work, although its size made it seem impossible. It was his lifelong task, his assignment from the great god, so he set about making the plans for the colossus that would take shape out of the living rock.

Pan changed. It had been three years since the night of the storm, and he thought that enough seasons had passed that people might not be afraid of him any longer. He walked through the town slowly, talking to people as he moved along, trying to speak gently and befriend them, which was not easy. He had decided, soon after the night of the storm, that he was a superior being, connected in some indirect way with the gods, and because the gods spoke to him alone he had no need of the people of Karnua. He now admitted he had been wrong. He needed to get over his own importance and be one with the town again. Pan still made mistakes. Instead of waiting for time to do its work as he grew older, he tried to rush into adulthood. He let his hair grow long until it hung down below his shoulders and blew wildly into his face. He wore a cloak of animal skins his mother made for him. It fell below his knees, which was much too long for a young man. It was the garb of an elder; he thought it made him look more authoritative. Pan walked among his neighbors in his new guise, and people soon discovered that although he was eccentric, he was harmless.

Not long after that the god Ahmun-Ra spoke to him again. Pan was out late at night walking along in the edge of the Bab toward the lion rock when he heard the familiar voice. "You are to call the people together to give them a message."

The boy stopped and looked up. Ahm was nowhere in the sky. "Where are you now, Ahmun-Ra? Are you sleeping on the underside of the land?"

"I do not sleep, Pan," was the response. "I am not like you, I am the creator, and need no sleep. Now listen and do not ask any more questions."

Pan listened.

"Call the people together and give them this message from me. They are to help you with the work I have asked you to do. They must not fail."

"How can I say that?" the boy asked. "Oh, that's a question." He lowered his head.

Once again he heard gentle laughter. "You do not have to do anything but tell them. That's all you need to do. It will be enough. Say exactly this: You are making a statue from the rock and they must help do the work and must pay for it as well. That is all."

"They won't like to pay - -" Pan started to say, but Ahmun-Ra cut him off.

"That is enough. Don't argue. Just tell them. They will do it."

Then silence returned, but it seemed more portentous; a pulsating, waiting stillness.

A few days later Pan went into the streets of Karnua. "Come to the water-fire, after Ahm has gone at the next dark, and I will tell you what the gods have asked us to do!" He called to people in the lanes and the market place. He went to the temple of Ahm, which was located where the original stone walls had stood, and repeated the invitation. The temple was only a small altar where the shaman began his ceremonies each morning, but it was thought of as the center, or heart, of Karnua. The water-fire, the one closest to the Great Water, was the only watchfire of the original four that remained in the same place. It burned on the very edge of the aboriginal stone circle, where the market place was located in Pan's time. The ancient walls had mostly fallen, but their ruins still marked the outline for the market area. The people of Karnua gathered there for festivals and all important meetings, and on that night Pan stood behind the fire on top of the only part of the old wall that endured so he could be seen in the firelight by all the folk who gathered. Their curiosity had been stirred, and anything out of the ordinary was better than life as it usually played out in Karnua. They came for fun and excitement, as well as to see and hear what the unpredictable Pan had to offer.

"I invited you to come," he began in the loud voice of a man, no longer that of a child, "to tell you that Ahm, our great god who made the skies and the land and everything that lives, has given me work to do. Not only me, but all of us! You know the lion rock that stands outside Karnua on the lower Bab side? We - all of us - are to work together to make it into a great monument to Ahm." Pan paused to look around. No one stirred; there was no sign that they understood.

"We all will sacrifice something for this work to be done. It will require lots of willing laborers and also a lot of deben to complete it. I ask you," he paused significantly, "The Great Ahm asks you, to give of your time and deben for this purpose. We must cut the rock, and we must have the tools to do it."

There was a small murmur among some of the people, but when his voice paused they all looked toward him expectantly. "The elders, if they will accept this office, will be in charge of the collection of deben to buy the things we need, and I will supervise the cutting of the rock. It will take a few years, but when it is complete it will be a glory to Ahm, a wonder to Karnua, and I am sure that all the villages up and down the Great Water will come to visit this wonderful creature and pay a tribute to Ahm there." He meant that visitors would pay in deben, although he didn't make that specific.

He was finished, or nearly so, and he shifted his position on the rock wall to indicate that he would soon climb down. "If anyone needs to know more about this, I will tell you all that the Great God Ahm has told me. For now, let us go home with the resolve to do what he has asked us to do."

He jumped down from the wall, and as he moved onto the sand he heard a glad sound. It was the kind of cheering that the Karnuan women did at their festivals and for weddings, and it rolled loudly out of the throats of the women while the men laughed and hit their hands together. Some of the men were also chanting, " Ahm! Ahm! Ahm! Ahm!" People started dancing to the rhythm, just as they did at the annual festival, and then others joined until many swayed and moved to the sound of hands clapping in time and feet swinging to the impact. Pan was stunned. They were celebrating! Like a festival! Then he recalled that he had not yet told them how much deben it could cost each family, or that the creature they would make was to be a lion.

It took months to get started. Pan had to design tools for stone carving and have them made by the coppersmiths of Karnua and other villages, including Harna. He also had a lot of stone hammers prepared for the basic chipping of the rock, and the elders gladly went house to house to collect the deben needed in the service of Ahm. They kept some for themselves, but everyone pretended not to notice. It wasn't a good idea to complain about such matters, as they all understood.   Knappers prepared flint and obsidian stones that were small but held up to the kind of work they needed; specialized work for the fine lines and small features that were essential for the transformation of the rock. He also ordered ropes for climbing the steep sides of the rock. Rope was a common product, although no one in Karnua had ever used it for climbing up and over huge rocks.

Banu, the rope maker, lived just outside town. He worked in many facets of the builders' trade, making good strong rope for use in construction, and soon became an important advisor for the lion project. Pan took the man into his confidence soon after they met. He needed someone to help him get the work started, and Banu, a tall, thin man with a short cropped beard and bright eyes, was easily perceptive and quick thinking. Pan went to enlist his support.

"You have to keep the rope from fraying on the rock. Otherwise you can never get enough to last for much time at all." Banu told Pan. "If you seal it with this stuff," he motioned toward a large vat of fatty-looking paste, "you can make it last a lot longer. Of course it will wear out in time, anyway."

"We'll need a lot of it for the quarrymen to hook onto while they work across the top of the beast," Pan told him. "It'll take years to do that, you know."

"So you've been telling me. But I still don't understand exactly what it's all for."

"It's just a lion carved from the rock. It's big, yes, but I know we can do it if we work together!"

"And you say it's to honor Ahm? Are you sure?"

"It's what I've always said. You've heard me!"

"I don't know," Banu ventured. "Such an image has never been tried before. Not around here, anyway. Why do you think you want to do it? Is it really for Ahm, or is it for Pan?"

"It's for both," Pan replied both honestly and carefully. "I need to do it; I'm not sure why. I thought if everybody believed Ahm wanted me to - - - and he does. He told me. Anyway, the plan comes from him, and it will be his as soon as it's done."

Bantu looked shrewdly at Pan. Then he asked, "Do you think he'll accept it? He could burn all of us down if he doesn't like it!"

"I think he'll like it just fine," Pan answered. "I didn't get the idea from my own head, you know."

"Ah, yes, the stick. Thought that might have something to do with it."

"It's a staff," Pan said pleasantly, "and it makes more of the decisions than I do! I don't know for sure where all the ideas come from, but someone talks to me through the staff." He had decided not to be clearer than that.

"I'd like to handle it," Banu told him. "I think it would be a good idea for me to take a look at that thing. You don't want to get into witchcraft, do you?"

"It's not like that at all. It's never meant to hurt anybody. Only to do things - like this lion. That's the main thing it wants me to do."

Pan placed the staff of the Great God Ahmun-Ra into Banu's hands. He looked quizzically at all the inscriptions running down the shaft, but felt and thought nothing extraordinary. "Nothing here that I can find," he remarked, taking a long look at Pan. "You sure about this?"

"Yes, I am," was all Pan could say. He took the staff as Banu held it out. They never talked about the validity of the plan again, certainly not after Pan laid it all out for Banu to see. He drew intricate plans in the sand first and then transferred the drawings onto flat rocks that were small enough to carry. Banu was impressed and finally agreed to help. It was the boy's mother who had serious misgivings.

"How will you make a lion?" she asked her son. "Have you ever seen one?"

"Yes, I have," he responded truthfully. He had not seen a live lion but had dreamed of them often, and had seen them in those dreams, running with flowing manes, huge eyes shining and tufted tails flying, or lying at the base of a large rock, sleeping in its shadow, and he felt certain that he knew lions and that he could make a good image, almost like a living lion, from that rock.

"Do you have enough people here to do the job?" Mera wanted to know. "They may start but a lot of them will drop out and leave it for someone else to finish."

"It will work. I'm sure of it. Ahm will be our guide," Pan affirmed his plan to his mother even though he felt some doubts himself. "It has to be done. You should understand that!"

"Yes, the will of the staff has to be fulfilled," she spoke softly. "It always wants to have its own way!"

"It's the will of the god Ahmun-Ra," Pan replied. "He gave me his name not long ago. Ahm is really Ahmun-Ra, or Ahm is short for it, anyway."

"Don't - don't tell anyone else!" his mother whispered. "Let them call him Ahm."

Pan took up each new responsibility with every appearance of a sure hand, although he was sometimes uncertain and at other times, almost defeated. Had he known what it would take to get the sculpture made he would have given up, but he pressed forward, driven by the force of the staff and his own consuming desire to accomplish the work.

As the chief designer, Pan knew he had to learn to cut stone so he could work along with the men who would cut the rock. He went to the quarrymen, the rock cutters; an art which had been established since ancient times. It was a long, tedious process, but men cut the living rock every day, and he asked if he could learn from them as they worked.

"Yes," the head cutter told him. "You can come any time to see how we do it. And if it suits you, you can learn to cut. But you must take care. It's a dangerous place for someone who has no experience with rock."

The next morning, very early, Pan went out to the quarry to begin his study. He arrived before any of the cutters and was walking through the maze of stones in varying degrees of completion when the head man entered.

"You are early, my friend," the man spoke in an amicable voice. "We don't start until Ahm's light reaches the deepest part of the quarry."

Pan saw that the light was not yet reflecting off the partially cut stones that lay in a pit along the bottom of a cliff. "I wanted to see it all before you started working," he replied.

The cutter smiled again. "Then come down into the pit and have a look."

The rock lay in what appeared to be wide stripes. Blocks that had been taken already created that effect. The stones that were in the process of being cut were large, but not as large as the picture Pan had of the stones he needed for the lion's forefeet. He felt some misgivings as he looked. Even with a great many men it would take years to shape the lion rock, without even considering the time needed to carve the intricate patterns that would give it the identity of a lion. The workday started soon and he was surprised again by the slow progress the cutters made. There were four seasoned cutters and one apprentice who had started a little more than a year before, a much younger man of Pan's age, who joked and cajoled his way through a morning of steady work. At mid-morning break they took food, and the young man came to Pan.

"I am Ketol," the pale skinned boy with red-brown hair said warmly. "They tell me you want to learn to cut stones to make a temple to Ahm."

"I am Pan, and I don't plan to make a temple. I want to make a lion."

"Lion? So that's what you're doing! I thought it would be a big building or something. What's the lion for?" Ketol asked innocently. He showed no awe or anxiety, which was a relief for Pan.

"It's just an idea of mine, I guess," Pan stammered a little. "It will take a lot of cutting to make, but I intend to do it anyway."

"What does a lion look like?"

"I'll show you tomorrow. I have a likeness I made."

"Does a lion eat men?" asked Ketol.

"It might. I don't know," was all Pan could say.

They finished the fish and bread and Ketol offered him some of the brew his father made. It was in a waterskin, but tasted much better than water. It was even tastier than the brew Dopan made, Pan thought. He also hoped that he had found a friend and willing partner for the undertaking he faced.

The quarry and the rock that would become a lion were, for Pan, like homes. He spent almost all his time in those two places, returning to sleep in his father's house at the dark, but always up and ready to go to work even before Ahm lighted the sky fields. He was happier than he had been since the great storm, which was now a major point of conversational lore in Karnua, and Pan held no small part in the legend. He was depicted almost as a god, and many people still reacted toward him with deference as he walked through the town toward his work each day.

Pan was well over his estrangement to most of the townspeople before Lep came to their door one night. He stood quietly outside as he asked to talk to Pan, and his father came in to tell the boy that their neighbor was waiting if he wanted to see him. Pan picked up his staff and stepped through the door with his father close behind, and they met with Lep on the doorstoop where Pan had stood to accuse the beefy man of witchcraft. Lep looked warily at both the staff and Pan as he started to talk.

"I am ashamed of what I did on the day of the storm," he began. "I had no idea that Karsha was misleading me. I know now. She's gone. I think she went to another town in the Wide Riverland with a man who came here to sell tools. I'm not sure." Pan felt a sense of pity for the man who seemed subdued by his bad fortune, but he wondered whether it might actually be good fortune to be done with that woman.

"She's a great beauty, as you know," Lep said. "You made the image of her and that must have been because she's such a splendid woman." He didn't look at either Pan or Dopan. "She's gone, and I'm not going to try to find her. I'll let her go."

Dopan wanted to speak, but couldn't find words either to praise or blame Karsha. Pan simply waited. This was all much more than he understood about relationships. Lep paused for a little, but soon spoke again. "I want to make things right between us. We're neighbors. Let's work together to make it right."

"Mera wouldn't like that, Lep," Dopan remarked. "You know you've done great damage to her." Dopan didn't mention his own injury.

The big man lowered his head. "Yes, true. Now I'll try to make it up to you. Maybe I can help you in some way. Your wife doesn't have to see me, ever."

Pan's head was racing. He needed men to help him work the stone. Lep was a hulking man who could do heavy work more easily than most, if he would allow the quarrymen to teach him. "I may have something for you to do," he told Lep. "I'll think about it and talk to you soon."

"I'll wait," Lep responded as he turned toward his house. Father and son watched him walk away; a quiet, dejected figure who had once been a combative and dangerous problem. When they went into their own house they made no mention of what Lep had said to the family. Mera didn't ask, but she watched them cautiously after the door was shut.

The work on the lion began some time later, after the season had changed again and the world was very hot. The head quarryman decided that he would let his men work with Pan late in the day after Ahm was walking away toward the end the Bab where he went beneath the earth, and the air was cooler. The master of the quarry held the right to ask his men to work from sunrise to dark, and it was he who would pay them for their work on the lion. He believed that the figure Pan was making was for the worship of Ahm, and he could gain the great god's favor. The stone cutters had the job of teaching their craft to all the men who were able to work, although they were a little reluctant at first. An entire village of quarrymen did not seem an advantage to them.

Almost everyone started work early in the hot season, with a long break in the middle so they didn't have to labor in the heat and flame that Ahm produced at the time of the year when his path was directly overhead. Most of the village returned to work when Ahm grew further away. It was an age old pattern, and they loved the mid-day rest. Lep was especially welcomed to the stone-cutting group, and he did a lot of the heaviest work of helping to lift rock that had been cut away.

The deben to buy supplies came in, enforced by the town elders. All the households paid a good sized tax, and the labor on the lion was voluntary from those same householders who paid for the equipment to do the work. It became, as Ahmun-Ra had promised, a project that everyone got involved with. There were huge fires to be maintained for the working of the copper tools which had to be remade often because they dulled so quickly. There were the dozens of men it took to drag the shaped stones into position, there was all the food to be prepared, water bearers for thirsty laborers, and many other aspects of a gigantic work force that were needed to make a lion out of the rock.

"The lion's body has softer rock than we usually work on," the quarry-master told Pan. "It won't be too hard to get it into shape, but it will take time. These things go slowly." Pan understood. He was learning, and had no need to rush. He would be proud to dedicate the colossal beast to Ahm, and Karnua would have a monument like no other. One that would last for eternity, he thought. It was a mind-boggling concept.

The days passed into seasons and the seasons into years. There was nothing particularly exciting about the work except for the times when Pan stood far off and looked at the animal that was growing out of the stone. He saw the beginning of gradual changes in the shape of the hind-quarters and the head; the slow, almost imperceptible shaping of the contours of the rock that made it come together as a replica of a great creature, as yet unidentifiable but certainly no longer just a rock. And although he appreciated the work that all the men were doing, he considered himself the creator of the colossus. It was, he told himself, his plan and his supervision that caused the work to go forward, and he felt great pride in it. The lion's feet were extended, his head gradually changed from craggy rock into a smooth featured lion face and mane, and his hindquarters with the tail wrapping around to his right rear haunch stealthily appeared out of the rock. As debris was produced it was hauled away into a large dumping site in the Bab.

"Why do you want a big bunch of hair at the end of the tail?" Ket asked Pan. "Shouldn't it come down to a narrow tip kind of gradually."

"It's the way I see him," Pan answered. "I may have never seen a real lion, but I think the tail part is right. I dream about him all the time."

"Well, you're the boss!" Ket joked. Pan felt the weight of responsibility as well as the honor of his creation and the work of hundreds of people all implied in that simple statement.

The lion's head was slow to appear. That part of the rock was much harder than the body, probably due to the fact that it had never been covered with sand and had stood in the light for untold ages, hardening and gradually becoming a different kind of stone to the softer, sand-covered body. Pan worked primarily on the head and face, chipping away at it, smoothing the contours after he had made as many stokes with the chisel as were needed to define the various parts of the lion's features and mane. It took years of persistent work; making the sad, constant eyes, which were each a little taller than the staff in actual size, and shaping the hair of the mane around the neck and face of the startling beast. At times the stone would chip at the wrong angle or too much would flake off in a spot, and Pan had to rework that place so it harmonized with all the rest. Improvisational sculpting became one of his strengths.

One afternoon, as the dark started to fall, Pan and Ket were digging along a far edge of the rock that had been cut away to make the floor around the beast, the still unfinished lion towering above them as they made the excavation in the soft sand. They were looking for evidence of something that Pan had been shown by the staff. The copper spade he was working with struck an object beneath the outer wall. Then, as he moved it to a slightly different location, it struck again. "Ket, come and help me here. I've hit something," Pan called. They worked together, and in the dim light began to remove hard sand that was starting to solidify around some old bones that gleamed up at them, glowing faintly in the dimness. The bones were well - preserved by the dry heat of the Bab. The young men worked as long as they could see, then went to one of the workshops for some torches to light the trench so they could study what they had uncovered. It took a lot more digging, but at last they stood looking at a large skeleton that lay on its side, clearly buried there for some purpose.

"It is a lion," Pan spoke softly. "I don't know how long he's been here, but it's been a long time. And people buried him! See the spears and the little stones?" There were obvious remnants of wooden shafts which had held the spear points that lay in a formation beside the great ribcage. And the amulets that Set had buried with the lion more than a thousand years before still bore the marks of Ahm the shaman had cut into them.

Ket was mystified. "Why would they do that? Bury it, I mean."

"They were honoring him for something, I think." Pan's staff lay on the sand just above the lion's burial pit, and it was speaking rapidly, showing him the past, the morning that the lion had been placed there. It was then that he grasped the importance of that enormous rock, and the reason he had been drawn to it. Men and lions working together had defeated an enemy.

The next day Pan returned to the grave early. He slid down into it and considered the bones of the long dead beast. He saw the skull with its gigantic teeth, the long bones for the front legs that had been stretched out ahead of the body, and he knew then that his decision to put long forelegs on his lion was right. He studied it all carefully, and just as carefully shoveled the sand gently back into the tomb and left the lion in peace. At last he knew for certain what a lion looked like.

There was a constant gallery of visitors from the very start. They would look and joke about some things, while other aspects of the lion confused them, or they simply stood and stared. The thing was beyond comprehension, and some were obviously troubled at a near-likeness of an immense lion standing alongside Karnua. What could it mean, and what kinds of trouble could it cause? Superstition abounded, and there was some consternation. "What if he makes it come alive?" an older man who believed in mighty acts from the gods asked some friends. "What would that great thing do for food? I hate to think!"

"We wouldn't have much left of our town in short order!" another teased him. "You could volunteer to be eaten first, of course. That would give some of us a chance to get away."

No one seriously thought that the lion might take on flesh and ravage the town, but it was fun to talk idly about it in the market and other places where people usually met. Not all the talk was jovial. No one spoke directly to Pan, or even within his hearing, but there was a lot of discussion about the great lion and its place in the local scene. Often there were no real reasons for objections, but objections were a part of human nature, so they took on a busy life as the work went forward. "What good will it do anybody? It will sit there and look awful for a long time. It's a really ugly old thing, now, isn't it?"

Another complained that all the work was a waste. "What does anybody want it for, anyway? It's just a misuse of time and deben, and there's no point in it."

"It's supposed to be in honor of Ahm," someone responded. "Otherwise, it would be a waste. But if they build a temple to Ahm here then it might work out pretty well."

Most people supported Pan's lion, but they weren't often heard from. No one paid much attention unless the dissenters were together and gossiping. Then all the naysayers held forth at length to oppose the development of the sculpture. Despite that, the work went ahead steadily. There was no more doubt in Pan's mind, and he supervised the rock cutting with a sure hand and eye. All the quarrymen were impressed, even Ket, who told him that the dead lion was indeed his inspiration. Pan agreed, but kept all the rest of his thoughts to himself. Villagers walked around and poked into things whenever they could, but Pan was not distracted by their attention. At times there were so many men working on the rock that it looked like an anthill full of very large, active insects. Some of the folk laughed or made fun, but no one spoke that way to Pan. His reputation as a friend of the Great God Ahm, or even possibly a god himself, was enough to keep them from complaining directly to the "Lionmaker," as many of the people called him. No one seemed to grasp the idea that it was all done for them.

There were other interesting things to use as fuel for conversation and gossip as well. "I wonder what he's going to do to find a wife? And when? He's twenty-three years old now," a woman asked her neighbor early one morning as they went to the pond for water.

"And what man would let his daughter marry that one?" her friend asked. "It may be good for him to be so close to the gods, but it's a dangerous place for most people."

"He might go to the gods themselves for his wife. Marry one of them," suggested the other. "Then where would they live? No one here would want much to do with them, that's sure."

"Well, I asked Mera about it the other day, and do you know what she said? She said, 'He'll have to decide for himself, of course, but I will be pleased to have him consult me! So would Dopan. We don't really know what he'll do.' That's what she told me!"

Choosing a wife was far from Pan's mind. He was totally occupied with the work, and he had to see it completed, even though it might consume him so that he would never lead a normal life. Pan grew older without taking a wife. The lion was not all that he cared about, but no one else knew what was in his mind or what he planned to do once the lion was finished.

When Pan reached twenty-five, after nine years of work with an uncertain crew, the animal had emerged from the stone, and yet he went up every day to tinker with it, chipping a bit of it here and there some days, but on other days he simply inspected without touching it with his chisel. He was finished at last, but he didn't want to let it go. Ket was also twenty five and had a wife and two children, and Lep had gone away to another village two years before. Some of the gossips said that he had found Karsha again, and that he went to be with her because she wouldn't show her face in Karnua. And time, at least for Pan, had resolved to a quiet and simple existence after the great inspiration, long labor, and completion of the magnificent lion. For him, the best part was that Ahm was satisfied. His staff became silent.

Hor-em-akhet, "Horus at the horizon," as the people called the lion, stood beside the village, its face toward the rising Ahm, forefeet extended to the dawn. The Great Water flowed beneath its feet a short distance to the east, and the plateau where the enormous triangular pyramids would rise during a later millennium stood above the Lion where the town of Karnua was located. Adventurous people from the Wide Riverland and the farther reaches of the Great Water heard about the colossal beast and many came to see it. A tide of visitors, some on foot or on donkeys but many in the small single-masted boats that sailed the Great Water, took long journeys to see Hor-em-akhet as he sat on the edge of the Bab gazing out toward the rising place of Ahm. The presence of the beast blessed Karnua with a vigorous income and sense of security. It seemed to offer a promise for a new and better world.

The future world eventually came to the place known as Karnua and left it empty. It gradually fell into decay and ruin, until at last the site became the home of the enormous pyramids of Giza. The Lion survived for centuries and then millennia, and like the pyramids, seemed to endure forever. The stories of Pan and the men who made the colossus sank into the west like the last rays of Ahm and would never be found again, but they were deeply inscribed within the Lion itself.

Chapter Three

2567 BC

The little boat rolled through the waters of the Nile. It flashed and glinted among the green-gray swells with its bright blue hull and red sail trimmed in gold. The river was still brimming weeks after flood stage, and the swift water bore the boat along toward the new necropolis where the great Pharaoh Khufu's astounding pyramid scraped against the stars at night, its peak so tall that if a man stood next to the foundation, the side of the tomb seemed to rise straight above him like a flat wall. It was the grandest of all the pyramids that had been created to that day, and history later proved that it was the grandest of all. Nothing like it had ever been seen on the face of the earth, and even its builders, the men who had done the work of construction, gazed in amazement as they looked at what they had accomplished.

The boat, small as it was, reflected some of the glory of Khufu, for it held two of his sons, alone in its hull as they plied the waters. Two similar boats, trimmed with less dazzle and style, held the brothers' retinue of followers and came along behind. Jed and Kafa, the princes, were at ease even on the swift water, and steered the boat with clever expertise. They were twins, now in their eighteenth year, but were easily distinguished one from the other. Jed, who became Djedefre I, a pharaoh of less renown than his father, was the taller of the two, with very black hair and narrow, close set black eyes that watched from under a wide forehead. He was as strong and muscular as his brother, but seemed a bit more awkward when he moved around a playing field, or when he wrestled. Kafa had the same black hair and eyes, but was more compact. He was also more agile and quicker with responses when doing athletics. He was a master of the small boat that has come down through history as a *felucca*, a single masted riverboat, and on that day he guided it with surety toward the dock just below the great pyramid despite the straightforward but deathly conversation the two were having.

"When it's done you'll be my first advisor and chief priest to his temple. We have to keep an eye on things there." Jed spoke just above the slushing sound of the water. "But I'll take the heat of the investigation if his priests or minions want to ask questions."

"It's not easy," Kafa remarked. "They watch him constantly, even while he's in bed or in the toilet."

"Especially then," Jed said with a short laugh. "It's the usual, that's all. No one really loves him, you can be sure. He's got a reputation."

"A mean streak. I have the marks to prove it!" Kafa grimaced. "He really hates me. You'd think he might be a little scared of us by now!"

"Probably is, but he's never going to let us know!" Jed commented with a shrug. "We can play him along for a while yet, but we have to do it this year. My astrologer tells me that this is my good year! Anyway, he hates me even more than he hates you."

Kafa looked up at the approaching pyramid that blotted out a large portion of the sky. "He wants to live forever, so we can send him there," he pointed to the monument, "quicker than he expects. Let his eternal life begin!"

"Yes, brother!" Jed smiled.

"I have friends who'll help. They know all about his tirades and the beatings."

"Just be sure you can trust them. Anyway, he's been pharaoh way too long. He's corrupted everything."

"Hold on. We're coming in." Kafa pulled on the sail's rigging and turned a little so they hit the dock with less force. Even so, he landed the boat at a faster clip than usual and it shuddered at the impact. Nubian slaves grabbed the rope that was thrown to them as the twins clambered out and turned toward Khufu's mortuary temple. Their retinue of guards, musicians, and slaves, including some lissome and beautiful young women, hurried along after them.

The mortuary temple for Khufu's pyramid was in its finishing stages, as was the monolith that towered above it on the plateau. The twins were there to inspect progress on the site and report to the king who rarely went out from his palace grounds. He was aging and suffered from some condition of his heart and was much too ill to travel, his doctors told him. He should relax at home and send for everyone he required to meet him at the palace in Memphis. The doctors, after being paid handsomely by some of the government ministers, had issued dire warnings to the pharaoh in an attempt to keep him confined so he wouldn't discover the extent of corruption in which most of the officials in the kingdom were wrapped. As a result of this wholesale involvement, they all protected themselves with bribes and cover-ups to one of the greatest extents anyone had seen up to that time, and the aging pharaoh was as much their victim as they were his.

Khufu had planned his eternal house so that it lay close to the only ancient monument that existed on the plateau at that time, the Great Lion, often called Hor-em-akhet, Horus on the Horizon, which stood above the Nile with its forefeet lying in a direct line to the dawn, the rising place of the sun god Ra. The statue was the first thing the god saw each morning as his eyes searched the horizon toward the west. The magnificent lion, a treasure from the distant past, had sat there for so many centuries that some of the people thought it had been created by the sun god himself, and was therefore to be venerated along with the pharaoh, who was the representative of Ra on the earth and a god in his own right.

Jed and Kafa walked into the temple to begin their inspection, but their followers waited outside in the courtyard except for two guards who hurried to catch up with the young princes so they would not be thought lax in their duties. If any mishap befell the sons of Khufu as they examined the temple where their father would lie during his preparation for the after-life, the guards' lives would be forfeit. The temple was a long, narrow structure that served as an anteroom to the pyramid as well as a corridor that led to its entrance, and it was the place where the body of the dead king would be taken immediately after his death so the internal organs, except for his heart, could be removed and stored, and the fluids and linen wrappings applied for mummification, a long and complex process. Everyone in the king's family expected to have the same thing done for their own bodies, but most of the inhabitants of Kmet, the ancient name for Egypt, had no hope of entrance to the afterlife. For them it was a situation of life ending where it had begun, on the earth, at the time of their physical death. There was no voyage among the stars and no eternal existence for common folk. That fact didn't distress anyone, however. Only the wealthy could afford the process of mummification, and few among the entire population were wealthy. The working class could not expect eternal life. That was a distinguishing element between the ruling class and the common people of the land.

In the days that followed the river trip, intrigue after intrigue developed within the palace at Memphis. Khufu, the aging pharaoh, waited there like an ailing spider with his web surrounding his throne, and anyone who wasn't wary might be caught and devoured almost before the victim could know what had happened. The queens, Khufu had three at that time, approached him carefully, as did all his children and various other relatives who lived in or near his palace. No one wanted to be called to appear before Khufu, and whenever a summons came, they wisely entered his presence with trepidation.

That included his two sons, Djedefre and Khafra, the twins born to him in his later years. They were the only sons still in favor, and he intended making Djedefre his heir, with Khafra placed in a major role as an advisor to the king. Khufu was always a severe parent, and he would have his sons beaten, especially the highly intelligent and headstrong Khafra, if they did anything that was less than pleasing. It was his way of ensuring that they were in his complete control and would never become a threat. Khufu had no intention of being murdered by his sons so that one of them could inherit the throne. "Keep them subdued, and always threatened, and they will never be able to think of overthrowing their father." That was the plan in Khufu's mind as he humiliated his children. It remained his plan until the day he died.

On that eventful day Khufu was holding court with a recalcitrant governor who had slipped in his tax payments and was now about to pay the price in full. The pharaoh was enjoying a game with him first, however, sporting with the man as he waited to spring the trap that would lead to another death.

The pharaoh liked to hold court in his dining pavilion, overlooking his garden with its lush ponds and green plants mixed with colorful bushes and trees. Every known bulb and flower that could grow in that climate was there, blooming and spreading around the graceful multi-columned building that was open on three sides. Its only wall was along the back, hiding the kitchens and storehouses. Khufu usually ate alone. He loved his food, especially when it was accompanied by music from a group of musicians hidden on the portico that surrounded the building. Large columns, heavily ornamented, held up the stone roof, and a beautiful floor of polished marble lay at his feet. Drifting curtains of soft linen covered some of the openings because Khufu liked to watch them billowing in the breeze, and his attendants, except for one taster and one server, waited on the portico to do his bidding.

He met Commander Nurifa in a large and comfortable seating area in the center of the pavilion, where he kept a throne on a marble dais that was a few inches higher than the floor. The pharaoh sat on the throne while the supplicant knelt at his feet.

"I expect, Commander Nurifa," Khufu spoke kindly, "that you have had some difficulty with your people - some sort of business problems I imagine." The pharaoh sighed. "They are common in the land these days."

"Oh, yes, mighty one," Nurifa lowered his eyes in order to look more sorrowful. He was a tall, thin, and sallow man with large grey eyes that looked deceptively blind. "I am desperately unhappy with the situation, but I have done and continue to do all I can. The needs of Kmet are always paramount in my mind, I assure you." He had played his best card moments before when he placed his well-documented account books into the hands of the king's stewards so they could be examined. The books showed the great losses that his lands and various other enterprises had endured during the past two years, and were sure to win him a pardon. No one, he knew, could possibly dispute the results of the hours of careful deliberation and figuring that had gone into those books so they would show loss despite the fact that he had received a staggering amount of money during that two year period.

"Well, come with me and we will eat and talk a little and forget these troubles," Khufu offered graciously. "It has been long since we were at meat together. I am sorry that I cannot offer you much, but I am restricted in what I can eat by my doctors. They will be the death of me, yet!" he quipped with a broad smile as he led the way into a dining alcove. The table was so laden with meats and fish and fruit and bread and flagons of wine that the governor could only stare at it all in silence. What did he mean, restricted? He recovered his voice quickly, however. "Do not make the pharaoh suspicious," his thoughts reminded him.

"Oh, mighty one, I am not worthy!" and he said it with conviction.

"I understand, commander," Khufu answered, "but you should eat and enjoy yourself while I have this bit of vegetable stew and a little bread. No wine for me. Not anymore."

"But, your divine grace," protested Nurifa, "how can I eat of this bounty while you are suffering so? I cannot." He bowed his head toward the stout, bull-like figure of Khufu.

"And how could you steal from me, from Kmet, in so profligate a manner?" Khufu asked in an ordinary and pleasant voice.

The commander paused. "But, your divine grace, I have just offered my account books to you. You can see that I have lost much more than I gained during the past two seasons."

"Ah, yes, your little story," Khufu smiled with pleasure. "It's a good one, too! But come now, my friend. Eat and enjoy yourself. You have earned this." And he said no more, but indicated for a slave to pull back a chair for the commander, who was forced to sit and eat as Khufu gazed at him with a smile. The tension was unbearable.

"I hope that you are not displeased with me, oh divine one," Nurifa made a small plea as he was eating, nearly choking on the food that was now tasteless and dry in his mouth, "I am so honored to share meat with you."

"You will notice, of course, that I have no meat," Khufu responded, an implacable smile still on his lips. "I am pleased that you are enjoying yours. But I need to warn you that some of the meat may not be entirely to your liking. I fear it is - - uh, a little contaminated."

"What do you mean?" cried the commander.

"Don't be too alarmed," Khufu said warmly, raising his hand in a gesture of dismissal. "It's only a small matter, really."

"What's a small matter?" Nurifa squeaked. "What's in this?"

"A little more - - flavor, I would call it."

Nurifa pushed the bowl away. "I won't eat it!"

"Oh, I think you've had enough, already," the pharaoh spoke heartily. He thought smugly of a cat who had trapped a mouse.

"Enough?" the victim quavered. "What are you saying?"

"At least you will be spared a more painful death."

The commander began to sob and beg, but the pharaoh insisted that he continue to eat, serving more of the food onto the unfortunate man's plate, smiling and speaking in the most conciliatory tones all the while. Nurifa refused to take another bite.

After the commander had slipped from his chair, gray eyes unfocused and staring, the pharaoh rose, walked to another alcove across the room where another table waited, laden with meat and drink. He sat alone, indulging in the feast until his advisor came to ask if his son, Prince Khafra, could have a brief audience. Khufu sighed but motioned for the prince to come in. Kafa entered and bowed low.

"Your divine grace," he said too rapidly to his father, "I am here to ask for your guidance concerning my future." He bowed lower.

Kafa glanced over the table quickly. Where was it, he wondered? He had had little time to prepare for this moment, even though he had gone through it in his mind often. When it actually arrived it seemed very sudden, from a totally unexpected source, and he was afraid. Khufu paused in his eating and looked for a moment at his son. He didn't believe a word of what he said, but what was the boy up to? He seemed agitated or frightened about something. "I have not changed my mind," he said abruptly. "Why do you bring this matter to me now?"

"I want only your reaction, my father. I know that you want a military career for me, but I would like you to consider a position in the temple of Amun-Ra. It would be in honor of your name."

"I have had greater honors, my son, if that is who you wish to be tonight. I do not need another. Whatever it is you really want can wait until another time."

"But it is not what I want, mighty king," Kafa said in an attempt at a more formal invocation. "It is what is good for all of us, for the nation - for all the people - - - for Kmet. If I were priest I could help the nation overcome -" Kafa struggled to keep his mouth working. He needed to pull himself together, and he took a long breath. Talking to his father had never been easy but at this moment he wanted to sink into the floor rather than stand nakedly before such power.

"Ah, and what do you want to overcome now? Out with it!" Khufu shouted, his anger rising. "You're nervous about something and you stammer like a child."

"I only want the country to be blessed because of your greatness, your valor, my lord, and I think I can do that - -"

"If that's your reason you can wait awhile. I'm still eating." Khufu reached for a bowl of his favorite meat, but as he did so he winced and suddenly gripped the side of the table. "What have you done?" he cried out. Khufu tried to reach his son with his heavy hand, but the young man stepped backward. "You snake! Come here, you bastard!" the old man bellowed. But Khafra did not move. The mighty pharaoh tried to stand. He struggled, but fell, uttering a cry. He hit the marble tiles hard, a crushing blow; the light in his eyes was fading. A small trickle of spittle tinged with blood dropped to the floor from a corner of the royal mouth.

"Father!" cried Kafa, apparently forgetting his place. He leaped toward the table but it was obviously over. "Play it out to the end!" he thought. And it had been fairly simple! Quickly he knelt over the dying king. "Don't let on that you know!" he said to himself, and kept the knowledge deep within his mind. The advisors and a doctor came rushing in from the portico. They gazed at the old pharaoh, touched his body and felt for a pulse. Nothing. The mighty had fallen and the pharaoh was dead. Anyone could see that. It was soon reported that death was caused by heart failure.

Later that night the queen met her twin sons in her apartment. They each lifted a glass of wine in memory of the dead pharaoh and then in salute to Jed, who, as Pharaoh Djedefre, had taken his place as the king. Kafa bowed low before him, as did his mother, and they spoke softly for a few moments. Then the queen stood.

"This morning, in this room," she said gently, "the great pharaoh Khufu told me that he was going to kill an asp tonight. I thought I might do as well and kill another." They all laughed quietly, obviously satisfied. Anyone who heard them would have thought they had recalled a fond moment in their lives with Khufu The Great.

In the days that followed the ascension of Djedefre to the throne of Kmet, the family thought little of the departure of Khufu. The priests and the embalmers at the mortuary temple took care of all the planning, and on the day of his burial in the grand tomb, probably the largest such structure ever built, the people of the nation mourned. Women who were hired for the purpose of weeping and lamenting preceded the pharaoh's body from the mortuary temple and up the ramp into the pyramid, while his sons and daughters and queens stood to one side, watching the spectacle with dry eyes and joyful hearts. The great loads of treasure and the many slaves who faced death that day entered behind the mummified body which no longer resembled the pharaoh. A chant intoned by the priests wafted, along with the strong smoke of the incense, from the opening of the tomb for a short time as they made their way into the burial chamber hidden deep inside the massive stones. When all had ended, the pharaoh's family stepped into the boats which were decorated and festooned for mourning and sailed up the Nile to Memphis where they gathered in the dining pavilion to celebrate the new pharaoh with a great feast. There was no mourning in that place. The people of Kmet, however, mourned for most of the next year. They venerated the late pharaoh in temples and homes throughout the land.

The staff of the Great God Amun was silent. It had not spoken for a thousand years. The Lion, that immense piece of statuary, had always watched on the shore of the Nile as far as the people of Kmet knew, and the stories of Gan and Pan were all but lost. A few of the legends survived, but they were told as amusing stories for children, and no one believed they were based in fact. The staff, as new and shiny as if it had been made very recently, stood in a corner of a farm cottage in the Nile delta; a very old cottage with sagging walls, a thatched roof and dirt floor, grimy with the muck of a few hundred years, filled with a ragged family with two children, some pigeons and a few goats. Everybody and everything, including head lice and other vermin, lived together in the lowly hut.

The peasant cottage was located in the tiny village that had once been Harna, now called Ranua, and it was only a shadow of what it had been. No one knew the history of the place; there was not even a story keeper in the area to recall the events of the distant past. It had not been abandoned, but as the river had changed its course through the delta, the town had lost its primary flow of water and there was now only a small trickling stream where one of the main bodies of the river had flowed in the past. The land remembered, but no one else.

The cottage stood on the edge of the water which moved sluggishly through a narrow channel, at times nearly dry. Only in the flood season was the stream alive and active, but even then the waters didn't reach into the cottage or water the fields that were behind it. The land was green, due to the underground water system that lay beneath the entire delta, but it wasn't as verdant as many other spots along the great river. There was no new soil deposit each year, and the land itself had grown worn and thin.

The family of Ser lived in the cottage, along with the few pigeons that sometimes roosted in the sagging beams which were situated low enough to narrowly miss the heads of the family as they walked through the single room. Three goats, the greatest wealth of the family, lived in a lean-to shed on one side of the hut, but the goats were frequent visitors to the family quarters, and there was one pig that Ser had found along the waterway and brought into the hut in order to keep it hidden.

Ser and his little wife, Uma, had two children; Wat, a small boy of ten who was stretching out to grow taller, although he was very thin, and Matu, a girl of twelve. She was short, like her mother, with a pretty face and deep, black eyes that glowed with vitality despite her meager allotment of food. She cared for the goats herself, tending them skillfully with all the strength and tenderness she had, for she loved her goats and understood that their welfare was of great importance to the family. Every year one or two kids were born, and they were sold at a market in the town of Enosa for the best price they would bring. She also milked the two nannies and the family got much of its nourishment from them. Any extra milk, which the nannies usually provided in abundance, was sold. The family land produced a little grain, which Ser planted and harvested, and they used most of that crop for daily bread and beer. They lived about as well as most of the peasants in the delta land of Kmet, and hardly knew that a better life was possible.

As she neared the end of her twelfth year, Matu was sought by a farmer who lived on a broader branch of the water. He had more land and an income from grain as well as goats. The aging man saw the girl at the market place, and noticed her beauty as well as her spirit, so he bargained for her although he was almost forty years and several of his teeth were already gone. Ser was glad to agree to the marriage, but Uma raised a fuss and Matu was distraught. She hadn't expected to have a husband for at least another season, and the older man was not at all what she hoped for. He had a wife already, and Uma was fearful that his first woman would mistreat her daughter.

"She keeps the goats for you," Uma insisted. "How can we keep the goats if she is married?"

"You can look after them as well as she can," Ser told her. "You don't have much to do here, anyway. And he will give us a good bride-price."

"She will be beaten, I know it!" Uma exclaimed. "You don't even care what happens to her!"

"What I do is none of your business, woman," Ser replied. "Go and get her ready. Wash her, and put something decent on her. He'll be here tomorrow morning." Ser couldn't recall the name of the farmer who was to buy Matu. He'd have to ask him in the morning.

Uma went out to the goat shed where Matu was milking and looked at her. She suddenly felt a pang of tenderness, which was usually not in her nature, and she reached out to stroke the girl's hair, gently, with a mother's hand. She withdrew her hand quickly because the hair was matted thickly with grime, and Uma felt ashamed. She would probably never see her again, and she felt, for the first time, a sense of loss. With a tearful sigh she returned to the fire near the door to bake the bread for the evening meal. Bread and beer, the daily food for the family, was a tiresome but essential task for women, and she thought of Matu in a strange house with a strange woman to work for, and a husband who would beat her. Uma began to weep. She fled into the darkness of the hut so Ser would not see. He would be angry and she wasn't sure what he would do.

"You have no need to fear," a voice came to her in the semi-darkness. "I have seen your tears, and I will give you what you desire. Matu will not marry Bolpa. He is already gone."

Uma looked around the little room with amazement. "Where are you?" she asked softly. There was no response. She was confused, but began to find hope that the voice had spoken truth. She had no idea how or where a strange man had come to know how she felt, but his words were reassuring. Her spirit lifted and she returned to the fire and the bread.

Later that night, as she lay beside Ser in a corner of the dirt floor, she heard the voice again. "You do well to believe, Uma." That was all, but she began to believe fervently. Matu would not have to go! She was certain although she had seen no one and had no proof. With relief she slept until the morning.

The next day everyone got up with the sun and went about their tasks. Everyone but Ser, who waited just outside the door for the farmer whose name he had forgotten, to come for Matu. The girl had taken the goats out to the back of the field where they fed on the green plants that grew there year round. She watched the little herd thoughtfully as she considered what her fate was to be that day. At mid- day when it grew too hot, she returned with the goats to the sheltering shade of a tree and sat through the afternoon until it was time for more milking. She wondered when she would be called to leave, but no one came, and she watched the path cautiously for any sign of the man she had to marry. The next day was the same, and the next. Finally, on the fourth day, Ser decided to go to the market place and attempt to find the farmer who had asked for his daughter. He went alone, and when he returned he told Uma a strange story.

"Bolpa is his name, I found that out. And I went way out to see him, out to his farm. But it was empty. No one was there, the whole place was deserted. Nobody in the area knew anything about him. I don't think he'll be coming back." Ser looked at his wife. "You got your wish," he growled.

Uma was thrilled. She went into the hut and looked around. "Are you here?" she asked. "Where are you? I want to talk to you again!" The voice was silent.

It was months later when she noticed the staff one early morning. It had been in the darkest corner, along with some other sticks that Ser used when he planted, but the staff glowed with a soft radiance that day, unlike all the rest. She took it in her hand and felt the smooth wood that seemed almost soft as it touched her fingers, and suddenly she could see clearly. Images and thoughts filled her mind with bright scenes and vivid colors. She dropped the staff, but immediately picked it up again. The flow of thought and imagery impelled her to continue. After about an hour of watching and listening, she knew what she had to do.

"Come with me," Uma told her daughter. "We have to get you ready!"

"What - is he going to come for me now?" Matu wailed.

"No - but you're going to a safe place! Come!"

She took Matu down to the small stream of Nile water and gave another command.

"Take off all your things. You're going to wash until you get clean!"

The girl had no choice. Her mother was strangely adamant. "Why?" was all she could say.

"You are going to the temple of Amun-Ra, and you need to be clean. So do I." Uma pulled her ragged robe over her shoulders and stepped into the water.

"The temple!" Matu was perplexed. She had never been there. "What's going to happen, Uma?" She never called her 'mother.'

46

They washed and scrubbed but without soap it was hard to get the stains off. Matu had never had a bath before, and she felt odd standing naked, splashing water over herself. Then they washed their clothes.

"Wait here!" Uma said. She hurried into the hut and returned with the sharp knife that Ser used to cut the grain. Matu wailed again when she saw it.

"No, no," Uma spoke soothingly. "Nothing like that." She knew that the girl was afraid her crazy mother would harm her. "We're going to cut your hair off. That's all."

Matu wailed again.

"We have to. It's too matted to do anything else. You have to be clean for the temple! You can cut mine off after I've done yours." She began cautiously pulling and cutting the strands of hair loose from the girl's scalp. "Hold still, Matu! I don't want to slip and cut off an ear!" Matu stopped wailing and stood very quietly as her mother gently trimmed the hair from her head.

"Now you do mine," Uma commanded. "But go slow and be careful!"

It took a long time, and both their heads had small cuts in several places as well as bristly bunches of hair they couldn't get off without injury, but the two women were finally free of their lice and dirt-filled hair, and they had washed themselves as completely as they could. Matu was amazed at how she felt, light and free, and Uma gazed in pleasure at the change that had come over her daughter. They dressed in the cleaner but still wet rags, covering their heads with odd strips of cloth. Then Uma went into the hut one more time and returned with the staff and a small pouch which contained all the money left from the sale of two kids only weeks before. It wasn't much, but would have to be enough. Late in the morning the two bald women set out walking toward the nearest temple to Amun-Ra in a city called Zau that lay somewhere beyond Enosa.

Uma stopped at the market in Enosa to buy a new robe and head cover for Matu. The girl couldn't go to the temple in rags, although Uma would. They bought a water-skin and filled it in the rivulet that flowed through town. When darkness came they slept in a stack of field hay near the path, and started again in the early morning, munching on a few dates that Uma had taken from a roadside tree the night before. The delta was hot, but intensely green, lush with bushy foliage and tall trees that swept the skies, fruit bearing bushes along the waterways, and well-fed cattle and goats in the fields. The colorless past was nearly forgotten as they anticipated Matu's future. The staff had shown a new life for the girl, which was now Uma's focus and delight.

The temple to Amun-Ra would best be described as colossal, especially for someone who had never seen such a place. Long rows of sphinxes on either side of a wide causeway led to the pylons that guarded the sanctuary. As they passed through the gate they entered a new world. Large stone buildings, all part of the complex, stood to the left and right of a central corridor that was open to the sky. Many pilgrims were there, moving across the center to various entries and enclosures that came together to present a vision of an eternal kingdom where Amun-Ra ruled alone. It wasn't a huge temple, but it was sufficiently grand to give pause to the young girl and her mother from Ranua. They stared at the height of the pylons, the finely crafted and sculpted stones which bore the likenesses of Amun-Ra and the pharaohs, the green lawns, and the fountains that flowed from the sacred lake; all temple designs that were common in Kmet at that time, except for the green lawns which were possible only in the delta.

The "house" for Amun-Ra was situated at the end of the causeway, in the center of the last row of buildings. It was a modest looking hall with a portico of three columns on each side, only large enough to house the statue of the great god in a niche that faced the entry. All was symmetrical and orderly; the religion was meant to inspire the people of Kmet to regulate their lives by its example.

Uma asked a young man where the priests were, and he pointed, after giving them an unpleasant look of appraisal, toward a building near the end that housed priests and the workers who kept the temple tidy. She took Matu's arm and guided her swiftly to the house, boldly walked through the open door and went inside. The walls of stone were plain, with only a small statue of the great god on a little shelf facing the visitors. There were two doors that led off the entry at opposite ends of the wall, but no one came forward to meet them. Uma clapped her hands loudly after a short time, and they heard someone moving behind the door on the right. At last a bald priest appeared, dressed in a soft gray robe, with sandals on his feet, and he stood considering them judgmentally. "What do you want?" he asked, a note of impatience in his voice.

"I have brought her - my daughter - to serve the great god here," Uma said firmly. "He told me to do this."

"How do you know the thoughts of Amun-Ra, woman?" he asked curtly. "We can't take in just anyone who comes here."

"The great god Amun-Ra has spoken to me. He told me himself."

The priest looked at her with something akin to contempt on his face. "How can you say this?" he asked sharply.

"It's true! Just ask him yourself!" Uma declared in a fiery voice. She showed such determination that he knew she wasn't going to back away.

"Wait here." The priest turned coldly and walked through the door. Soon an old man who looked quite tired appeared. He spoke to them softly.

"What is this you say, my daughter?"

"I have come to bring Matu to Amun-Ra as he asked me," Uma responded. "The other priest doesn't want to believe me."

The old man looked first at Uma and then at Matu. He paused a long time. "Where do you live, my daughter, and do you have a husband?"

"I am from the village of Ranua. My husband is there."

"He didn't come to bring his daughter to the great god?"

"No. Amun-Ra spoke to me. To me only, and I brought her myself. We walked yesterday and all morning today."

"Are you hungry, my dear?" he asked kindly. "We should have some food and talk."

Uma thought of Matu. The girl must be hungry. She admitted that she was, too. "Yes, we are, sir. That would be good of you."

"Follow me," he said, and led them through the door he had entered. The next room was a quiet workplace and library where a few priests were reading at tables, and one was copying a large scroll silently. They passed through without a word and came to a second large room that was empty of people. It was furnished with chairs and stools for sitting, and there was a place with a fire in the center. A large hole in the roof carried off the rising smoke. They turned through a door on the right and came into a room with a dozen tables. One wall was open to a large garden filled with the color and fragrance of multitudes of flowers. The old priest sat them down and provided a basin of water for washing. Then food came, wonderful food. Rich meat such as they had never tasted, and breads and fruit, along with goat's milk and cheese, something they had never known before, and then a sweet with honey and figs. It was heavenly. After they had eaten the priest spoke again.

"Now tell me all your story, my daughter," and Uma started at the beginning, at the point where Matu had been sold to the farmer. She told of the entire series of events that had led them to the temple. Matu listened as her mother talked. She had no idea that things like that had happened, and was a little concerned about the possibility that Uma had invented the story for her sake. When Uma finished, the priest stood and held out his hand. "Let me touch the staff," he said gently. Uma placed it into his hand.

For a short time the priest examined the rod with no apparent reaction. He looked at the inscription running down from the tip, and he held it in various positions, with one hand and then both. After several long minutes he turned slowly to Uma with a dazzled look on his face. "Where did you find this?" he asked with a tremor in his voice. Uma knew that she had won.

Two days later Uma left the temple in honor, wearing a new robe that was embroidered with bright designs, her head wrapped in a silky scarf, and she carried the great god's staff with dignity. All the priests were lined up along the causeway. Matu stood nearest the entrance to the house with the old priest, who was the head of the order for the temple. He took Uma's hand as he assured her, "We will honor your daughter as we have promised, and will deliver her in purity when the young husband who is seeking her comes to make his claim. She will live and learn with us until then."

"Be safe, and come back to see me if you can," Matu said as she lowered her head.

"May Amun-Ra guide you," the old priest said, and Uma was off, walking swiftly toward the pylon, past the honor guard of priests. The staff was silent, but it vibrated in her hand, and she felt its power as she walked.

The court of Pharaoh Djedefre I was alive with intrigue and spies. After he had worn the double crown for only a short time he had no idea who his true friends were. He sat on his throne pronouncing judgments for situations he had little information about, and his capricious decisions went every direction as he tried out new ideas and experimented to find his way among the bold factions that vied for his favor. He had never had a chance to learn judicial procedure. His father had seen to that. The pace of intrigues had gradually quickened, and there was no one for Djedefre to turn to for help. He was literally lost among the jackals who were attempting extortion, mayhem, enslavement, and worse.

Prince Khafra, his brother, understood the situation better. He had had time to watch and learn. The prince began to develop a system and philosophy for ruling that was rather too close to the ways Khufu had employed for Djedefre to accept, and the two began to drift apart in every aspect of their lives, largely because Khafra saw no harm in continuing some of the old alliances and practices of Khufu. Djedefre was far more altruistic, and Khafra told him that he would weaken the nation and go down in history as a failure if he acted on his impulses. Pharaoh did so anyway.

The lavish palace of Memphis was not as impressive as the final home Khufu had built for himself on the plateau overlooking the Nile in Giza. Accordingly, Djedefre had determined to make his own tomb less imposing than his father's. It was located in a funerary complex on the western side of the river a short distance north of the great pyramid of Khufu. The pharaoh had no desire to emulate his father with such an improvident, expensive tomb that would bring Kmet's economy even greater problems, and he told the priests that a lesser site and smaller pyramid were suitable for his own eternal dwelling. Khafra, on the other hand, thought that succeeding pharaohs should make ever more extravagant monuments as time moved forward, and was critical of the way his brother limited power and prestige and royal privilege. Djedefre had a lot of ideas that Khafra considered weak.

"Why did you meet the emissary of Punt as an equal? You're a powerful king and such people should be afraid of you! You're far too easy when it comes to negotiating their contracts!" Khafra fumed one evening after an audience the pharaoh had given Punt's ambassador.

The brothers were enjoying a dinner with music and dancers on the portico of the pavilion Khufu had used for some of his court functions. Towering torches lit the area, and the pool sparkled in the flaming light. There was a warm breeze that fluttered the linen drapes inside the pavilion, wafting them toward the portico at times, undulating and sinuous like the dancers who swirled around the royal party. Perfumed flowers and women cast their scents into the soft, dry air, and the jangle of bells on pretty ankles attracted subtle attention. It was just another night in Memphis at the palace of the pharaoh. And, just as any night, there was an argument.

"A reduction in their allotment is acceptable considering the circumstances," pharaoh said evenly. "I investigated the situation before he came, and was willing to settle for less. To do anything else could enslave them completely."

"But now everyone will want their allotments reduced. You can't do that. It will bring Kmet to financial ruin!"

"I appreciate what you're saying, but we have a large store of gold and other metals in the treasury all the time. Why should we drive our subject nations to death? They have reasons to hate us already, and if they joined together they could win!"

"You don't speak as a pharaoh when you say that!" Khafra stated flatly. "Not one of your advisors would agree!"

"Fortunately, I am pharaoh. I can do what I want, even if my advisors don't like what I do!"

"And then where will we all be?"

The pharaoh was silent. Khafra appraised the situation. No need to offend him completely.

"There is no more reason to argue, my lord, my brother. Come, let's talk about other things." Khafra backed away amiably. For that time.

"Good. Enough of this! Here's the new dancer they found! A really luscious bit. Let's see what she can do!"

She was a beauty with passionate eyes and seductive motions, but she twirled artlessly to the rhythm. Khafra soon became tired of watching her clumsy efforts. His eyes swept the crowd furtively, looking for someone, anyone. He needed some new blood to whet his appetite. Tedium had gradually overcome all his excitement for the women he knew. He watched and waited. There was surely someone there among the guests. Then his eye caught sight of a girl standing behind a group of Commander Anrom's men on the opposite side of the pool. She was just out of the torchlight, dimly visible, but as she swayed to the music he could see that she had possibilities. He leaned forward to get a better look.

"Don't lean too far. You'll fall off the chair. She is a beauty!"

"Not the dancer!" Khafra laughed. "She's nothing. The one over behind Commander Anrom. See her?"

"Not very well. Too dark."

"She looks interesting at least. I don't think I've ever seen her before. Wonder who she is?"

"I don't know. You'll find out, of course."

"Yes," Khafra affirmed. "I will."

The inquiries Khafra made were not terribly discreet. He had no concerns about anyone else, not even the girl. He simply intended to use her as he had the others - or he might not even like her after he had seen her in full light. Why shouldn't he go after whatever he wanted? He was the brother of pharaoh and in the highest position of authority after the king. The result of his questing was that she was the wife of a young assistant to Commander Anrom, and had come the day before with her husband to Memphis. He smiled subtly at the idea of a naive young woman, an ingénue, and better yet, a newcomer. He sent a servant with a message to the Commander.

Matu walked anxiously through the apartment in the palace. They had arrived in Memphis the afternoon before, but she had seen nothing of the city or its people except for the dinner at the pharaoh's pavilion last night. "Where is Redha?" she asked herself. He promised to take her to see the sights in the afternoon but hadn't come back yet. The Commander didn't ever keep him this long! She crossed the small reception room to the balcony to look down on the passageways below, searching for him to come into view. The sun was dropping rapidly, almost set, and she was troubled. The lunch she ordered was on the table, growing tasteless and congealed; still he didn't come. She went inside and sat on a sumptuous chair to wait.

It was dark and the lamps had been lit before she heard the door open and the sound of Redha's voice calling. "Matu, get the things you need to travel! We have to go home. There's a problem that Commander Anrom needs me to take care of. Hurry! We have to leave now!"

"What is it? What's wrong?" Matu asked him with alarm.

"It's better if I don't tell you yet. Wait 'til we get home. We'll talk about it then!"

"But why?" Matu was unable to grasp the situation.

"Don't worry. We can talk about it later. Just get ready to leave!"

She hesitated. "Why should we have to go? Can't someone else do it?"

"No! It has to be me! And you need to get your things together."

She made an effort to accept the information. "What should I take? Everything?"

"No – no the servants will pack most of it in the morning. Just whatever you need for one night on the road. We may have to stop to rest – to camp – along the river."

"I don't want to leave my jewelry, Redha! I don't want to lose it!"

"Yes! Take it with you, and maybe some other clothes too! But we'll be home tomorrow night."

"Why can't you tell me?"

"I just can't. Anyway, we have to go as soon as possible!"

Matu went into the bed chamber to pack a few things. "I haven't even had a chance to see Memphis, or not much of it!"

"I'm sorry about that," Redha called from the reception room. "But your chair is waiting downstairs. The carriers are waiting."

Matu looked her things over and picked up another dress and some towels and soap. She had to keep herself clean. Then she got another toga for Redha, grabbed the box of jewelry, and shoved it all into a small valise with a silver handle.

"I guess I'm ready," she told him as she entered the reception room. "I only wish I could have seen Memphis!"

"You are sweet," Redha told her as he enclosed her in his arms for a moment. "I'll make it up to you, I promise."

"I know," she told him. She put on a smile.

Then they swept out the door and away from danger.

Matu was soon to become a young woman when Uma left her at the temple in Zau, but the priests regarded her as a child because she knew almost nothing about the worlds of language, science, and philosophy. Most of the men at the temple were helpful, and when they discovered that the girl learned quickly they gladly engaged her mind with all the things they knew and taught. She was especially adept at learning to read hieroglyphics and went through the scrolls in the library briskly. She studied philosophy too, and developed skills in debate and speech that rivaled many of the visitors who came to the temple house. For three years she worked her way through the many entangled philosophical concepts of the times. Then Uma appeared again, suddenly. She was much the same scrappy little woman, but she dressed in clean, simple robes and had a new bearing of authority.

"Ser is gone," she told the girl when they had retreated into Matu's tiny room. "He left just after I brought you here. Wat was alone when I got back. It's better." She paused a moment, then continued. "You know the priests gave me money? A lot of money, I mean."

"No."

"They did. To honor Amun-Ra, they said. So I used a little of it and we have a big goat herd now. Wat takes care of them."

"You must be all right, then."

"We are. I hid most of the money. Nobody knows where it is. If you ever need it, you can have it."

"I don't need money, Uma. I'm happy here."

"You won't always be here!"

"Maybe." Matu was thoughtful. "Where could I go?"

"Maybe you'll get married."

"Who would want to marry me? I'm kind of unusual. A peasant girl who can read."

"And think. That's not a bad thing, Matu. But that's not who you'll be forever."

There was a silence.

"I've changed the house. Fixed it. Made it bigger, and we have a new building for the goats. Wat does a good job with them."

"I'm glad. I always liked the goats."

"So does he."

"Do you think Ser will come back?"

"No, Don't think so. But if he does, Amun-Ra told me to run him off fast. With the staff." She laughed at the idea.

When the gong sounded, Matu took Uma to the dining room for the evening meal. The priests made way for the small woman and her pretty daughter, and they were led to sit at table with Zarrax, a place of honor Matu had never before been assigned. The men were in awe of Uma and the staff, and watched her closely as the meal progressed. Zarrax treated her as a visiting dignitary, and paid careful attention to whatever Uma told him. The one thing they were all aware of, except for Uma and Matu, was the staff of the great god, casually leaned against the side of the table as though it were an inconsequential object.

Uma spent a few days at the temple, often with Zarrax in his office. No one had any idea what they talked about, but some of the priests thought it must be the words Amun-Ra had spoken, and why she had come to visit at that particular time. Everyone, including Matu, was curious. Just as suddenly as she had arrived, Uma told them she was leaving, and the honor guard of priests stood along the causeway once again as she walked past. This time Matu walked with her mother to the last pylon and stood inside the gate as Uma began the two-day journey back to Ranua. Many of the priests wondered why Uma had not resettled at the temple herself, but knew better than to ask. Uma had a way of dismissing idle curiosity that was not always pleasant.

A few months later, during the cool season, Matu was outside in the courtyard reading in the sun, an impossibility most of the year. The sky was fresh and clear and cool. Blazing winter flowers glowed in the stillness of the afternoon. It was a peaceful, almost sleepy time, and Matu tried to concentrate on a new scroll she was attempting to read. A young man wandered into the garden. He was not tall, but had the bearing of a man of importance, and was obviously strong and muscular, not at all like the priests who enjoyed heavy meals and little physical activity. He stood watching her with an honest stare. Matu looked back at him with a smile as Zarrax came toward the man, bowed in greeting, and led him away toward his office deep within the temple house where Redha, the young man, asked Zarrax about Matu.

"She is studying with us," the priest told him, and took up the subject they had met to talk about.

"I would like to know more about her," Redha insisted, and the priest responded easily. "You should talk to her yourself, then."

The business discussion didn't start well, due to Redha's preoccupation. Zarrax attempted to get onto the topic several times, about some temple lands that Commander Anrom thought should be taxed, but couldn't get anywhere. Redha's head was in the clouds, so the priest sent him back to the garden alone, something that wasn't usually done.

Approaching the table where the girl studied, he said, "I am Redha. I saw you here when I came in."

"Yes, I saw you looking at me. I am Matu." She unconsciously swept her hair back from her face.

"Where is your father, Matu?"

"I don't know. He was in Ranua the last I knew. I am alone here."

"Who can I speak to then?"

"To me. I will answer."

"You will answer for yourself?"

"There is no one else unless you wish to speak to Zarrax."

"He sent me here to you."

54

"Then you will have to speak to me."

"I will. To you alone, Matu." They both smiled. "I ask you to be my wife," he said, watching her raptly.

"I am pleased, but don't know how to answer you. I really belong to Amun-Ra. My mother left me here as she was told to do."

"Do I need to ask Amun-Ra?" Redha questioned. "I don't know whether he will answer me."

"He will, if it's about me."

A puzzled Redha continued. "You are very important, then?"

"No, not important, just his responsibility, I think. I don't know what else to say."

"Will you come with me to ask him?" Redha suggested.

"I have already asked. While you were inside with Zarrax."

Redha was at once surprised and pleased but didn't tell her. "Well, what did he say?"

"He didn't say no."

After Redha left the temple he walked along the river to think about the girl who spoke for herself. He stopped close to the water and listened to its hypnotic flow. Some superstitious people thought it dangerous to spend much time with the songs of the water, but Redha had always loved them, and he listened again with renewed interest. The water and the land seemed animated and palpable. The trees, mostly date palms, spread their fronds above the path, and the undergrowth rustled with all kinds of life; human and animal and serpent and bird and even the smallest insect, all together, clustered along the banks, nourished by the water and the plants. It was a rich, green milieu of vitality, and few people who lived along its watery waysides knew them as well as Redha. He had lived there all his young life, and had no desire for anywhere or anything else, except now, for Matu.

Evening faded and night settled down. The stars above Zau always blazed in a particular splendor, and the path of white light that gleamed among them was more brilliant than any he had ever seen. Spangles of starlight sparkled in the undulant waves and rivulets, danced across to the opposite shore, and shimmered in the tiny canals that flowed inland from the moving tide in a display that was like no other. This was his world, and it recreated this vivid extravaganza every night.

Very late, Redha returned to Zau and found his way to the temple. He was not to be deterred. He strode through the pylons and up to the temple house door, but it was shut. Bolted. He pounded on the door and waited. When the door finally opened, an unhappy priest with a carefully shaved head glowered at him. "What do you want?" It was more of a warning than a question.

"To speak to Matu!"

"She has closed her door for the night and I can't call her."

"Then Zarrax! I'll speak to Zarrax!"

"Everyone's sleeping. Come back tomorrow." He started to close the door.

"Matu!" Redha shouted. "Matu! I've come for you!" He shoved the door open and sent the priest sprawling on the floor. "Matu!" he shouted again. It was Zarrax who met him as the young man charged through into the library. "She'll be here in a moment. Calm down, son."

"I'm sorry – I just had to come for her!"

A sleepy Matu entered from the other side of the room. "Redha! Why are you here now? Is something wrong?"

"No, nothing's wrong. I've come back for you! We can be married tonight!"

"I thought you'd be back, but I expected to see you tomorrow," Zarrax intervened. "You understand that she can't go with you now, of course. It will take some time for her to prepare."

Redha smiled. He felt embarrassment rising up his neck and onto his face. "I'm sorry to act like this. I'll come back tomorrow."

"You have no need to be sorry, does he Matu?"

"No. But I do need time, Redha, to get myself ready."

"Yes, yes, you do. I know. I guess I've made a fool of myself."

"Not at all, son. No, not at all. I'm glad to see you happy," Zarrax assured him. " Matu, you should go back to your bed, and I'll talk to Redha."

The girl turned without a word and left the room.

"Come and sit here. I have a few things to tell you." When they were settled at a table, Zarrax asked, "Do you know that Matu's mother is the voice of Amun-Ra?"

"The voice?"

"Yes, she speaks for the Great God Amun-Ra. Actually, he speaks to her and she carries his messages."

Redha considered for a moment. "How do you know this?" He asked.

"Amun-Ra himself told me," Zarrax replied. "Uma, her mother, carries a staff that is the gift of the god to us. She hears his words through the staff and tells people what he's saying."

"I don't understand. How do you know that he actually speaks if you can't hear him yourself?"

"I have heard him. Directly, not through Uma. I held the staff and he talked to me. Does that make a difference to you – about Matu, I mean."

Redha paused to take it all in. "Maybe it should, but I don't care."

"Uma told me you would come."

"Why didn't you say that this afternoon?"

"She didn't give a name. She said, 'A young man' and I think you're the man."

Redha had no idea what to say, so he accepted the wisdom of Zarrax's words. He must be the man, if the whole thing was real. At the moment nothing seemed to be a reality except for Matu, and he was satisfied with that.

Zarrax continued. "Come back in five days and she'll be ready for you then." It was a dismissal. Redha left.

"Five days, then," he said, and went to the door.

Uma stood facing the water, holding the staff in her hand. The night was moonless and dark, but she had no fear. She had stationed herself on the eastern bank of the river, just across from the pyramid of Khufu and the ancient lion. The two gigantic forms faced her across the eddies on the water, black against the starry sky. Uncountable points of silver light bathed the river and the trees along the shore into a shadowy, indistinct fusion of shapes. Only the monoliths rose above the jumble with clear lines and sharp focus. Uma waited. More than two hours passed before she felt the staff tremble and heard Amun-Ra tell her that they were coming soon. She remained there, with her back to the pathway that was the main road to Memphis, like a statue of a woman holding a tall staff in her right hand.

Matu was leaving Memphis without having seen the city. She rode through the dark in her sedan chair, Redha walking swiftly beside her. The two young slaves who carried her seemed tireless and did not speak to each other or to Redha as they moved along. The road, actually a broad, sandy pathway, was smooth and straight along that side of the river, and they made good speed. Redha had not yet considered stopping for a rest when he heard a voice calling from along the darkened riverbank. A woman's voice was calling. "Matu! Stop here," and his wife, who had been napping, startled into full wakefulness.

"Uma!" she exclaimed. "Uma, where are you?"

"I'm coming up to the road." A moment later her mother appeared, a slight, plain peasant woman dressed in a simple robe, carrying an oversized staff. Redha regarded her for a moment.

"You must be Matu's mother," he said.

"I am. You need to send the slaves on to Zau. Without Matu."

"What? Why would I do such a thing? Matu can't walk all the way."

"She could if she wanted to go to Zau, but she can't go there. Neither can you! Now send them on!"

"No!" He said loudly. "That would be foolish."

"Send them!"

Matu climbed out of the chair. "I think you should send them on alone, Redha," she said quietly. "She knows something we don't."

"You don't have time to stand there. Do it, or I will!" Uma threatened.

Redha was speechless. He heard Uma issuing orders to the two young men. She placed the staff in front of her face as she told them they had to go on alone, and they left without hesitation, still carrying the empty chair. Uma spoke to Redha again. "You'll understand soon. Don't let that trouble you any longer. Now come down to the riverside with me. We'll walk there for a while."

They descended to the water and Uma led them along the bank, moving stealthily north. They walked in silence for about half an hour, when the sound of men marching quickly came from behind.

"Stop! Stand still, facing the water!" Uma ordered. "Wait here until they pass."

There were several men, moving as fast as they could along the soft, sandy road. They hurried forward, paying no attention to the three who waited at the riverside. "They didn't even see us, hidden among the rushes," Redha thought.

"They'll come back when they discover she's not in the chair. We want to be as far away as possible by then," was all Uma said as she moved forward. "Let's go!"

58

The starlight seemed to provide just enough illumination for them to walk comfortably through the stalky reeds and bushy growth, and the three fugitives continued on toward the north as quickly as they could. After about an hour, Uma stopped. She held the rod up and listened, slowly making a full circle before speaking.

"No one is coming behind. I can't hear the soldiers, either. They've gone on, I think."

"Does Amun-Ra have anything to say now?" Redha asked curiously.

"No!" was all Uma could manage in response.

The three continued walking for a little while, but Matu began to stumble, so Uma stopped under the cover of a small grove of palms and they sat on the ground to rest.

"How long do you think it will be before we get to Zau?" Redha asked his mother-in-law.

"We aren't going to Zau," she said curtly. "You must have figured that out!"

"I must return!" he insisted. "I have work to do for Commander Anrom."

"If you go there they'll find Matu and take her from you," was all Uma said. Redha didn't reply, but he realized he had no more duty to the commander. His duty was to Matu, and his career had ended.

Matu heard the exchange. What could Uma mean? Everything fell into place then, and she understood that the flight from Memphis was for her protection. Someone powerful – was it the pharaoh himself? – had wanted to take her into his entourage of women, his concubines, and Redha had decided to flee rather than allow her to be taken. She felt a sense of devotion that she had never felt before, and leaned against him as she closed her eyes in sleep.

The first faint glow of dawn was in the east when Uma called them to get up and walk again. She brought water up from the river but had no food. "We'll find some soon. There's a village nearby," she told them. Within an hour they had eaten and were on the path again, this time walking toward the west where they crossed the river in a small boat and continued on the opposite side. She covered Matu with a simple dress and told Redha to take off his outer tunic, the one that indicated his rank, weight it with rocks and drop it into the water. They went on, looking like the people of the land, even as far as Matu's hair, which was shining and clean until Uma rubbed a little sand into it to give her a proper peasant look.

They came to Enosa at last. Matu was too weary to go on without a rest, so they ate and drank some beer at a stand near the market. They hid from the sun and slept in an alcove of the temple until late in the afternoon, when Uma took them back to the path. She headed south instead of west toward Ranua, as Matu had expected. They walked with a new energy for less than an hour until they reached a place where two small streams, part of the delta system, converged. There was a tidy farm house partially hidden by tall bushes which sat low to the ground, with two large rooms that extended on either side. There was a large herd of goats to greet them. And there was Wat, looking tall and very thin, as he stepped out the door as they arrived. He smiled shyly at the sister he hadn't seen since the day Uma had taken her to the temple in Zau.

"It's yours now," Uma told them. "Wat and I will go back to Ranua tomorrow."

Matu was stunned. Uma had planned for everything.

Wat had prepared a cooking fire behind the house, and a table under an arbor of vines. They ate roast chicken and drank large mugs of fresh beer, although meat of any kind was not a usual meal for peasants. "You are a clever fellow!" Redha spoke agreeably. "This is great!" He lifted his mug in appreciation.

Sleep came before the sun sank below the horizon. The house was small, but Uma and Wat had given it a good cleaning. There were comfortable beds and pleasant breezes which came from the delta to cool them through the night. It was all better than they could have guessed, and the next morning Matu went with Wat to milk the goats. No one ever knew that this was the renewed creation of the farm where Matu would have lived in squalor had she been forced to marry Bolpa, the man Ser had bargained with for his only daughter.

The hideaway was isolated. They heard no rumors about the search for Matu, nor were they disturbed by travelers along the little road; only the nearest neighbors passed by. Redha, the nature lover, adapted quickly to his new situation. He loved the farm and the water and the small trees that grew on the banks of the stream, and he was learning about the goats as well as how to plant some small crops to add to the human and animal food supply. He watched the night sky, always looking for some new movement among the stars, and the luminous moon was his friend and confidante. He talked to her whenever she came into view, and often stayed up late watching as she slid across the star-field and dropped into the land of the dead, only to arise and return the next night. The phases of the moon were wonderfully fascinating to his mind, and he had theories about her that could have filled many 'scientific' scrolls, if only he could have written them down. Redha wasn't as clever as Matu with hieroglyphics. Mathematics was his strength.

He went into Enosa twice a week to discover what he could, but the town was far from the main channels of the river, and little news came into the backward country. If Commander Anrom was searching for him, there was no evidence of it. Redha believed that the commander, who tacitly understood his situation, was assisting him by looking the other way. And no news at all came from Amun-Ra.

Uma returned to the farm after four weeks to talk with Matu. She waited with her main arguments until Redha was away in Enosa. "You may have to live here a long time," Uma explained, "and I want you to be happy. You can get whatever you need. Gold is hidden under the floor just over there," she pointed to a spot along the wall, "and there is more inside the foundation of the goat shed on the right side of the door. Just don't ever let anyone know you have it! Redha can exchange it – I think Enosa has a shop or two for that. Maybe not legal, but he can find someplace. And whenever you dig it up, be sure to repack the top. No one could ever find it then." The floors of the cottage, as in almost all the houses in the delta, were sandy soil, often covered with woolen carpets, swept clean every day. "There is a place in Enosa where you can buy scrolls, but hide them carefully if you have them here! Redha can find them for you, too. He'll know how to do that."

Matu, who held her mother in high regard, now placed her among those who consorted with the gods. "I will do as you say, Uma," she inclined her head to her mother. "You've done far more for me than I've ever earned."

"Nonsense!" Uma exclaimed. "You're my own daughter. I have the power to do things, and I would be useless if I didn't. No more of that talk!" Uma didn't like praise. She often thought of her life before she discovered the rod, or it discovered her, and was ashamed. "We'll all work on this together," she said, "When Redha gets over the idea that I'm too – ah – forceful."

Matu laughed. "He's still a little scared, you know. He will get over it, I promise."

"When are you going to have a baby?" Uma asked abruptly. "I want to have a grandchild!"

"I don't know. Redha asks me that, too. We'll have to wait and see."

"Not too long I hope! Who knows what will come in the future?" She looked at Matu. "You don't want to talk about this, do you?"

"I just don't have an answer, that's all," Matu replied with her usual honesty.

"Then we'll let it wait!" Uma said enthusiastically. She had no desire to cause Matu any more frustration. The abrupt upset of her entire life, and Redha's as well, was enough for anyone.

The days passed with very little change, except for the seasons. The delta was usually hot, except for a few weeks in winter when there was a chill at night. The water flowing throughout the lands made it a garden that produced much of the food for Kmet. Small farms were everywhere, and there was generally a peaceful and contented approach to life. They were not yet engulfed in the wars that would come to later generations, so most of the farm families were reasonably prosperous. The people of the land had very little concern for Memphis and the rulers who lived there, but Matu sometimes trembled at her own escape. She longed to visit Zau and the priests at the temple that had been her home, but said nothing. It was safer to stay in out-of-the-way Enosa.

In Memphis, the pharaoh and his brother Khafra were working their way through a morning audience for citizens of Kmet who had civil disputes. Khafra thought it tedious to hear the complaints, so he sent them on to another authority whenever possible. He always maintained a strong degree of separation from those who dogged him with their questions and concerns.

For issues that interested him, Pharaoh Djedefre heard them to the end, often pausing to ask questions, and after a time of quiet deliberation, he spoke the words that were law for anyone he held innocent or responsible. He was not inclined to be indulgent, as Khafra sometimes suggested, but rather judicious in his work, and he took it seriously.

He had been pharaoh for about seven years, and had decided hundreds, if not more than a thousand quarrels. With a reputation for fairness and thoughtful answers, he was pleased to take his place as judge from time to time. On that particular day the pharaoh was in the midst of listening to an argument from a minor landowner when the heavy doors suddenly swung open and a small woman holding a glowing staff stepped into the hall. The guards rushed toward her, but the pharaoh was intrigued and told them to move aside. He beckoned for the woman to step forward, but she stopped well short of his throne. She didn't bow or give her name, or offer any polite words that might excuse what she had done, but a strong, strange voice came from her lips. It penetrated the depths of the place and all who were present heard her solemn words.

"The Great God Amun-Ra," she said, "does not care who sits upon the throne in Memphis. He has no more concern for a pharaoh than for a farmer or a slave. He is outraged, however, with the plot to desecrate the Great Lion which sits on the Western Bank. It was dedicated to him! Do not do it! It will be to your everlasting ruin if you do!" She did not seem to address the pharaoh directly, but looked past him into the deeper regions of the hall. Prince Khafra and a man who had been making an appeal to him stood there.

She banged the staff on the floor and sparks came from its tip. The marble floor cracked in the place where it was struck. "Do not desecrate it!" she repeated, and the staff came down again. There was thunder, unlike any thunder the banks of the great river had heard since ancient times; the night of Pan and the storm. People were shaken by its roaring under a cloudless sky.

Uma turned her back on the throne and its occupant, as well as Prince Khafra, and sped out the doors into the entryway where the citizens of Kmet waited for their opportunity to stand before the great judge. She was soon engulfed by the crowd which didn't understand what had happened, and disappeared from the palace and the city, never to return.

Amun-Ra didn't speak again for several years. When he did speak, Uma immediately responded. She traveled from Ranua to Enosa that same day, but this time she hired a chair, and two men carried her all the way. It seemed a luxurious way to travel, but she was unable to walk that far. Age and infirmity had caught up with her.

On arrival she went in to Matu with her message. "The Great God Amun-Ra has told me that I must surrender the staff to you, Matu. From now on you are the one he has chosen to speak his words!" She thrust the staff forward into the face of her daughter.

"No! I can't! How can I do this? I need to stay here with Redha!" Matu protested.

"It is not a choice, Matu. He has chosen you and you must obey. It is not such a terrible burden! I held it for many years."

Matu sank onto the floor beside her mother. "No! I can't! Please don't ask me to do this!"

Uma looked down upon the woman who cowered at her feet. She felt pity, but knew that any argument would be useless. "It is the decision of Amun-Ra, not mine. Listen to him! He has chosen to speak to you now."

"I won't take it! I won't listen. It's too much for me to do!"

A disembodied voice came to them suddenly. Even Redha, who was standing outside the house, could hear it. "Uma has completed her work. Now it is Matu who will take up the staff and speak for me. Take it, Matu. It is what you have been prepared to do." Matu did not respond except to bow her head and shudder. "Take it, my daughter. It is now yours, and the task will not seem too difficult."

Redha entered the room and looked at Matu. She raised her eyes and he nodded, pointing to the staff. She rose reluctantly; Uma handed the rod to her. Matu was resistant, and at first the staff could not speak, but gradually it began to vibrate in her hand and the new bearer began to see the images and hear the assuring voice of the great god. It was not long before Matu was listening with fascination to the revelations Amun-Ra offered, and she grasped the rod firmly with both hands as though she feared being swept away by the flow of understanding and knowledge. She felt alone in an open space, unencumbered by any surroundings, floating freely above the world and its influence. Then she gradually returned, through the kindness of Amun-Ra, to the waiting world, having become in those moments the new voice of his power in the land of Kmet.

Pharaoh Khafra sailed majestically down the river on his barge, a floating palace. He was surrounded by his personal entourage of lovely young women and the usual sycophants – men who were endlessly in his wake and agreed with whatever he said or did. Khafra loved flattery. He had made sure years before that no one would question his decisions, and now there was no one who could. Every person on the barge hated him, which he understood well enough, but they were constantly smiling and appeared to be light hearted and even happy. Musicians played relaxing music and slaves served the rich food and wines that he loved, but life was hollow and he continually faced the dreaded fear of poison, a method he had used frequently to rid himself of combatants and threats to his throne. He sometimes recalled the final meal of his father, Khufu the Great, and at times even allowed himself a fleeting memory of Djedefre, his twin brother who had died ignominiously at his hand. As time passed there was nothing he would not do to preserve his position. Most of his family was dead, removed in one way or another by his fear of treachery, and he was loath to eat or drink for that reason. The pharaoh was captive within his own prison.

Khafra had forgotten the strange woman who had burst into the judgment chamber and pronounced doom upon his plans. He had dismissed her warning as a fluke and gone ahead with his own destruction. The Great Lion had become a creature of doubtful origin; a fanciful representation of himself as the god Ra who watched the sunrise in the east and guarded the horizon on the west. At his bidding teams of sculptors had cut away at the lion's head and remade the creature into his own likeness. He had intended that, but had not intended for it to become his nemesis. Now, whenever he visited the place, its too small head on the immense body gave him a sense of his own lack of proportion. He had no spirit left, only an empty shell of a body, aging and vulnerable, to carry him into the afterlife and whatever his fate would be there.

The barge sailed smoothly up to the long pier beside his nearly completed pyramid. Hundreds of men were working on its outer 'skin,' the smooth white limestone covering that blazed intensely in the sun. Workers and tradesmen surrounded the pyramid and the mortuary temple that stood nearer the river. The great pyramid of Khufu reared up on the right, still glorious in its primary position, and Khafra glowered whenever he saw it. Khufu was something he could do nothing about, and his pyramid would almost eclipse Khafra's splendor except for the fact that his image on the lion figure was a great sensation, despite its improper scale, for all the world to see. Khafra's face would stand there forever while Khufu would be seen only as a geometric design with hard edges. An apt description of the arrogant old man, he told himself.

The great god Amun-Ra had not forgotten Khafra, however, and his day of retribution was at hand. Matu walked and waited, staff in hand, below the shining pyramid, near the giant creature that had been a lion but was now something alien on the plateau. She did not look at the sculptured beast, but toward the mortuary temple where Khafra now waited for a moment as he walked off the barge and stood facing the line of temple priests who were bowing. He had not yet spoken to the head priest, but watched them with a kind of amused pleasure as they twitched slightly from the effort they were making to remain with faces near the ground. His own retinue had been told to wait on the barge until the pharaoh had gone inside the temple.

Khafra was in no hurry. He waited for some time before he acknowledged the line of men in supplication before him. It did them good, he thought, to teeter a little before his presence. It was true respect that he sought, not the quick ducking bows of the palace court. At last he spoke, "Arise," and as the head priest raised himself upright, all the others did the same. Many were red-faced and blinking.

"I am deeply honored, your majesty, by your visit. We are all honored." The priest was in good form.

"Tell me your progress with the temple. Be quick. I don't want to stay here long. I need to get on up to the necropolis."

"It is finished, gracious one, and awaits your coming."

"I suppose you all look forward to that."

"Oh, no! Do not mistake me! I mean that we are ready to serve you, but that we expect it to be long in coming."

Khafra laughed, but didn't say what he thought: "You can hardly wait to eviscerate me! You charlatan!" The pharaoh was in a particularly bad mood.

"Why are so many priests required? There are more than twenty of you."

"We all have our special roles to fulfill, great one. We study and work together to understand our calling." He didn't add that there were only sixteen that day.

"I certainly expect that you should know your duties by now. See that a lighter crew is arranged. There is no need to pay for so many, just to wait for my demise!"

"I will eliminate all but six, if that would please you, great lord."

"That would." Khafra wondered what he must mean by 'eliminate.' It was an amusing thought.

The pharaoh turned his back to the priests, who waited mutely to follow him into the temple. Khafra wanted to look upon his own face, the giant face which crowned the body of a lion. But as he gazed, his attention was taken by the sight of a small woman with a staff in her hand who looked back toward him across the sand. Then he heard the voice.

"Khafra," the stern voice spoke. "This woman is Matu. Do you remember her?"

In an instant the pharaoh remembered. She was the one he could never find although he had searched for more than two years. She had tried to humiliate him!

"Yes, that's right. She is the one," the voice agreed. "Now she is here at my bidding to bring about your end."

Startled, the pharaoh pointed his hand toward Matu and tried to shout, but he had no voice. Then he stumbled and fell to the ground. "It's all because of that woman," he wanted to scream, but no sounds at all came from his mouth. Everyone tried to crowd around him, to raise him to his feet, to comfort and cajole him, but they could not. Confusion ruled the moment, and they all jostled each other while the pharaoh sank into a kind of stupor. He was aware of nothing but the voice of Amun-Ra, the calm but sinister voice which spoke to him of all his misdeeds, almost cataloging them in order, as the once-mighty man suffered the pains of his conscience and his fears.

Pharaoh Khafra lived for over a year in that condition. He did not seem to be aware of things that were around him, although he ate a bit of food now and then. He could not see and he could not speak. Tears seeped repeatedly from his blinded eyes. A small movement of his right arm seemed to be all that was left, and he sat, day after day, in a soft chair next to a window where light poured into the room. Nothing seemed to occupy his hours, and he died a slow, sorrowful death, enclosed within his own thoughts and memories.

Matu walked away from the scene when Khafra fell. This was her first and final mission. She never heard the voice of the god again, and at her death the powerful staff disappeared from human knowledge until it came to life centuries later as it lay under the sands between the forepaws of the beast who later became known as The Great Sphinx of Giza.

Chapter Four

1403 BC

Prince Tuty of Kmet peered around a corner of Khafra's magnificent pyramid. He waited quietly in its shadow while a small herd of antelope skittered across the stony ground on their way toward an ancient watering hole. The hole was often dry, but just after the coolest time of the year a little water, deep enough for drinking, pooled in a sandy pit where a large pond had once sparkled year round. The animals were in constant danger from crocodiles when they had to go to the river to drink, but now Prince Tuty lurked in the shade, presenting another kind of danger. His spear was ready and he took careful aim. With a strong thrust he sent it flying, but it fell clattering onto the pebble-strewn sand. The antelope fled.

Tuty swore in the name of the pantheon of gods that Kmet worshiped as he walked swiftly across the foundation stones to the spot where the spear had fallen. The sun was high, rising to its zenith, and Tuty was hot and tired. He called to the two slaves who waited beside the pyramid, and together the three young men descended the slope. They came to Hor-em-ahket, the part lion-part human figure who guarded the entrance to Khafra's tomb, as the mighty heat of Ra threatened to overpower them.

"You seem tired, my prince. It's been a long morning." Yu, the slave who spoke, was a very tall young man from central Africa whose father had been king over a multi-tribal land until Kmet had overpowered his army and brought the royal family to Memphis. The king had been executed because he refused to grovel before the throne of the pharaoh, and his family had been placed into various positions of servitude. Yu, who was four years old at the time, had become the slave-companion to the prince of the same age, and the two had grown up together, along with another boy whose ancestors were from the land of Canaan in the far north, born into slavery in Kmet. They were now the protectors, constant companions, confidantes, and friends (although no one would have the audacity to suggest the latter) of Prince Tuty.

"It's too hot," Tuty agreed. "Why don't we all take a little rest? You have the water?"

"I have," Alaem, the other slave, told him. "Where can we find a shady spot?"

"Just there, next to the beast. Between his front legs." The forelegs were tall enough to provide a strip of shade along their length. "Pass the water around!" Yu said quickly. " We all need a drink!" They shared the water and sank onto the hot sand. They talked of general things that were of interest to the prince; the rules for hunting his father, the pharaoh, maintained, and the growing scarcity of the game the royals liked to hunt.

"I missed that antelope," Tuty admitted. "I don't know why. Did you see the throw I made? Was it too weak? It fell far short of the herd."

"It was thrown hard enough but didn't have enough loft," Yu told him. "Aim it a little higher and it should come closer to hitting the mark."

"I don't want closer, I want to hit it exactly right."

"I think you know what I mean," Yu told him jovially. He took unusual liberties for a slave, but they were granted by the prince.

They were quiet for a time, and then heard Alaem breathing deeply in sleep. Gradually the heat and quiet overwhelmed all their swimming brains, and sleep came gently on the warm breeze. It was a long time before Tuty awakened to the mid-afternoon world. He saw Alaem sitting up and gazing toward the face of Khafra that seemed to float in the heat high above them. Yu continued to sleep. Tuty waited quietly as Alaem got up from the sand and walked toward the face that loomed there, then held out both his hands toward the ancient image. He didn't say anything, but seemed almost to pray to the old god who stared placidly over his head, eyes fixed on the far horizon toward the east, gaze constant, unwavering. Tuty became curious. "What are you looking at, Alaem?"

"I thought I heard him speak to me, my prince. It was just a curious dream, I guess."

Tuty laughed . "What do you think he said?"

"I'm not sure. It was strange. He seemed to tell me to dig in the sand under his chin. He said I'd find him there."

"Well, are you going to dig?"

"Do you think I should?"

"Why not? You'll never know unless you do it."

Yu sat up and looked around. "What are you two talking about?"

"Alaem wants to dig up the sand under his chin," Tuty explained, pointing to the head that stuck up above the sand which buried most of the lion-body. "He says he'll find the old guy down there."

"That's no place for him to spend eternity!" Yu responded. "You'd better dig him out."

"He says that old Khaf told him to do it."

"Yes, I can still hear him. He's telling me I have to dig him up."

"But how could he be down there?" Yu asked logically. "He's buried inside, up there."
He pointed to the glistening pyramid.

"Maybe he got out!" Tuty laughed loudly. "Let's find him!"

"It's not like that at all," Alaem declared. "He needs me to dig. I guess I'm supposed to
find something there."

"What?"

"Don't know. I might dig all the rest of the day and find nothing. That's what I think."

"Do you want to do it or not?" Yu asked.

"Yes, yes I do. It may take a while. If you don't mind waiting, my prince." He
remembered his place just in time.

"We'll help you, at least until we get tired," the prince told him.

That decision having been made, they found some small rocks for scoops and started
digging beneath the chin of the ancient god; the pharaoh who had ruled more than a thousand
years in the past and was named on the ever-growing list of the multitude of gods who watched
over the land of Kmet.

Alaem became more excited as time passed, but the others grew weary and stopped the
work to watch the young man from the north as he bent his back to the task. He seemed driven,
as though encouraged by an unseen force, and Prince Tuty was at first amused and then
concerned as Alaem gave himself so wildly to the work. The prince was about to call a halt to
the whole thing when Alaem reached through the sand which was falling back into the pit they
had managed to dig and gradually pulled a long, dark shining rod from its tomb. It was nothing
spectacular, the prince noted, but it did have an unworldly sheen, and Alaem seemed enlivened
as he held it in his hand.

"I will hold it," Tuty declared pompously. Alaem handed the staff to the prince. He felt,
but could not show, his reluctance.

Tuty turned the staff in his hands and gazed for a while at the glyphs that started at the
top and descended to the hand hold far below. It was a curious object, but the prince could not
find anything extraordinary about it. After a short time he tossed it to Yu, who immediately
passed it back to Alaem. The boy from Canaan gripped it firmly and looked off toward the river.
The staff was whispering, but its message was clear. "Come down to the water." Alaem felt a
great desire to follow its instructions, but he waited for the prince to give the next direction.

"Let's go down to the river," Tuty said abruptly, as though he could hear what Alaem heard. The slave started off before the words were hardly finished. "You are eager now!" The young prince joked, but he was watching the actions of his slave suspiciously. What was the fixation with that thing, he wondered.

At the bank of the river they stood a little back from the water. There was no need to excite the crocs. They watched the endless flow and the small ripples and waves that moved across the surface in silence. Their boat was docked at the old temple below Khafra's pyramid, and they were some distance from it. There was nothing unusual to be seen where they were. Tuty was wondering why he had taken them to that spot when an enormous hippo, a rarity in the waters that far north, began to climb up out of the water on its stubby legs. Tuty and Yu ran up the bank, but Alaem stayed put. The fat creature, its rippling folds moving loosely as it walked, came bobbing along up the sand until it stood about thirty feet away, making strange, low noises in its throat. Yu and Tuty, from their more distant position, shouted to Alaem, but he was unaware. The hippo was making a wild, threatening call to the ears of the prince and the tall slave, but it spoke intelligibly to Alaem.

"Come to the great hall of the gods tonight at the middle hour. Bring the staff. I will be there to speak to you. Come alone. Tell no one."

The clumsy beast turned back to the water and gradually submerged itself beneath the gliding surface. Alaem ran up the bank, clutching the staff, to a harsh greeting from Tuty who dashed up as the creature disappeared. The prince had actually feared for the life of his friend, but could not express it, so his rebuke came out in anger. "You didn't obey me! You must always do what I tell you!"

"Yes, my prince. I am sorry. I was too stunned to think. I didn't hear anything but that hippo."

"Very well, then. But get hold of yourself. I don't want to have to find someone to take your place!"

In the darkest hour of the night, Alaem left his post outside the door of the bedchamber where Tuty lay fast asleep. The hunting day had tired the prince, and he wouldn't awaken until Ra rose above the horizon with his flames and heat. Yu was sleeping on the other side of the passage. Alaem waited for the guards who patrolled the surrounding corridors to pass, and when he knew he was alone, crept along to the great hall of the gods. It was an unusually large indoor space with a high ceiling supported by a multitude of columns, filled with wall paintings and all kinds of statuary. Alaem didn't like to go there, but the hippo had commanded and he obeyed. The hall was mostly dark as he entered. He could see two priests with a torch near the altar of Amun-Ra, engaged in conversation, paying little attention to the hall or anything that might happen there during the hours of the night. He stood just inside the entrance, out of the light, holding onto the staff with all his strength.

"Do not be afraid, my son," a voice came to him. "I am here beside you, but you cannot see me. The others cannot see or hear me at all."

"Who - - " Alaem started, but the voice interrupted. "Do not speak. Just ask your questions in your thoughts. No one will hear that way. They have no idea we are here together."

"Who are you?" Alaem asked within his head. "What do you want with me?"

"I am Amun-Ra. There is no need for fear. I have spoken to many people in the past. They have come to no harm. You are my chosen for this time."

"Why me?"

"Why not? I need you to act for me now. That's all. It isn't difficult."

Alaem was silent. He was confused. Amun-Ra was the chief god, the creator-god of Kmet.

"Do you want to know what you are to do?"

"I was expecting the hippo to be here."

Amun-Ra laughed. Humans were often such delightful creatures. "Yes, I thought so. But it was my voice you heard from the hippo. I am here."

Another silence.

"Do you want to know what you are to do?" Amun-Ra asked again.

"Yes – I guess so."

"That is enough. You are to help the prince. He will become pharaoh, and he will need you, and Yu, also, to be his companions and friends. It will not be easy."

"But he isn't in line. His brother is the next one."

"Nevertheless, Tuthmosis will be. He needs to be prepared. Many things will happen that could lead him astray."

 "Shouldn't you talk to him, then?"

"I have chosen you. My reasons are my own. I will give you information to give to him, but do not tell him it came from me. That is important."

"What do you want me to tell him?"

"Nothing yet, but wait a while. You will have to tell him many things over time."

"But he will be pharaoh and I am his slave."

71

"You are actually more important than he is, but he doesn't know that, and neither do you. Not yet. Now you must be patient and wait for me to speak again."

Alaem couldn't believe anything that was said. His eyes searched for the one who was speaking, but the darkness was too deep. He could only make out the two priests, who were preparing to leave, by the light from the small torch one carried.

"It is hard for you to believe. I know this."

"Yes," Alaem acknowledged. "Very hard."

"Just remember that the future of your people is in your hands."

"No!" he spoke the word aloud. "Now what have I done?" he asked himself. The priests had heard him, but he was quickly rescued. At that moment a falcon came soaring through the door, crying shrilly as it made its way to a perch on the far side of the hall. The priests made a joke about it, laughed, and dismissed the voice they heard as a part of the falcon's cries.

"How can the future be in my hands?" Alaem asked silently. But there was no response. Amun-Ra had gone. The slave didn't hear from him again for more than a year.

The festival of Min, the fertility god, was among the oldest celebrations in Kmet. Everyone enjoyed a time of revelry, drunkenness , and erotic play during the festival days and nights. It was a special time for farmers because the pharaoh himself took a scythe, pretending to be the god Min, and cut some wheat from a chosen field at the opening ceremony, if such serious words could apply to the activities that were the norm for Min's antics. Everything was over-the-top, and moral values were often put aside for the three days Min ruled the land. Everybody loved it.

Tuty was no exception. He led parades in the guise of Min, dancing along the streets in costume, indulging in bawdy play with the crowd. He never seemed to grow tired in the role. People tossed full heads of wheat and bright flowers in his path, watching in fascination as he scampered mischievously along the way. Yu and Alaem, ever present, walked or ran along the sides of the streets, protecting the prince from any overt female who attempted to grab him as she revealed more of herself than was acceptable for public entertainment. It was during this celebration that Amun-Ra spoke to Alaem after his long silence.

The last morning of the festival had begun. Tuty was not in good shape. He had a hangover headache and refused food and tea, but prepared himself for another day of amusement with a large quantity of beer. He looked into a small bronze mirror at his eyes, puffy and almost closed to keep out the light. It was no good, he decided, and fell onto his bed again. It was then that Alaem entered.

"Go away!" Tuty complained from his bed. "Why are you in here? You can't burst in any time you want to!" He was aggrieved.

"I have a message for you, my prince. It's important."

"What?" the princeling moaned. "It can wait!"

"I think you had better listen to it, my lord." Alaem was very formal, which caused Tuty to pay attention.

"Out with it, then, whatever it is! Who is it from?"

"I have no name, my lord."

"Then why in the name of Ptah do you think it's so important?"

"The message is that you will become pharaoh, my lord." Alaem said it in a matter-of – fact way, but it was received as too much information on a bad day.

"By the gods, you must be insane!" Tuty shouted. "That's treason! You know it is!"

"I don't mean to offend you, lord, but I have it on good authority by an augur of omens who refused to give me a name."

"It's insane!" Tuty repeated, but his eyes were opening fast. "Where did you see him?"

"It was a woman. At the palace gate. She seemed to know that I could contact you."

"Have you ever considered that she saw you with me in the parade?" Tuty was sarcastic. "That's not hard to understand."

"I think she was real. She was – ah – unusual."

"How so?"

"She dressed in a strange robe. And she had large hands and almost flaming eyes." Alaem had tried to think of things that would bring life to his story. He had rehearsed it many times, but had never spoken a word of it aloud to anyone.

"There must be lots of women with large hands and flaming eyes during Min!"

"I couldn't take my eyes from hers, my lord. She was hypnotic."

"So you think she spoke the truth?"

"I don't know. That is for you only to know."

Tuty waited, considering the possibilities. He trusted Alaem. That much he was sure. Why would the slave give him this information if it wasn't true? He struggled to think as well as he could for the condition his brain was in, and decided that he'd best wait to consider anything further.

"Well, keep it between us, then. And I mean that! Don't even tell Yu!"

"I will do as you say, my lord." Alaem bowed very low and left the room. Tuty began to prepare himself to participate in another day of reveling. Both his demeanor and his mind had changed.

In the darkness late that night Amun-Ra came to a sleeping Alaem and jarred him awake with a loud voice. "What do you mean, telling that boy that he is to become pharaoh? I told you not to say a word! How can I use you if you do things like that!?"

"I thought he should know. My first loyalty is to him. Now will you let me go? I don't want to be your messenger."

"You are not wise. You could do great damage."

"Say what you like. I owe it to him to tell the truth."

The great god was silent for a long moment. "That is a noble trait, son. I admire you for it. Even more than I did before. But let me know when you want to divulge secret information and I may tell you why you should not, or I may shut you down permanently."

"You alone have to make that decision. But I will be loyal to him! Now you know it! I hope you don't ever say anything again that I can't tell him. I'll never hide it!"

"Obviously, I had no reason to tell you not to fear me." Amun-Ra seemed to be thinking aloud. "But it is not such a great damage. Maybe it will even help him a little. I would like to know why you told him now. A lot of time has passed."

"I don't like to see him carrying on the way he does in the parade – and most of the time during Min, really. He needs to know that he will be responsible to people someday, and he shouldn't want them to remember him as the almost naked boy who played with them on the street when he hands down a decision of life or death."

"Very well put. You have been thinking. I almost agree with you. Let us leave it there for now. I will return soon to instruct you." Amun-Ra was gone.

"Things are getting closer. You need to pay attention." The voice of Amun-Ra woke Alaem in the night four months later. "He is seriously thinking about his accession to the throne."

Alaem waited in silence.

"The prince will soon begin to notice your people," Amun-Ra said quietly. "He has heard a lot about them already, but he is unaware that they are your tribe."

"I don't know what you mean."

"The Hebrews, as they are called, are growing rapidly. Soon they may be a force that will have to be controlled.

"We are slaves. Why do we need any more controls?"

"You are a great people. Great in number, anyway. And you are a threat."

Alaem almost laughed. "We can do nothing. The soldiers have the power. They're everywhere."

"Ah, yes. But the Hebrews hate them."

"What are you trying to tell me?"

"There is a great struggle brewing. It may not come for a while, but it will come. You will need to have the ear of the prince who will be pharaoh."

"I seem to have it now."

"Do not lose it! It could be a tragic loss for Kmet as well as the Hebrews."

"Please don't talk in riddles. Speak plainly."

"You are also willful and disobedient."

"Find someone else." Alaem turned his face away.

"You know that I still believe you to be the best. Hear me now. Prince Tuthmosis will soon be drawn in by people who want to keep the population of Hebrews from growing. They are a powerful lot, and will not sit by and watch any longer. They will advise Prince Tuthmosis that when he is pharaoh, which will happen in a few short years, he must find a way to stop the Hebrews from growing in population and strength."

"How will he do that?"

"He will find a way. There is much talk about it already."

"What is my place in this?"

"You wield greater influence than you realize. He will listen to you. Tell him not to harm the Hebrews, but to send them away!"

"That's a lot to ask. Why would he listen to me? I have nothing to give him."

"He will listen in time," Amun-Ra responded. "And do not make up any stories about soothsayers. That will never do."

"I'll do what I can."

"Just wait until he asks you."

"He never will."

"He will."

Amenhotep the Second never did acknowledge Tuty, nor name any successor to the throne. The aging pharaoh always suspected that Tuty had stolen the life of his chosen heir, but he had to walk carefully. He wanted a member of the family on the throne of Kmet, and Tuty was all he had left. Tuty, on the other hand, had a strong sense of his own importance and a desire to promote himself, although he tried to keep that hidden from his father. He conducted what he called 'the family business' with a cool reserve and a hand that easily opened to receive whatever gifts a supplicant deemed proper to give. For him it was an almost effortless game, and he grew to love politics. The men who pre-paid for his services against the time when he would be pharaoh were generous.

Tuty met regularly with men who had all the essentials to buy a government: money, and with the budding pharaoh on board, power. Their meetings were secret, but word got around anyway. The old pharaoh heard the rumors, which he suspected were true. He sent spies to follow his son, who reported that everything the king supposed was true even though they didn't actually do their job and follow their target. Everyone was trying to take advantage of the situation to get whatever money they could for themselves; the palace world was filled with double-dealing. It was a short time after the meetings started that Alaem asked the prince about the 'Hebrew problem.'

"I don't know anything about that, but I have heard some rumors. Why do you ask?"

"I am a Hebrew slave, as you know, so I am interested in what could happen to my tribe."

Tuty didn't know, but he didn't tell Alaem. If he had ever been told, he ignored the fact. "Alaem, you will never come to harm. I'll see to that!" the Prince of Kmet promised.

"What about all the others?"

"There's no need for concern for anyone. I'll take good care of all the slaves in the kingdom. I expect that they will be happier and much better off when I am pharaoh."

"As you say, my lord. I'll expect that, too."

"You seem distressed about something else - more than a slave problem. Tell me what it is."

"I've had another message.

"From the fortune telling woman?"

"No. From the great god Amun-Ra."

Tuty laughed. "It must be an interesting message in that case. What are you trying to get me to believe?"

"The first message was actually from Amun-Ra, my prince. I made up the fortune teller woman."

"What?!"

"You would never have believed me if I had told you the truth. As you see, it all came out exactly as he said."

Tuty was confused and shaken that Alaem would tell him such a story. "How do *you* receive messages from the great god?"

"I don't know, my lord, but he has talked to me several times. He wants me to give messages to you."

"How has this been happening? How long?" The prince was on guard. This slave was trying to play him for a fool, or was telling him these things for a subversive purpose, he was sure.

"Since I pulled the staff out of the sand. You remember that day?"

"Yes." The reply was tart and hard. "Does he talk to you all the time?"

"No, not very often, but it's all related to you. He wants me to give you his messages."

"This is outrageous! He should speak to me himself! Why have you withheld this information?"

"He told me not to tell you where the messages were from."

"Messages! How many?"

"Only the two so far, but I think there will be more."

"And exactly how does he talk to you?"

"I hear his voice. He's just there – in the air, I guess."

"Have other people heard him speak to you?"

"No, at least not that they knew. Do you remember the hippo we saw just after I found it?"

"Yes."

"The voice of the hippo was actually Amun-Ra. He told me to meet him that night, and I did. He told me he spoke through the hippo."

Tuty took a long time to respond. Alaem was good at this. He seemed to believe what he was saying. No! It was impossible! But - - what if all of it was true? But how could it be? The Great God Amun-Ra would never deal directly with a slave and let the prince dangle. His thoughts were evident in what he said next. "Where is the staff now?"

"It's in the passage, under my blankets there."

"Go get it." Tuty had to get Alaem out of his confidential role as his personal slave. His trust in the friend of his youth was suddenly gone, and the prince was angry.

Alaem went out to get the staff, which seemed lifeless as he brought it to the prince. Tuty held out his hand. "Give it to me," he said in a strange, stern voice. The prince held the staff for a few moments, then looked at Alaem with an awful face. "You have deceived me and failed me. I will call the guards and they will take you to the prison house." Alaem fell to the floor to beg for pardon but Tuty had made up his mind. "Don't come any nearer," he commanded. And then he screamed for the guards.

"You would not listen," Amun-Ra said in the darkness of the prison. "You told him everything I said you should not, and now, here you are."

Alaem refused to respond.

"There is no reason to be silent, my son. You have lost your influence with the prince, and the staff is gone, but you can still hear me. I know you can hear me."

"Just leave me here. I don't want to listen to you!"

"I cannot leave you. I am the creator who made everything that is on the earth, and you are part of that creation. You are foolish, but no worse than any other man, and actually much better than most. Now stop moping and listen."

"Why? What can I do here?"

"I can change the mind of the one you call Tuty. I will do so if we can work this little tiff out together. Do you want to try?"

Alaem waited a while, silently wondering why this persistent god was – persisting. "What do you want to do that for? Tell me your reason."

"I will only tell you that it is not because Tuty will be pharaoh, or anything to do with royal clap-trap. As I said before, I am interested in you – yourself. You are far more important than all this squabbling. More than all the royal heads in Kmet. They will meet their match soon enough."

"That's hard to believe."

"It is true."

"Why am I still part of it if I can't be trusted?"

"Oh, but you can be. Stop the moping, as I said before, and I will tell you what you need to do."

"Will you tell me the truth about all the riddles you keep hinting about?"

"Some, maybe, but certainly not all. That is my best answer."

Alaem spoke slowly. "I might as well. Go ahead."

When Amun-Ra visited Tuty later that night, he was in the guise of the seer Alaem had described. Tuty and his friends were having a midnight supper in his private rooms when the woman with flaming eyes appeared at their table unannounced. "I will speak to you," she commanded the prince. There were no guards present; they were outside the doors, but Tuty could find no voice to call them.

The woman seemed to grow in size, at first only a little, then to the top of the high ceiling in one sudden motion. Tuty and his friends were aghast. "You will listen to me!" she said in a low, rumbling voice. "Your servant Alaem is in the prison house. I saw him there. You will send for his release now, or there will be disastrous consequences. Do you understand?"

Tuty nodded, his head jerking wildly. He was terrified.

"Alaem will not return to you. He is to be left in peace to go where I send him. If you do not obey, none of you will see the dawn. I will wait until you have ordered his release." She immediately reduced herself to the size of a normal woman and sat down at the table with the men, nodding at Tuty to call the guards. His voice was thin and shrill, as the guards heard. They came rushing into the room, sensing that something was wrong, to find the woman sitting next to the prince, smiling decorously as the young man gave his orders in a panting, breathless voice, and the guards went off to the prison house. Then the woman, with only a short word of warning, departed. "I will be watching you," she said as she moved toward the door.

Alaem walked out of the jail, having been released just as curiously as he had been imprisoned. He was free, but waited sleepless on a public bench near the old temple of Niwt-Imn that stood beside the river. Early the next morning he went down to the water, as he had been told, to the boat landing. Yu was there to see him off. They didn't wait long. A small ferry came alongside and Alaem stepped into it. They crossed the river with only a scant cargo and two other passengers, to the western bank; the place of the dead. From there he disappeared into the desert; he didn't see Thebes again for many years. The one thing of value he brought with him was the staff which Yu rescued from the remains of the garbage fire after Tuty commanded it must be burned. The staff was intact.

The tiny settlement of Mut, in the oasis of Dakhla, was named for the world-mother goddess. The village, still in its early stages, was nothing but scattered mud-brick buildings, a temple of stone to honor Mut, and sandy paths that connected the village with the lake and some cultivated land on the far side. It lay several days journey from Thebes, isolated and almost unvisited by the outside world. Alaem joined a party of desert traders for the long trip. They used small donkeys to carry their goods, and traveled slowly, ploddingly, across the sandy wastes and rock hills. There was little food or water, and from Alaem's perspective they moved along as if in a bad dream. He sometimes saw the cold face of Tuty before him, like a mirage on the sand, and began to believe that the prince had never really been a friend or anything but a more or less kindly slave master. At least the prince had treated him better than other men might have, until their final moments together. That was small comfort. Alaem was headed to a place where Kmet's authority was almost non-existent, an oasis in the great and wild desert where other Hebrews had taken residence to escape from slavery; a place where he would be free of the past and live without fear. That is what Amun-Ra had told him.

After eight miserable days, the caravan arrived at Mut in the mid-afternoon, a time when the day was hottest and a dry wind blew sand into the faces of the men and donkeys during the final hours of their journey. There was plentiful fresh water at Mut, and more food than Alaem had seen since he left the palace. He rested for a night in a tiny hovel that belonged to another Hebrew, and began to feel better. The head of the village soon discovered that Alaem had no skills which would be useful for a life in that remote place, so he was offered apprenticeships in several different kinds of trades. He quickly chose baking as his calling, and later that day he went to work with Kep, the baker of Mut, a sturdy man with strong hands and arms, who lived with his wife and several children in two rooms at the rear of his bake shop. Alaem was given a place to sleep on the floor in the oven room. He placed a worn wool blanket on the floor, leaned the staff into a corner, and was home.

Baking started before dawn. Alaem had to be ready to load the ovens at least an hour before the town came awake. He didn't like that aspect of the job, but he loved the shaping and changing of the dough into something that was fresh and delicious to eat, and he began to look forward to the time just before dawn when he watched the light change in the eastern sky, from azure to rosy-pink to the bright blue of a full day. He saw the lake through the open door of the oven room, and it reflected the colors in the sky as light increased and the stars faded from sight. It was a gentle, peaceful time, cool and soft before the heat and glare of unrelenting sunlight spread over the town.

Alaem was surprised that time didn't stop. He thought life would become terribly monotonous, but there was always something new to learn about the baking process, and people from town to talk to as they came by the shop for daily bread. There was rarely any news about the outside world, but when the caravan arrived, about every two months, the inhabitants eagerly digested the latest reports from Thebes. That was how they learned that Pharaoh Amenhotep II had died and that Tuty, now Tuthmosis IV, was the king. It made little difference to most of them, but Alaem felt a strong tug of desire to see his erstwhile friend in all the glory of his new position. He could hardly imagine how the boy must be taking his place in that august world of ruler-gods. He smiled to himself. He knew Tuty well, probably better than anyone except for Yu. His thoughts moved to the tall dark-skinned friend he had left behind and he became a little more subdued. He wondered how his best friend was faring in the new world of Tuthmosis IV. The baker's apprentice thought about all of that for several days, but other things began to entertain his mind, and he started to feel possibilities for happiness that he had never encountered before. When he finally became aware of a pleasant young woman among the customers who visited the shop every day, he suddenly realized that he desired her.

"Do you think people are suspicious?" Tuthmosis IV asked pointedly. "I had nothing to do with it! You know that."

"Yes, my lord, I know," was all Yu could say. He had never told the pharaoh that he saw two men leave his apartment early in the morning on the day Prince Amenhotep, the heir to the throne, died. He had put it together as soon as he heard the terrible news, and waited, half expecting Tuty to be apprehended for the crime, half hoping he would be caught, but it was not to be. The old pharaoh had apparently chosen to ignore this act of treason almost in the same way he ignored small family squabbles. No noticeable suspicion had fallen on Tuty until after his father, Amenhotep III, perished and the rumor mills went into operation.

"I need to do something about this! Do you have any ideas?" Tuty seemed exasperated.

"Not now, my lord, but let me think about it for a little while. Perhaps I can think of something." Yu kept his other thoughts to himself.

"Good man! Do your best thinking." Tuty remembered Alaem, too. He was still confused by the slave's pretended relationship with Amun-Ra, but missed his friend and companion. Alaem would have come up with a fairly easy solution to this problem! He was clever; too clever. Too bad he had disappeared. "I don't want to have to deal with it much longer," he concluded to Yu.

The business of ruling Kmet went on as usual, but the pharaoh was increasingly anxious about quelling the gossip that surrounded his throne. He resolved to settle the rumors as well as the Hebrew problem, which he was pressured to do on a daily basis, before he completed his first year in the lonely but exalted position of Lord of the Universe, as he thought himself to be. He acted on the Hebrew situation first.

"It is a problem that can be solved," the pharaoh told his advisors. "It only needs strength of purpose. We can do it." The population of the Hebrews in Kmet was growing far too large, nearly ten thousand by the last census count, and people feared the audacious Hebrews who did not know their place as slaves.

"Yes, my lord, but when will we start? Many people are very concerned about this." Vizier Hinha looked up at the pharaoh gravely. The large audience chamber was empty except for the guards and the seven men who sat below the dais. They were all watching Tuthmosis with carefully serious expressions.

"Tell me what you propose as a solution," the pharaoh responded to Hinha.

"I don't have a precise proposal. We are all hoping that you, our mighty king, will know what is best to do."

"In other words you want to place the blame on me in case the plan goes wrong. There is no need to protest. I know what you're doing."

"With my greatest respect, your divine grace, we understand the peril of making a decision about this, and we would all accept the wisdom of our highly exalted king, if you would be willing to tell us what you have decided you will do." Commander Vobolpo stood and bowed after he spoke. He had been hounding the pharaoh in private sessions to take a decisive action.

"Ah, Volpo," Tuthmosis smiled darkly, using a diminutive for Vobolpo's name. "What would you counsel me to do in this setting? I wonder if it would be the same as you spoke to me about in private yesterday?"

Vobolpo pretended not to notice the insult. "I am sure that I didn't counsel anything that would harm your grace or Kmet, my lord. I intend only good to come from my advice."

"So the death of all the Hebrew babies would be a good thing?"

"That isn't at all what I mean, my lord. None of us want to do harm to the slaves, but we have to find a way to protect Kmet, to protect the future of our nation and our own children."

Another commander, Le'atus, stood and bowed. "If it please you my lord, let it be announced that the plan came from your council and that you are hesitant to make it law. But let it become a law, if you please, my lord."

Tuthmosis sat up straighter. He couldn't very well bandy with Le'atus. The man knew far too much about him and his accession to play with him as a cat with a mouse. He would make a formidable enemy, as would some of the others in the group.

"I will not be told, even by my council, what I must do. It will be for me alone to decide this matter."

Le'atus bowed, even more deeply. "As you wish, my lord."

Yu, who stood in back of the dais behind the king, watched the process of the discussion and the deliberate attempts to bait the pharaoh with intense interest. He would be the one Tuty would come to in the end, and he would have to tell his master and king, his closest friend, what should be done. It wouldn't be an easy job. He wished once again, even after more than two years of wishing, that Alaem were there.

The caravan arrived at Mut about a month later, and the terrible news spread throughout the oasis. The Hebrews wailed and cried, not so much for themselves, but for others. They were far from Thebes and the river valley. They wept for their kindred, the population of slaves who were surrounded by the forces of Kmet. The pharaoh had committed a terrible decree against them, and the tribe had been violated wherever they were in the land. The shrieking and lamenting went on for days, and the people of Mut who were not Hebrew eventually became annoyed by the constant sounds of suffering they heard. Most were empathetic, but there was a need for life to return to normal despite Thebes and Tuthmosis IV. The threat would hardly touch anyone in Mut. That seemed sure.

Alaem was greatly distressed. He thought that Tuty could not be behind such a thing, and believed that the evil men the new pharaoh had consorted with in the past were now calling in repayment of the riches they had heaped upon the young prince. The pharaoh had been captured by wealth and power long before he had a chance to think things through.

Although the peril existed, Alaem and Rachel were married in Mut, and set up life in the tiny house Alaem built. It was unusual because it had a floor, and an opening in the back wall; a window to allow better light and air circulation into the dwelling. Rachel was one of the happiest brides in Mut. She had found an unusual husband, a man who had once been in the world of power in Thebes, associated in some distant way to the pharaoh, and was now developing a steady bread business that would sustain them for a lifetime. She was content.

Amun-Ra, however, was not. He called to Alaem one morning as the young man was building the oven-fire before dawn. "You know what the pharaoh has done." The god stated.

"Yes. An awful thing! Could you have stopped him?"

"That was the job I wanted you to do."

"Why are you blaming me? I had no idea what would happen. You seemed to know something about it, though. And you could have found someone else."

"In a way I did. I spoke to Yu. He has agreed to keep the pharaoh from enforcing this abomination at least for the present time."

"Is Yu alright?" Alaem asked eagerly.

"Yes, he is still the same. But he misses you. The one called Tuty misses you, too."

"I think of them both sometimes."

"I am sure you do." Then Amun-Ra abruptly changed the subject. "Your wife, Rachel, will soon bear a child. A girl. She is important."

"No! You can't have my children! Stay away from them!"

"I will never speak to her, but she is important."

"Why do you say that? You're the problem, you know. She'll be put into danger!"

"I will take care of her. She has a major role in the departure of the Hebrews from Kmet."

"Please, please, let her alone. She isn't even born yet and you've just told me you'll take her. Why should she have to do anything about our people leaving Kmet?"

"She doesn't have to. She will not even know it! I cannot force her to do anything, and you cannot stop her!"

Alaem was nearly overcome with frustration and fear. "Please, just let us all alone. You told me I could live in peace here. Don't go back on your word."

"I have no intention of doing that. I ask you to be reasonable about what you are saying, too. Think of the needs of your people instead of yourself!"

"I can taste the fear for my family when I talk to you. Please let us alone! I've done all I could to make amends for my mistakes!"

"Do not be afraid, my son. I know you well and still believe in you. You are good, a much better person than many I have to deal with. Go easy, and think before you speak."

Alaem was silent for a rather long time. He couldn't let his protests form in his mind because even that would be heard. He had dreadful doubts. Amun-Ra finally continued:

"Yes, I understand. It is difficult for you, and frustrating. So I will tell you what will likely come about. Your daughter will have a good life here until she marries and then she will be taken to Thebes. No – no, do not interrupt. You will all be taken. The one you call Tuty will be gone, and Thebes will force all the Hebrews back to the river valley. Then the law will be carried out, but your children and grandchildren will be safe. They will not fall to the swords of Kmet. And one of them, your grandson, will become the leader of the Hebrew people, but you will not see that. He will live to be an old man before he does great things. He will take the Hebrews out of the land and return with them to their own place, the land of Abraham and Jacob. And he will become one of the greatest men who has ever lived."

"Your words offer a little comfort. I will trust you to keep them. I only wish - " he stopped without finishing.

"Do not lose heart, Alaem. You will do well here, and will not faint when you are taken back to Thebes. Do not lose heart." Amun-Ra seemed to move away, and Alaem impulsively knew that he would never speak to him again. He felt a surprising new sense of quiet pride. The baker went to the open door and lifted his face to the sun as it rose above the hill on the eastern side of the lake. He gazed into it as the ancients had, trying to see Amun-Ra there, but he knew that the god didn't live in the sun, nor did he rise with it in the morning. He was independent of all the creation and apparently could be understood only by those who believed. What a puzzle things were! He realized that now he wanted only to go home every day to his sweet young wife and give her all the things he could to make her happy for the time they had left in Mut. In a state of unexpected calm he went through his daily routines, baking bread that people needed and loved as if that had become the fulfillment of his life and his hope.

Pharaoh Tuthmosis spread the word around the nation of Kmet that he had been ordained as pharaoh by Hor-em-akhet, the man-lion that crouched on the bank of the river just below the pyramid of Khafra. He carved his story onto a stele, a stone tablet that was placed between the forepaws of the great beast, and left it there for the world to see. The stele detailed how he had fallen asleep under the shade of Hor-em-akhet, and the creature had spoken to him through a dream, asking to be released from the sand that engulfed his body. That was partly true. Tuthmosis had recently ordered his slaves to dig the monument out of the sand so its magnificence could be seen once again, but it wasn't Tuty who received the message from the gods there, nor did he truly care about the beast itself although he elevated it to a superior position in the realms of deity. He made Hor-em-akhet into the greatest of all the gods, placing him above even Amun-Ra, the creator.

Carefully phrased, the stele implied that Tuthmosis was in league with the gods and that they spoke to him asking for favors. In return, they offered him the honor of becoming pharaoh; eventually to achieve the stature of a god. It was an egocentric and daring maneuver. No one believed it, certainly not Amun-Ra.

"Names are important," Alaem said to all the people who could be wedged within the walls of the little house. "We have a history that needs to be continued. That's why we have decided to name her Jacobed, to honor our ancestor Jacob. It may be a new name, but it is from an ancient source."

Kep, the baker, and his family were there, along with Adam, the new mother's brother, and his wife, who was another Rachel. Others from the Hebrew community waited outside, and some were able to see into the room through the window at the back. Naming ceremonies had become an important event in the lives of the people of Mut.

"I name you Jacobed," he spoke to the baby he held in the crook of his arm. "I give you this name to be an encouragement to the people of the Hebrew nation, and to honor Jacob, our father. May the god of the Hebrews give you his blessing, and may you grow into the best woman you can become!"

A shout of celebration rose inside and outside the tiny mud-brick hut. It was also a cry of defiance, but no one from Thebes was there to witness, for which all the people of Mut were glad. Isolationism was still their way of dealing with the world at large, and they had become adept at it, although they loved the caravan and the news it brought.

Life in Mut went on quietly for a long time. Alaem's son, Jacob, was born, and another named Abraham. Although he couldn't explain why, Alaem felt it necessary to keep reminding the Hebrews of their beginnings. Names, being the primary association that identified a people, were important. For him, those three names signified a return to the old ways; the long-held beliefs of the Hebrew people, and the continuity of the faith that had kept them joined to each other while they were slaves in Kmet. Alaem was not a son of Kmet, and despite the times that the god had come to him, he had never come to a conclusion about who the god was or why he would seek a Hebrew. The man never knew or understood Amun-Ra's true nature or identity.

When Alaem was nearly forty years old, the Hebrews from Mut returned to Thebes under duress, and although they were subjected to the law, even the law that required the killing of their infant sons, they developed a resistance toward their captors and refused to accept complete submission. Many chose death instead.

Alaem and his family were somehow overlooked. He was declared a freedman, so his children were not as threatened by the "slave laws" during their earliest days in Thebes. He was soon a baker in a much busier shop than the one in Mut, and had several assistants to help him produce the large quantity of bread the government required. One day he had an almost unexpected meeting at the shop. He was puffing the fire with a bellows when a tall, thin man came through the kitchen.

"Alaem!" Yu shouted above the clattering noise. "Alaem! My oldest friend! I've been searching for you!"

Alaem responded with a glad cry and embraced the serious and official-looking Yu. "It's wonderful to see you again! I hoped we'd meet, but I had no idea where to look! Tell me about things – what happened when I left?"

"I thought you were dead for a while, but I had a 'visitor,'" he emphasized the word, "who told me that he had sent you off in the wilderness. I never expected to find you again until I read your name on the list."

"We need to have a good talk! Can you come to meet me here at sundown?"

"I will, unless the pharaoh needs me!" Yu responded. "Then you can tell me about everything!" He added with a congenial voice that implied a concealed meaning.

"I will. Everything! How good it is to see you again! And you can tell me everything, too!"

The meeting was what anyone would expect of old friends. They talked through the night, getting and receiving news, mostly about Tuty and his troubles as pharaoh. Alaem was subdued when he heard how Tuty had tried to save the Hebrews from the vicious men who demanded death for the children born in slavery. But it was beyond the pharaoh's ability to do much by that time, and the dam burst on the pharaoh's passing. The monstrous law that Tuthmosis IV signed was fully enacted then, and the weeping of the Hebrews could be heard throughout the river valley night after night. " It was almost more than a man could bear," Yu told him. The final act of intolerance came with the rounding up of the slaves from all the hidden places and forcing their return. Where was Amun-Ra during that time was the question that Yu and Alaem shared.

Jacobed, who was twelve when the family was taken to Thebes, married a few years later and became the mother of Miriam and Aaron. Her oldest son was protected by a special word from Yu, a vizier of the city of Thebes; a powerful man in Kmet. Her youngest son, Moses, was saved from the decree because she hid him in el nil, the great river, where he was discovered by a daughter of pharaoh and raised as her own. Jacobed herself became the baby's nurse.

Despite severe suffering and a long struggle, Moses was able to lead the Hebrew people out of the land of Kmet, later known to the emerging world as Egypt, and up to the border of the land of Canaan.

Chapter Five

1323 B C

The yearly festival of Hor-em-akhet was held during Shemu, the harvest season, when el nil flowed the lowest of any time during the year. At some uncertain time in the past, an earlier pharaoh concluded that Hor-em-akhet was the god of the deluge, the annual flooding that ensured a good harvest, and the god's importance was instantly elevated. In time, Hor-em-akhet was honored not only for the flood, but for all the seasons of the year; Akhet, the time of the flood, Peret, the time for sowing the seed, as well as Shemu. They were all a part of the annual offering of new soil which the god graciously provided when he was pleased with his worshippers. When he was not pleased and the deluge was either nonexistent or inadequate - in rare cases it was too full - the people suffered varying degrees of famine and life was hard. Gradually, the part lion-part human beast who sat on his haunches above the flood evolved into one of the greatest powers of Kmet, even more honored at times than was Amun-Ra, the originator, according to the believers at Karnak, and god of all things.

The Pharaoh Tutankhamun, who eventually attained greater renown than any other pharaoh, built a palace on the western side of el nil, the wrong side for a living habitation, near the great beast Hor-em-akhet. During the annual celebration of the god, he and his wife, Ankhesenamun, sometimes occupied the royal house for a few weeks. It was a new idea, building a palace on the necropolis side of el nil, but the royals were young and filled with optimistic new concepts, and its placement suited them. Tutankhamun wanted to be near the source of the blessing of the deluge during the festival. Most of the celebrations were carried out at the place where the gigantic image of the god crouched on the sand, gazing toward the sunrise every morning. His lion shape and human head signified the eternal union of the lion and mankind, as was foretold by the stars that were grouped above the eastern horizon, according to ancient lore. His name, Hor-em-akhet, meant 'Horus-on-the-Horizon,' a descriptive name that specified a god who ruled the morning rising and the evening setting of the sun god, Amun-Ra; a position of great power and importance.

The pharaoh and his entourage traveled from Thebes on an immense river barge, a floating palace, with many smaller barges and boats trailing along behind. There was always music, dancing, and feasting as they traveled easily down the stream toward the north, following the will of the river, carefully guided by the omens and the soothsayers who came with them. The water was usually smooth and placid; the trip could get monotonous.

"What do you think about this, Hessie," the pharaoh asked his little wife as they sat alone on a well-shaded balcony behind their apartment. "We could go on down the river after the celebration and see the far shore. It's a ways, but I've heard about the beautiful water up there, out in the sea. And the weather's cooler."

"Are you suffering from the heat again? I hope it's not the fever coming back! You know how you get then!" she fussed.

He smiled, but only a little. "Hessie, don't go scolding me about my health. I do everything I can."

"What did your doctors say this morning?" A team of doctors studied Tutankhamun every morning. They looked for any signs of sickness, especially the fever, that he might come down with.

"I had an all clear."

"Moon," she replied, her large eyes examining his face, "Is that really true? Sometimes I think you don't tell me everything they say."

"Ask them." He gave her an encouraging smile.

"I do, but they always seem to slide away into their reports and prescriptions. I don't think any of you are honest with me."

"Well, you know I get the fever sometimes. That's enough, isn't it?"

"They only tell me because they can't hide it! It's like a game you all play around me."

"You have all you need, Hessie. I'm supposed to take care of you, and you all take care of me!"

"Just tell me if you start the fever again!"

"You'll be sure to know. That's something I can't hide."

Tutankhamun suffered from serious attacks of malaria he had contracted as a child. They seemed to grow worse every year. The fever season was the same as the season of Shemu; there was cause to worry. The truth was that the pharaoh had been feeling unusually warm, even for the season, in the late afternoons. He had avoided telling the doctors so far. The people of Kmet, especially the ruling class, expected, demanded, the pharaoh to be strong physically as well as authoritative and decisive. There was no place for frailty in the ruling monarch, and someone could dispatch him quickly if he displayed weakness. There were always men who kept watch for any possible opportunity to do so.

The festival was a four day event featuring games and races and processions, as well as feasting and dancing and stealthy encounters for sexual dalliances, not like the open atmosphere of the Min festival, but one that was more seductive and clandestine. That appealed to many people, especially those who could not or would not openly display themselves during Min. As was the custom of the times, everyone looked the other way. The pharaoh himself had no need for outside entertainment. He was happy to be with his wife or the scant number of concubines who were a part of his 'ordinary' life. Hessie and Moon were not simply married; they were the best of friends and in love with each other, a situation that was rare among the royals.

The celebration began with a throng of people waiting on the shore of el nil or standing among the pyramids on the plateau, along with a sizable number who were waiting in boats that drifted lazily on the waters of the river. This was only the third festival for Hor-em-akhet that Pharaoh Tutankhamun had attended, and there was a watchful expectation throughout the noisy crowd. In mid-morning, trumpets announced the entrance of the pharaoh and the priests who had been assembled from the far corners of Kmet, more than three hundred, clad in white linen, each carrying a small offering of food and drink. Pharaoh Tutankhamun, glistening in a golden kilt, the tall double-kingdom crown planted on his head, led the procession. The crowd cheered and banged on anything that would make noise as the train of officialdom approached the statue from the riverside. The mighty god stared constantly above their heads, eyes fixed on the eastern horizon, silent and brooding as always. The sound increased to a steady, thumping roar as Tuthankhamun walked down the sand between the forelegs of the beast and placed his own offerings just below the towering head, bowed in an unheard prayer of thanksgiving, and returned slowly to his place in front of the assembled priests. Then the head priest of the temple took his turn down the aisle toward the silent god, repeating the movements of the pharaoh. Gradually, in slow and solemn parade, each of the other priests approached the chin of the god to offer his own gifts as a representative of the people. Trumpets continued to sound at intervals, adding to the noise. The congregated people began to drift away even before the tenth ordinary priest had made his approach. There was much more to do and to see at the celebration.

Public entertainment had become like a carnival. There were all kinds of booths and vendors selling everything from the cheapest trinkets to valuable jewelry and art. A papyrus with your own cartouche painted on it was a great attraction, as were decorative henna designs applied to the hands and arms and feet. There were always foot races and throwing contests, shooting, wrestling, and boxing, but the greatest attractions were the chariot and horse races that even the pharaoh had been known to take part in. Food pavilions abounded, offering the best of Kmet's provender as well as some of its cheapest, if not the worst. Beer frothed from all the cups and mugs that were filled each day – you had to bring your own drinking vessel – and meats rolled in flat bread were consumed by the hundreds. It was one of the greatest festivals that Memphis knew at that time, and it was the newest, having been established in very recent years.

Hessie waited at the palace. Moon had gone to do his duties at the festival, but she was concerned. He hadn't been well that morning, she thought, because he hadn't spoken to her before he left. She herself was often delicate as far as health was concerned. Her second miscarriage had been only weeks before, and she had spent nearly a month in bed, weak from loss of blood and a great depression that settled over her whenever she thought of her chances of producing an heir for the throne. That was her primary job, and she knew it. 'When I am completely well we'll try again,' was her firm resolution. In the meantime, Moon was spending his nights with one or more of the concubines, purportedly protecting Hessie from a pregnancy that might come too soon and result in another loss. She sighed inwardly and waited for the announcement of his return, but he appeared a few moments later without fanfare, silently opening her door and entering on bare feet. He looked terrible.

"Hessie," he smiled self- consciously as he spoke, "it's a huge crowd and they're unusually enthusiastic." He sat on a divan spread with silk cushions. "Ra's very hot today."

"Yes," she responded quickly. She didn't want to talk about his fevers again. He didn't like that. "Was it fun at all?"

"You should go out there some time, maybe in the evening after he's almost gone. You'd have a good time."

"Well, you can tell me about it, anyway. Did you see Ay this morning?"

"No, not yet today. He'll probably come round later."

"You can be sure."

Ay, the primary vizier for the pharaoh, was a source of agitation for both of them. He was always mostly concerned about the line of succession and kept it at the front of every meeting.

"Do you want some tea or beer? What about food? Did you eat this morning before you went?"

"We can eat later this afternoon. I think I need a little sleep first. These things are tiring."

"Maybe you need to eat. That will make you feel better. Then you can sleep. What do you think?"

"Good. We can eat now. I'm hungry. You must be."

"Moon, are you getting sick? I really want to know."

"It's just a light touch of the fever. I think it'll go away before long."

Hessie looked at him with frightened eyes. "A light touch?"

"That's what the doctors said this morning. Let's forget about it now. I took the medicine. It's really awful!"

"I saw you as you left earlier. I watched from my balcony. You were splendid!"

"The crown's too heavy. I want to make one that's lighter, maybe made out of thin wood with an overlay of gold. This one makes my neck tired."

"Ask Ay. But he won't let you do it."

"I think he will. He's interested in other things, not in traditions."

A servant knocked and entered, bowing low and averting her eyes. "Would my Lord the Pharaoh, or Lady need anything?" she asked.

"Yes," Hessie spoke quickly. "We want some lunch. A little meat and bread with lots of fruit."

"And beer," the pharaoh added.

"Yes, my lord." The servant ducked out the door.

"Would you like a game of senet while we eat?" Hessie could play the game for hours.

"Good. I'm ready to win again." He gave her a wink with a cautious smile.

"So be it, my lord," Hessie replied with bowed head.

On the second day of Hor-em-akhet's festival, the pharaoh participated in a shooting contest. He chose it among the many events offered for the day because he was reasonably good with a bow and would not likely be too humiliated if a peasant should defeat him. In the past the contests had been set up to ensure the pharaoh's victory, but Tutankhamun had declared he wouldn't allow that. He would be as vulnerable to defeat as anyone, he insisted, but it was not to be. As soon as the young king placed himself as an entrant to any contest, Vizier Ay and his servants made sure that the other contestants were informed that they were required to lose. It was an important thing for the pharaoh to be triumphant in any activity he set out to accomplish. Tutankhamun was sometimes surprised that he was victorious, but could never catch the culprit Ay in any fault. The king knew, but was unable to prove that his wins were assured.

"Excellent shot!" the pharaoh exclaimed to the young athletic man who was his opponent. "Where did you learn to shoot?"

"My father taught me, my lord," the man said, bowing. "He and my fathers before him have always been excellent shots."

"Where are you from, friend?" Tutankhamun asked.

"We are from the delta, my lord. A place called Zau."

"I have heard of it but not been there," the pharaoh replied. He loved to talk to real people. "Tell me, have you ever been to the great sea that lies beyond the delta?"

"No, my lord, I haven't, but people I know who have been there tell me it's a wonder."

"So I've heard. Well, it's my turn to shoot again. Perhaps we can talk more later." The pharaoh turned toward the target, pulled the arrow back and took aim. He didn't hit the center, but was close. Not as close at the contestant from Zau, however. The pharaoh smiled about that. Let Ay come try to fix this one!

His rival took careful aim, then relaxed his arm for a moment before he started to aim once more. Suddenly he cried out and fell, his left leg gushing blood. There was a lot of confusion. The king ran to help the man, but some of his guards came swiftly and blocked him before he could get too close. He shouted at them, but they persisted, so he had to struggle to get through. "He's hurt!" the pharaoh exclaimed. "Someone shot his leg!"

An athlete from another target range came running toward them. He was strong but small, and his efforts to get close to the victim were forcefully refused. "I shot him by accident! My arrow went wrong! I want to see how he is!" the athlete cried out. He was restrained by some of the men, and Tutankhamun was forced away from the scene by his protectors. He managed to turn to watch the spectacle and it was then that he saw Ay in the distance, coolly surveying the result of the 'accident'. Moon hated him.

The pharaoh rested in his palace for most of the afternoon. Ay did not come although he had been sent for. The vizier seemed to be missing and no one knew where he was.

"He's out planning some new nastiness," was all that Moon told Hessie.

"Could you stop him?"

"Yes, I will when I find him!" Moon threatened, but he knew it would be nearly impossible. Ay was constantly insinuating his controls into any situation he could, making himself a contender for the rule of Kmet. He had made decisions for the boy-pharaoh when he had come to the throne at age eight, and wanted to continue even though the pharaoh, who was now eighteen, was old enough to take all the responsibility on himself.

Moon was quiet for a while, waiting for the right moment. Finally he spoke again.

"I want to escape for a little while," he told Hessie. "What do you think?"

"What do you mean?"

"I want to sneak out of here! Let's go out to the festival!"

"That would make quite a stir," Hessie answered. "And it could be dangerous."

"I think we could get away with it. I don't mean to go as myself. We'd have to wear disguises."

The idea was planted, and Hessie regarded him watchfully. "Are you sure?" Her meaning was actually another question: "Are you well enough to do it?"

"I feel better now than I have for the last couple of days. It would be fun! Let's go!"

"How would we get out – and who would take us over to the celebration? It's too far to walk, especially to walk back in the dark."

"I have all that covered. We would go out the back, through the kitchens, and I would drive a little cart over – then we'd leave it with a vendor to guard. Lots of people do that. It's really easy."

"So you say. What if you're recognized?"

"We have to leave that to fate. I can take care of it anyway. Just assume the attitude of command. I've learned how, if you haven't noticed."

Moon seemed certain, and Hessie, who had been so concerned about him, let down her guard. "If that's what you want, we'll do it! Just tell me when you want to go."

They left the palace through the kitchen doors late in the day. The light was still strong, but the heat was diminishing as they climbed into the cart Moon had ordered under the name of Ay, and set out to the festive grounds. Hessie looked a little strange as a peasant, but Moon took the part easily. He had applied some small abrasions and other marks with makeup, and had conscripted an old kilt from a servant. They both wore leather sandals, not the golden ones Moon wore for public appearances, and they walked with a less pronounced step, more typical of the peasants they saw at the festival. They carried only a few bars of silver, small and inconspicuous in a pouch Moon tied around his waist. It was the best they could do in a hurry, and it seemed to work. There was a place to park the cart near some outer pavilions, and they paid the boy who had the concession more than he was used to getting, not knowing how much other people paid for the service.

The shadows of evening were long across the sandy paths, and Hor-em-akhet's face was darkened as they moved from place to place, looking in wonder at the great number of things that were offered them in such a limited space. They stopped to eat some of the bread and fruit, washed down with beer although they hadn't known to bring their own mugs. They were lucky; a supply had been left by previous customers, and the vendor filled two jars with his sweet, strong brew. It was rougher than what they usually drank, but tasted of adventure and intrigue. They drank well.

Hessie saw some trinkets she liked, so Moon opened his pouch and drew out a silver bar which was much more than the things cost. The vendor smiled, tucked it away with a polite 'thanks' and turned to the next customer. Having never shopped for anything they wanted or needed, they had no idea what to do. They walked on.

Street performers were abundant, some on stilts – which they had never seen before – and some doing magic tricks or music, others gymnastics and dancing, until it all swirled inside their heads along with the strong beer, and they felt tired. It was at that particular moment that a child grabbed hold of Hessie's hand and asked them to go with him.

"My grandmother has a booth over there," he said convincingly. "She sent me to find you and bring you to see her."

"Let's go!" Moon responded in a happy, carefree voice. They crossed to a side street and entered a pavilion with a low tent flap folded open for access. It was completely dark inside. The child led them out another opening in the back of the tent, where a woman sat at a table under the stars, a torch on her right side, some trinkets spread across the tabletop. Her head was bowed and she didn't look up when she spoke.

"You have come to me at last," she said in a deep voice. "There is no need for you to hide. I know who you are."

There was a long silence. Then she continued. "Sit there. I will speak to you."

Hessie and Moon sat at the table, silent and wondering, still affected by the strong beer. They had no sense of apprehension or fear.

The woman raised her head, her eyes were aflame, and she spoke again in an even deeper voice, echoing from somewhere outside herself. "I am Amun-Ra," she declared, "and I do not customarily speak to pharaohs." Moon felt a sharp sense of anguish. He hoped to go unrecognized.

"You have come in disguise, but you cannot hide your true selves from me." The woman was suddenly as big as the courtyard where she was seated. It could hardly contain her presence.

"Tutankhamun, Pharaoh of Kmet," she seemed to thunder. "You have come here seeking truth. I know it. I will give you truth. You are in danger, not from people, but from that which you carry within your body. You will soon pass this life for the next, and you will at last be free. But, I will warn you that the carter will come for you and take all you have except your forever spirit. He will be the destroyer of your earthly house, but will also be a blessing for the many who will follow you."

She turned to Hessie. "Ankhesenamun, faithful wife. You will despair, but you will find comfort again. I will give you a talisman of our visit, and it will help you remain strong." She held up the glowing staff, almost twice as tall as Hessie. "Take it! Many have held it before, but none more deserving!"

Hessie took the staff without hesitation and without taking her eyes from the woman who filled the courtyard. As the staff passed from her hand, she became normal size again, sitting across the table from them. "Go now with my blessing. I will see you, but you will not see me." The torchlight flickered and was out. They stumbled to the door and out into the dark street, Hessie gripping the staff with one hand and Moon's arm with the other. Then they turned and fled as quickly as they could to the place their cart was waiting and on to the palace, filled with confusion and wonder, but not fear.

Moon slept well that night, better than he had for many weeks. Hessie, on the other hand, seemed to hear voices and thoughts assailing her as she attempted to drift away in sleep, but the oblivion of sleep refused to come. The pharaoh was up early the next morning. He sent for Ay and waited. The vizier finally arrived with much complaining, but Tutankhamun silenced him.

"I have made some decisions," he said to the wily vizier. "I am appointing an heir to the throne. I do not want to trouble my wife further about producing a living son." His voice was flat and curt, and Ay took notice.

"Who is your appointed heir, my lord?" he asked with constraint. "I think we should discuss an appointment of that nature together before a final decision is made."

"I am pharaoh," Tutankhamun said firmly. "I will decide."

Ay was silent.

"I have decided to appoint my wife, Ankhesenamun."

Ay gasped audibly. "She is not a qualified appointment, my lord. She has no background for such a position."

"It is useless for you to argue. She is my appointed heir. She is the daughter of a great pharaoh, Akhenaten, and she has always discussed affairs of the nation and advised me during my years as pharaoh. There is nothing more to be required of her, and I am telling you, not asking, that she is to be my successor. Within the hour my scribes will complete the documents that I will sign to make her my heir."

"Have you told your wife? What does she say in this matter?"

"That is none of your concern. From this time forward you will cease to be vizier. You are now officially retired. Ankhesenamun and I will rule the nation of Kmet together."

Ay was unable to speak. He bowed low before the pharaoh and started to leave.

"You are not yet dismissed!" Tutankhamun hissed at him in anger. "There is one more official thing that you must do. I have had this prepared for you to sign." He shoved a papyrus document toward the man who stared in disbelief. "It is your agreement to termination of your position. You are not required to sign it, technically, as I have signed already, but it would be a great service to Kmet if you did so."

Ay took the thing into his hand and read a part of it. Then he dropped it to the floor and turned with a red and furious face and left the presence of the pharaoh, never to see him again in life.

Later that morning Tutankhamun made ready to leave Memphis. His time was ending, as he well knew, and he needed to be in Thebes as soon as possible. It would take days, but he had to get back before Ay had his chance to attempt overtaking the throne. Hessie, who had not yet been told of her succession, watched with concern as Moon snapped at the scribes who took dictation, telling them to hurry. It was uncharacteristic of him, she thought, and did not portend favorably.

The long trip on the barge brought about significant change in the pharaoh. He could not bring himself to tell Hessie that she was to be the next ruler of Kmet, but he hinted now and then. She didn't take it agreeably.

"Why are you telling me that you might not be pharaoh much longer? Did you really believe that sorceress at the festival? All she did was play some magic tricks!"

"Yes, I believe her. I don't know how much longer I'll be the king, but I know that I'll be stronger now than I ever was! Ay had better not try to do anything to alter my decisions."

"Don't say those things, Moon! You know how that hurts me! I don't want to live without you."

"I'm sorry, my dear love, but it's all there for us to know. Amun-Ra told me! What else do you want to think?"

"I – I can't think." And she wept. Moon comforted her.

The days passed slowly on the water. There was no sign of any disturbances on the shore as they glided along, but Tutankhamun began to feel anxiety the closer they got to Thebes. Small groups of peasants along the banks stood in salute, and the larger villages poured their entire populace out to the riverbank to shout and throw blossoms into the water as the pharaoh passed. He was much loved, Hessie knew, and she sorrowed as they floated slowly between the tall, green palm trees that thrived along the sides of the wide waterway. Finally, on a very early morning eight days later, the royal crafts arrived at the dock of the royal city, and they disembarked into their litters for the last trip to their extravagant palace. They were feted with banners and flags, musicians and dignitaries greeted them as they were carried to the very doors, and the young pharaoh stepped from his chair as a figure of authority and power that none had seen before. Horemheb, the first general of the military forces was there to meet him, and he was quietly impressed by the change that had come over the boy, as he thought of the king. It wasn't until the next day when he heard that Ay had been dismissed that he understood the newfound independence of the sovereign.

The palace was tense. Ay had not appeared, but he was in contact with most of his friends and some of his enemies in an attempt to remove Tutankhamun from the throne in any way that it could be done. He was not at all adverse to assassination. Hessie, who moved through the days in a dream-like state, came to believe that Moon's acceptance of his near demise was only a fabrication brought on at the festival, so she became more cheery as time passed, and they began to enjoy life again.

Finally, after waiting for nearly a month, Tutankhamun, Pharaoh of Kmet, had the courage to tell his wife what he had done. He was afraid that she would discover his decree before he told her, so he set about to make it a mutual declaration. Hessie was appalled. She had no plans or desire to rule.

"Why would a young woman like me want to be a pharaoh? I know that Hatshepsut was a long time ago, and that she accomplished more than the men, but her name was nearly obliterated after she died. Why would I want that? I only want to be your wife and when we both die we can go through the next life together. Forever. That's all I want!" She wailed the final words.

"I can't do anything else, Hessie," he told her. "I don't want to pressure you about having more children and I can't leave the kingdom to Ay or anyone else. That's what he wants! With you named as my heir I'm assured of the future of Kmet, which I'm very serious about. Please think about it some more and then, if you don't really want the job, I'll find someone else." He gave in.

"I will think about it, Moon. I will, and if I can find a way to do it for you, I promise that I will agree. For now, let's leave it aside. We can both be happy again."

When Horemheb got word of the plan for succession he came to meet the pharaoh.

"My lord," he started with a soft voice, "I am told that you have placed your wife, the Lady Ankhesenamun, in the position of your heir to the throne of this land. I must ask you your reasons, lord, and what you think the consequences of your choice might be for the people of the land."

"You can very well guess my reasons, so I need not tell you. As for the consequences, The Lady Ankhesenamun is far more qualified for the job than anyone else in the kingdom. Do not dispute my word on that!"

"Yes, my lord." Horemheb bowed. "I will ask you then if the lady is in complete agreement on this matter."

"General Horemheb, that is not, nor should it be, a concern of yours. I am satisfied. You should be as well. Is there any other subject for discussion at this time?"

"Not at this time, my Lord."

"That is all, then, General." The king rose from his throne and the general bowed. Tutankhamun passed from the audience hall without another look.

There was no more time. It had run out. On the next morning Pharaoh Tutankhamun had a disastrous accident while racing his chariot across the desert near Thebes. He was thrown from the vehicle and smashed his left leg - just above the knee - on a sharp outcropping of rock that the winds had swept free from sand. His leg cracked, he could both feel and hear it, and he was carried back to the palace where physicians attended him and tried to set the bone. The king was in agony, which was soon exacerbated by an onset of malaria, and within ten days he had been carried away by the combination. Hessie was bereft and without hope. She was able to bear up while Moon lived, but the instant he died she began to weep, and wept nearly constantly for the next two days. Nothing seemed to be able to revive her until she was called into audience by the Vizier Ay who had retaken his old job. She became angry, then furious, as she thought of that 'old fool' disregarding his dismissal, and she prepared herself well for her interview. She hid a small dagger under her mourning cloak.

Ay rose and bowed to her as she came forward into the audience hall. He was not audacious enough to sit on the throne, but at a table just below the dais, and he looked triumphant as he greeted her. "My dear, what a terrible loss. Both for you and for Kmet."

"You have no idea," she said as she glared at him. "Why are you here now? You were dismissed!"

"General Horemheb and I thought it best for me to come out of retirement, my dear. Please, sit here with me for a while. We need to talk."

'Clever,' she thought, 'bringing the army into this.' "I have no need to sit," she told him.

"As you will, then, my lady. As you know, the Pharaoh Tutankhamun has named you as the heir to the throne of Kmet."

"Yes."

"You have been, ah, upset now for two days. I think it time for you to consider your duties if you are to be pharaoh."

"You snake!" she exploded. "I will take on my duties when I have properly buried the pharaoh."

"You are still too upset for duties now, I see. Well, perhaps you can consider some other things at this time. The general and I have been discussing this situation, and we feel that you are not entirely yourself, and that we should offer our assistance for an interim period. Would that be a suitable solution for you, my dear?"

"You will not! I am now pharaoh, and I forbid you to take any part of the ruling of Kmet from this moment!"

"Well spoken, but the general and I do not agree. You are still - -"

"I care not whether you agree. You are an evil man, and I am only sorry that you have brought the general into partnership with you."

"It was the general's idea, my dear. He has a new plan for Kmet. Do not say anything more that you might regret later." Hessie was stunned, but did not speak. Ay continued. "We have had a few meetings and have decided that you will be most unsuitable for the throne, and I know that you will come to agree with that conclusion as soon as I tell you the rest of the story. The general has pledged the army to stand with us, and we will jointly advise the government until we find a new pharaoh who will meet the requirements of the military and can assume the throne."

"What are the requirements?" Hessie asked him in a cold, stark voice.

"You have no need to trouble yourself about that now. I know that your heart is in the preparations for your husband's funeral and that - - "

"To you he will always be called by his title, The Pharaoh Tutankhamun, nothing else!" she bellowed.

"Of course, The Pharaoh Tutankhamun's funeral, then. We do not expect you to enter into matters of government at all. As I said, you will not become pharaoh. There are many reasons for that. Now you know and you can rest with the understanding that you will never need to assume the throne."

Hessie began to cry, sobbing faintly. Ay leaned over to pat her arm. She struck at him violently, suddenly, and with good aim, but his heavy belt deflected the dagger, which broke with the strength of her thrust. It clattered to the floor and she spat into the face of the future pharaoh of Kmet. He grabbed her arm, but let go quickly, and laughed.

"I had not expected that. There is more to you than I knew. A spitfire. Well, let's keep it our secret, my dear, and we shall see what happens next. It may be a secret for now, but I will reveal all if you try to cause an upset. Remember, Hessie" - he used the familiar name as an angry epithet - "I am in charge now!"

Hessie was able to sleep that night. Getting her blood up with Ay and his insolence had helped her overcome the initial shock of Moon's death, and she mustered her courage. The next morning, however, was a different story. She awakened with the dread lifeless feeling that had been her constant companion since he died, and she wanted to hide from the day that was to follow. How would she manage to get through it? Then she thought of Ay and Horemheb and strength returned to her mind and body. She must repel them! She had no desire to be pharaoh, but knew she had to act in some way to prevent them from destroying the memory of her beloved. She wept a little more, then pulled her mourning robe over her shoulders and went into the sitting room to think. A servant brought her food and some tea, which she found she wanted for the first time since Moon had gone. She ate with dispatch, which pleased the waiting servant immensely, and then set out to make a plan. She was disturbed by a caller. General Horemheb had come to see her. She sat upright on the chair and told the servant to let him enter.

"My lady," he bowed. "I have come to offer my respect to you and to the Pharaoh Tutankhamun." Horemheb was very smooth. "Your great sorrow has come to my attention, and I want to assure you that I will personally do whatever I can to assist you in your plans for the funeral of our fallen pharaoh."

"Then you will call that terrible man off!"

"You mean Ay. I am sorry that he upset you. He had no business doing that. I told him that he should speak very carefully."

"As you are doing now, general?"

"If you wish, my lady," he bowed again. "I may be your best hope of survival through all this," Horemheb spoke candidly.

"I do not particularly wish to survive."

"But you should, lady. There is much that remains for you to do."

"Then you will be good enough to give me an example, I'm sure."

"You will need to oversee the planning of the funeral for our Pharaoh Tutankhamun."

"Will I be allowed to do that? To do whatever I think best for him?"

" 'Whatever' may be a tall order, but the things that are important will all need your approval."

"What do you consider important, general"

"The tomb site, the furnishings for his afterlife, the rituals to be said and done for him when he is buried, all that sort of thing"

"He's in the mortuary temple now. How long will that take?" She was surprised that she could speak so calmly.

"It will be about two months, I think. A pharaoh takes a long time, as you probably know. He has to be wrapped very carefully."

"So I have about two months to find a tomb and get it decorated and ready."

"Yes, but I will personally assist you."

101

"No, I will find my own assistants. I'm sure you and Ay have other things to do." She scowled.

"As you wish, lady. But please keep me advised about your progress. It would be a bad situation to leave a pharaoh waiting for his tomb."

"You should have thought of that before!" Immediately she wanted to recall the words, but Horemheb ignored them.

"Please call for me if I can offer any help for anything, my lady." The general rose and bowed and a servant let him out through the nearest door.

The morning passed as Hessie considered who she could rely on to find a tomb for her Moon. She had thought of no one when a servant came to tell her that Vizier Ay wished to speak to her. "He said it is an urgent matter, honored lady." The servant bowed to the floor.

"Send him in. I'm ready for him now."

Ay appeared and the instant he saw her he knelt on the floor with his head low. "My lady," was all he said.

"Get up!" she barked. "Why do you want to see me this morning? Didn't you have enough yesterday?"

"My lady," Ay spoke from his kneeling posture without looking up. "I have come to beg your pardon for the things I said yesterday. I will apologize more, but you can't possibly understand the pressures that caused me to speak to you in that manner, and I am humbly sorry."

Hessie realized it was an act. "Get up and speak your message before I have you removed."

Ay glanced around, taking in the two servants who stood near the door. No one there had the strength, physically, or the spirit to do anything about him with the exception of Hessie. He slowly got to his feet. "My dear lady," he lowered his head again. "I have come to ask your pardon."

"You do not have it!"

"But still I ask. It was my concern for you that made me speak without regard to your feelings."

"I will believe that when the gods stop laughing! Now, what else do you want?"

"You are harsh with me, and I can't blame you. Do you have a dagger in your possession today? If so, thrust it into me, and I will not complain."

"You make me quite ill" she told him. "Either say what you planned, or leave."

"Then I will say that I have spent a long night in sorrow and struggle. I have offended you when I should have offered my help and my heart. I will go now, lady, but the next time we meet I hope that you will think more kindly of me."

"Go! If I never see you again I will be pleased. Go!" She turned away. Ay headed for the door slowly but with purpose. He was going, and a servant opened the door quickly to let him take his leave as soon as he would. In the passageway, Ay smiled. It would take some time, but he would eventually win.

Hessie had visits every day from both Ay and the general. She began to wonder why they gave her so much attention, but her mind, apart from bouts of grief, was filled with the preparation for her Moon's burial. He had to be sent off splendidly. She was offered a small rock chamber that was cut into the western valley; a place of mostly small rooms with no decoration, to prepare for his eternal home. She had no idea that it belonged to Ay and was the place he had planned for his own burial until her need came so suddenly, and he had offered it as a gift for the Pharaoh Tutankhamun.

She always imagined, as she thought about it, that she would be there with her Moon, and that they would spend their eternity among the things she used to furnish it. Hessie wanted, literally, to be sealed inside with her husband and to die there so they could be together. She cared nothing for mummification for herself, only for her presence there, and she dreamed of the day, soon to arrive, when she could get inside just before the final closing of the door and the seals were placed on the surrounding sill. That dream kept her going.

Just two weeks after she directed the start of the decoration for the tomb, Horemheb came for his daily visit. He came right to the point.

"We have chosen Ay as the next pharaoh," he said quietly. "But I must be honest with you. We have chosen him because he is old and cannot live much longer. Soon the throne will need a new occupant."

Hessie made no response.

"He has a need to justify his place on the throne, as you well know, my lady. He needs a connection. We hope that you will be that connection." He said it gently, without force of guile. "We offer this to you. You will once again be the pharaoh's wife, and the life you have known will endure at least as long as Ay is on the throne, and you will be able to honor our great Pharaoh Tutankhamun every day. All the people still love him." It sounded so simple.

Horemheb was completely taken by surprise when Hessie answered. "I will consider this, general, and I will take the matter seriously." The general had expected to find a wall of anger and resentment, and had prepared some strong arguments to support his case, but she had taken charge of the situation easily and naturally. So it was that Hessie prepared for the funeral for Moon and her marriage to Ay at the same time. No one else knew that she had been in conversation with Amun-Ra who told her what she must do to avenge her beloved, who seemed to be the only pharaoh the great god had ever liked.

Hessie had free reign for Tutankhamun's burial preparations. Ay gave her the best that he could offer at such short notice, and she took it skillfully. She had little time to decorate the walls of the tomb, but managed to get some large pictorials of her cherished one in various scenes from his short life. She had lines of baboons; the creature that led the dead pharaohs to paradise, placed above his head in memory of his favorite childhood pet, Kula, and murals of Tutankhamun with Osiris, the pharaoh on his throne with his wife standing in front of him, and the two of them sitting in the garden; as many memories as she could pour into the space in the few days she had left. As it was, she could decorate only the burial chamber itself, all the other walls were left barren.

The collection of tomb furnishings was incredible. Tutankhamun was buried with a proper store of lavish treasures. Amun-Ra insisted that it must be so, and Hessie was happy to oblige. A large golden pavilion held three smaller ones, each fitting inside the others, decorated on all sides with golden goddesses. There was statuary of gods and animals, small and large jars, stunning jewelry, some of her very own that she gave to him as a memory of herself - also to wear in her own afterlife. There was his bed and his chair, his chief servants replicated in realistic poses, and a resplendent pure gold sarcophagus that fit inside the heavy stone receptacle which was to be his conveyance into eternity. The most amazing of all was the mask of his face, wearing all the symbols of office, articulately and accurately shaped in solid gold with lapis lazuli decorative stripes and facets. It made her smile and weep at the same time.

The morning was hot and fine. The vault of the sky was deeply blue and radiantly clear above the rock cliffs along the sides of the valley of tombs. A small breeze stirred the dry air, and people gathered along the road to the valley very early. They had come prepared for the whole morning with water skins and food, sunshades, and flowers. They waited quietly; this was no celebration. At last the procession climbed up from the river, a large contingency of priests followed by the elegant gold-encased body of Tutankhamun. Ay, his successor, rode in his canopied chair beside Ankhesenamun's, each carried by four slaves. He looked haggard and very old, as was befitting newly acquired burdens of government and his age, but his bride-to-be was as lovely as ever. She didn't smile, nor did she weep, but gazed straight ahead at the golden figure of her dead husband as they slowly followed the curving trail that wound into the valley.

No one in the vast audience was allowed very near the burial place, but they could see the dark entryway, the door to death, that lay down several steps below the narrow pathway that passed among the tombs. No one but closest family, friends, and officialdom, as well as the artists who prepared the young king's place, had seen the interior, and its secrets remained unknown to the gallery who watched from the slopes of the parched hills. Death was always mysterious, but the death of the pharaoh was unparalleled in its depth of secrecy. Drums tolled the step that the procession kept as they marched to the place where Tutankhamun would finally and forever disappear from view.

The cortege and its followers stopped at the entrance to the tomb. Tutankhamun was taken in hand by an honor guard of highest ranking officials who touched his coffin as it was carried by the strongest young slaves Ay could find, and they all descended the steps and passed through the door to the beat of the drums. The Lady Ankhesenamun stood rigidly at the top of the stairs, waiting for the drums to cease before she returned to her chair to watch as the treasures she had selected were taken inside, and the door sealed at last. She would not leave until she was sure that all was in order, and guards were placed beside the door; guards who had loved her husband in life and would now protect him after death. It was not only their duty, it was their honor to serve their king as he began his eternal voyage through the stars. For the lady it was like a dream - an obstinate, confusing dream. No matter how much she believed that Tutankhamun would be greeted by the gods and accepted as one of them, she felt a terrible urge to scream out his name and recall him from the house of death. She would if she only had the power.

Five days after the solemn funeral, Ay prepared for his wedding to the bride of the former pharaoh. He dressed himself in a new golden kilt, his head newly shaved – he was almost bald anyway – and he had drunk potions and eaten certain foods that would improve his ability to act as a husband should as soon as the wedding celebration was complete. Hessie had asked him to keep the celebration simple out of regard for her deceased husband, and he agreed. Fewer than five hundred guests were invited, and the menu was kept to a minimum; roast fowl and joints of mutton and ox, a variety of garden vegetables and lots of rice and bread. There was also wine, or beer for those who liked it better. Then the sweets would be presented, figs and honey, dates laced with sweet liquors, sweet cakes, and as a finale, ices from the land far away where the mountains were cold in all seasons. The ices were infused with honey and other sweet liquids, and they were always a big hit at royal affairs.

The bride, Ankhesenamun, was dressed in the simplest possible ensemble, with only one small amulet around her neck, and Ay was disappointed. He wanted her to be a show-stopper, but could do nothing about it after she had made her appearance more than an hour late. She sat with him on the dais and greeted people without much warmth, and began to look tired and seemed withdrawn far too early.

"Can you attempt to be more cheerful?" he asked her quietly, but she ignored his request and turned away to greet someone he didn't know nor care to meet. She was not the young woman he had watched sitting beside the Pharaoh Tutankhamun, but he was determined not to show his displeasure to his guests. He would settle with her later.

Far earlier than he expected, Hessie turned to him with a near-smile and said that she would like him to take her to her bedchamber. Ay suddenly felt quite young again, and smiled warmly. "Of course, my dear," he whispered clearly. "A fine idea."

They arose and she took his hand, rather disarmingly, he thought, and they walked together across the audience chamber as their guests threw flowers in their path. At the door to the bedchamber, Hessie paused.

"Just let me go in first, for a little. I'll be ready soon. Why don't you count to a slow one hundred?" Ay opened the door and watched her enter. She seemed altogether lovely again, he thought. He did a rather too quick count, but knocked on the door before he opened it. "Do come in," she said in a low voice. The room was dim, but he could see her plainly, sitting on a low chair beside her bed, in no way prepared to welcome him there. She held up her hand.

"Stop where you are!" she ordered. He moved on another step.

"Stop!" she said again and her voice seemed so harsh that he obeyed. "I will tell you this one time, and do not want to repeat it again. I married you, yes, but I am not your wife. I am the wife of Tutankhamun and will never be wife to another."

"What do you mean?" he leered at her. "You're legally mine!"

"If you step forward again I will use this," she held up a long dark staff that seemed to glow from within. "It can do a lot of damage. Now listen! You are to leave me here, now. Do not come back to this room again, ever. It is mine, and you have no rights within it! I will never pretend to be your wife again!"

"Then why did you marry me just now?"

"I did so to protect myself and the memory of my dead husband! You have no hold on me. I will never truly be your wife!"

"You're an evil bitch!" he shouted and strode forward toward the chair.

In a flash Hessie held out the staff, pointed it directly at him, and he felt a charge as though it had fired something, he did not know what, into his chest. He sagged but did not stop.

She watched him take another step. "The next one will probably kill you," she said in an even tone. Ay stopped. He couldn't imagine what was happening. How had she found that thing, and how did it work? At that moment a most fearsome apparition entered from the opposite side of the room. It was a woman with flaming eyes who stood as tall as the ceiling. She spoke to him in a voice that echoed inside his head for the rest of his life. "Ay, loathsome pharaoh of Kmet!" she said.

He looked at Hessie who seemed surprised to see the woman but was obviously not afraid. He looked back at the woman. "Who are you?" he demanded.

"You have no need to know. Only this will I tell you: Do exactly as my daughter Ankhesenamun has told you. If you ever enter this room again or apprehend her in any way, you will forfeit your life! Remember that." Ay collapsed on the floor.

Then the woman was gone and Hessie stood above him with the staff in her hand. "Come," she called her serving maids. "Take this man out into the passage. He can find his way from there." Ay was carried through the door and dumped along the wall, where he lay in confusion and pain for nearly an hour before one of the palace servants came along and saw him there. He called the guards who took the pharaoh back to his own quarters.

Ay made no accusations against Hessie. He never spoke to her again, although he saw her once in a while on the palace grounds or in the dining room with her friends. She had become a celebrity with a devoted following, and he took careful pains to avoid her at all costs. Nearly four years later, Ay passed on suddenly one night, and Kmet had another funeral for a pharaoh. It was nothing like the last one. There were few mourners, and only one of his four wives, Ankhesenamun, attended. She also planned the whole thing so he would not receive any undue honors, and she was cheered to know that he had met his doom at last. After a short time, life and merriment continued at the palace. Horemheb chose himself to be the next ruler, and everyone, with few exceptions, was happy again.

Hessie lived for many years, outlasting even Horemheb, and was finally sent to her eternal habitation by a great crowd who knew and loved her well.

Chapter Six

982 B C

The capital city of Tanis glowed in the subtly golden evening light that streamed across green fields where rivulets of water made the delta into a perfect garden. It was farmland, and almost everything that could be grown anywhere on the earth prospered there, a feast for the eye as well as the palate. Tanis itself was not an imposing or magnificent city, but it was the place where the power of Kmet dwelt, and had certain aspects that made it an international city, one with no small claim to prominence.

Thebes was another capital of the nation, far to the south, and still held considerable power, but it was in Tanis that the inheritors of the kingdom stayed, and from Tanis their influence was sent abroad. Tanis was a new city, built less than a century in the past. It did not have the provenance of once mighty Thebes; the guardians of the monuments there had become primarily keepers and protectors. What the world considered to be the true power of Kmet sat on the throne in Tanis.

Princess Ka 'artia, a strong-willed girl of sixteen, was the third daughter and sister to several sons of the Pharaoh Siamun. She was as physically exquisite as her will was strong, and was always the apple of her father's eye. The king doted on her wishes repeatedly and unstintingly - she was a clever beauty he could never allow himself to disappoint. She had a passion for all kinds of animals and her menagerie filled a large part of the lower quarters of the north wing of the palace. All kinds of creatures, small and large, were included in the collection, and she wanted to be sure that she knew all about every one of them and visited her private zoological gardens every day. Her father indulged her with such beasts as gazelles and peacocks, simians of all kinds, canines, and even zebras and giraffes, exotic animals that made heads turn to look twice whenever they were on public display.

Ka 'artia, or 'Artia as she was most often called, led a happy and eventful life. Her multiple interests kept her attention, and she had no reason to doubt that she would have a contented future until the morning she met with her father when he told her he had arranged for her to marry a future king, Solomon of Israel, a distant country that she felt sure was as unsophisticated as it sounded. She immediately reacted with a strong "No! I'll never do it!" To her amazement, her father turned with his full authority showing in his face and said, in a calm and steady voice, "You will." 'Artia realized that she had gone too far. She bowed low in submission as her father turned away.

"I'll never go, Rina! I promise you that I won't! He may be the pharaoh, but he can't make me do this!" 'Artia exclaimed firmly to her personal maid. She had flung herself across a divan in her private chambers on the upper floor of the north wing, just above her treasured menagerie.

"Do you think it's that bad to marry a prince? He'll be king one day soon."

"Don't try to make me believe it's going to be good! I know the kind of man he is! I've seen enough of those little royals around here, and I can't believe my father, or should I say 'The Pharaoh,' would offer me as a prize to one of them! It's barbaric!" 'Artia was not at all weepy, but she was plainly angry and hurt at her father's lack of concern for her welfare.

"Now, Miss, be sure you know what you're doing. Don't try to be defiant. It will only make a barrier, and you don't want to do that." Rina began to smooth the girl's hair, very gently.

"What can I do? What do you think is the best way for me to get him to see my position?"

"I don't know yet, Miss. Let me think about it a little while, and you think, too. I'm sure you'll find a way."

"Have you ever heard of a Prince Solomon? I haven't. He's a Hebrew is all father told me."

"No, but then I don't go in the circles you do, Miss. You might ask your Lady-Mother about it." Rina was always careful to speak about the queen with a title, even though she was closer to 'Artia than her mother had ever been.

"The queen wouldn't know. All she can ever think about is either Ennes or Kon. Daughters have never been of much interest to her!"

"I'll ask around a little. Someone in the kitchen may know something. They usually get the scuttlebutt when a prince is coming. They have to know what to feed him!"

"Well, see what you can find. I want all the information I can get." She paused for a moment to consider. "Rina, I heard somewhere that these Hebrews have a god they can't even name. It's supposed to be a terrible thing to say his name out loud, anyway."

"People do strange things sometimes, Miss. I don't know anything else."

"I can't imagine such a thing! I could never believe in a god I couldn't name!"

"You won't have to, Miss. You can take your own with you."

"I don't know how they'd feel about that. If they're crazy like that they probably wouldn't let me. Bring my own god, I mean. And there wouldn't be any temple, either."

"If you aren't going to go anyway, why should that be a problem, Miss?"

"You're impossible!" She paused for a moment. Rina continued brushing her hair. "Rina, do you remember that time last year when we were going past the market and they had a slave there, a girl about thirteen you thought?"

"Yes, Miss, I remember."

"And the way all the men were eyeing her; some of them even touching her."

"Yes, Miss."

"Well, you know how I yelled at them, and someone asked me if I wanted to buy her?"

"Yes, Miss."

"They said she was a Hebrew, Rina. They said the slavers had found her alone in the desert. She'd run away or something."

"Yes, Miss."

"I should have bought her."

"Why do you say that, Miss?"

"I need someone who knows about the Hebrew country now. I don't know whatever happened to her. Do you?"

"No, Miss."

"I watched you talking to the men, Rina; the slavers. You paid for something. I thought you were buying her for me."

Rina was silent for a little while. "I did buy her, Miss, but not for you. I sent her to a good woman I know who needed a maid. That's all."

"How did you have the money to pay for her?"

"The pharaoh has paid me for a long time and I've kept it all. I have money left."

"But why did you do it?"

"You know why, Miss."

The princess knew that Rina had been a slave herself. The head servant on the queen's staff had bought her when Ka 'artia was born. The pharaoh had given Rina freedom at Ka-'artia's insistence when the girl was only ten years old. It wasn't a lengthy story, but it had important significance for the princess every day. She paused and took a short, gasping breath before she committed herself with the next thought. "I want you to come with me when I go to marry that Hebrew Prince."

"I will, Miss. You could never stop me."

"And I want to take that girl back to her homeland."

Rina waited. It was a typical response; she understood it well, but she wasn't sure it could be done. "I don't know if I can get her for you, Miss. I told the woman she could have her as long as needed."

"You can. Tell the woman that I command it. And I will pay you a better price than you paid for the girl. The pharaoh will pay, of course. He'll have to do that much for me! I want to talk to that slave about the place she came from, and she can tell me what she knows about the Hebrew royalty."

"That's good of you, Miss."

"No. Not really. It's just necessary. How else will I get any information?"

It was four months of negotiation and preparation before the Princess Ka 'artia was ready to leave Kmet to go to Israel, up to the city of David, and into the palace of the king. She had changed quite a lot, in her mind at least, and had heard good reports about the young prince and his influence in the surrounding area. His father, the powerful King David, won battles, it was said, and although he was not a direct threat to Kmet, her father considered it an important enough matter to send his best-loved daughter to influence Prince Solomon and to obtain his promise of a secure relationship between their nations. Ka 'artia, he was sure, would have a wonderful effect upon the young man.

Much consideration was given to the bride's trousseau, and the queen paid decisive attention to each item that was included. The city of Jerusalem had a very different climate to Tanis, and no one knew exactly what to expect. The slave girl, Netele, a recent acquisition for the princess, was consulted. She was native to the region in the hill country near the Hebrew capital, and knew the climate well. So many warm things were constructed for Ka 'artia that it caused her to wonder how cold it might get in that far-off place. She had never experienced winter temperatures. Not only was all manner of special clothing part of the package, but linens and bedding and towels, soaps for cleansing, and perfumes that were especially alluring, were part of the whole, and no young woman the queen knew about was given a finer collection for her send-off. When the day arrived, the princess was taken to the shallow waterway that flowed through Tanis and boarded on a flat barge that sailed slowly on the crest of the river as far as Rakotis. There the entire party transferred to three smaller sea-going vessels, and moved onto the Great Sea for a voyage that would last nearly ten days. The ships from Kmet were all majestically fitted out with blue and red sails and golden flags that flowed in the strong currents of air. 'Artia, Rina, and Netele boarded the center ship, the largest of the group, and as they slipped gently away from the docking area they felt the roll of the water beneath their feet. A sense of homesickness as well as unsteady stomachs sent them below to the royal enclosure in short order. 'Artia was soon recovered and walked freely along the decks, but Rina and Netele suffered, mostly in silence, for the first few days of the voyage.

After five days on the water, 'Artia decided it was time for her to interview Netele. She had wanted to ask her questions as soon as the girl arrived at the palace about two weeks earlier, but Rina had warned her that Netele needed some time to adjust before the princess set out enquiries that might unnerve the shy young slave. Netele approached the interview with lowered eyes and a voice that could hardly be heard. They sat together in the salon, a situation 'Artia thought would promote an easy conversation, but it did not. Netele was obviously so alarmed by the princess that she could hardly move, let alone tell anyone about her observations concerning King David and his son Solomon. Little was gained that day, and 'Artia soon decided to stop the interview because the girl sat with a downcast face and claimed no knowledge about anything in Israel.

"She's afraid of you, you understand," Rina told her princess. "I don't think she'll be able to get past that very soon. In time, maybe, but not now."

'Artia considered. She wanted information but had no way of getting it – unless Rina would do it for her.

"Then you must ask her for me. Get her to tell you what you can, and you and I can talk."

Rina was doubtful, but agreed that it might be the only way the girl could be persuaded to speak about anything she could remember. The next morning 'Artia announced suddenly that she was going to the deck and wanted to be alone. Rina didn't question her resolve, and soon she and the little slave were cleaning the princess' cabin and fluffing her bedding on the small balcony that opened above the shining waters of the Great Sea. As they set to their tasks, Rina began a light-hearted dialog to which Netele responded cheerfully. It was a good time to ask careful questions about Netele's past, and Rina gradually came to the heart of the matter.

"Did you ever see King David?"

Netele dropped any remnant of shyness. "Oh, yes! I saw him lots of times! He was always going places where he could talk to people."

"Do you know anyone who talked to him?"

Netele's eyes were wide and glowing. "I did! I talked to him myself! He was walking through the gate one day as I was waiting to go in, and he saw me. He left all his men and came right up close and spoke to me. He asked me my name and who my father was. He was one of the kindest people I ever saw, and his eyes smiled. They really did, and I think he actually liked talking to me!" It was obvious that the memory left her with compelling impressions. "In a little while he left, but I never forgot. I tried to see him whenever I could, and another time he smiled at me when I called his name, but he never spoke to me again."

"Maybe he will when you get back to the city."

"I'm a slave. He won't even see me now."

"You're still the same, Netele, and he might."

"No, I'm a slave. I don't have a life of my own anymore. I belong to the princess."

Rina leaned over toward the girl. "You'll get your life back, you will! I'm sure of it."

"I don't know how."

"Princess 'Artia will protect you, she told me she would. She likes you."

"How do you know?"

"She told me. Anyway, if you can tell her anything about Prince Solomon, she'd be grateful. I know her. She'll always treat you well."

Netele seemed to take that information seriously, and she smiled a little at Rina. "I can tell her something, if she wants me to."

"Oh, yes, she does. And you can believe what I tell you. She's very kind."

When 'Artia returned from the deck, Rina spoke out. "I think that Netele has something she'd like to say to you, Miss. I told her you wanted to hear what she has to say about King David and the prince."

"Yes, I do!" 'Artia responded. "Please tell me, Netele."

"Do you want to hear about when I talked to King David?"

Rina nodded from the side. "Yes. Please!" 'Artia answered.

The girl told her the same story she had related to Rina as the princess listened thoughtfully. Then she asked, "Do you have any other stories about the King or Prince Solomon?"

"She does," Rina encouraged.

"Yes, about the prince. I can tell you things. What I've seen myself. I saw him several times, and he was always the same, the way he looked and acted. I think everybody likes him, and to me, he is wonderful!"

"Did he ever talk to you?"

"No, but I watched for him a lot. He liked to go to the markets and public places. He was always with lots of people, and women all loved him, I think. Everybody did. Anyway, they acted like they did."

"That's good, Netele, but what did you see about him that caused you to be so happy when he was there? To think he's wonderful?"

"His eyes smiled, like the king's."

The voyage wasn't unpleasant for the princess. She enjoyed the days on the sea with no land in sight, sitting on a chair on the top deck near the rail, watching the water in its endless movement. The crossing was storm free, which allowed for a lot of deck sitting, and the princess came to feel as though the wash of the waves against the hull was the most pleasant and calming thing she had ever heard. The sun was hot in the afternoon, but she found a shaded place which faced toward the east and sat there as the hours passed. She loved the water and the waves and all the small bits floating on the surface. They told her that land was near, but it was always beyond the horizon until the final day when hills appeared in the distance, a line of insignificant bumps on the eastern horizon, and she watched them grow, slowly but steadily, until their features came into focus although they were nestled quite a way inland from the still far-off shore. "A new land, a new home," 'Artia told herself as she watched the coastline draw nearer.

At last she saw a city gathered closely around a little harbor; it was the city of Jaffa, the celebrated port of Israel, but to Ka 'artia it looked miserable. She recalled the white quay shining in the sun at Rakotis, her place of departure, and had a sinking feeling that Israel was no Kmet. There were no buildings of style or importance, and there seemed to be no civil order in the place. The natives she could see from the deck looked disheveled and dirty, a far cry from her homeland and most of the people she had seen there. The new life in Israel looked rather hopeless for a while, but she mentally shouldered her responsibilities once again and waited for the final docking in her cabin with Rina and Netele. "It will all work out," she told herself for the hundredth time. "I don't think I've seen the best of this place from the docks."

The royal company remained on board for that night. It was late in the afternoon when they arrived, and Prince Solomon had determined that his princess should not be required to ride onward until the following morning. The city of Jaffa had no decent hostelry fit for a regal lady. Early the next morning Ka 'artia called Rina to help her dress. She put on a new outfit, one that would be suitable for the eyes of this new land, as she had been told. Kmetian women usually wore only small white linen coverings, as little as their kind of modesty allowed, but in this place women were much more concealed. She chose a soft blue robe with a silver belt, and Rina exclaimed about the effect it presented. "You're a stunning beauty, Miss! You should have worn this in Tanis! Everyone should see you now."

"Do you really think so, or are you just telling me that?"

"Do I ever 'just tell you' anything, Miss?"

"No, Rina, you don't. Thank you."

Netele, who had come to trust 'Artia, told her much the same thing. "You are perfect, Princess 'Artia."

An officer from the crew knocked on the door. "Prince Solomon has arrived, my lady," he bowed and held the door as the princess stepped past him, followed by Rina, and Netele - who couldn't stop herself from going. She strode briskly up the stairs to meet the future.

Everyone in Israel knew the history of David, the King, and his son Solomon. It was a lengthy and rather twisted tale of love and murder and revenge, but that had all been long ago, and the country was once again united. David was getting old, Solomon was still young by royal standards, and their similar but vaguely different styles for governing were a fresh new venture for the kingdom. When Solomon was younger, before he could even recall such things, his older brother Absalom had been named successor to the throne. Absalom had become angry with his father, then greedy to possess the crown, so he had revolted and gathered a large army in order to take his rightful position as king by force. Absalom was a very handsome man, beautiful, as he was described by historians, with long flowing hair and a strong athletic body. At the end of his revolt, his hair was caught in the twining branches of a tree as he rode swiftly beneath it, and he was run through by a sword on the orders of Joab, the general of David's army, although the king had specified that his wayward son should be spared. It was a terrible blow to David, who loved his son, and he mourned Absalom for a very long time.

Solomon, it was commonly agreed, was even more beautiful than Absalom. The prince and new heir to the throne was a strongly charismatic and striking figure, not only within his own kingdom, but in the world at large. His father loved him with all his heart; he had no other son who was as gifted as this young man, and David was filled with joy at the prospect of Solomon becoming king.

David had gone to the extreme of having the first husband of Bathsheba, Solomon's beautiful mother, killed in battle so that the woman could be free to marry again. It was an act they paid for dearly, for their first son died at birth, but Solomon came along soon, and David immediately loved him. When the young prince was old enough, the king declared him his heir, and Solomon began to learn the duties of a monarch. He also learned the privileges, and was given much latitude by his father.

It was onto this stage that 'Artia, the daughter of the Pharaoh of Kmet, walked that morning, and took her first look at the man who was to be her husband. Solomon was waiting for her, smiling and attentive. He was concerned about what kind of woman the daughter of pharaoh would be, and his smile widened as she approached. For her part, 'Artia was astounded. Solomon was more than a prince. In her eyes he was the most handsome man she had ever seen, and the words of Netele came rushing back; 'To me, he is wonderful.' 'Artia was completely taken by the man she saw, and even if he already had three wives it made no difference. He was hers. For the first time in her memory she was speechless.

They rode in a cumbersome wagon-like conveyance that could hardly fit the path. Solomon and a company of soldiers on horseback travelled with them throughout that day and the next before arriving at Jerusalem, the capital of united Israel, late in the night. Whenever he could, Solomon rode close beside the wagon and 'Artia told him all she could about Kmet and her life there. Solomon was unusually intent, she thought, and listened and asked so many questions that she sometimes became confused about which ones to answer. All the while she kept watching him gratefully. It wasn't every princess who went to a foreign land to marry a future king and found such a man as Solomon waiting at the end of her journey. She was more than thankful, she was ecstatic. Nothing went wrong during the journey, and she began to wonder whether she might be dreaming. The land went past, green and bright with plants and trees and small villages. The sky was as blue as the skies over Kmet, and she felt the blessings of Amun-Ra pouring over her as they traveled over the byways of Israel. She was able to ask the prince a few questions, but spent most of her time answering his, a position she enjoyed in most companies. They stopped the first night and tents were set up beneath the gibbous moon and intense stars. A small supper of bread and cheese and soup was provided, and 'Artia slept the night through on soft pillows, covered with woolen blankets in her own tent, with Rina and Netele nearby. It was late the next evening when they climbed to the heights and arrived at the city in the hills. The King, they were told, awaited them.

"I must look untidy," Artia told Solomon. "I don't want to meet the king looking like this!"

"Not at all," he assured her. "You look wonderful! He's waited up late to meet us." So they went to the audience immediately and 'Artia met King David.

An old man, still stalwart and very much in control, sat on the throne-chair inside his lengthy hall. His hair was long, but finer than Solomon's, grey and soft in the candlelight. Although his face was not lined, he looked tired, but his wide blue eyes smiled. 'Artia was startled as she looked into them and recalled the words of Netele. He was like Solomon in so many ways, she thought, but unlike as well. Then she saw his hands, strong and brown, with a shape that was attractive, and realized that Solomon had a younger looking set just like them. 'Hands are important,' 'Artia said to herself.

The three of them stood together to drink a cup of greeting, and the old king smiled fully upon 'Artia. "Welcome to Israel, and to this house," he said with a vigorous voice. "You have been long-expected, and are now a part of our little family. Be at ease among us, Princess Ka 'artia. That is a beautiful name, one to match a lovely princess. Be happy with us."

'Artia bowed before him. "It is an honor, your grace, to be with you. My first days in your country have been wonderful, and I believe I shall remain happily with you for all my life."

"And you are a well-spoken lady, indeed. You are more than welcome, my dear. We shall all love you, I know."

"My father," Solomon spoke to the king, "She must be tired from the long journey. Will you excuse us now so the princess can rest?"

"Certainly, son. I have no desire to tire this beautiful lady longer." He chuckled as he said it.

Not knowing what to say, 'Artia bowed again, smiled broadly at the king, and allowed Solomon to lead her away to her own chamber where Rina and Netele awaited her.

In the light of morning Jerusalem took on a different character. It did not seem so welcoming. Hard, cold-looking stone lay everywhere, across the ridges of the hills, tumbled into the surrounding valleys, and built into the walls and the buildings of the city. Small, scrubby trees grew in the crevices of the stones, and there was little grass or other plants to relieve the stony silence of the place. 'Artia looked across the city from her balcony and felt a sense of loss for her menagerie and the lovely gardens and trees of the delta and the palace at Tanis. The king's house, as they called it, in Jerusalem was no match for the palace of Kmet with its myriad rooms and halls. She breakfasted on the balcony, and the food, while it seemed vaguely familiar, had a foreign taste. Different spices, she thought. The lentil broth with egg was good, and she loved the little cakes full of nuts and sweetened with honey; certainly different to Tanis. The morning wine, somewhat watered but very sweet, was unusual as well. Solomon is here, she told herself, and smiled with satisfaction. 'Artia had never known that kind of love before, and it was stirring strongly within her chest – the heart, as everybody knew, was the seat of emotion. She plunged into the day.

After breakfast Rina helped her place the god shelf on her small dressing table. It reflected in the polished bronze mirror, enlarging the miniature figure of Hor -em–akhet the princess had brought to represent the Great God Amun-Ra. It was to the great god that she offered her daily oblations, as Rina had taught her from her earliest years. Hor-em-akhet was the physical appearance of Amun-Ra, Rina had told her long before, and it was he who ruled the two horizons where he rose in splendor each morning and descended at the end of his long trek across the sky-path. Rina was exceptionally devoted to Amun-Ra, and 'Artia followed her example.

"I hope that Solomon doesn't object to our god," 'Artia spoke softly. "He means a lot to me – Amun-Ra, I mean. And of course," she added with a laugh, "Solomon."

"If he objects just keep your god-shelf to yourself," Rina told her. "No harm in that."

In a very short time 'Artia became settled in Jerusalem and was a favorite of the king during dinners and celebrations. She often sat at his hand, usually on the left, but on some occasions on his right, which was a distinct place of honor. She hardly saw Solomon alone, and felt that was a bit strange, but all the customs of this 'house' were very different to those in Kmet.

Two weeks after her arrival, 'Artia and Solomon were married. Messages were sent to Pharaoh Siamun and the queen, and return messages were soon received, along with rich gifts. All was in order, as far as 'Artia knew, and she was happy beyond her dreams. The small troubles started a little later.

For the first few days following their wedding, Solomon and 'Artia continued to dine at the king's table at his invitation, and share in his stories and music. It was always a highlight when, after the dinner was concluded and the guests had already enjoyed much conversation, the king asked for his harp, and the sound of his voice and the strumming of the delicate strings filled the hall with a magic that 'Artia had never before experienced. King David was one of the greatest minstrels anyone had ever known, and they listened and applauded for more until the king finally tired and slipped away to sleep. The spell of the music continued to fill the hearts of the listeners as they left the hall and went off to sleep soundly through the Judean night. It was indeed a mystical experience, and 'Artia wondered what the source of the power could be, but no one could tell her. Even Solomon was reticent, so she waited for time to reveal the secret.

Conflict came first, however. 'Artia was invited for an 'audience' with Prince Solomon's first wife; the chief wife as she was called, and the princess was taken aback with the demand as well as the affront she received. Merbaba had married Solomon when he was only seventeen, many years before, and had borne him three children in that time. She met 'Artia in the little reception room that lay closest to the door of her apartment, not the inner room where distinguished guests were usually invited, and without any customary greeting Merbaba leveled complaints about her husband's newest wife's behavior.

"You seem to think," she told the princess, "that the prince is solely yours. That is not the case. He is mine, and as I am first, Solomon is mostly mine. He has three other wives as well, and each will have her share of his time, and you must not interfere with the arrangement we have all worked out. He spends most of his days, as well as nights, with me, and after that he will go to the others as he has time and inclination. You will not likely see him often, and when you do, you will always defer to him in every matter - he is to be king. I have heard that you do not do this. Only I am able to discuss matters with him as an equal, and you should keep your place."

Artia was angered. "Only I among his wives," she responded tersely, "am truly a princess. I am daughter of the Pharaoh Siamun of Kmet, and I see no reason to defer to you or even to the prince in any matter which concerns me alone. I do not expect you to call for me again. I will not respond. Furthermore, I will speak to Solomon about your words, and allow him to settle this with you."

She turned to go.

"I haven't yet said all I need to say!" Merbaba spoke sharply.

"You have said all that I will hear." 'Artia walked through the door as Merbaba fumed.

Rina was silent as 'Artia told her about the encounter. "Do you agree that I did the right thing?" the girl asked her.

"I can't say, Miss. I wasn't there so I can't judge your actions."

"Then you think I shouldn't have walked out?"

"I can't say, Miss."

"Rina! You do have an opinion. I know it! Now tell me so I can consider it."

"I think that you have some questions about what you did, Miss, or you wouldn't be forcing me to say something about it."

"Rina! Tell me. I'll take it as a friendly bit of advice."

"Are you sure you can do that, Miss?"

"By all the gods, Rina, you do exasperate me sometimes. I know you don't want to criticize me, but tell me!"

"I really can't Miss. I wasn't there."

"You know I value your opinion or I wouldn't stay on this so long. I want you to tell me if you think I was wrong – or right, or anything you think." She looked imploringly at her servant. "You're really like a mother to me, you know."

Rina sighed. "Yes, I know, Miss, but I don't want to disagree with you. You're very clever and I'm not. You know what's best about these things."

"I really think that you usually know the best. I depend on you."

Slowly Rina faced the princess. "I think you could have stayed and tried to help her. She's afraid of you."

"Afraid? She didn't act that way at all."

"Who is King David's chief wife?"

"It's Bathsheba. You know that. Oh - I see what you mean."

"Yes, Merbaba is afraid that you'll replace her. The king or the prince can choose the wife he wants as his – sort of like his ambassador - I guess, and you are the most likely of them all."

"Merbaba has been until now?"

"Yes."

"I can't stop him if he chooses me."

"No, but you can assure the woman that you aren't trying to take her spot. Be kind to her."

"Thank you, Rina. You see, I told you that you know about things that I don't understand."

"You'll learn, Miss. You will. Thank you, too. For telling me."

"What?"

"That you depend on me."

"I really do. And I meant it about being my mother. You are – you're mine."

Rina could feel the emotion welling up. She couldn't speak for a moment, but whispered a quick, "Yes, Miss. You're my sweet girl, I know." It was the nickname she had called the princess as a baby.

'Artia didn't say a word to Solomon about the encounter with his chief wife, but she sent a message to Merbaba three days later, inviting her to come for lunch in her apartment.

Another summons was issued. 'Artia received it the same day that she sent her invitation to Merbaba. It was from the king, asking the princess to meet him for breakfast the following day at mid-morning. 'Artia had no idea what time mid-morning was, so she sent Rina on an investigation to learn the time that King David usually breakfasted. It was, the maid reported, at the fourth hour of the day. 'Artia was early, but waited in the passage until a servant notified her that the king had entered his small dining room. She was led to the table where a spare breakfast was laid, and the king stood to meet her as she entered. He bowed, as she did to him, and asked her to be seated before he sat in his unadorned chair. It was an uncommon thing, she was sure, for the king to show such deference.

"You are looking especially lovely this morning, Ka 'artia," He loved saying her name, which he thought to be exotically beautiful. "I hope that you are finding real happiness among us."

"Yes, my lord," she told him honestly. "I am very content." She didn't offer any hint that her own Rina made all the difference between agitation and contentment.

The king eyed her steadily for a moment, then asked, "Are things going well with Merbaba?"

'How does he know'? she started to think, and then realized that the woman had probably gone to him for solace. "I am working that out, my lord," she smiled brightly at him.

"Merbaba doesn't understand who you are, my dear, or she would be more careful. She is not very – ah – sophisticated about royalty. None of us are, actually. I am only the second king of Israel, and was a sheepherder before that."

"My lord," 'Artia spoke carefully, "You are one of the greatest kings of the world."

"I want to be, but at times it is a heavy burden, far more than I could have known. I try to be fair." He spoke the last word gently.

"You are, I'm sure you are."

"What can you tell me about your meeting with my daughter, Merbaba?"

"I am sorry I left her in such haste, and I have already sent her an invitation to lunch on the day after tomorrow so we can talk in a more productive manner."

The king took a long look at the young woman who sat across the table from him. "You are wise to do that. I hope that you can help her with her concerns. But there is no denying that Solomon will favor you. He's told me that already."

"I am honored, but I don't know if it's the best thing to do."

The king laughed. "Don't tell him that. He won't know what to think. He wants to place you on a pedestal for the world to see. I'm only afraid that he will ignore his other responsibilities."

"I think that perhaps I can guide him now that I understand the situation better. I had a talk with my maid, Rina, and she explained it all to me."

"Rina. I don't think I know her."

"She's been with me since I was born. She's really been a mother to me."

"She sounds like a good advisor. I'd like to meet her."

"I'll bring her to you whenever you say, my lord."

119

To Rina's everlasting amazement, she soon became a favorite of King David. He found her sensible and direct opinions much to his liking, and she was often invited to sit with him at table to discuss all manner of ideas and questions that interested the aging ruler. It was her guileless transparency that intrigued the king, and he talked to her about the things that were nearest his heart, not only for himself, but for the nation of Israel.

After some months of what the king termed 'consultations,' he offered Rina an apparently insignificant gift. They were sitting with a group of his closest friends and counselors when he reached behind his chair and brought out a long, dark rod that was inscribed from the top down with what seemed to be hieroglyphics.

"This came to me from Kmet," he told her, "and I think it fitting that a native of that country should have it. I was told that it had a hidden power, but that power has never been revealed to me, so I want you to take it and see what you think." He handed the staff to Rina.

"Who gave this to you, my lord?"

"He told me he was a priest of Amun. I don't know much about him except that he came as ambassador from the court of Pharaoh Psusennes the Second. He wasn't here long. Some trouble at home caused his recall, but he gave this to me before he left."

"It's a curious thing. I'm not sure what it could be."

"I give it to you, and you can do as you please with it. I have some strange idea that it wants to go back to its homeland, but I can't understand why I think that." His eyes smiled although the rest of his face was serious. He placed no value in foreign gods or idols.

Rina turned the staff in her hand. "I'll take care of it, my lord, and if I ever go back to Kmet I'll be sure to take it with me."

On a hazy day in the season that followed summer, Prince Solomon took 'Artia up from the city to the hill of Moriah, a fabled place in the history of his people. It was to that hill that their god had sent the patriarch Ibrahim with his only son, according to the reckoning of the Hebrews, to make a sacrifice. There was a flat stone outcropping on the hilltop that was to have been the place where a sacrifice would be made. Ibrahim thought that his son was to be the sacrificial victim, but his god had other plans and placed a ram at the end of the stone altar in a briar bush. Then the god told Ibrahim to sacrifice the ram instead of the boy. The patriarch had no difficulty making the substitution. Prince Solomon wanted 'Artia to learn more about his people, he told her, and the short trip was to be a starting place.

The little stream called Kidron rippled along on their right, the olive tree covered slopes of a long hill rose beyond, and a blue sky filled with wispy clouds sheltered it all. It was an occasion that included a basket filled with favorite foods and wines, and a large woolen carpet to sit on.

They rode leisurely, along with a few military guards on donkeys. It was a lovely day, marred only by Solomon's casual remark that he was taking another wife in two weeks' time. 'Artia was stunned. She didn't ask him why, but he attempted to explain the reason to her anyway.

"It's purely political, 'Artia. I have to do this so we have an alliance with the Ammorites. She is the daughter of the current ruler – he's not really a king but he calls himself one. He was the military man who won the most battles and made himself the ruler. That's all. We don't want to fight with all our neighbors, so it's a good thing for me to marry this woman and make a treaty with the Ammorites at the same time. It's all political."

"Are all your marriages political?" she asked.

"Yes, I think they are. But ours is different. I'll admit it was supposed to be only a political union, but when I saw you, I knew."

"So you brought me up here to tell me?"

Solomon smiled with his entire face, not only his eyes. "Guilty," he said cheerily. "I thought you would take the idea better outside the house." He waited for a response but none came. "It won't change anything between us, but something else might."

"Now you want me to ask you what could change things."

"Yes."

"Well then, what?"

"I want you to be my chief wife, to be my companion at court functions, and to help me when I become king. You are the brightest and best, 'Artia, and I want you by my side at all times."

"Except when you visit your other women."

"Well, that would be awkward, but you know what I mean."

"I understand, Solomon, and - well, if I have a choice I need to think about it for a while."

"Do you want me to give you a choice?"

"No," 'Artia heard her own voice saying, "You need to decide for yourself."

"I was expecting to tell Merbaba soon. She's a good woman, you understand, but is nothing like you."

"Please – please wait to tell her for a few days. I want to talk to her first."

"What do you mean? Do you want to tell her?"

"Oh no, but I've never talked to her when she wasn't angry. I want to try again."

"When will you see her?"

"I don't know. I've invited her to my rooms a few times, but she's always refused to come."

Solomon made a mental note to talk to Merbaba immediately upon arrival at the king's house. It had always been his opinion that wives should have little or no contact with each other, but if 'Artia wanted a meeting, Merbaba should go to meet her.

The river valley and the delta of Kmet had attained the wonderful green-yellow hue of the season of Peret, when crops grew to their ripest. It was followed by Shemu, the hottest time of year, when the harvest began. The countryside sweltered in the heat, but the people rejoiced. Harvest during a good year was the greatest time for celebration. There would be no suffering because the crops had developed to their fullest and richest potential. The nights were warm, and sleeping atop the house on a roof porch was comfortable. There was also freely flowing beer, and all the bread anyone wanted; there was even a little meat now and then. It was an opulent, plentiful time, and the nation felt secure.

The palace in Tanis was vibrant with other news that surpassed even the best harvest season they could have. Solomon, Prince of Israel, along with his beautiful wife Ka 'artia, Princess of Kmet, were about to arrive for a visit. An advance group of priests and scholars, workmen and cooks had been in the city for nearly three weeks setting up the required kitchens and a place of worship of the highly unusual Hebrew god, all working together for a successful venture for the royal family as they sailed, more or less serenely, across the Great Sea.

The god–whose–name–should-not-be-spoken was revered by the Hebrew people, and his edicts about living, as well as food, were carefully honored and obeyed. The prince could eat no swine products, and all other meat was strictly kept away from dairy foods. They required two kitchens for that purpose, to the confusion and amusement of the Kmetians, but the Hebrews were insistent, as was the pharaoh; the needs of his guests were carefully accommodated in every way.

The long voyage from Jaffa was not as peaceful this time, and even Ka 'artia felt the swells and plummets of the water as it crashed against the hull. The storm was windy and wet, but not overly wild as storms go. Solomon, along with 'Artia, sat on the deck under a canopy as much as possible, and watched the progress of the wind-blown waves. Rina and Netele suffered more than anyone else in the company, and everyone was glad when they reached the calm waters that lay close to the shore of Kmet and the pretty little port of Rakotis. Solomon watched from the deck as the ships came in close to the town, and was impressed by the white stone quays and the little houses and shops that huddled amid the greenery next to the landing.

Their arrival in Tanis was a royal reception with music and dancing along the riverside as they were taken in litters to the palace, just a short distance away, and greeted there by the pharaoh and his queen. Drums and gongs played as they walked down the sphinx-lined corridor to the entrance area of the palace which was open to the sun. It was a magnificent place, so very unlike the king's house in Israel, and yet not as grand as the palaces of Memphis and Thebes. Kmet paraded its wealth before the prince who seemed to take it all in without any sign of resentment at such a display. He, as a man, could hold his own in any company, and he knew it. 'Artia knew it as well, and was magnificent in her obvious pride. The Pharaoh Siamun watched her silently and knew he was right. Here was a suitable husband for his brilliant daughter.

The official visit was planned for about two months length, not long enough to travel all the way to Thebes, but Memphis was close, and the overwhelming pyramids of Giza and

Sakkara were within easy reach. They traveled in the royal barge, a floating palace with its numerous rooms and apartments that rose to four stories above the water. A kitchen suitable for the Hebrew prince was tied to the barge, and meals were prepared there by his own staff. Everyone on board followed the dietary laws that Solomon observed, so there was no need for concern on his part. There was a merry atmosphere all the time, and celebrations sometimes lasted into the late hours, the coolest time of the day. Three smaller barges filled with servants and supplies followed the royal palace upriver toward the south. They came first to Hor-em-akhet with his gigantic neighboring pyramids, and the prince took it all in. These things were super-human. The royal party landed and walked among the colossi.

"They were made by pharaohs long ago. I think they were buried there more than two thousand years in the past. Not all at the same time, of course. They were made for a father and his son and his grandson, each following the other." Pharaoh Siamun described the scene as succinctly as he could.

"What about that?" Solomon pointed to the statue of Hor-em-akhet as he spoke. "The beast with a man's head."

"It's one of our gods, Hor-em-akhet. He guards the rising place and setting of Amun-Ra, the great god who rules the sun. It was once believed that he was the sun, but now we know he only rules its movement."

"I've heard of both those gods. I have learned as much as I could about our world, and Kmet is a very old place, indeed."

"And Israel is now ascending to its own prominent position. I know that." The pharaoh spoke with authority. "And I'm glad that my daughter is happy there."

"I'm lucky. She's a truly remarkable young woman. And wife." He added the last quickly. "But why do you think this beast had to be a lion?"

"Lions are a symbol of power and authority, and when the pharaohs started in this business they needed to represent themselves as having those qualities. He's only an extension of what we think we were and are." The pharaoh laughed a little, as though he had told a joke.

"Lion's, eh? Well, we have a lion symbol as well. The lion of Judah, a strong and mighty warrior. We're still in the warrior phase, I fear."

"I imagine that a lot of kings think of themselves as lions." The pharaoh gave another short laugh. "It's a popular image."

The servants, who remained on the barge, stood at the rails watching the scene. Rina was beside Netele as they regarded the monuments gravely.

"How did they make them so – big?" It was the only word Netele knew to describe the size of the tombs.

"Nobody knows, little one. They've been there nearly forever, you know."

"Really? Forever? I thought somebody had made them, but it must have been the gods."

"No, I don't mean forever that way. Men made them, but a long time ago."

"Oh, - how?"

"Nobody knows now. It was a secret at the time, I think, and that secret is lost."

"They look scary."

"Do you think so? To me they look kind of ugly. All white and gray and serious."

"Yes, they do, but scary too."

"Maybe they are, a little."

Late that night Rina awakened in the tiny room she shared with Netele. The girl was sleeping, but Rina thought she heard someone call her, and she got up from the floor to look out the open doorway. The moon glided above, reflected in the ripples of the water that lapped along the shore; the face of Hor-em-akhet seemed to possess a dim light of its own. Rina looked carefully. She was not given to imaginary visions. The eyes were bright in the face of the beast, growing brighter as she stood watching, and then she heard her name again. She was drawn toward the immense statue, and stepped out onto the deck as if pulled by a force that compelled her body to move forward.

"Rina, daughter of Kmet," the voice said. "I call you now to hear me."

"I'm dreaming," she told herself.

"This is no dream, my daughter. I have chosen you and brought you here to listen to my voice and do as I ask of you. You are at the source."

"I don't - - -"

"Don't speak aloud. Only think of your words and then I alone can know them."

"Who are you, lord?"

"I am known to you as Amun–Ra."

Rina sagged against the railing.

"There is no need for fear. You are safe with me. But Kmet is no longer safe. It will be swallowed up sooner than you think."

"How? How can Kmet be 'swallowed up'?"

"In many ways, but that is not yet. You still have some time."

"What can I do? I'm simply a servant of a princess of the land. I don't know what I would be able to do."

"Guard the princess well. You have her love, you know, and her trust."

124

"Yes, I know."

"And you have the trust of David, the Hebrew."

"The king?"

"Yes. He is in need of watchful care."

"How can I do anything about him?"

"Stay close to him."

Rina had no way of knowing what that meant, and Amun-Ra did not explain.

"And keep close to Netele as well. She is important."

"How is she important?"

"I cannot tell you all the ways, but she is. She will speak for me soon."

"How can she do that?"

"Wait another year, and then take her to the king with the rod in her hand. She will give my words to him"

"I don't understand. How will she know your words?"

"Just watch and see."

"How do I know I'm not dreaming?"

"I will speak to you again soon."

"I hope you do. I need to know I'm not losing my mind."

"I will, and you are not."

Rina felt the withdrawal of Amun-Ra's presence, and when she looked again at Hor-em-akhet, his eyes were dark. The woman drifted back into the room and lay down on the soft rug on the floor, her head working. But she had no idea what to think, and gradually sank into sleep once more. Netele slept on in youthful innocence.

The next morning Rina awakened to see the sun shining into the face of Hor-em-akhet, and her mind flew to the memory of the night just passed. Was that a reality? She didn't think

so. Her memory of the conversation was vivid, but she believed it to be a dream. Netele, a large part of her disbelief, was up and gone already. She moved to the door and walked along the passageway to the latrine. As she walked she heard a faint sound that seemed to follow her steps. When she returned to the little room, she heard it there, a soft humming, and searched around to find the source. She soon spotted the glowing staff that the king had given to her. It lay on the floor, tucked between the blanket and the wall. She reached for it and as her fingers closed around its base she began to see images, some she recalled and others were new; the staff

125

showed her a flow of her life's experiences and then looked into the future. Some of the things she saw there were impossible to accept, so she put it aside, although that was difficult to do, and prepared herself for serving the princess' breakfast. The day had started, but she stopped to confront the night before. Contrary to her practical nature, she reached a decision that it was a reality.

The days and the long nights, when there was a lot of feasting and celebrations, passed quickly. Tanis was hot, much more so than Jerusalem or anyplace they had been in the land of Israel, and Solomon began to weary of the intensity of the sun and the terrible heat. 'Artia had always loved the harvest season, but now had a different awareness of the heat, and grew tired of the weather as well. She began looking forward to their return to what was often called Zion, not only for the climate, but for the fellowship of the king and his extended family of advisors and friends. They had become, in the time she had been among them, her own.

Rina was anxious about meeting the king again, and how she should approach what she thought could be a problem. Rina had never attempted to use feminine wiles as 'Artia so easily could, and believed that she had no subtlety at all. She might blurt out anything, she feared, and would in consequence damage the cause she had been assigned. She approached the city with some trepidation.

Fears were unnecessary, she soon learned. The king called for the royal couple and Rina to meet with him as soon they could, so on the morning following their arrival, the princess and Rina went to the small dining room to breakfast with King David and Prince Solomon, who had been in conference for more than two hours prior to the arrival of the women. David embraced them both, and to her surprise – as well as the bemusement of the others - asked Rina to sit at his right hand. He pressed her for her accounts of their travels far more than he did 'Artia. After a lengthy discussion of the visit, the king dismissed the couple but asked Rina to remain so that they could talk about "things," and got to the point.

"I have missed you," the king told her with his eyes smiling and attention focused only on his single-member audience. "I realized after you had gone that I needed you, and determined that I should ask you to be my wife. I know that is not something you had considered, but I do need you, Rina, and I do want us to marry."

Rina was troubled. "But, my lord," she spoke tremulously, "I am not a person who could marry a king. I was once a slave."

"I know, but that makes no difference to me. I want to be close to you all the time. I am old, it's true, but I can still honor a wife with my love and concern."

"You have many wives," she blurted, and then thought better of it. "I'm so sorry. I mean you seem to have all that you need with the lovely wives you already have."

"You don't understand, Rina, I want you to be my wife. I don't care how many others I have now."

"My lord," she said carefully, "I'm sorry I spoke. I don't doubt your sincerity, but I need to think about what this means. I have to find out whether I'm able to be the wife of a king. You know that I have never married, and that 'Artia has been my life."

"Yes, and I will ask the princess her permission if that will help. You could still be as close to her as you are now."

"Thank you, my lord, for this great honor."

"There is no reason to thank me, Rina. I wouldn't have asked you except for my need for you. You have come into my life, and I am forever grateful."

"And I am grateful to know you as well, as a friend, and now – well, I don't know. I think we could continue as we were."

"If you cannot marry me, then I hope that we will, but still I will ask."

Rina gave him a rare smile. "You are a wonderful man," she said, "and I am honored."

Amun-Ra's input was anything but predictable. Rina came to him at the little 'temple' that she kept in her room. She told the great god all that had happened.

"Yes, I know," he responded. "He wants you for a wife. He has many others, you know."

"Yes, but that isn't a problem for me. To be included is still a flattery. Of course, I don't see how I can marry him; after all, he's a king, and I'm not a fit wife for a king, no matter how many others he has."

"He chose you. You did not choose him."

"I don't think I could handle it well – being a wife to a king."

"Do not be afraid. Most of his wives have less understanding than you. And he loves you."

"Do you really think so?"

"Now that you ask me so plainly, I will respond plainly. Yes."

Rina stopped her denials, but still thought warily. "I need to know what I can do for Netele."

"I think that you are the one who can speak to the king now. I don't think there is a need to ask Netele. You can tell him what I tell you."

"What will you want me to say to him?"

"I will let you know when the time comes."

The answer was hardly satisfying, but Rina didn't argue. "I still need to think – I'll tell you when I have decided in a few days."

"You have no need to tell me. Tell David, and I will know." Amun-Ra was gone.

Rina sent a message to the king telling him that she was considering his proposal, and that she could give him a response the following afternoon. That much she could say, for she hated lengthy struggles over decisions. 'Either you do or you don't' had long been a favorite aphorism.

King David sent a reply that he would willingly await her decision, and when she was ready he would welcome her immediately. The next afternoon as the sun had declined halfway to the horizon, Rina appeared in the great hall. The king saw her as she came in and rose to greet her. They went into a small room at the rear to talk.

"Please sit here and tell me what you have decided," the king told her quietly as they passed through the door.

"I would like to stand, if that is right with you, my lord," she answered as she turned to face the man with the smiling eyes who watched her every move intently.

"I will marry you, my lord," she said softly, and David, who waited as if to receive a blow, swayed backward a little, then reached out and took her arm.

"You have made me happy," he said as his voice rose, "extremely happy. And I want to make you happy as well."

"You do, my lord," she answered, "you always do."

The word spread speedily through the king's house. Rina, the servant of the pharaoh's daughter, was to marry King David! It was like a firebrand to many who heard, and was greeted by disbelief among advisors as well as the women who were known as "The King's Wives." There was to be an addition to their family, and although some were pleased, the over-all reaction was one of disbelief and sorrow. How could a woman from such a lowly position be allowed to enter their world and become a full-fledged wife to the king? It was fuel for the best gossip that had come their way for a very long time.

'Artia was bewildered at first, but as she thought about the situation, its natural occurrence was obvious. It was she who had first brought the king's attention to her servant, and it was Rina herself who had shown her worthiness in the eyes of the king. She deserved this happiness, 'Artia was sure, more than anyone she had ever known. She went to Rina as soon as she could to embrace her and let her know what came from her heart.

Netele was another matter. She had placed King David on such a high pedestal that his choice of Rina for a wife came as a terrible blow. This woman, no different or better than herself, had been successful in getting the attention of the king! How had she managed to do that? Netele was definitely one of the naysayers in the many factions that surrounded the throne. She was jealous.

'Artia insisted on making plans for the wedding just as her mother the queen had planned her marriage to Solomon. She arranged for the dress Rina would wear, and for the details of the wedding feast that would follow the vows. She herself sewed some of the fine things Rina would need as the bride of a king, and had the ladies of the court assist her in all the other preparations. 'Artia organized the event with natural skill and her love for Rina both playing a part in the things she did. Rina, as well as the king, seemed completely happy.

The wedding itself was scheduled for three weeks from the day Rina had agreed to the marriage, and on that morning 'Artia acted as her maid to prepare her for the wedding. She dressed the bride in a new cloak of silk and soft linen and placed jewels from her own collection around Rina's neck and arms. They walked together with some of the ladies of the court to the small 'temple' that stood just outside the king's house. Rina and 'Artia entered its simple doors together. Solomon was there, but the king had not yet arrived, so the priest spoke to them, especially to Rina, about things that were essential for the rite.

"I will lead you through all of it, and all you need to do is respond to what I ask you and say the things that are needed each time."

Rina nodded, and then David entered, dressed in his finest kingly robe, deep blue and richly embroidered with pearls and other precious gems, wearing his golden crown on his silvery-white head. Rina was amazed at how youthful and beautiful he was. They stood together before the priest as he led them through the opening words of the ceremony of marriage; a rather short prelude, Rina thought, to such a lofty and enduring life change. Then the priest stepped to the side, and Rina and David faced each other, clasping right hands, to repeat the most solemn vows of the day. They were first intoned in Hebrew, which Rina hardly knew, and then she was asked to repeat her vows in Greek, the common language of the world. She promised to be faithful to David alone, and to serve him as his wife for all her days. She made her vows with a sincere heart. Then the priest came to the final vow.

"Rina, you must now take an oath of loyalty to the king. Your oath will be taken "before the Holy one of Israel, the God of Abraham, Isaac, and Jacob." Rina hesitated. She hadn't known this was part of the wedding. She faltered a moment, then heard the voice of the Great God Amun-Ra. "Speak the oath, Rina, my daughter," He said.

"You are here?" she asked aloud. David looked puzzled.

The voice spoke again, and although they seemed to be slow and deliberate, the responses between the great god and Rina were flowing lightning fast. "Yes," Amun-Ra said, "I am the Creator God and I am always with my children."

In that instant, Rina understood, and enlightenment welled within her body and her spirit. She lifted her head, changed forever, and in an exultant voice repeated the oath carefully and sealed it with the final words: "I take this oath before the Holy One of Israel, the God of Abraham, Isaac, and Jacob."

David squeezed her hand.

Chapter Seven

402 BC

Menebaq awakened slowly, the sounds of the battle far away and dull in the distance. He tried to move but couldn't find his arms to lift himself, so he opened his eyes to see where he was, and the memory of his last moments in the mêlée suddenly emerged. He was lying under some brush near the base of a tall palm tree. He recalled rushing toward the bushes to escape from a Persian warrior running in his direction, swinging a fierce battle-axe in his hands. That was the last thing he had known. The Persian must have hit him, he realized, and his head throbbed as if to confirm the understanding. He looked a little further off, across the river toward the west where the golden rays of the sun were shining above the points of the gargantuan pyramids and the sphinx, and thought of the great god who ruled the heavens, now descending in his golden chariot into the western horizon over the desert; all powerful, but totally unconcerned about the battle and the dead who were lying all around, he was sure. Menebaq couldn't see the dead; he couldn't move, but he could feel their presence, a collective woe of the spirit that seemed to pulsate in the brilliant sunset as Amun-Ra made his way toward his nightly habitation. The god obviously didn't care about them at all.

The soldier lay still. He was too tired to do anything else, and he drifted in and out of sleep or consciousness, he didn't know which, until it grew dark and the battle ended. There were no more sounds of horses pounding the earth, or clanging chariots, or shouting, or the screams of the dying. No more sounds. It gave him a kind of comfort, but he had no way of knowing who had won, or if the battle would be joined again the next morning, or if a surprise attack at night was in order from one side or the other. It hardly mattered anymore, he thought abruptly, and the furious zeal that had created such a strength in him melted away. He was surprised that it no longer mattered. "I must be dead," he thought. "Really dead." Then he fell into oblivion again.

Only a few months before, the determined men of Kmet rallied to fight off their oppressors, the Persians, who had conquered their land a century ago, but gradually became weaker and were now vulnerable to a new challenge. The nation was fighting for its birthright against the malevolent government that had taken everything away. They gave no thought to the fact that Kmet, in its time, had enslaved and occupied many peoples, mostly near neighbors, who had been assimilated into the country and were now Kmetians like themselves. That was far in the past and they had no certain knowledge of those times, but the invasion of the Persians was relatively fresh in their memory, and now they had a chance to fight off the invaders, and they took it with new strength and vigor.

The Persians were also much weaker than they had been when they conquered the land. In the battle known as Marathon, three decades after the fall of Kmet, the Greeks had defeated the Persian Empire, which had steadily declined from that time. At last, a Prince of Kmet had emerged in the city of Sais, and he succeeded in bringing the country to rebellion. They realized they must fight to overthrow the Persians, and came together with sworn oaths to accomplish that goal. As he lay there, Menebaq had no idea whether or not they had succeeded, but they had shown their collective strength and the will of the people to the Persians, at least. "If not this time, then next time," he said to himself. He was thirsty and needed water, but it was far away, and he could not get there. "I'll never know," he said again.

In the late night a small group of people moved cautiously across the battlefield without a torch despite the darkness that enclosed everything. They were quiet, whispering once in a while, turning the bodies that lay in the field, moving carefully and systematically through the area. There were other widely scattered groups doing the same, from one end of the dreadful scene to the other, and it looked as if they were searching the dead for whatever small riches they could find, but that was not the case. They were mostly women, sifting through the remains of the terrible scene to find anyone who might be living yet. They found only a few, but when they discovered a survivor, they gave a low call and some other women came and lifted the suffering man to carry him off the field to the safety of a place along the bank of the river where he could be treated for his wounds by a physician who worked through the night to care for the living and assist the dying. It was a compassionate thing to do, perhaps the only benevolent thing to come out of all the destruction of the previous day.

The women came at last to Menebaq who was unconscious but still breathing, and one of them called softly to the three who waited. They wrapped the young soldier in a blanket, which they used as a litter, and carried him away from the brush under the tall palm to the courtyard of a small house where the living and the near- dying mingled around a fire, many lying on the ground in an unconscious state. It was in that place that Menebaq was given water when he awakened an hour later, where his head wound was closed as carefully as the skilled doctor who lived in the house was able, and where he was expected to die. But Menebaq lived on into the morning and through the next day and then through more days until the doctor began to believe that he would survive the horrific gash of the axe. The soldier finally stayed on because he didn't know where else he could go, and the benevolent doctor allowed him to remain. Menebaq's home was destroyed; the town where he had grown up had been burned beyond recognition, and his parents and younger sisters could not be found. Kmet had been victorious, the Persians who survived the battles were driven out, but for Menebaq the situation was complicated by the fact that he was not yet well enough to work. He had been trained as a metal smith, but the destruction left him no place to mold and shape metal, so he simply stayed at the house of medicine and did the few things he could to help other men who were recovering from maiming and mutilation – loss of limbs and eyes, and shattered bones were the most common injuries. As soon as he could get up and around, Menebaq helped to heal; washing and tending wounds, giving or applying medicines, and talking quietly to the injured men despite his broken cranium that looked like a puffy white trench across the back of his head. In the process of assisting the doctor he decided that he wanted to become a healer.

"Why do you want to learn medicine?" The doctor asked. "Do you have any skill with writing or reading?"

"No," Menebaq admitted, "But I will learn to do it all."

"I have to be honest with you. I'm not sure that you can. Your wound was serious and that kind of injury often prevents people who already know how to read from being able to do that anymore."

"I want to try!" Menebaq was determined. "If I can learn to read, will you let me read the things you have in your library here? Medical information, I mean."

"If you are able to read them, then of course, read everything you can!"

"How can I find a teacher?"

"Are you able to pay?"

"No, but I will work for someone if they teach me to read."

"I don't know anyone, Menebaq. I wish I did. But you need to heal a little longer first."

"I'll try to find a teacher myself, if that's alright with you. When I'm ready."

"Yes, yes, you do whatever you can. I wish you luck."

"Thank you, doctor. I think I can find someone. I'll start looking soon."

Menebaq was sixteen when he fought in the great battle that won the independence of Kmet. Despite his youth, he was, for all practical purposes, an adult. He was free, but the wound kept him from enjoying the sense of freedom that some surviving soldiers experienced. He was unsteady when he walked, his eyesight was not good, his hands shook most of the time, and he had a more or less permanent headache, all attributed to his hurt. Even with those limitations he regained health a little more each week and his outlook was always optimistic.

One bright morning five months after he had been carried to the house, Menebaq went to the alcove where the doctor kept his scrolls. He wanted to look at one or two just to see what he was to face when he started reading, but he was shocked to discover that he couldn't even fix his eyes on the figures. They were dim as they squirmed and seemed to recede and then draw closer, and he realized that he could not focus on anything that small. It was a jolt - he squinted and tried until his head started hurting too much. Then he rolled the thing up and replaced it on the shelf, not knowing what to do.

"I'll just have to wait awhile and then look again," he decided in the sensibly matter-of-fact attitude he had adopted since his near death on the field of battle. "If it's to be, it will be."

While he was there he looked around the space - a large common room, examining the chairs and the table more closely than he had before. It was a pleasant room, full of light and fresh air from a large opening in the wall that was limed around the edges. What had the doctor called it? He couldn't remember the word but thought he would ask again.

He heard a faint sound, a sort of whispering, that came from somewhere behind a table that stood under the opening. He looked down and saw a long wooden stick, dark and yet glowing softly. He found himself drawn toward it and reached to pick it up. There was no immediate flash of thought or energy as he did, but he felt a gentle warming in his distressed brain, and it calmed him. His headache began to subside, and although he didn't know it, his steps were steadier as he carried the staff from the room into the courtyard. There was by no means a sudden or even rapid improvement, but Menebaq felt better, surer, than he had before, and his confidence was roused. "I have to wait, but I'll do it," he told himself again, but this time he really believed it to be true.

"What is this?" he asked the doctor, who looked at the staff for a moment.

"I don't know. I don't remember, anyway, but I think it's been here all the time. It must have been in the house when I came here a few years ago." Then the doctor saw the look on the boy's face. "If you want it, it's yours to keep." Menebaq was delighted with the gift.

Over the next months and the changes of seasons, the young soldier kept his thoughts to himself. It seemed to him that he was hearing a voice, an encouraging voice, in the night especially, and he felt that it was urging him on toward his goal of learning to read and finally to become a physician. He waited a long time, nearly a year, before he looked at a scroll again, and this time the lines stayed in their places and he could actually see the figures as they ran along the sections on the papyrus. He was even more pleased by that result, and began to look for a tutor in earnest. The priests in the local temple of Amun-Ra were the closest and probably the easiest to ask, he decided, and set out a few mornings later to walk the short distance to the waterside temple. It was very near the scene of the battle where he had been found, and as he moved along the dusty path, clutching the staff to assist his legs and feet, he started to remember the unspeakable things he had experienced there, and his head felt heavy as he stumbled along, but the staff held him up. He walked past the tall palm tree and the bush where he had fallen under the axe of the warrior. He felt another tingle of sorrow, but nothing more except for memories of his family who had lived far away from this riverbank hell, and he tried not to imagine the fiery horror of their ending. He deliberately turned his thoughts toward possibilities, and went on his way.

The temple to Amun-Ra was built on a foundation of sturdy stone above the high water level of the annual inundation. It was a large and rather gloomy-looking place, facing the east with its back toward the great river. There were several buildings in the complex, but none were so imposing as the hall of the gods where the altars for Amun-Ra, Mut, Min, and Hathor were located. Menebaq looked inside at the wide aisles and the statues and candles that cast dim lights and shadows, and he noticed a few sky-holes in the high ceiling that let in shafts of vivid light from the sun. They met the floor like a staccato smattering of spot-lights, and everything around them seemed darker and withdrawn. It was a dramatic effect, but caused Menebaq's brain to reel, and he stumbled away from the entrance with a queasy feeling.

He went on, searching for the priest house which he found at the very back of the temple grounds. It was unassuming at the entrance, but when he stepped inside, the huge corridor- like room was filled with constant sunlight. Its rear wall was open to the river and the sky, and he could see the water flowing along far below, the three pyramids on the plateau across the water, and the mighty sphinx, the lion with the head of a man, standing eternally present on the western shore. The priests lived and worked in that room, their tiny individual cells opening through many doors along its sides. Their cooking fire was located outside at the back, on the brink of the river, but there were two inside fire pits below ceiling vents, one on either end of the huge central room. It was an enormous space but still almost cozy, Menebaq thought as he took it in for the first time.

A priest dressed in a white toga met him. "What are you seeking here?" He asked with an attitude of near exasperation. "We can offer a meal, but no place for anyone to stay."

"I want a teacher.' The simple truth was all Menebaq could say.

"You want to learn?" The priest was close to sneering.

"Yes, to learn to read."

"I don't think anyone here can help you."

"Why not?" Menebaq asked quickly before he could think of any other response.

"You should go somewhere else. A school comes to mind."

"I have no money to pay for a school."

"We have no time to teach," the priest told him.

Menebaq stood where he was, making no movement to leave. He didn't say anything more, but watched the priest closely. Then he held up the staff just a little from the floor. The priest pulled back.

"Is that a threat?" he demanded.

"Oh, no!" Menebaq told him with alarm. "I was injured in the battle, right outside over there." He pointed the direction with the top of the staff. "Sometimes my arms jerk a little, and my feet, too." The priest was now convinced that he was simple-minded.

Some other men had gathered close by and one of them, a young man near the age of Menebaq, stepped forward. "Do you really want to learn to read?" he asked. "It isn't easy for anyone, you know."

"I know, but I want to learn so I can study to be a physician."

Some of the priests smiled knowingly, but the young man continued, "Why don't we sit over there and you can tell me more about this," he said.

135

"Yes, I need to sit for a little while anyway," Menebaq replied. "I got kind of tired, and it's hot."

"Then we'll have a cool drink and talk. And I think a little food, too." He led Menebaq to a chair that was filled with cushions. "Now tell me all about yourself."

Two days later the future physician entered the priest's house as a student of young Nemko, a priest-on-probation at the temple; a small man with large open eyes and a pointed chin, from the peninsula of Italia in the far north, across the water. He had been brought to Kmet by some traders who kidnapped him with the intention of selling him as a slave, but had escaped from them at the town of Rakotis on the shore of the Great Sea, and wandered, half- starved, into the temple of Amun-Ra at Zau three years earlier. He could read Greek well and seemed destined for great things, but decided he wanted the simple life of a priest and had been sent to the North River Temple to serve Amun-Ra there. He had been rescued by the great god, he believed, and had a burning desire to rescue others.

During their first lesson Menebaq showed Nemko his wound, a long, white, sickly scar that covered most of the back of his head. No hair ever grew along its furrow, and eventually the skin there looked as though no blood at all flowed through. It was a miracle he was alive, and Nemko felt an instant kinship to his young soldier-student.

The ancient science of Kmet had changed and grown over two millennia, but despite the changes no one understood the function of the brain. Some scientific thinkers began to believe that it was an important organ, the seat of reasoning, they said, but others discounted their theories. "We have always known that the heart is the center of thought and reason," they insisted. "It is with the heart that men understand and have emotional feelings. Our holy writings tell us that." There was little evidence for argument on the subject, but Menebaq was in a unique position to know that the ancient lore was wrong. Not only did the brain control thought and intellect, he reasoned; it controlled movement, vision, and speech as well. At times he believed he could feel his injured brain struggling with concepts and ways to express them.

Menebaq applied all the skills he knew to learning to read. First he memorized the letters of the Greek alphabet, the common language of most people who lived around the Mediterranean Sea, and began working on basic vocabulary words. It wasn't too difficult. He spoke most of the words already, and had a sense of the language from the common speech. But it was very difficult to learn verb and noun forms and new words that were uncommon, as well as the styles and idioms of the language. "I can't learn everything now," he told his teacher. "I can only get the basics and start using those first." Menebaq deftly began the painstaking process, opening his mind – and his heart – to learning, a process that he never left behind even as he advanced in age. He loved the thrill of discovery, and for him, learning to read and speak a language – any language – was like a voyage into a distant and astonishing land that opened as a bright sunrise without clouds. It was a progression that not only gave him much needed information but provided the final touches of healing to his brain. He used its increasing capacity as it became available, and the more he learned, the more his damaged mind was eager to achieve. In his later years he came to look upon the battle injury as one of the greatest blessings the great god had ever given him.

Nemko was a man of many talents. The priest had a fervent interest in art which was fed by the designs and imagery of the pyramids and temples and other monuments, and he began to sketch as well as sculpt some amazing pieces that delighted the eye and helped to bring Menebaq's imagination into focus. Both the teacher and the student loved to see the natural as well as the created splendor that surrounded them, and Nemko became especially enamored of the great sphinx which stood across the river within sight of the temple. He crossed the water as often as he could to sketch and measure and climb over the giant beast, and he learned its beauty and dimensions as well as its hidden powers.

Menebaq studied language with Nemko for more than two years. He learned a lot of Greek as well as the ancient Hieratic and the newer Demotic languages of Kmet, and was finally readied to pursue a medical diploma. One thrilling day he stood in the courtyard of the home that he shared with the doctor and many other patients to receive praise and the funds that were essential for his training; funds which the doctor had secured for him in some unknown way. By that time he was a fully functioning and articulate young man, but his head still had a patch of sickly white skin across the back where no hair would grow, and he suffered from headaches all too frequently.

Menebaq had no idea what the staff he had found actually was, but he would never have abandoned it. He listed it first among his possessions, and guarded it carefully on the long trip upriver to Thebes. Soon after his student left, Nemko received an unexpected summons from the pharaoh himself to come to Thebes. The young man with roots in Italia had come to the attention of the leaders of the land due to his artistic designs, and the Pharaoh Nakhtnebef, one of the last native pharaohs of the kingdom of Kmet, called for the best talent in design to come to the southern capital and present a plan for a grand new project the king would build there. Menebaq was surprised to hear from Nemko so soon after leaving the delta; the teacher and his student met again in Thebes amid the urban center of the diminishing kingdom and developed a friendship that lasted while they both lived.

"I'm here to design a road, maybe the greatest road in the world. Pharaoh Nakhtnebef wants something spectacular to link the temples of Niwt-imn and Karnak. He finally chose my plan over all the others." They were sitting together under a canopy for shade outside an ancient bakery along the shores of el nil, just in front of the entrance to the beautiful Niwt-imn Temple, eating bread and fish and drinking a strong ale.

"That's a great honor, then. What's your plan, if you can tell me?" Menebaq was excited and happy.

"Well, it's a long roadway that replaces the dirt path between here and the Karnak Temples, and I made a plan to line it with sphinxes! Each one will be exactly two full lengths from the next! It'll be a fantastic road, paved with stone, and the priests from both temples will use it for ceremonial movement, especially during Opet."

"Giant sphinxes?" Menebaq asked in surprise. He was thinking of the Great Sphinx of Giza, trying to imagine a strip of larger than life lions along the road.

"No, No," Nemko smiled widely. "They'll be normal size! Just think of the alabaster sphinx at Memphis, and they'll be smaller than that!"

Menebaq had never seen the great art of Memphis. "Oh, yes," he said, not willing to show his ignorance of the world that Nemko seemed to know well. "That sounds like such a big job!"

"It is, but I have a huge crew. Lots of men to do the sculpting according to my design. Now tell me how your studies are going." Nemko demanded in his tutor voice. "Are you able to keep up with all the others?" The question was offered out of concern, as Menebaq knew, but he was chagrinned at the need for it to be asked.

"I think I'm holding my own place," he answered truthfully. "We're studying anatomy right now, the first part of it anyway, and I understand it well. I'm hopeful."

"As you should be. I firmly believe that you will succeed. I know how you work!"

The Academy of Medicine met in a new building in Thebes. It was constructed of common mud-brick, but had a stone facade decorated with a relief of Amun-Ra, the creator god, as he was acknowledged in Thebes. He was considered patron of the art of medicine as well as many other things, and his attributions were lofty, especially for Thebes, which was accustomed to the presence of the plethora of gods who protected and sometimes befuddled its citizens. Amun-Ra was special. Nearly everyone acknowledged his supremacy. He was above all things, and creation belonged to him. Unless, as it sometimes happened, a person was a follower of Ptah, a deity popular in Memphis, who was considered the creator god there. Menebaq hailed from the region above Memphis; he was one of those who supported Ptah as the highest in the order of gods, and did not accept Amun-Ra as his equal. When it came to a discussion of the gods, Nemko declared his support for Amun-Ra, as he believed it was he who had rescued him from slavery. The priest and the medical student developed a system for argument that was new to them, but they enjoyed the times when they could talk about their favorite gods with such intimacy, as though the gods were their personal friends, and although they disagreed, they continued to be best friends themselves. As it turned out, Nemko was right.

Twelve years passed from the time Menebaq had gone to Thebes, and he had accomplished so much that he could hardly grasp it all himself. He was already a physician of renown, skilled in all kinds of medicine, but with special skill in helping people who were suffering from anxiety or depression. He was known as a healer of minds, but he made no claim to that distinction. He had developed a method of treatment that worked with many troubled clients; he simply listened and asked only the few questions that were pertinent to each situation. He did his work well, and developed an enthusiastic following of those he helped and those who wanted to understand how he helped. He lectured once in a while, but never claimed any special talent for the work he did.

Menebaq was also an outstanding surgeon and diagnostician, and he was right far more often than he made a mistaken conclusion. The medical community regarded him with awe, and he enjoyed watching over the health of many famous clients. He didn't attend the pharaoh, however. That would have required all his time, and he wanted to work with as many patients as he could. Medicine was his calling, his special gift, and his greatest love.

One late night after a particularly difficult case had required his attention for hours, he arrived home to find his wife and children sleeping, so he went into the garden with a jug of ale and sat looking at the trees and flowers that grew there. While musing about his life, he felt an urgent call, almost as though it were audible, from the nearby garden house. The doctor went to the door and peered inside. In a far corner, leaning against a workbench, stood a glowing rod. He entered the shed and reached for the rod, which he recognized as the staff he had found so long ago in the house of his physician and friend near the delta. The staff throbbed in his hand, and he stood dumbly before it, not knowing what to do with the thing. Then he was drawn away. Still holding the staff, he was transported to a place he had never seen; nothing like it existed anywhere in the world that he knew, and he became vaguely uncomfortable. He paused for a while in a boundless open field where a softly sunrise-mauve sky glowed all around. Then he saw a creature, a sphinx, like the ones Nemko had placed along the causeway between the temples, and thought that he was dreaming. The sphinx suddenly sprang to life, and stared at him with flaming eyes. It stood on its four feet, walking slowly toward him. "I'm dreaming," he said aloud, but he knew he was not.

"It is no dream, Menebaq," the sphinx said as it grew nearer. "I am Amun-Ra."

Menebaq was so stunned he couldn't speak.

"I am the creator of all you see and all you know," said Amun-Ra. "There is no other."

Menebaq had the sense to bow to the ground.

"There is no requirement for that," the sphinx said. "You see me now as some humans think I am. I am not. No one can ever see me as I truly am."

"Why have you brought me here?" Menebaq faltered, his voice trembling.

"I have called you to myself because I have need of you."

Menebaq was silent. How could such a creature need him?

"I need you to carry my message to the cities of Athens and Sparta. Kmet will require their help in the very near future."

"What is this place?" Menebaq asked.

"Listen to me! Tell your mind to listen now as you have never listened before. I saved you from death in the past, you know. There is no Ptah. There is only myself."

The doctor finally understood the folly of his arguments. There was no Ptah! It was a revelation. He bowed again.

"Hear me!" The command was not loud, but the message was clear.

The man lifted himself from the ground and looked into the flaming eyes. "I will hear, lord," he said with conviction.

"You will arrange for yourself to go to Athens and Sparta. I will prepare them for your coming. Tell them this: 'Amun-Ra has need of you in Kmet! Come at once!'"

"I – how will I get to Athens and Sparta, lord. I am no traveler."

"You will find a way. Go and do it!"

Menebaq found himself back in the garden house, holding the quietly glowing staff in his hand. He considered the possibility of hallucination, but decided he shouldn't take that chance. He had no desire to go against the will of Amun-Ra. He never defended Ptah again.

Nemko had nearly completed the Avenue of the Sphinxes. It had to be ready by Opet, the time when Amun-Ra was brought from his temple in Karnak to Niwt–imn to consort with the goddess Mut, his wife, and the city reveled in their coming together. It was in the season of Akhet, the rising of the water, a season that was equated with life if the river was full and generous, or death if it did not rise to expectation, that Amun-Ra came from Karnak. Opet was the greatest party of the year, devised to please or appease the god, and nearly everyone participated in the celebration. In actuality it was hardly noticed by the god who was not quixotic nor vainglorious, but when he did step into human affairs, things changed quickly. The new avenue that Nemko had designed rang with voices of priests and the crowds as they followed the barque, a symbol of sailing on the water, for the entire distance. Amun-Ra stopped along the way at various chapels, also designed by Nemko, for food and drink and rest, and the priests of his temples enjoyed the libations and provender as much as did the great god himself. Other parades followed, day after day, sometimes for as many as twenty seven days. It was a tiring event, but not for Amun-Ra. He was carried everywhere, feted and fed and adored by the pharaoh and the priests and the masses. The actual purpose of Opet was obvious; it was a renewal of the king's right to rule, and each year the pharaoh was crowned anew during the festival, in full view of the god Amun-Ra and his goddess wife, Mut, who gave their blessing. Their son, Konshu, was also privy to the ceremony, which was a family event.

Nemko had not seen his friend, the good doctor Menebaq, for months. He had received a short, cryptic message from the doctor stating that he was going away for a while just before he disappeared. He promised that he would return, but Nemko wondered by the time Opet arrived. It was almost a full year's cycle of seasons, and Menebaq had not come. The river was high and boats sailed easily along the water, many coming from Memphis and other places in the north, but Menebaq was not a passenger. Nemko went home tired every night. The long work was over but the celebrations seemed to take more of his energy, and there were no messages and no sign of his friend. The priest-designer watched his children playing in the garden behind his house, his two wives always scurrying around keeping the household in order for the great man who spoke regularly with the pharaoh, but the man himself was growing dispirited and concerned. He had no idea where the doctor had gone, and no one else seemed to know, either. He had not booked passage on a boat - Nemko checked - and no one reported seeing him walk or ride out of the city on a donkey, but he must have done one of those things. He was not there.

It was a few days after the celebrations were over that Nemko received a note. "I have just returned. My trip was a success. Meet me after your work day in our favorite place next to Niwt-imn." The sign for Menebaq's name followed.

Nemko dropped everything and went immediately to the bakery café in front of the temple. It was now the terminus of the avenue he had built, and he sat under a shade canopy for the rest of the day, watching the people pass up and down the avenue, walking between the solid lines of the sphinxes. It was nearly dusk when Menebaq appeared. He approached in his usual manner, unhurried and seemingly unconcerned, and sat down across the table from his old friend.

"Where in this world have you been?" Nemko exclaimed. "I have been looking for you for months!"

"You have? I sent you a note saying I would be gone for a while."

"A while! You didn't say a whole year! What happened?"

"It's a strange story. You won't believe it."

"I will if you will tell me! Out with it, man!"

"Amun - Ra took me away."

Nemko stared at him. "What?"

"You heard what I said. It's true, and I must tell you that I have come to believe in Amun-Ra without any reservation."

Nemko could hardly stand it. At first he was nearly furious as the anxiety of the months flowed over him. Then his reaction turned to laughter. He shook from laughing and sat for a brief time, watching Menebaq with unbelieving eyes. "You're telling me that you have been spending your time at Karnak with Amun-Ra?"

"No. Oh, no. I've been to Greece. He sent me there, not to Karnak." Then Menebaq faltered. "It's hard to explain. But tell me what you've been doing, my friend. I need to catch up on what's happened in Thebes."

It was more than Nemko could bear and he became agitated, rapidly growing more upset until he was quite angry. "I can't believe you! Tell me what you've really been up to! You owe me that at least."

Menebaq was startled. He had never thought that his friend would react this way. Then he perceived the reason, and was sorry he hadn't told the designer the whole story before he left. "I'm sorry, Nemko. I didn't do things very well. Please listen and I'll tell you now."

He started at the beginning and told it all. The designer was amazed by both his calling and his mission. He sat silently when Menebaq ended as the world turned to darkness around them. "So there is to be war," he said at last. That wasn't exactly what he meant to say, which the doctor understood, but it was the final stage of Menebaq's story, and Nemko had finished it with his solemn declaration.

They ordered food, discovering that after so much news they had worked up an appetite, and as the night wore on they set out plans and contingencies that would make their lives easier in the future, even with the world at war.

The Achaemenid Empire never gave up. Kmet had long been a part of their holdings, and each succeeding king could not or would not believe they had lost it forever, so the empire sent a series of invading armies into the struggling nation in order to bring them back into the fold by force. The great river and its fertile valley, along with the other riches of history and precious metals, were a prize that could not be ignored. The Persians were fierce about maintaining control of the wealth that remained in that land. In the first year of King Xerxes the First's reign, the new king of the Achaemenid Empire ordered another invasion of Kmet, and sent an army which was commanded to fight to a successful conclusion. The forces marched across the eastern end of the Great Sea and set out to enter the land from Gaza, an ancient city in the edge of the desert which had long been under Persian control. Kmet was always watchful at the border, and as the Persian army amassed on one side, the defenders prepared their resistance on the other. The unknown equation at the scene was the Greek force Menebaq had supposedly secured which was slow on arriving, and there were whisperings that they were not coming at all. That might have been true except for the hatred the Greeks bore for the Achaemenids, the overwhelming motivation which sent Greece into the fight at last.

The easternmost point of Kmet, an imaginary line somewhere in the eastern Sinai Peninsula, was like the rest of the overwhelming desert that flowed across the entire continent except for the sand that stretched along the coast of the Great Sea, which was interspersed with sparse sea grass and scrubby bushes that seemed to always be dry, rattling in the winds that blew in from the water. There were small dunes that lined along the shore, but in those times the sea did not rise, even in a storm, to reach far enough inland to touch the dunes; they existed from a time in the past when the sea was deeper and its waters were stormy.

Nomadic tribesmen lived in tents among the dunes; dull, sand blasted, worn-out tents made with almost colorless lengths of woven goat hair. The families who lived there were nearly the same; dull, sand-blasted, and worn. Life for them was hard, and they had little fresh water for themselves or their goats. The children in the families served as the goatherds, standing near the small flocks that ate from the scrubby bushes until all the green tips were gone. When one area was depleted of its nourishment, the families packed their tents into small bundles and headed to a new place where they could find goat food. The families themselves fed on those very same goats.

Menebaq came up from Thebes to ready a chain of medical stations near the border where they planned to engage the Persians. He wanted to be there when the Greek armies arrived; to see his countrymen surge forward as they joined with the Greeks - he alone had been instrumental in convincing them to fight alongside his people - and to care for any soldier from either side who fell injured in the battle. He watched the nomad families with concern. They were in harm's way, and someone had to warn them of the impending disaster that could destroy their very lives. That someone turned out to be Menebaq. No one else in the forces near the sea shore seemed at all concerned about the few goat herdsmen who lived there.

The doctor went alone to speak to the nomads, who shook their heads to tell him they didn't understand.

"I am trying to tell you that you are in danger," he spoke slowly and carefully, but the men continued to shake their heads.

"Kibbta waw umna," one said, and he pointed to the others. They smiled congenially and handed Menebaq a jar of some sort of brew for which he bowed low in thanks. He knew that making a connection would take time, but he had little of that.

"Many soldiers will be here soon, and they will kill each other on the sand," he explained with slow words and a few graphic motions. The men grinned and repeated the motion, that of a man slicing another with an axe, but they obviously didn't know what they were doing. Menebaq tried again.

"Your families, your children and your wives, will be slaughtered by the Persians," he said clearly, and some of the men repeated the word, 'Persians.' They had heard it before. They smiled broadly as they said it.

"Oh, let the nightmare take them," he thought, but immediately was saddened. Why should these poor scrabblers become victims? He had to find a way to make them understand. He bowed again and started with another attempt. "You must leave at once!" He stood tall before them and waved his arms toward the west. "You aren't safe here now."

The men stood and waved their arms toward the west in imitation as though they were doing a kind of dance. They still smiled, and tipped their jugs of brew toward their mouths. Menebaq took a sip from his while pretending to drink a lot more. It was crude, as he expected, but not without some flavor and a bit of a jolt. He smiled, too, before he realized the situation. Not smiling was the best way to conduct this business. He needed to be serious.

"I need to speak to you seriously," he said, but knew that the words were unheard. "Soldiers, war, death!" He spoke very deeply and maintained a grimace. The men loved it, repeating the three words with the same distressed aspect Menebaq had shown them. He gave up. "I have to give it some thought," he said to himself and left the men in the little tent to their evening meal, which they invited him to take with them. He shook his head and smiled, feeling like an idiot, and withdrew from the tent. It was no use. They seemed to speak a different language, one he had never heard. He was puzzled, but as he recalled the words they had spoken with each other, he flashed upon a sudden realization; they were speaking a dialect of the ancient Hieratic language he had worked so hard to learn years before.

The next afternoon he walked to the tent again, feeling the heat of the sun on his head and shoulders. It wasn't the fiercest time of year when the sun was bright and burning, but was still uncomfortable for him to be out walking over the sand at mid-day. Menebaq was excited to speak to the goat men again because he felt sure that they could understand him when he used the ancient tongue. As he approached, the men came out to greet him. They were more than friendly and nearly overwhelmed him with their strong hands that struck his shoulders and back in greeting.

"I came yesterday," he opened, and the men took immediate notice. "I came to tell you that you are in danger here." He didn't know how to say some of the words, but tried to string enough together to get his message across. "A huge army with soldiers and weapons will soon have a battle in this place, and you must move on. You will not be safe. The Persians are the enemy, and our soldiers, men of Kmet, will fight them off, but for a while you need to be somewhere else." The men stirred and nodded. Then their head man spoke in the same language but with a different accent and simpler vocabulary.

"Now we hear you, friend. We are glad for the warning, but you need to know that we cannot leave now."

"But you could all die here! You must understand me and leave at once!"

"We cannot. Our herds are all we have, and they haven't finished grazing in this place. It will be for a few more suns that we need to stay, and then we will move on toward the rising place." He motioned toward the east.

"But you can't go there! That's where the enemy is lying in wait even now. You must turn west."

"We cannot. All the land has been grazed for this season in the setting place and we would starve because the goats would starve. We will leave here soon, and we will go toward the rising."

"The battle will be here! Upon you! They will kill you!"

The goat men looked at each other, and then they all shook their heads.

"We stay because we cannot go. They have never hurt us before, and they won't hurt us now. We thank you for coming to say these things, but we will be safe. We do not fight the - - the Persians." He grasped for the word that he had heard but almost never said. He gave a quick smile. "We are safe. It is bad that you are not."

Menebaq bowed toward them. "I wish it to be as you have said, friends." He turned and walked away toward his own tent that was set up for the coming carnage, sad in his mind and heart because the goat men, he was sure, would not survive the battle.

The doctor waited day to day for over a week. The Persians could be heard at times, marching and singing, clanging their swords together and shouting, just beyond sight across the border, hidden behind some sandy hills. They had not yet attempted to step onto the soil of

Kmet. Soon, he knew, they would. The area was tense, the waiting almost intolerable, as the Persians played a game of intimidation.

Late that night Menebaq slept fitfully in his tent. In the very early hours of the morning he woke up enough to hear movements outside. It was a stealthy sound, but seemed to be a large company moving across the sand, making as little clatter as possible. 'The Persians have sneaked across the border!' he thought with alarm. And there had been no sighting of the Greek armies! His two associates, young men who were students of medicine, slept soundly. He opened the flap a little to peer outside.

The moonlight was bright but not yet at the full as he looked across the desert from the dune where his tent was located. Columns of men under the banners of Athens and Sparta were marching along as quietly as they could through the sand, trying to hide their presence as long as possible. They were a substantial army, moving like specters across the land, heads high and bodies erect as only the Greeks could march, pointed toward the east and the confrontation that would surely come at dawn. Not one of the soldiers noticed the face of the man watching from a small tent next to a squat dune that was covered with as yet ungrazed bushes and grass, but Menebaq's heart leapt forward toward the host and his mind offered a prayer of thanks to the Great God Amun-Ra whose plan had come to fruition at last. He watched from the tent, his attention fixed on the columns of strength that foretold the fall of the Achaemenid Empire and the certain escape from its hawk-like clutches for Kmet. He was nearly overcome with the thrill and the joy of it all.

The Persians had intended to wear down Kmetian resistance slowly, by menacing from a distance and waiting to carry out the threat, but were at a loss to explain why none of their spies had mentioned anything about the large Greek army until the night when boats landed along the shore and men jumped out prepared to do battle. Persia had been forced to start the action immediately in case more defenders were on the way. It did not go well for the Achaemenid Empire from the beginning.

Battle opened before dawn. In the half-light the Persians came roaring toward the border, swinging swords and axes, screaming with full force, but the combined armies of Greece and Kmet were ready. They loosed a salvo of arrows that were aimed high enough to strike the lines of onrushing men before they were close enough for hand to hand brutality. Some men fell, but most screamed even louder and continued to advance at the same pace. There was an onward rush of enemies from the side as well, as the Persians attempted to encircle the entire defending army, but Kmet spread out quickly at the flanks and toward the rear, and the invaders were unsuccessful. Persians who were caught near the rear of the battle were either killed or captured, and no one came to their aid. The Achaemenid's had all they could do to keep the front lines advancing steadily and try to drive their opponents into the sea or a retreat.

The Persians were as formidable as they had always been. They had a strong fighting force, but they did not own the spirit for self-preservation that was vital for Kmet. Even the fiercest Persians recognized that their victims were fighting for their lives with such determination that they were almost inexorable. The empire had told its soldiers they could win the battle easily, that Kmet was weak and disorganized and would not last long before the strength of Persia, but the reality was quite different. The assailants felt the fury of Kmet immediately and intensely.

Menebaq watched the battle begin from the front of his tent, a white banner flying above it along with the ancient insignia for a medical unit. He knew that it made no difference to the Persians, but the flags were there to attract the attention of the defending armies in the hope that wounded would be brought to him for tending.

In the earliest hour of combat the initial drive was far away, but as the time dragged along some Persians broke through the lines and the fight moved quickly toward the little tent beside the dune. Persians on horseback came through, riding hard and striking as they came. Swords and axes and pikes were their weapons of choice, and they skewered as many as they could. It was a gruesome thing, and the doctor watched, along with his medics, as the horsemen ran through the staggered lines and slaughtered anyone who couldn't jump aside fast enough. One young soldier, their first casualty, was struck in the back with a pike not far from the tent. Menebaq and his men ran to seize the victim from the place he fell although he was already dead. They carried him as fast as they could, looked at his sightless eyes, and placed him gently between the tent and the dune, a place that would be harder for the riders to smash through. As they laid him there, Menebaq caught sight of the staff lying inside the rear opening of the tent. He grabbed it, and with a strong thrust, forced it deeply into the sand outside the front entrance. It was an act of defiance, as he saw it, but it was a signal that seemed to spread across the field and in a few minutes men carried the fallen to the sanctuary that had been created for the healing of the wounded. The medical tent was busy from that moment on.

A general took notice of Persian horsemen running amok inside his lines and called for the best archers; in a few minutes several riderless horses needed to be brought off the field, and they came to stand behind the dune next to Menebaq's tent. It was a place of refuge in the midst of the horror that was taking place on the opposite side of the low sand hill.

The battle stormed on for hours. All was confusion on the field much of the time, but Menebaq returned to it frequently to rescue fallen men when he caught a glimpse of them from the door of his tent. He brought in a Persian or two, one cursing and causing an awful clamor, the other quietly accepting his fate. The doctor's clothes were soaked in the blood of a hundred men, and his face was taut with anguish at times, but the tent remained a place of sanctuary where men were usually quiet as he worked with them even though he had to cut off a few limbs that were too mangled to repair. Some died as he attempted to save them, but most did not, and his crew worked solidly through the long hours of the day, hardly noticing the tides of war that were surging in the arena outside their door.

A child, a son of the goat herders he had warned to leave, was brought in. He had been struck by a heavy wagon that was lumbering through the scene to bring new weaponry supplies to the soldiers of Kmet and Greece, and the boy fell beneath it. His father carried him into the tent with a short request for the doctor to do what he could, but the boy was dead. Apparently unmoved, the father took the child in his arms and carried him away. It seemed to Menebaq that it was like something the man did nearly every day.

Late in the day the battle sounds seemed to ebb away, and the defending soldiers could be heard shouting in the distance as they chased the Persians, attempting a renewed massacre as the defeated army ran in full rout toward the border where they thought they might be safe. That was not the case. Kmet and Greece followed the retreat and killed as many as they could before darkness made it impossible to define foe from friend, and they returned, exhausted but victorious, to their own side of the imaginary line that had been made centuries in the past. Menebaq did not have the privilege of stopping, but worked on through the night, and many more survivors were brought to him so that the area around the tent couldn't hold them. He worked up and down lines of wounded men that stretched far out into the torn and ragged desert where they had fallen. The next morning found him still tending the wounded, and he spent the early hours of that day examining and treating as well. When he was too tired to go on, he directed the men to come closer to the tent, where he slept for an hour before he began to patch up those with less threatening wounds. It was even more hours later that he encountered a young Persian who watched him with hate on his face as the doctor examined his broken leg and a long gash on his side. The blood had dried and the doctor attempted to wash it away to get a better look when the soldier suddenly pulled out a thin knife and stabbed the tired doctor through his heart. Menebaq fell against the Persian, who was held down by some Greek soldiers and run through by their swords, but the doctor died as well. There was silence in the tent. The two young assistants took the bodies; Menebaq to a place inside the tent, while the Persian's body was tossed out the door as far as they could throw him.

Despite the sudden grief, the men who remained were treated and sent to find their commanders, until at last the tent was empty except for the two young medics and the remains of the good doctor. A ragged little man appeared at the tent flap then, and spoke to the men about a place of burial for Menebaq. "He tried to save my son," the little man said in the common tongue, "and I would like to bury him here beside the boy." He took them to the top of the dune where a new grave had been dug, and indicated that he would like to place the doctor there as a memorial for himself and his tribe for the doctor's kind acts. The medics spoke together. They had made no other plans for Menebaq's remains, and this seemed a respectful choice, so they helped carry his body to the top of the dune where some men from the tribe dug another grave, and they all stood in silence as Menebaq, still covered with the blood of countless soldiers, was lowered into his final place of rest. When it was over, the medics left the area to find their commander and prepare to go back to Thebes.

The goat herders waited for another day and then wandered away slowly toward the west without their goats. They had been stolen to feed the battle-hungry soldiers. The herders, however, were happily carefree. The Persians had paid them well to spy against Kmet. They had reported the size and movements of all the units as well as the arrival of the Greeks, and were amply rewarded. The best part was that the Persians lost the battle, so no one knew of the herders' part in the invasion, and they were absolved of any reprisals or other complications stemming from their involvement in the war. They went to the coastal village of Rakotis first, and then south into the fresh water delta where they found ample grazing land and used a portion of the money to buy many more goats. They prospered in their new home.

One of the young medics took Menebaq's staff to Thebes where he intended to give it to the doctor's family, but he grew attached to the staff along the way and decided to keep it for himself.

Chapter Eight

332 B C

For millennia the nation of Kmet continued very much the same. The government was mostly stable, moving forward century by century while remaining broadly constant. Citizens enjoyed freedoms that were perhaps the most generous in the world at that time; religion followed consistent patterns and kept the same gods for multiple centuries, although there was a tendency to enlarge the pantheon of deities by combining the names of existing gods to create new ones. Work and matters of finance were static, and even the beautifully crafted sculpture and wall paintings looked almost identical for three thousand years - with the short-lived exception of the Pharaoh Akhenaten and his ideal of realism. Whims and fads regarding the nation's way of life were few during that long period of passing history. Stability was honored and maintained along with a painstakingly slow development of social conventions and individuality.

Unchanging continuation came to a halt rather suddenly when the Persian Empire invaded the land, and never returned in exactly the form that was lost. Although Kmet remained reasonably stable during its annexation by the Persians, a foreign power ruling in place of a native pharaoh was a difficult blow for the nation. A short time after the Persian aggression ended, the Hellenistic period began, and everything was altered; the world turned upside down. The people of Kmet welcomed the Greeks as deliverers so they hardly saw the drastic changes coming.

One of the most obvious transformations was in the nomenclature which had developed gradually over the lengthy span of history. In a very short time the lion statue on the west bank of

the Nile changed in name from Hor-em-akhet to Sphinx, and the proud name of Kmet began to metamorphose into the Greek name for the country, Aigyptos. The dynastic form of government was forever distorted as well. The country had not yet recovered from the Persian invasion when the Pharaoh Nectanebo II, the last true pharaoh with Egyptian ancestry, lost his throne in 342 BC, and the home-ruled dynasties that had endured for over three millennia failed at last.

The Greek armies, under the direct leadership of the young King Alexander of Macedon, appeared near the border of Egypt during an adventurous campaign to wipe out the Persians, and set siege to the fort at Gaza, one of the strongholds of the Persians; a place that could withstand an assault for a long period of time. An assailing army, especially in a desert landscape, would need to find water and provisions in order to sustain an attack on such a fort. Everyone had always accepted those two aspects of battle as fact. Alexander proved otherwise. He simply sent miners into the earth to dig tunnels beneath a part of the outer wall, and in a short time the barrier collapsed, the army smashed into the fort, and the end result was that all the defenders were slaughtered and the women and children taken as slaves. Soon after that the victors moved across the border into the ancient land of Kmet, where they were welcomed at Pelusium, a fortified anchorage on the Great Sea, as any wise magistrate of a severely weakened state might do. The Greek king took a strong liking to the people. He traveled on toward the west with his army, and soon came to the tiny port of Rakotis, which to his mind became an ideal spot to build a new city that would showcase his power. He would call it Alexandria. He studied the landscape around the port, and called on his surveyors to set up sight lines for streets and public spaces.

Amer, an assistant on a large survey team, waited on a sandy waste outside the village for his crew. They told him to keep their equipment under his watchful eyes while they set off across the landscape to find another sight-point, and he had been lingering there for over an hour. Some children, laughing and sometimes throwing pebbles in his direction, were hiding behind a grassy hillock a short distance away, and he could hear the sounds of gulls and other sea birds above the wind that blew across the grasses from the west, strong and robust in the warmth of the sun, calling to him to come out to the water's edge and find his way onto the sea. He had never been on the water, but was fascinated by the thought.

He saw some men on horses approaching in the distance and watched them casually as they rode swiftly across the landscape. They stopped a short distance off, and he became aware that they were inspecting him. Two of the men urged their horses closer and hailed him as they came forward.

"You – you with those tools – who are you and what are you doing here?"

"I am Amer," he told them. They were obviously a military patrol. "I work with the surveyors. They'll be back soon. These are their things." He gestured toward the equipment.

"Where are you from?" the first man asked.

"I am from the village. Rakotis. I started with the surveyors just a few days ago."

"Do you think we can use him?" he asked the other.

"I don't know yet."

"Amer," he spoke slowly, as though the man he addressed might be thick-headed, "Do you have any education? Do you know how to read and write?"

"Yes. I know. I can write in two languages. Copt and Greek." Copt was a derivation of the native language of lower Egypt.

"Are you very good in Greek?"

"Yes, my Greek is good."

The men looked him over, studying his every move, it seemed. "I think he could do," one of them said lightly.

"Come with us, Amer," the other man told him.

"I can't. Those children hiding over there will steal all these things. The survey crew will be angry."

"Come with us. I'll leave a man here until they get back."

"Where?"

"No questions, just come along."

Amer was placed on a horse for the first time, and was led away a little too fast. When one of the men saw that he was struggling to stay on the animal, he called out and the group slowed. They rode a short distance northwest, toward the sea, and stopped beside a group of large yellow tents that bordered the dunes along the beach.

"Wait here," one of them said , and they went inside leaving Amer, sill on the horse, with one guard. The horse stood very still as though it was afraid the rider might fall. Before long two of the men returned, helped Amer off the horse, and pointed him toward the tent. "Go in there. They're waiting for you."

Inside he found a second level commander of the Greek army who occupied a classic Greek chair. He was drinking a cup of Greek wine and eating what could only be assumed to be Greek bread and cheese. He took a long look at Amer. His face held no expression but curiosity, and he neither approved nor disapproved, but began to question.

"You say you speak Greek?" he asked in Greek. Amer answered in the language, and the second level commander asked him about speaking and writing in Copt.

"Do you ever use that language, sir?" Amer asked.

"Answer the questions you are asked. There is no reason for you to ask anything."

"I use both languages, sir." Amer replied.

"Read this and tell me what it says." The commander held a paper out and a soldier took it to Amer who read it aloud in Copt and translated immediately.

"Yes, that's what I was told." The commander turned to the man who had decided to bring Amer in. "He can stay. At least for a few days. Then we can decide."

"Follow me," the man told him. Amer was taken from that tent to another, a scruffy looking place with rows of cots along one side. "You will sleep here." He pointed to a cot. "Your outfit is in the trunk there. Report back to the commander as soon as you are dressed." All was business in the Greek army. When he had changed, Amer looked, and started to feel, Greek.

151

The work at Rakotis continued for several days, and Amer was kept busy running errands and translating communications. At first all his translations of the commander's communiqués were checked for accuracy by an old priest from Tanis, but as the days went by, the checking slowed to only an occasional inspection. The commander had learned that he could trust his translator.

Amer often had to deliver verbal messages; many local people for whom messages were intended could neither read nor write in any tongue. Their only line of communication was through the translator. After each delivery he was questioned, and apparently he had done a proper job. He was sent on one job after another. Eventually, Amer came to understand that his post was secure.

During the fourth week of his service the camp became agitated. People were scurrying around in a state of anxious watchfulness. Amer listened and tried to hear what was happening, but no one spoke about their disquiet. At last in the mid-afternoon he heard a loud thrumming of horse's hooves. He managed to sneak a quick look through the tent flap and saw a young man with golden hair and a very crooked nose. He was riding a fantastic stallion, and Amer knew that he was watching the great man, King Alexander. Everyone bowed to the ground as the king approached the officer's tent, and when he entered he clucked an order that must have meant 'get about your business.' They all rose and pretended that he wasn't there, except for the highest officers who took him to one side and sat at a long table to talk war, or so Amer hoped.

In actuality it was a mundane talk about the plans to reorganize the government of Egypt, including the trip some of them would take to Memphis to set up the new administration. King Alexander was often adamant, and Amer could hear him shouting at some points in the conversation. The king could use common Greek, but usually spoke a dialect from his particular area of Macedon, so the messenger-translator had a difficult time understanding what he actually said. Amer also had to pretend to be busy with other work, as all the men were doing, but in truth all were listening in on the planning session.

The next day Amer was told that he would travel later in the week to Memphis, where he would continue to work in communications for the second level commander Menos, his boss. Amer was overjoyed. Going to Memphis had been a life-long dream, and he planned to make the most of it. King Alexander was going to be in Memphis, also. He planned to set up a government for the renewed nation of Egypt, and Amer was proud to have a place in the latest development of his native land's journey into the modern era.

The military contingent sailed down the Nile to the ancient capital city. On their way they passed the monuments that lay in the area called Giza, the antique home of Karnua and Pan and the stone lion he made. Although most of the men didn't realize it, more than two thousand years of history surrounded them as they left the Great Sea and sailed southward. Amer traveled all the way on the lower deck of the barge, but he was lucky to be on the western side, and had a magnificent view of the gigantic pyramids that the long ago pharaohs who were now gods had built. Then, hard alongside the water, the oldest stone creature of all, the Sphinx, stared fixedly toward the east with wide eyes open, keeping his thoughts to himself.

Memphis was more than he had expected. Much more. The streets were alive with prosperous-looking people, and traffic was always packed into the narrow streets and alleys.

Litters went flying through the streets, and men on foot or on donkeys zigzagged everywhere. Women, too, were present among the crowds, often attending to their own stalls filled with goods that people seemed to crave, and trade was spirited.

To Amer, the wonderful buildings were the most amazing part of the whole. The palace of the pharaoh and the temple to Ptah were the most outstanding, but all the larger buildings were made of stone, some with marble facades, and the look and feel of wealth was deeply imbued upon the entire city. The great river divided to the south, just above the city, and half of it flowed along the western flank of the place, lined with wharves and landings. It was a highway both to the north and south lying provinces of the land. No one would have guessed that the country had only recently been through a time of turmoil. Memphis stood above it all, and the business of growing richer, both for individuals and the nation, was reflected in its clamorous action.

King Alexander was anointed Pharaoh of Egypt in Memphis just after Amer arrived, and the day was one of festivity and loud, boisterous adulation by the crowds who came into the city from all the surrounding countryside. They danced and celebrated around large fires late into the night, and everybody had too much beer before the last of them went home to sleep it all off and try to get back to normal the next day. Starting a nation over again was a heady experience.

Amer settled into work at a small office within a large government building, along with two other translators he supervised, and began the task of converting all the new codes of law that the king devised from Greek into Copt. It would take a long time, he knew, and he set to the job with fervor. He would live in Memphis for at least a year, he assumed from the amount of new copy-work that poured out from the central offices each day. There was already enough to fill his days, working along with the other two copymen, for half a year. But there was a sudden interruption.

Amer heard the news after a few weeks in Memphis. He was going to Siwa. He knew of the place, but never had considered going there. It was too foreign; they even had a separate language that was almost impossible to understand. No one left Siwa if they had been born there, as he had heard, and many of the visitors who went decided to stay. The place was enchanted and was dangerous for normal people to wander into. But King Alexander was going, and his boss, Menos, was going along as communications officer. He had selected Amer over the others to have the honor of the trip. Even so, Amer had mixed feelings. To his mind, Siwa was a shadow world and should be avoided, even though he had a greater desire to go there now. Of course, he didn't have a choice.

The temple of Amun-Ra in Siwa was on the rocky hill of Aghurmi, a short distance from the lake. An oracle lived in the temple; a priest who channeled the great god and spoke his answers to questions from any creditable man he thought the god would notice. The seer, supposedly chosen by Amun-Ra, had a powerful position in the community and in the land of Kmet, as Egypt had been called when the oracle came into being. Everyone believed he was the voice of Amun-Ra, and he told fortunes for the most influential men of the world at that time. King Alexander had come to Siwa for the purpose of meeting with the oracle at the temple and having his fortune read. It was, of course, a very personal thing, so no one but the soothsayer and the king were present when the god Amun-Ra spoke through his medium. The problem was that Amun-Ra had nothing to do with it, and it was he who spoke to Amer in the quiet of a back room in the temple while the oracle was dealing with the king.

The translator had come to the temple with the king's entourage, along with Commander Menos. He wandered away quietly just after Alexander went into the inner-sanctum to hear his fate; he later realized that he had been called: the voice of the god came to him from a shadowy doorway. Although Amer didn't yet know what it was, the staff was there, glowing in a blinking pattern like a signal on a dark night, and it attracted Amer's eye. He reached to take it in his hand and collided with Amun-Ra at the same time. The god, in the shape of a lion with flaming eyes, was incensed, but not by Amer.

"He is not my voice." the lion growled. "I do not speak through him."

"Who are you?" Amer quavered. He was in near panic.

"I am Amun-Ra, the one who is being impersonated in there. There is no need for you to fear me. But that priest should!"

Amer was unsure. He was still terrorized, even though the lion was not menacing. "But the god has always spoken through the oracle," he stammered. It was the first thought that came to his mind.

"I have never spoken through the priests! They have all been imposters. I have never come to speak to anyone in this temple before today!"

"You are speaking to me?" Amer felt a sudden rush of disbelief.

"Yes, Amer, to you alone."

"Why do you speak to me, lord? I am no oracle."

"That is the reason. You will not pretend to know my voice as all the others have done. I do not make decisions for people. I only guide them to the right ones if I they will listen. And I do not tell them the future. Not often, anyway. They all have to live and to learn as you do, Amer."

"I'm scared. I don't know what to say."

"You do not need to fear me, son. I know you well. You have not allowed life to make you hard-hearted and angry, and you are here with me now for that reason."

Amer bowed his head. "I still don't understand."

"You are stronger than you think. When things change, use your good sense to do what is the best for everyone concerned."

"How will I know what's best?"

"I will speak plainly. The king who is in there now," he moved his head in the direction of the inner temple, "will not survive long. When he is gone, you will be free, and you can go where you will. You will find that true when it happens. But keep this confidential, always, or you could get into trouble."

"He will die?"

"Yes, but that is still a little while. For now he will pretend to be my own son. Come with me and listen."

Amer gasped. He found himself standing beside the lion in a dark stone-walled room faintly lit with two torches fastened to a far wall. The king and the oracle were facing each other on a circular dais in the center. A small, shining chest lay at the oracle's feet, and they were earnestly talking.

"They cannot see or hear us," the lion told him. "But we can listen."

"I will do as you need, mighty king," the priest was saying. "I will declare you as the son of Amun-Ra-Zeus. As an official declaration."

"You are sworn to secrecy on your life."

"Yes. I will never speak of it unless you tell me to do so."

The lion spoke to Amer. "That is how the oracle always works. Each time a new one starts he learns the tricks of his trade soon enough. I have never told any of them the future of their clients."

"Why do they do it then?" Amer asked him.

"For the gold. Listen now."

"I will make the announcement today, and as soon as you hear of it, you can make your statement. No one will ever know anything else. On your life, priest."

"Yes, lord. I am not one to tell more than I should."

"Enjoy the riches." Alexander turned away. He was disgusted with the man even though he had used him.

"My pharaoh," the priest bowed as the young man swaggered away.

"We will leave this place." Amun-Ra said to Amer. "It is foul."

They were in the dark entry room again. Amer was bewildered. "That is how they do it, always," the flaming-eyed lion said. "Even when they make no arrangement, the priest tells them whatever they want to hear and then he receives gold. It will have to stop soon. This is a false temple."

Amer showed no reaction at all, but was overwhelmed by the situation. He waited for the lion to direct him.

"After Alexander, you will take up your life in Egypt again, first in Memphis and then in the new city, Alexandria, and will find there the people and the place you need to be to help govern the city and the nation as it should be done. The Greeks have changed things, but that will not cause you or the people to suffer, even though the house of the pharaohs is now over. The Greeks will prepare you for the future. And you alone know that King Alexander is no god."

"I will remember."

"Take the staff with you, Amer. I will guide you through it at times."

Amer took it in his hand; a long slender pole with the strange writing flowing down from the top. "I will, lord." He was shaking.

The lion faded rapidly from view, and Amer, stunned as he was, knew he had to return to the men who waited for the king in the front enclosure of the temple, but none of them noticed when he rejoined them as the Pharaoh Alexander came through the outer doors.

The word soon spread that Alexander was declared to be the son of Amun-Ra-Zeus, a trinity of names to represent the three gods encompassed in the god-king, but only Amer knew the truth, although many others guessed.

The entourage left Siwa the next day. As they rode out through the streets, the people came together along the route to shout praise to Alexander, "The Great One," as he passed them on the road. The King acknowledged the accolade, and waved a friendly hand to the crowd. The scene was to be repeated in Memphis and the villages and towns along the road to the city. Amer looked at it all with new vision and thought about the words of Amun-Ra.

Pharaoh Alexander, the newest pharaoh-god in the Egyptian hierarchy, ruled in Memphis for only three months after his remarkable trip to Siwa. He set up an entirely different system of governance that placed one Greek and one Egyptian at the helm of all the administrative departments, and made edicts about nearly every aspect of life for the people. It all sounded clear and agreeable, and no one questioned the new laws, for they were issued by a duly anointed pharaoh and had all the power behind them that had been amassed by the legion of kings who preceded Alexander. It was a tidy business, and in the end it succeeded into a new system that was more efficient and practical. About the only thing that Alexander could not accomplish was an audience with the gods who could tell him more of the history and the customs of the Egyptians, but he made sweeping decisions anyway, believing himself to be appointed to the task by fate if no one else. He succeeded, to a point, in getting the nation back on the right path, although he couldn't altogether stamp out the corruption that lurked beneath the surface. It was a time-honored custom, and everyone accepted that the people who governed should have the largest share of the bounty of the land.

All was moving toward a conclusion, however, and Alexander left the capital city, never to return, in April of that year. He set off for the lands that the Persians had conquered in the past, then went to India, and ended in the city of Babylon when he met his sudden demise at the hand of a poisoner. Egypt mourned his passing, and then set its mind to accept the new force that was about to reign; the Ptolemies.

Perdikkas, a man of uncertain authority, took the rule of the empire of Macedon immediately after the death of Alexander. He was, officially, a regent to look after things until the slain king's son was old enough to accept his father's mantle, the child having been born after the death of Alexander. But Perdikkas was ambitious and made other plans. During the absence of a true king, the regent appointed Ptolemy, a general who had worked closely with Alexander, to become the governor of Egypt, called a satrap, and rule there in his place. The general also had other plans. So it was that the next dynastic power, the Ptolemies, entirely Greek and foreign to the ways of their new kingdom, eventually became the pharaohs of the vast land of Egypt.

Amer, in his simple life in Memphis, knew nothing of those things. He only knew that he needed to codify the new laws as rapidly as possible, and drove himself and his small workforce to do the job as he perceived it should be done. Commander Menos, his superior, had gone to Macedon to honor the fallen king, and although Amer waited for a full year, Menos did not return. The translator operated as though he was subject to an authority figure, but over time he became one himself, almost without recognizing that fact. He directed the men who translated with him in their work, and they eventually got down to the smaller projects, what he considered the lesser points of law that King Alexander decreed, soon after the full realization of his position was revealed to him. Amun-Ra spoke.

"You are soon coming to the end of the work you started," the god told him one day while he was alone in the untidy office. "You will need to place yourself in a new position."

Amer was startled. He hadn't expected to hear from the lion, as he thought of Amun-Ra, again. "I don't know what to do," he finally answered. "It's not clear to me."

"Would you like an idea?" the disembodied voice asked.

"Yes. What do you want to tell me?"

"Do you know that Macedon has sent an army toward Egypt? They plan to take it back into their possession, and the satrap, as they call him, will need advisors."

"I don't know how to advise a man like that. I only know the codes of law I've been working on."

"Exactly. You alone have read the whole thing. That is right, is it not?"

"Yes. I've read it all. I needed to check on the work."

"Then you alone are the only living authority who understands the organization of the new government that King Alexander wanted to use for this nation."

Amer considered that statement. It was true, he recognized, but he didn't feel like an authority. "I can't remember it all," was his only response.

"But you know where to look for whatever is needed. You also made the index for the codes."

"Yes, but I'm not a student of the law."

"You need to give yourself more credit. You are the only one in Egypt who has all this information at his hand, and Ptolemy will need to know how to use it, and how you can help him. He needs you."

"You say a war is coming?"

"Not a war you should be in, Amer. You are needed in another place. Go to the court of the satrap and tell him about the work you have done and what you know. He will understand all the rest."

"Does he know that Perdikkas is advancing?"

"Yes, he knows, and is marshaling his own troops at this moment. It will be about three weeks before the Macedonians are close enough to fight. Ptolemy will likely send his armies out to meet them. Anyway, you need to get over to see him, and you can tell him the new rules for dealing with the country. Start with the basics first, and get into the details later. He will willingly listen to you, I am sure. He was close to Alexander, one of his bodyguards, in fact, and respected him."

"Have you talked to him?"

"No, but I sent him a few messages. He is expecting someone to come to his aid soon."

Amer changed the direction of the encounter. He had misgivings. "I thought you didn't like Alexander. Why should we follow his new laws?"

"I do not like or dislike anyone, just what some of them do. And his new laws are good ones, as far as they go. I think Alexander did as well as anyone could in his peculiar position. It would be hard for a man to rule the world."

Amer didn't ask any more questions.

It didn't take Ptolemy long to dispatch the army Perdikkas brought. The fire of King Alexander still burned within the new Egyptian ruler and his troops. The discouraged army of Macedon had little left to fight for. Their great hero-king was gone, and the interloper, Perdikkas, was seriously unpopular due to his short temper and vicious treatment of his men. Some of the men deserted to the cause for Egypt and the promise of land along the fertile Nile River Valley, which was enough for any mercenary who wanted a more stable life to consider carefully. Other Macedonians plotted against Perdikkas and assassinated him before the conflict with Egypt could be concluded. That was the end of direct Macedonian influence in Ptolemy's affairs; he soon became much more interested in securing the riches of his new land. He declared himself the new pharaoh and was acclaimed by the Egyptian people.

The temple of Ptah in Memphis was an ostentatious structure. Its only competition for supremacy in the city was the royal palace itself, and the high priest of Ptah was nearly as royal as any pharaoh. Ptah was considered to be the creator-god by the citizens of that city, although most of the country accepted Amun-Ra as the greatest of the gods and was therefore venerated as the creator of all things. A small but important rivalry ran between Memphis and Thebes in this regard, but the Egyptians were somewhat easy-going about their pantheistic beliefs and did not object to having a few extra gods and goddesses around just for the sake of security and comfort.

The temple of Ptah was a dark place; he was the god of the underworld and it seemed a good thing to keep his temple darkened so he would remain contented. As a result, Ptah never saw the light of day, and his rituals were conducted without the benefit of torches and candles. Only enough illumination was included so the priests could see in the gloom. There were no flowers or other bright things in his décor or his rituals, only shadowy stone walls and floors, colorless and cold. Ptah did not love things that were radiant or luminous. There were mostly windowless rooms deep inside the temple, and it was in such a room that a council of the highest ranking priests was holding a meeting. They sat in a circle facing each other, except for one door-watcher at the entrance.

"He has come out of nothing, I believe," the high priest was speaking in a somber voice. "No one knows anything about him, and I don't think he is attached to any power in Memphis or Thebes. Our man within the court has no previous knowledge of him."

"Why then does the pharaoh favor him?"

"It seems that he has received some kind of message or revelation about this new man. He believes that his choice is ordained by one of the gods."

"Do you think he is any danger to your position?" a small priest with a prominent lisp questioned.

"No, I can't see how he would be, but the new pharaoh is an unknown equation in all this."

Another priest, a younger man with immaculate robes and shifting eyes added his thoughts. "We must go carefully, your highness. We may not know anything about this one, but his association with the pharaoh is powerful enough. We don't want to cause suspicion of any kind."

"We have never done that, Daket, and I have no intention of stepping out too soon. Just watch him and find his weakness. Every man has a weakness. We all know that."

They laughed softly, creating a strange sound that the room rarely heard.

Historically, the high priest of the temple of Amun-Ra in Thebes had often become pharaoh. For one extended period of time in the past, an entire dynasty had been carried forth with one high priest after another succeeding into the title. The priests of Ptah had never been able to gain that kind of political power, and they were now eyeing the prize with fervent hope.

"I think we might be able to have him removed, permanently, if we act quickly. We don't want him to be given any more power than he has already been offered." Daket was often outspoken.

159

To their surprise, the high priest was not critical of the suggestion. "He hasn't yet been offered anything, but will be soon. I have considered what you suggest, and it could be a solution. But if we do it, we have to find someone who is very professional. It shouldn't be done in the slipshod manner of our last effort."

"Surely, your highness," a quiet priest who sat watching the door a short distance from the others remarked, "we cannot be blamed for that. We contracted a man who came with high recommendations. We had no way of knowing he was a drinker with a loose tongue."

They all laughed softly again.

"Well, Tambel, you weren't blamed, were you. I know you thought you had found the best. And he did a good job, initially. He was quick and efficient then." Laughter again.

"We should wait. No reason to go after him yet. Wait and see what happens." If any of them could be considered sympathetic toward intended victims, it was Olwen, a large man with a chubby body who seemed to be poured into his robe. He was always barefoot, and might have seemed an ascetic but for his appetites. He loved the pleasures of life and indulged himself readily.

"Waiting too long will do no good," the high priest responded. "You are cautious about these things, but I wonder why." The high priest fancied the pretense of piety and kept his own immoderations well hidden.

There was a movement of some sort, no one could ever recall exactly what happened, but a large lion appeared mysteriously in the center of the circle, facing the high priest. His eyes were red-fire, and his voice was strong and firm. The priests recoiled as one.

"Be on your guard, priest!" the lion growled. "You are the one who should be cautious."

The high priest was so terrified he could not speak.

"Know this," the lion continued, "Amer is mine and you will not touch him! He is following his own destiny."

The priest tried to ask the lion who he was but his voice could only squeak.

"You are frightened now; just wait until I have finished with you!" the lion informed him. "You are fit for very little in this world! Amer will make a fine vizier to the pharaoh, but you would poison the entire world if you had your way."

The insult was greater than the priest's fear. "Who are you?" he demanded with a gasp. "You are not Ptah!"

"Indeed, I am not. There is no Ptah! Priests have invented him for their own purposes. There is no one but myself and there never has been. I am Amun-Ra. And you, more than any other men, should fear me!"

Most of the priests cowered before him, knowing they had met more than their match, but two men looked at him with hostility. One was the high priest.

"We have served Ptah here in this temple for entire lifetimes. How can you say he is not here?"

"I am Amun-Ra, and I alone am the creator."

A sly look came into the priest's eyes, and his fear was replaced with cynical thought. "He is jealous," the priest believed, but said nothing.

The lion spoke again. "You are wrong. I am not at all concerned about Ptah because he is not real. I have no reason to behave as humans do. I am who I am, and if you are wise you will leave your petty thoughts and accept truth."

"My lord," the priest rose from his chair and bowed before the lion. All the others did the same, some with shaking bodies and hands.

"You are still a false one," Amun-Ra said sadly. "You will never change. But I came here to say this: you will leave Amer alone. He is mine, and you cannot harm him. If you attempt any action against him, you will answer to me. His service to the new pharaoh is his decision alone. You will not interfere."

The lion was gone just as suddenly as he had appeared.

Amer felt as though he was being weighed in the balance of the gods. The pharaoh sat on his throne considering, while he, the subject of consideration, bowed his head and said nothing. 'Something is wrong here,' he thought, but gave up the idea. It was a false hope, to expect the pharaoh to take him as an advisor, but he could only wait. It seemed a very long time.

At last Ptolemy spoke. "Amer of Rakotis," the pharaoh said formally, "We receive you as the Vizier of the Law. You are to interpret the law so that we may understand it and act accordingly. Will you do this?"

An astonished Amer found his voice and answered, "I will do it, my lord." He had not expected to made vizier, only an advisor of the law.

"You will need to respond to requests in a timely manner, knowing that the justice a petitioner seeks from pharaoh is the foundation of Egyptian law and public order."

"I will always do my best, my lord," Amer replied. "I may, at times, need to reference the scrolls of the law to provide an answer, as you understand, my lord."

"Yes, that is why we ask these questions. An accurate response in a timely manner is what we want."

"Yes, my lord."

"That is all for this moment, Amer, Vizier of the Law. You will be summoned at our pleasure to offer explanations and interpretations, which we will then consider before making a decision on any point of law. You will also understand that your interpretations may not always agree with ours, but that is of no consequence when we judge cases."

Amer understood there would be no disputing the pharaoh's decisions, even if he turned the law upside down. The pharaoh was the final word. He bowed before the throne and left the audience chamber in a daze. He had no idea of the opposition he faced, only of the future which looked bright before him. Opposition was not long in coming.

The high priest had almost recovered from his fearful encounter with the lion. He knew that he was playing a dangerous game, but gambled that Ptah, the god he continued to honor, would protect him. He fully expected to win against Amun-Ra. The high priest decided to challenge the new vizier whenever he could in order to show the young man's incompetence. He had his own ideas about law, and believed that the new pharaoh needed to be informed by those who long honored their god of the underworld. He knew that Ptah was of utmost importance in the conduct of the human soul, the Ka, into the world beyond this life, and no vision of a lion with bright eyes could shake his belief.

On the next petitioner's day, the high priest and his company of brother priests entered the audience chamber to await the appearance of Pharaoh Ptolemy, and to listen with care to all the requests presented as well as to the advice Amer, the Vizier of the Law, offered. And they had set a trap. An entanglement of laws based on a fictitious situation was all they needed to confound that young man and to end his career as suddenly as it began. The high priest was ready.

As Amer left his apartment that morning he decided to take the staff he discovered in Siwa with him as a badge of authority. It came from Amun-Ra and the god had told him to use it. How to use it was the question. I'll learn in time, he thought as he walked along the quay next to the Nile until he came to his favorite place for a morning meal, with riverside tables and a canopy over all to protect customers from the sun, which was hot already. He guzzled a barley soup and followed it with beer and bread, listened to a conversation between three men at a table close by, sat in thoughtful consideration for a time, and then dashed off for the 'morning circus' as it was commonly called; the pharaoh's infrequent public judging of civil cases. This was a time-honored duty that the people expected the pharaoh to perform at least once a month, although in recent times it had become delegated to only two or three days a year.

Amer hurried into the palace for the opening of the court at the third hour of the morning. He changed from his street clothing into the official garb of the Vizier of the Law, a strange looking costume he thought, that included a large head covering and generally contributed to the 'morning circus' theme. He entered the court just before Ptolemy stepped onto the dais.

The vizier engaged in only one consultation during the first hour of the proceedings, but shortly into the second hour a contentious argument arose between two brothers the pharaoh was dealing with, and Amer was called as a legal expert. The hall was filled with people of all kinds, peasants and businessmen, wealthy and poor, and he noticed a group of priests far in the back. He was startled and looked again, carefully checking his eyes to be sure, for watching with the priests was the lion, Amun-Ra, eyes bulging and blazing as he looked solemnly toward Amer.

"Proceed, my son," Amer heard the god's voice saying, so he turned again to the pharaoh amid his confusion and tried to clear his mind. Twin brothers were arguing. Each was declaring that he was the firstborn, and that he had the right of inheritance from their father who was recently deceased. It was all the guards of Pharaoh Ptolemy could do to keep the brothers from overstepping their privilege of petitioning before the king.

"I have a sworn affidavit from our father saying I was the first," one of the young men shouted. A guard held him in check or he would have shoved it into the pharaoh's face.

"I have the authentic statement from my father," said the second. He held it up for everyone who was interested to see.

Ptolemy looked pleadingly toward Amer, who took both the papers in hand and looked them over carefully. He wanted to appear to weigh the matter well before he advised the king. He looked attentively at the young men, and then surveyed the room slowly, cautiously eyeing the crowd. He saw the lion waiting at the back of the room, his eyes were glowing faintly still, but they held less fire. He heard the voice again; "No one but you can see me now. Soon I will reveal myself to others." Amer wondered what kind of pandemonium that would create.

The vizier turned to the pharaoh and bowed. The young petitioners were quiet at last, and with carefully enunciated and dignified words Amer spoke. "This case is fraudulent, my lord." Ptolemy was startled. "How?" he demanded.

"These men are not the heirs of their father. He is living yet."

"Do you know this for a fact?"

"Yes, my lord, I do."

A strong protest arose from the two brothers, and the priests in the back went scurrying toward the door just as Amun-Ra appeared in front of the exit, apparently seen only by those who were attempting escape. He was blazing with an inner fire that caused his entire body to glow. The would-be escapees stopped in their tracks.

"Give me your evidence," Pharaoh Ptolemy said, trying to dismiss the confusion at the door.

"The man in the back, the one in the blue tunic, is the father of these twins."

The pharaoh peered across the room toward the man. "Bring that man to me!" he called from his throne.

Guards loped down through the hall, nabbed the distraught fellow and swiftly deposited him, now in a groveling position, before the king.

"Is this true?" Pharaoh demanded. "Are you the father of these petitioners?"

"No, lord, I am not!"

Amer heard the lion growl.

"He is not our father!" the twins shouted.

"I believe I can clear this up, my lord, if I may call some witnesses," Amer declared.

163

"Yes, do that! I don't want this court to become a circus."

"Bring all those priests here!" Amer called to the guards at the back. "Bring them.!"

The parade of priests moved slowly, warily, past the lion who looked into their faces with sad eyes. "Speak the truth," Amun-Ra said to them.

"May I ask these priests some questions, my lord?"

"Yes, get on with it!"

"Are you the priests of Ptah?" He spoke calmly and without rancor.

"Yes," one of them whispered. It was Olwen.

The high priest spoke then. "I am the high priest of the temple of Ptah, and I demand to know why we have been called as witnesses."

"Because you know the truth of this case," Amer said evenly. "You are also the instigator."

"How dare you - - -" the high priest started, but the lion was abruptly standing beside him, and his voice checked. The high priest knew at last that he could no longer maintain the deception. Amun- Ra could destroy them all.

"What is all this?" Ptolemy was growing impatient. He couldn't see the lion. "Clear this up immediately!"

"It is a simple case of fraud, my lord." Amer bowed toward the pharaoh. "These priests bribed the twins and their father to make a false case that could not be solved using the codes of law that are now in place. The law states that the oldest son will inherit at the death of his father, but does not foresee the kind of case that was brought here today. I am not sure why this was done, but I think it was to discredit my appointment as the Vizier of the Law."

The pharaoh paused as if to debate within his own mind, then stood, and the crowd waited in awe. A pharaoh had no need to stand except for a sentence of death. "Is this true, priest? Did you bribe these men?" The high priest could not speak, so Olwen gave testimony.

"Yes, it is true, lord."

"Do you all agree to that answer?" Under the searching eyes of the pharaoh they all nodded or in some way assented to the response, even the high priest, as the lion watched them.

"Take them all," Ptolemy said to his guards, "and lock them together in the prison-house. Keep a guard posted so they do not attack each other or make plans for further false testimony." He turned to Amer. "How did you know this, vizier?"

"When I went to a coffee house this morning, my lord, I sat across from these three," he indicated the father and his sons, "as they discussed the plans for their testimony today. I heard the entire plot laid out."

The pharaoh laughed. "You were lucky, then, vizier. But you do know how to put on a good case! As far as it goes, I would have divided the inheritance equally had it been a real case."

"You are wise, my lord," Amer said, bowing humbly toward the king. Amer didn't believe in luck.

The fate of the deceivers lay in Amer's hands. The pharaoh wanted nothing to do with them after the fiasco they had made of his court. "Punish them as you will," he told his vizier.

"I will have to be lenient. I can't impose a heavy punishment on any one of them."

"Do as you like. I have no patience for that sort of thing. They intended to harm you, but used my court to do it! I would probably send them all to the executioner."

"I will find a suitable penalty if I am to choose, my lord," Amer agreed.

Amer considered the punishments carefully. The men were staying in the prison house until he made up his mind, so he didn't want to take long. Balancing the sentences with the crimes was not easy, but he made the decision in less than two days.

The priests and their bribed victims were taken to the audience hall once again, but no audience awaited them. The pharaoh was notably absent; the lion in full view. He waited next to Amer as the youthful vizier read his decision.

The farmer and his twin sons were fined the exact amount of the bribe that had been paid to them, but were not imprisoned, which they knew was a gift. They also had to pledge never to be false witnesses again. Heavy retribution would certainly fall on them if they repeated the offense.

The priests were distressed with the logical penalty Amer set out for them. They were all exiled from Memphis forever and sent to become the lowest ranking priests of Ptah at a small temple in Rakotis, where the new city of Alexandria was building, along the shore of the Great Sea. They were also cautioned against returning to any of their criminal activities, and warned that any wrongdoings would bring the full weight of law down upon them. The session was short and Amer breathed more easily when it was completed. He had never expected to become a judge.

"You have done well," the lion said as the prisoners left the court. "You are going to be a wise magistrate." That was the last Amer ever saw or heard directly from the god, although a fiery lion often appeared in his dreams.

Chapter Nine

326 A D

The Christian disciple Mark, whose Gospel account is recorded in the Bible, came to the splendid city of Alexandria on the northern sea coast of Egypt and established a church there in the year 42 A D. It grew rapidly as the new faith took hold and advanced throughout the region. By the time of the First Ecumenical Council of Nicaea in 325 A D, the church was a place of importance in the city. The Christians were not always popular with the government, and at times they were under scrutiny from Rome, but the church prospered, not only in Alexandria but in other parts of the country as well, and many thousands of converts were added to the faith in the three hundred years from its introduction to the occasion of the Council in Nicaea, a city in the far-off northern realm of Bithynia on the Black Sea.

Astormen, a young servant of the cleric Athanasius, who was, in turn, a servant of Alexander, Bishop of Alexandria, was in attendance at that council meeting throughout the summer, and watched from his position in the gallery close behind his superior as the debates and decisions unfolded. It was sometimes hot and muggy in the church, and Astormen, as well as many of the delegates themselves, was prone to get a little sleepy in the late afternoons. Athanasius was not one of them. He was a firebrand of rhetoric, and took after his fellow delegate Arius with withering denouncements and accusations. Some of those watching felt pity for the Arians, as the followers of Arius were called, but in the end the Arians were put down by the literalists, and the doctrine of the absolute, innate deity of Jesus of Nazareth, whom they all called the Christ, was confirmed by a thunderous majority; all but two voted with Athanasius. The emperor himself stepped into the picture after the vote and banished Arius to Palestine where he was to work with the poor and needy.

On returning to Alexandria, the victorious holy men took up their administrative positions again, Alexander firmly in charge as bishop. Athanasius waited, not so much in the wings but in a pronounced place of importance, to take on the job as soon as he inherited, which would be as soon as Alexander died. Everyone loved Alexander, but Athanasius became a little impatient to take the throne and the office in the direction he wanted to go. Bishops were men of importance, and were privileged to sit on actual thrones to conduct the business of the church.

In time the situation changed; Bishop Alexander passed on to his place in the Kingdom of Heaven. His successor, it was rumored, took his office in a midnight ceremony where he was consecrated bishop before any opposition could come to the fore. To his credit, Athanasius eventually became a much revered patriarch and served the church of Alexandria as well as the whole nation of Egypt with fervent resolve and control. But not everything was under his absolute authority, he found, and despite his best efforts there were some situations that existed, having been in place for millennia, that he could not condone but could not inhibit, either.

Just before dawn on a placid morning during the season of Akhet, the time of the flood, a small group of peasant farmers approached the Great Sphinx carrying an assortment of grains and wine, ready to offer them to the god Hor-em-akhet, as they still knew him, and to proffer supplication for the success of the flood and subsequent planting and harvesting of their crops that year. They were descended from ancestors who had done this act of entreaty for as long as the chain of life had brought them to this place on a sun-drenched morning.

In the past there had been hundreds of groups coming every week to beseech the god; there were fewer these days. The new religion discouraged such things, but many still came to perform the rite as it had been done since the earliest days when Hor-em-akhet was defined as the god who blessed the flood and its subsequent results of planting and harvesting. It was a lifeline that extended from the ancients, and peasant families still followed the practice.

Astormen, whose multiple relatives were mostly peasant farmers, came with his brothers and their wives and children to offer obeisance to the great god, and the men approached the immense form that morning at the moment when the sun sprang above the horizon. The women and children waited at a discreet distance, as the lines of priests had done centuries before, while Astormen and his brothers walked slowly, with measured steps, between the long forelegs of the statue that gazed serenely above them into the light of the new sun of the morning, toward the remains of earlier sacrifices lying on the sand just below his bearded chin. The air was warm but not yet hot as it would soon become, and the men were unhurried. They wanted to do this business correctly.

"Put it here, on top of this one," Astormen's brother Hani told him. "We want to get it in the middle."

Astormen hesitated. He had no desire to cover anyone's gifts, so he put theirs just in front of the other. "I think it's better here. It doesn't really matter, I suppose." He spoke quietly to his brother.

"It's fine. Let it lie."

Some other farmers approached at that moment.

"Greetings, Aboleb," the brothers said in the same voice. "It's a good morning, isn't it?" Hani added.

"We hope. We need a good crop this year. It wasn't so good last time."

"Not for anyone. We hope for the same," Astormen answered. He turned toward the Great Sphinx and bowed. "Bless us now, Hor-em-akhet. We need a fruitful season."

All the men bowed before the god, and as they moved away between the long legs, another group arrived with an armload of offerings. They had walked out to the end, nearly past the paws of the beast when Astormen saw him. Athanasius waited there, marking on a long piece of papyrus that would eventually be rolled into a scroll. He looked up and scowled with disapproval.

"Why are you here, Astormen? Have you been bowing before this false god?"

"I have been bowing, but he is not false."

"Abomination!" shouted the bishop. "You have committed an abomination before the Lord! Your sins are great. You know the truth."

Astormen looked at him with new eyes. He had never been accused before. "I only do what is right, your grace," he spoke gently. "I have never made a claim to the Christian religion, as you well know. I am here because I am a follower of my god."

"You also know," Athanasius said severely, "that your god is false. Admit it!"

"I cannot, your grace," Astormen responded carefully. "I am a believer in the ancient religion of my people, and will not deny that."

"I will deal with you tomorrow," his superior said in a cold voice. He turned abruptly and left after marking his scroll again upon seeing another family coming to pay tribute to their god of the harvest.

"What will he do?" Hani asked.

"He'll probably lecture me and when I won't give in I'll be dismissed."

"Then you'll have to come back and work the farm with me," Hani offered more jovially. "We can work it together."

"Wait until I see what he says before I do anything else," Astormen told him.

The family left the presence of the great god and set out on a small felucca down the river. They travelled slowly, celebrating with food and drink in honor of Hor-em-akhet for the rest of the day, until they finally reached their farm near Alexandria. Astormen continued on later in the evening, walking home to his tiny room behind the church of St. Mark.

The day was bright and already hot when the assistant to the Bishop of Alexandria walked to his post the next morning to meet his fate. Bishop Athanasius was not yet in his voluminous office, many times the size of the space Astormen called home, so the assistant set about shelving a set of scrolls that were left from his last work day; records of meetings that the bishop had been reviewing. He worked his way through the entire batch but still no bishop was to be seen. Then he went to work on another project that needed his attention, the cleaning of his own desk and sorting through all the drawers to find any detritus that needed to be discarded. The bishop insisted on tidy work and workspaces, and he knew well what could happen if the hidden jumbles were found when Athanasius was looking for some other, less significant item that he needed. That was soon over; there were few unneeded items that wanted relocating or discarding.

He wandered outside to the green of the garden that opened to the sun. Astormen loved the garden, even on a hot day, and waited on a stone bench in a shady place beneath the branches of a tall tree. His mind wandered for a bit, but refocused on his current situation, and he began to speculate a little wildly about the absence of the bishop. Could he be ill? Should a doctor be notified? Could he be so angry that he refused to face his sinful assistant? Astormen had no reason to believe otherwise. Finally, in the distant gateway he saw a figure in black approaching. It had to be Athanasius, he knew the gait well; but the man's head was bowed and covered with a cowl of some sort, and he carried a long staff in his hand. He did not use it for walking, but held it carefully, almost reverently, Astormen noted, and he walked slowly as one in great sorrow or pain. The bishop came along the stone walkway and without looking up entered the door that led to his office. Astormen hurried across the garden and followed the bishop inside. He waited quietly in his little anteroom for the bishop to summon him, but all was silent and no summons came. He sat at his own desk and started to write some notes about the coming day's activities, then, feeling compelled, got up reluctantly and knocked with a small tapping on the bishop's door. He heard shuffling from the other side, and the door opened widely. Athanasius was there, distraught and red-eyed, regarding him with a drawn smile. "Astormen," he said hoarsely, "please, enter. I have had an encounter and I am not myself."

"What has happened, your grace?"

"I have been wrong." He looked toward the floor. "I am ashamed."

"How - - have you been wrong?"

"My brother Arius – I hated him."

"But he was wrong, you said."

"Yes, he was wrong, but not as wrong as I have been. I must go to him and ask forgiveness."

"Are you feeling all right, your grace? Do you need to visit a physician?"

"No. I have met a physician, and at last I am cured."

"I don't understand, your grace. When did you meet a - "

The bishop interrupted him. "All is well, my friend. I am well, also. Now. And I have no need of further treatment from a doctor, but I must go to Arius because I have sinned against him. Would you come with me, please?"

Astormen felt a surge of pity. "Yes, your grace, of course I will, but I am concerned about you."

"You need not be, my friend. And please, do not speak of me as 'your grace.' I have been anything but gracious."

"What happened to you last night, yo-. " Astormen stopped in mid-word.

"I met – well, I met – here, take this for a little while and tell me what you hear and see." He held the staff out toward Astormen, who took it into his hand. The wood felt warm, even for a hot day, but he detected no other sensation as he held it.

"It feels warm."

"Then he will not speak to you. Well, that is all I can say. I have no other explanation. Let us begin our preparations to go to Palestine. I must see Arius as soon as I can." He took the staff from his assistant and started shuffling things from a shelf in the desk. He pulled out the scroll he had been writing on the day before. "Burn this," he said quickly, "and there are more things that need to go with it."

They walked all the way to Palestine - a long, hot journey, but as they moved along day by day the bishop became lively again and smiled and laughed at everything he saw that pleased him, and there were many. He walked with the staff in his hand, using it as anyone would, to steady himself in the rough places and to push up hills, and as a brake when descending hills. Astormen had a walking stick, too, which helped him out during the long days of hiking, but it was not at all like the staff the bishop carried. Athanasius seemed to regard his staff as he would a person. They passed the borders of Egypt, where the battle with the Persians had taken place far in the past, and took shelter in the shade of a dune during the hottest time of the day when walking was difficult. They passed the heaped ruins of the old fort at Gaza, and walked on into Palestine freely. No one impeded their progress and no one questioned their movement across the land. They came to a place in the rough road where they could go to the right or left, and were told by another wanderer that the road to the right went down to Beersheba. Athanasius felt a great temptation to follow it, but turned left instead to walk through the valley that stretched from south to north across Palestine, and followed the track north past groves of oranges and pomegranates and dates, taking pleasure in the fruit they got from the local farmers.

The bishop chose a camp site every night, and they felt safe in each of them despite the desolate places where they were sometimes located. No animals or men troubled them in any way. It was an idyllic time, Astormen often thought, and he learned from the bishop as they walked along. Athanasius was a master teacher. He offered the wisdom of ancient wise men, and filled his pupil's mind with some of the best lessons the chastened man had learned.

One night in their camp the bishop asked Astormen, "I often wonder what you thought when I accosted you after you had made your offering to Hor-em-akhet."

"I was afraid of what you might do. I thought I needed the job I had in your office." Astormen spoke openly and fearlessly.

"What did you think I would do?"

"Send me away. My brother said I could work the farm with him, but that's not what I wanted to do."

"What do you want to do now?"

"To continue as I am. Your assistant."

"You can certainly do that, and more if you have the desire. I think you would make a fine deacon or even a priest one day."

"But I would have to change my religion." He paused for a moment. "I guess I've already started to do that. Just from the things that have happened since and the talks we've had along the way."

"I think you have, but it's not important to me now. Of course it would be the thing to do if you were to work in the church, but I have come to grips with the differences in religions, and no longer condemn people for their beliefs. I hope that you'll convert, but you can continue to be my assistant as long as you want to, anyway."

At last they headed into the hills, which looked small from the valley where they had been walking, but spread into huge dimensions and difficult pathways as they climbed among the stony slopes. One mid-afternoon a few days later they finally attained their destination among the rock-strewn hills and entered the holy city of Jerusalem. The city had no walls; they had been taken down long before. There were large piles of rubble lying about, but there was also new construction, and some recently laid streets ran straight into the heart of the mass of rocky remains and newer buildings. Jerusalem was in the process of rebuilding.

Bishop Athanasius began looking for Arius immediately, and after they had searched out the house where the man lived, he went in alone. Astormen waited outside in a small garden entrance. There was no sound or movement from within for a long time. He sat beside the gate, anxious, for nearly two hours before the two men emerged together.

"Please, come into my house," Arius extended his hand toward Astormen, who watched the two together with wide eyes.

"All is well, Astormen," the bishop told him. "We are reconciled."

"Come and eat with us. It is my privilege to have you both as guests." Arius spoke heartily, seeming to be glad for the company.

The house of Arius was small in comparison to the lavish palace that the bishop held in Alexandria, but the welcome was genuine and the food much better than the bread of humility they had eaten all along the trek. They devoured pheasant and some wild boar along with a rather large amount of regional wine which was as good as anything they could find in Egypt. The talk ran to the sites and beauties of Jerusalem and did not touch on the past or any theological issues. Astormen was relieved and happy.

As they left Arius that day, the two men who had been so bitterly opposed embraced each other and gave promises of meeting on the morrow for a tour of the city, especially the sites where Jesus was reported to have walked. All was mended, as far as Astormen could determine, and Athanasius seemed more good-humored than he had ever been.

The remains of the old city of Jerusalem were easily walkable if people stayed on the modern, straight streets, but getting onto the winding ways that were often interrupted by piles of rubble was difficult going. They toured with Arius for several days, always seeking some site where Jesus had walked or preached or stayed. One was the Mount of Olives, which was bordered by the Garden of Gethsemane. The garden was quiet, and overgrown with weeds. Age-old olive trees extended their twisting branches above the undergrowth, and the Mount of Olives, the opposite hillside whose lower slope was also covered with the trees, continued the grove up to the oldest cemetery in the region, the only place where the walls had not been demolished by the Romans in their destruction of the city two and a half centuries before.

Reports circulated that the emperor had plans to build a church at the site where Jesus had been crucified and buried, and Arius took them through broken streets to the area. Athanasius walked around the remnants of the garden, now small and overgrown, peered into the stony tombs that lined the bottom of a mounded hill, and as he walked he waited for insight about the death of his lord in that place, but none was forthcoming. He had to leave without the reinforcement he hoped for, but soon found it at a different site.

"I must tell you my brother, that I am a little disappointed," Athanasius spoke to Arius. "Do you find things here that cause you to believe it's the site of the Lord's passion?"

"It's a lot different now than it used to be," Arius tried to explain. "But I have never found anything here that said 'yes' or 'no' to me."

"Then I wonder why it's been noted that he was brought here to die?"

"There is an inscription somewhere down below, in a little cave, I think, that has a name on it. Some think it says 'Jesus,' but others say it's really 'Joshua.' It's hard to read, anyway. Come on down and take a look."

They moved across the abandoned garden, through an opening on the opposite side, and down some dark steps into a cave. There was no torch and very little light from the open doorway.

"Go up and get a light of some kind for us, Astormen," the bishop told him. "We want to see what's here."

The assistant climbed up the steps into daylight to find a torch, which was not easy. There was no one else around, but he followed their route back to the street and came to some old men sitting on benches outside a half-ruined house.

"A torch?" he asked in tortured Arabic. Then he tried another common language. "Lumen?" He pointed toward the entry to the garden. One of the men shuffled into the house and returned with a rather feeble flame, which Astormen accepted as he paid the out thrust palm. He returned to the cave slowly because the thing sputtered as though it could go out, but he kept it burning. Inside, the torch made a better show of the place. Athanasius grabbed it eagerly and exclaimed as he saw the name smudged in charcoal over a small opening into a tomb.

"It says Joshua, I believe. Did they call our lord by that name?"

"It's a derivative of Joshua, yes, and some people did call him that," Arius responded. "I have been told that, anyway."

173

"It's only a small opening, like they would have had to push a body in on a long board. That's not the way he was said to have been buried. He was laid on a stone shelf. This is not the place, then."

"And there's no groove for the closing stone to be rolled into place. It looks like stones were simply piled up across the opening. See these large rocks all around?" Arius was looking at the piles of rubble that were heaped against the rocky face of the tomb site. "It isn't right, is it?"

"Is there any other connection?"

"Not that I know of."

The two men looked at each other with gloomy faces. They took the torch and left the area and did not return.

Bethlehem lay a day's journey to the south of Jerusalem. The town where both King David and Jesus were born was a tiny village on the top of a hill with steep valleys descending to small, walled winter pastures that spread out below. They passed through the grubby street that was the main market place, lined with a variety of little worn out houses and shacks, to a rocky point at the edge of the hill just before it dropped into the valley. Arius guided them further, into an entrance on the far side of the rock; a low, natural door which led to a steep ramp that descended onto the floor of a cave.

"One thing sure," Astormen noted, "animals live here." The place smelled rank.

"Of course they do." The bishop was ahead of him as they peered in through the door. "All the accounts of Jesus say that he was born in a stable. Didn't you know that?"

"No, can't say I did. I haven't read them."

"If you're in this land you should read them. It would help you understand why we want to find these places."

"I will. Give me the book and show me where."

"You have no Bible of your own?" Arius asked.

"He is not yet Christian," Athanasius said.

Astormen laughed. "Not yet. Leave it to you two and I will be soon."

Astormen didn't want to go into the cave; he suffered from a fear of closed places, but he bravely followed his mentor through the door and down the ramp. There was only a little light from an oil lamp placed high in a natural niche in the wall, and it took a while to adjust to the gloom and the stench. Athanasius was enthralled. His heart told him that he had found the true birthplace of his lord, and he probed the dark corners of the cave until he found the small alcove where a moldy, dirt encrusted manger rested, half filled with hay and waiting for the cows to come feed there. As he knelt in the squalor of the place, his face took on an enchantment that

174

Astormen had never seen. Arius came to the manger and knelt beside his brother, and together they spent a time of silent contemplation on the mystery of god made flesh.

Some things did not change. Astormen stayed in a tiny room out behind the laundry shed of a guest house, while Athanasius lavished in a large suite with a balcony that overlooked the brook and the Mount of Olives on the opposite side. They did not usually take meals together, either; the bishop dining with the wealthy guests and Astormen taking a tray from the kitchen into his room. Neither man thought a thing of the situation, but Arius might have made an issue of it had he known. Things were not perfect between the two powerful theologians, but there had been such an improvement in their relationship that no one would have questioned the fact that their faith had come to the rescue, and they now regarded each other as equals.

The emperor himself had taken matters into his hand once again and cleared Arius of any wrongdoing. An ecclesiastical court would soon convene and allow the excommunicated cleric to return to his work in Alexandria and be in full communication with all his brothers. These things were all moving together at the time of Athanasius' visit to Jerusalem, and the bishop was greatly relieved that the rift had been healed. The church and the newly enlarged Diocese of Alexandria could only benefit from the renewed fellowship of all the brothers.

Time seemed to dictate that he should return to Egypt sooner than later, but Athanasius suddenly had another idea. He wanted to visit and experience all the places he could think of where Jesus had lived or preached or healed. That was a big order, but Arius set about creating an agenda for a lengthy trek across the land, starting in Jericho, not because it was a prominent place Jesus had visited, but because of the story of 'The Good Samaritan.'

Bishop Athanasius carried the staff, leaning upon it at need, throughout all his walking adventures in the land of Palestine where Christians believed that Jesus had come forth into the world, where he had died, and where he had come forth into life again. It was a story, a belief, and a foundation for whatever the bishop did, and it was his purpose to learn as much as he could about the man Jesus while he had the opportunity.

On a morning when the summer season was more than half over the three set out together, descending the long hill trail that led to the Jordan valley and the remnants of Jericho, an ancient place that figured prominently in the history of the country and the Bible. Astormen knew the 'Good Samaritan' story well; it was illustrated on Athanasius' office wall in Alexandria. A picture there, a simple drawing, depicted a poor, besieged man lying beside a path with his savior leaning over him, a look of earnest concern on his face. What he did not know was the history behind the story; one of racial tension and hypocrisy, which was the real meaning of the tale and the purpose of Jesus' lesson.

Jericho was almost tropical. Hot and arid in the afternoon sun when they arrived, green trees and verdant crops stretched along the road in the river valley, and flowers that prospered in drought were blooming in abundance around the heaps of ruins that had been a succession of towns which were all called Jericho. Everything else was watered from the flow of the tiny Jordan River. No one knew which was the earliest site among the ruins; the place where the Israelites caused the walls to fall down, and no one seemed to be concerned about it. It was all

Jericho, and it was a sweltering jungle compared to the ultra-dry heat of the surrounding uplands. They found lodgings in a large guest house that offered an ancient pool for swimming.

"It may not be as clean as you would like, but it's about the best inn here," Arius told Athanasius hesitantly.

"No matter, we need to stop somewhere, and it's better than sleeping on the ground."

"And there's a pool for swimming. Or, if you don't swim, you can cool off in it."

"Do you know about the food?"

"I think it's decent. I've never been here, but people I know tell me it's good enough."

The depth of the pool was a sickly green color with a strong odor of decay, but most of the water looked clear. They enjoyed the luxury of a cool, if pungent, bath before they went to the dining terrace for a questionable dinner relieved only by good bread and the fresh fruits of the area. None of them felt very well the next morning.

Astormen soon discovered that Arius had a habit of praying very early in the morning, sometimes before dawn. He carried a small silver cross, about five inches tall, with him everywhere. It was wrapped in a silken square of soft blue color, and he sometimes set the cross against a tree or a rock with its foot on the cloth, and knelt before it to pray. Where there was no object to lean the cross against, he laid it flat on the earth with the cloth beneath, and leaned over it as he prayed. It was not many days before Athanasius joined him at his morning prayers, both of them humbled before the cross and toward the other.

Their journey continued along the river valley where the local people pointed to several sites which were all candidates to be the place Jesus had been baptized in the Jordan River by his cousin John, and they trudged along wondering whether uncertainty would mar the entire trip.

The group soon turned inland and headed for Hebron. This was not a stop to recall an event from the life of Jesus, but for historic purposes. The cave of the patriarchs was located in Hebron, and both the bishop and Arius wanted to see it.

The cave was a great surprise. It was surrounded by an immense stone wall, four to six feet deep on every side, and sufficiently tall to discourage any would be invaders had it been a fortress. The wall was erected by Herod The Great, as he called himself, King of Judea, and protected the holy shrine of the tombs of the patriarchs. It was watched over by local families who were a kind of honor guard for the patriarchs buried there, although the families were Arab, not Jewish. They would not permit the Egyptian men to enter until Athanasius pulled some coins from his purse, 'sufficient to pay for several nights' lodging,' he later said. Then they were given the finest treatment money could buy from a boy who proclaimed himself their guide.

The cave was a complex of two chambers, one just below the other, and was difficult to get into. A single trap-door in the floor inside the walls opened to the first, and from that a narrow hole in the bottom dropped into the second. To get to the lower level, a ladder was let down into a moldy space that smelled of ancient decay, where some old bones were lying in a rectangular stone enclosure in the far corner. That was all, but it was significant for the two men who went inside. Astormen declined. He had no desire to go into such a place again. He had not seen past the trap-door, but thought that inside the cave it would be difficult to get a decent breath of air, so he gladly waited outside under the limited shade of a half dead tree until the others completed their visit.

Athanasius took a torch from his guide as he descended. Arius followed, and then the boy guide came last. He didn't really like going down into the tomb, but his father had told him he must do it, anyway.

"How many are supposed to be buried here?" Athanasius wanted to know.

Arius answered, "Well, there's Abraham and his wife Sarah, and their son Isaac and his wife Rebecca, then Jacob, along with Esau and their wives – all the patriarchs of Judaism. And a lot of people think there are more, but I don't know. And it doesn't seem a good idea to ask. He wouldn't know, either." He gestured toward the guide.

"So at least eight?"

"Yes, eight or more."

"Not really that many bones."

"Some have probably decayed completely. It was long ago," Arius responded.

"How did they happen to be buried here?"

"You must know your New Testament better than the books of Moses! Abraham bought this cave, and there was a field above it. He bought it all. It was the only land he ever bought that we know of."

"That's good planning. Like the pharaoh's. To get ready for eternity."

"Actually, he bought it for Sarah when she died. He lived a long time after that. They used it for a family crypt. A lot like today."

"Now they're all in there together," Athanasius shook his head and smiled. He recalled that Sarah, especially, had been a difficult woman.

"Until the end of the world. Then they go on to their reward."

"Most religions have that in common."

"Yes, but most don't have to depend on god's grace to get to heaven. They try to do the right things to earn it."

"Well, we know that Christians are different. You and I have shown them that."

"Maybe we haven't shown them our best, though. We had a terrible row, you remember." Arius frowned at the thought. "That's all over now. It is for me, and for you, too."

"Yes, it's all in the past. Let's leave it there."

They climbed out of the tomb slowly, almost regretfully. In the presence of such giants of faith they had confirmed their reconciliation.

The Galilee was a region of peace and beauty. So many events from the story of Jesus in the Bible had taken place there that they could hardly find all the locations. Arius, who seemed to know even more about the life of Jesus than Athanasius, led the way.

They decided to tackle the places rather than the chronological accounts and thus avoid repeated crossings of the same landscapes, but the starting point for either would have to be Nazareth, the town where the Virgin Mary first encountered the Angel Gabriel, who told her that she was to be the mother of the son of god. They agreed on that point, so Nazareth was the first objective in their path across the district. It was a town that reminded Astormen of Bethlehem, but enlarged and at times nearly overrun by crowds. The market area was dingy, a mass of dirty canopies with withering vegetables and barely surviving poultry for sale beneath them, along with various fabrics and household items. It was depressing, Astormen thought, when compared to the fine items of every kind that were available in Alexandria. His idea of the world at large was that nothing compared favorably with his own city, and for the portion of the world he had seen, he was quite right.

The people of Nazareth, as in the rest of the Galilee, were not Christian. They knew a profitable thing when they discovered it, nonetheless, and during the past century a fine business had developed serving the Christians who came to the town seeking information about Mary and the place where she lived at the time of the announcement, as well as Joseph and his carpenter shop and the house where Jesus grew up 'in favor with god and man.' It did not take them long to set up a trail for visitors to follow, led by guides who received handsome rewards for taking pilgrims to the holy sites. It was a good business, and there was no concern about the fact that different guides selected different sites for all the early events in Jesus' life, but a gradual consensus developed over time due to the fact that the visitors compared notes with each other and were angered when they had been led to diverse dwellings posing as the place where Mary lived at the time of her conversation with the Angel Gabriel.

When Bishop Athanasius, along with Astormen and Arius visited, however, there was not yet a consensus among the guides, and the bishop was especially distressed to find that he had been taken to the carpenter shop cum residence of Joseph, the place where Jesus had lived as a child, which were different houses visited on different days where he was led by different guides.

"It's a treachery," he fumed to Arius. "How can we or anyone else believe what they tell us? How do we know that this is even Nazareth? It could be any town."

"There must be a way to find the true sites," Arius responded. "We just have to be patient."

"You're right, of course," the bishop replied. "We must ask more questions and try to find an honest man among them."

They found one, an honest man who told them that no one had any idea where the holy places venerated by Christians were located. "It would make it much easier if we knew," he conceded.

"Don't you have records? Were there no titles written to indicate who owned the houses and buildings? What about looking into those."

The man answered truthfully. "Your world is very different to ours," he said. "If no one has claim to a piece of land by living there, it's available for the taking."

"There are no rules, then? How does property pass from one to another?"

"It doesn't really matter to us. Usually it's by inheritance. The oldest son always inherits the house his father lived in. It is our way. But when it's land that's never been occupied, you can claim it for yourself if you want to."

"How can you claim it?"

"You build a house on it and live there. We always honor that."

"Can a man sell a house or land?"

"He can, but it's a private arrangement, and might not hold if someone should inherit the property. Even if it was bought years before."

They left Nazareth, if it were really Nazareth, and walked thoughtfully across the Galilee toward the great lake in the west, called 'The Sea of Galilee' in the Bible, but named variously Kinneret or Gennesaret by the native population. It was a place of beautiful, brilliant skies above the blue water that could often become seriously disrupted by wind in stormy weather. There were hills in the distance, and mountains beyond them, shaded in blues and grays with white on the tops in the coolest season. The lake was the source of the River Jordan, which flowed through a deep cleft in the land southward into the far-off Dead Sea, a place of desolation surrounded by desert.

Athanasius had to imagine the Dead Sea, but it was not difficult since he had seen the Jordan in the desert near Jericho, and soon he was happily rereading the Bible passages he had brought to study at their source; the sermon on the mount, the feeding of the thousands, as he preferred to think of it, and the account of Jesus in the storm on the sea, as well as other timeless and wonderful stories of the miraculous events in the life of the son of god, and he was content. Arius read them too, and if he did not feel exactly the same as Athanasius, he did not say. It was far better to allow the past with all its pain to slip away, and to become a new creation once again, reborn in the love of the church as well as the fellowship of the bishop. There was nothing profitable in allowing the old fight to continue, although in their own hearts both men held tenaciously to their original positions. Compromise in public became the order of the new day.

Sunshine flooded their road for the return to Jerusalem. The days were getting a little shorter, and the cooler weather had begun to set in, but mid-day was still hot as they walked down the long path from the Galilee to Jerusalem. There was a lot to see that they hadn't noticed before, side trips to hill towns or the flat topped mounds which held millennia of information about the past and would become archaeological 'digs' in the future.

One day they stopped in a tiny village near the road and went to the well for water. Arius looked around for a short time, gazing at the small, dusty hovels scattered nearby, and turned to the others with a smile.

"I think this is the village where Jesus talked to the woman who was getting water from the well."

"He asked her for a drink and then gave her what he called 'living water.' An unexpected encounter, but he spoke to her plainly about himself," Athanasius recalled.

"She was considered a loose woman by her neighbors. You remember what he said to her?" Arius responded.

"Yes, to tell her husband, and then when she said she didn't have one, he told her that she was truthful. He didn't condemn her."

"No, he didn't. He told her that he knew her well. That was what got her attention."

"You're probably right. Sometimes I wish I really understood everything he meant. Some things are puzzling. Like that woman."

"It all depends. Jesus didn't want to hurt her, he only wanted to show her who he was. And she seemed happy about that."

"Maybe he told her other things, too."

"Whatever he said, it caused her to think."

"And all the town. She told everybody. I think that was important."

"Do you think it was only a story?"

"I have never known what to think about the things he said or did, or the stories he told. Sometimes I can't tell truth and stories apart. He was unpredictable."

"Of course he was."

Astormen couldn't follow the flow of the conversation very well. He determined that he needed to study this book if he were to travel with the bishop or meet with people who discussed such things.

Everything that surrounded them as they walked toward Jerusalem was of interest and consumed a lot of time, but the wanderers eventually entered the holy city from the north, and found their way through the narrow old streets to the house of Arius. Astormen and Athanasius left him there, with long good-byes and sincere wishes for reuniting soon in Alexandria, and went on their way. All was well, Athanasius felt within his own heart as he led the way down through the hills and into the long valley, headed south for home. They camped for the first night beneath two picturesque pomegranate trees along the side of the pathway.

"I know it's a big question, but what do you think you learned on this trek?" Athanasius asked Astormen after they had eaten a meal finished off with a hearty drink of local spirits.

"Oh, I can't say all the things," Astormen responded. "There's so much. Like a new world."

"Have you thought any more about converting?" the bishop asked.

"No, I can't do that. You tell me there's one god. I believe you. But if god is one, then why do we have to replace his name with another? I think god understands my question."

"You really have learned, Astormen, and you are wiser than many men of ancient years. Yet you still have questions. So do I. It's the human condition. I can only tell you that I don't know very many answers. God alone can give you that. In time you will know. God hasn't spoken to me directly on this journey, but has been with me all the time. I am the one who has learned the most." Athanasius unconsciously pulled the staff closer.

"What you have learned, bishop?"

"Ah, yes. I have baited you, and you ask, but I'm not sure I can answer fully. I still have to find out so much more." He paused and prodded the fire. "But this I do know; I'm not a good man. I never was and I never will be. It is only god who is good. But I'm no longer an imposter. I was before. I thought I was doing everything right, but it was all wrong. I'll always hold you in high esteem, as I know god does, because you are a child of the one god. And that is true for my brother Arius as well. He is the man I thought was wrong, but he was not as much as I. Now I know it, and god knows that I know it, and we are happily involved in the process of changing me so I can think more like a Christian should. I don't know how to say it more plainly."

It was plain enough.

Chapter Ten

1384 A D

Arabic is a language of utter beauty; the sounds of its words easily lend themselves to poetic articulation. Natives to the language praise the virtues of their vernacular as a vehicle for lyrical expression, and much has been said about the lilting verse of original Arabic cantos and quatrains. Sadly, that expression is lost when translated into other languages. The flow of words is important to the rhythm of patterns and phrases as they fall on the ear; Arabic has one of the most mellifluous sound sequences of any language of the world. Not only is the language known for its sonority, but form is one of its foremost attractions. The shapes of the letters, their curvaceous lines flowing from right to left, are the artful patterns that provide a great splendor to the idiom. Changes in stylization have become evident over time, but classic shapes of the Arabic alphabet are still the most predominant expressions of the art of its calligraphy. Arabic is stunning in written form.

Both writing and worthy writers are raised to a high level of prominence within the Arabic world, and the styles used are often expressions of the mystery and exoticism of their language. There are many illiterate people in the Middle East, but even though they cannot communicate through written words, they have an affinity to language that is unusual, and the *fellahin* of Egypt are often able to speak and understand words and phrases of many diverse languages as they have need. Literature of all kinds has long been a source of pride and dignity in a place where pride and dignity had some of its deepest origins among humanity; where the ageless monuments reveal the glories of the past, and truth and beauty are still reflected from them.

History, in all its amazing facets, has also been an important study in the land where, among few others, the written record of the world had its beginnings. One of the greatest of the early historians, and an artist of Arabic language expression, was Tariq al Maqira, born in 1374, who recorded events of the period of the Egyptian past known as the Fatmid era.

"This is the mosque of your ancestor al Maqira, you know," his father told him as they removed their shoes near the grandly beautiful entrance door. Tariq was ten years old. "You must go carefully when you enter this place."

The boy looked up with a sincere face. "I will, Father," he said without a smile. "I didn't know that this al Maqira was an ancestor. Who is he?"

"A grandfather from long ago, and his memory still lives in Egypt."

Al Maqira was among the first *caliphs*, the Fatmid title for ruler, to be born in Egypt. He succeeded his father at age fourteen near the end of the first millennium of the Christian era, about the four hundredth year of the foundation of Islam. He had a highly irregular caliphate according to popular understanding, and the tremendous mosque built in his honor was not completed until many years after his strange disappearance. No one, except his assassin, ever knew what happened to him. He rode away on a donkey into the Muqattam Hills to the east of Cairo and was not seen again, but his bloody cloak was found soon after.

"I've learned about him in the school," the boy spoke as in a dream. "He has the same name, but I didn't know he was an ancestor." Many Arabic names of the mighty as well as the lowly are the same.

"That is only for us to speak about together. You have no need to tell anyone else."

"Yes, I will remember that," the boy answered. He knew that he had received an instruction.

"Get yourself washed now. It is prayer time."

The boy hurried to do as he was told.

Tariq al Dah ibn Ali ibn Amr al Farid ibn Muhammad al Maqira, the full name of the boy, studied at an Islamic school of law in Cairo – a school that extended from early education through university level - and eventually became a historian of renown as well as a Muslim preacher. He used the power of language in his oratory and his writing. He finally became known primarily for his interest in the Fatmid era, the era when the infamous al Maqira was caliph for a few years. He also wrote a continuing history of Egypt from the beginning of its Islamic past up to his own time.

It was early morning and the school day was opening. The master entered to greet his students and stood at the front on his own dais. "Good morning, men," he said to them all, although some were only boys. "You have need to think wisely today. I will lead you in a discussion regarding the social implications of the late Fatmid Caliphs, as well as educational and scientific advances during those times. Be sure to mention the caliph and the specific dates of his rule as you respond. That discussion will take place after the prayers. Study the writings well until that time."

The room settled into quiet thought, each student going through his collected notes, each attempting to put a well-presented question for the professor together before the allotted time expired. Although they were told that they would be examined, they all knew their learned teacher sought questions; excellent questions that indicated their interest and ability regarding the subject at hand. No one intended to be placed in the awkward position of failing to live up to expectations.

Tariq, at age fourteen, was in the middle of the class age-range, and had a terrible fear that he would never measure up to the requirements of this teacher, ibn Katab. He had been taught by his own grandfather and the finest scholars of Islam at the time, but this man challenged him as no other had done. Tariq moved through his lessons and found a specific question he wanted to pose and set out to write it with all the erudition he could muster. He had no idea that all the young men in his class were fearful that he, one of the younger and least experienced, should outperform them all.

The pattern of days flew by with only small conflicts, but Tariq felt them all as though they were an end to themselves, and he strove toward perfection as only he knew how. His reputation as a scholar developed and went before him as he honed his mind and body to accomplish his goal. He simply wanted to be the best. Tariq completed his studies for the year with an exemplary promotion, and he set out to start his education again as though it were a new beginning at the next term.

Although he participated in athletic events and other activities designed to keep his mind sharp and clear, he was primarily a student, striving with all the intellect he owned to gain a new understanding of his religion and the world around him. Religion was always the major focus of education, and he thoughtfully considered his duty to Allah all the while he studied Koran and history and sciences. While the European world lingered at the end of the Dark Ages, learning had awakened in Egypt - had erupted actually - and it was the center and the motivation of every young man who had the opportunity to study and become an important part of his mosque and, therefore, his society. Religion was at the heart of life for everyone.

"I think a trip to Alexandria and Tanta would be in order," Al Dah, Tariq's father, told him one evening as they ate their meal together. The women were not present, as was the custom. "I have business to attend to there, and you should come with me. It is time you stepped into the world around you and learned from life."

Tariq's heart fluttered. "I would love to go," he said, but he had misgivings. How would he continue his regimen of study if he took an extended time from books?

"Excellent!" his father answered. "We will leave in two days' time."

"Father, I need to take some books along, if that is alright. I don't want to get behind on my reading."

"Yes, yes, of course. Bring them." Al Dah was a little impatient. He thought Tariq spent too much time with books. He favored education, but saw the boy getting into deeper and deeper study without much else in his life. It had become a problem.

"When will we return?"

"I'm not sure, but I think within six days. Do you have something else that you need to do?"

"No, but I don't want to be gone too long. I'll have to work harder to catch up, I think."

"Catch up with your reading?"

"Yes. There's a lot."

His father didn't know how to respond. He didn't want to tell the boy to stop studying so much, but he was concerned about the books for many reasons. He wanted Tariq to be a whole person, not only a scholar. But for the present he decided to let it go.

"I'll get you back soon enough, you can be sure," he said jovially and turned to his meat.

Alexandria was a different city to what it had been in the days of the Ptolemy's. A gigantic earthquake in the distant past had sent the palaces and temples and even the great library remains, which had already been destroyed by fire in Roman times, into the sea. The lighthouse called Pharos, one of the seven wonders of the world, had taken the plunge as well, and now a smooth sandy beach with scattered buildings along the quay and a large mosque toward the west end were the structures that rose along the waterfront. Nothing of the grandeur of ancient Alexandria remained, but there were shipyards and large warehouses, and commerce flowed along the streets and alleyways of the neighborhood.

It was business that brought Al Dah to the city, but pleasure waited there as well. The gambling halls and taverns were well known, and were frequented by most men, Muslim or not, who took a few days for business there. Pleasures of another kind; the flesh palaces of Alex, were legendary - at least by reputation - to almost every man in Egypt, and were gossiped about by the women as well. Al Dah had no intention of taking Tariq to that kind of establishment, but he was sure that Tariq knew what was available, and should the boy show an interest? Who could say? He smiled to himself when he thought of that possibility. He would certainly need to feign surprised concern if the boy should ask any questions.

Tariq went with his father to the first round of business meetings; discussions about his trading enterprise and the expected revenues for the coming months, and they went faithfully to the mosque that sat beside the waterfront for prayers. It was a large, rotund structure with hanging lamps and colorful carpets laid out on the cold marble floors. It was a palace of sorts, a place to meet and greet Allah and to spend a few minutes or hours of friendly conversations with the men of the city who were much more worldly-wise than the men of Cairo seemed. But Tariq missed the college and the amazing lessons he always encountered there, as well as the connections with brilliant students and teachers. Academia was his great love, and he longed for the stimulation of ideas he exchanged with everyone at the school, which he thought of as his 'business.'

Tariq was twenty-two when he first met his life's challenge. He had long been a part of the Hanafi school of thought regarding the Muslim religion; a more liberal and arguably more reasonable reflection of Islam than the other three major schools under that religious umbrella. Tariq accepted the ideals of his school with ease. He had grown up under the shadow of protection that religion afforded him, and he was wholly convinced regarding its statutes and tenets. He had no idea, despite his intellect, what the rest of the world outside his own thought. It came as a shock.

The day was hot and fine. No clouds of any kind obscured his contemplations, and Tariq was happy. He was soon to be married to a girl he had never seen, but his father assured him that she was a beauty, and his thoughts were toward her that morning. He went down to the khan to buy a suitable gift for his bride, one he would give her on their wedding day after they had escaped the celebration and could be alone and express their love for each other in any way they chose. Privacy was always hard to come by, but he had secured an apartment for himself and his bride from his father; an addition to the family house where he had lived all his life, and she would come and adorn it with her presence and her beauty. He could hardly wait. The days seemed to creep along as he anticipated his future, which to such a great extent involved the as yet unseen woman who would be his own.

The khan was swarming; people pushing against each other in the narrowest of passages that led to tiny shops and their numerous so-called bargains. Tariq was seeking a jewel of some kind, hopefully a pearl pendant, but he wasn't sure that his money would go that far. He would have to negotiate industriously; a common rule of shopping anywhere in the Arab world. He turned down an alleyway that was empty except for an old man, most likely a beggar, who sat along one side with a few trinkets to sell. He walked swiftly, avoiding the man, but just as he was past, the old man called his name.

"Tariq," he asked in a full but gentle voice, "Why are you in such a hurry? Do you not want to see what I have to offer?"

Tariq turned to face the man. He was obviously aged, but his face was unlined and he smiled with the warmth of a sunrise on a cold morning. "I think I have just the thing, and I will let it go for a very good price," the beggar said.

"Do I know you, Father?" Tariq asked. "I apologize for hurrying by so quickly." He gazed at the man, who returned his stare, and Tariq thought he saw a spark of light in his eyes. "Yes, you know me, but by a different name. But let me show you this!" He held a gleaming pearl set in rich gold, many sizes larger that Tariq had ever seen. "I took it myself, from a very large oyster," the old man chuckled at the thought. "He did not want to let it go, but finally he gave in."

"What do you want for that?" Tariq asked in bewilderment – or possibly enchantment.

"Simply put, You!" The man said.

"What do you mean?"

"I want you to speak for me. Now and in future days."

"What am I to say for you, Father?"

"Write the words I want you to record. That's all. They will be different depending on the situation."

"I'm sorry but I don't understand what you mean."

"You are right. You do not understand, but you will soon enough. For now, let me tell you something. You will not need this pearl. The woman you have succeeded in winning is gone. I am sorry, but that is how things happen sometimes. Her father will tell yours all about it soon."

187

"Gone? Where?"

"She has died. She was never very well, a fact her father concealed from yours, but she has gone now, and is resting. You no longer have need of this pearl, do you?"

Tariq was confused and grieved at the same time. Finally he said, "Why should I believe you?"

"Because I speak the truth. But I do have a present for you. Come take it. That will convince you."

Tariq felt both a reluctance and a compulsion to accept any gift, but he stepped forward. The strange man leaned toward the wall and pulled on a long, lean stick. He held it out and Tariq accepted the offering. He had no idea how to think or react. The staff felt smooth and warm to the touch; somehow it comforted him. It was only a moment before that he had been bereft, but now he found a new purpose and power growing in his mind. He was also torn by the conflicting feelings.

"Now go home and meet your father," the man said, "but do not tell him what I have told you. Wait for him to get the message first. And you will soon be rewarded with a different wife. One who is not ill. She will be the woman you want. Go now." The man's eyes glowed as he spoke.

Tariq stumbled away, astounded by the chance meeting, carrying the astonishing staff of Amun-Ra which buzzed slightly in his hand. There were no pictures or voices that came from it, but it offered him consolation. The brief contact with the old man had started simply, but his mind groped to find a rational explanation for the gravity of the entire event. He didn't know how he should perceive it.

Tariq started dreaming. At first he thought the dreams were caused by the jinn, evil spirits who were thought to bring nightmares, but the dreams were not bad. They told him mostly of the past but sometimes of the future, usually in small, apparently unimportant situations. The first, which was prophetic, came soon after he was in possession of the staff. He was alone on a road in the countryside in the dark of night. He took a turn in the road and saw a small cottage that seemed to wait for him a short distance away, and walked toward it expectantly. There was a lamp burning inside, and a shuttered window kept out the night, but he could see through the walls and found a sleeping child there, along with a wakeful young woman who was expecting him to enter. It was peaceful, charming, and very puzzling. He felt that it was a true-life cameo, and that he would someday come upon it in reality.

Weeks later Tariq went to the khan again. He walked down the alleyway looking for the unknown stranger who had gifted him with the mighty staff, but the place where he had been was empty. Tariq paused there, sensing a residual presence from the man, and moved his sandaled toe idly along the dusty wall. He caught something on his foot and leaned down to pull it out of a crevice. It was the pearl, as large and luminous as it was before, and it seemed to smile at him from its golden chain. He put it in his pocket and the final sadness of his loss left his mind.

"I have found another wife for you," Al Dah told him a few weeks later. "She isn't sick. I told her father that if she didn't pass your mother's inspection you would never marry her!"

"Thank you, Father," Tariq inclined his head respectfully. "I appreciate your effort on my behalf."

"It is my pleasure, Tariq. You have always done the right thing and made me proud."

"When will this wedding be, Father? I'm involved in classes right now, so if it can be held after two months, that would be best for me."

"Yes, I told him that. She'll keep, Tariq. She has to get herself ready, anyway."

"Do you know anything about her?"

"First, she's not sick. I made sure of that. And she's a pretty thing, her father says, but you know how that is." Al Dah added. "I told him you were strong and good–looking, but I spoke the truth, of course." He offered a wide grin.

"They say I look like you," his son replied.

"So you do, my boy. And I am proud. He also said she would be a dutiful wife. That seemed important to him. Anyway, your mother will find out everything."

Tariq married a few weeks later, and although she was no beauty he was earnestly fond of his wife, and even respectful of her wishes, which was an unusual mark for a man in Egypt at that time and for many centuries to come. They got on well from the start.

He lived in the apartment of his father's house with his wife, and she shared the common kitchen and the household duties with Tariq's mother and sister. It was difficult for Bapset, the new wife, for a time; her mother-in-law, although she had approved, was not a kind or considerate woman, but it all sorted out for the better when Tariq took a position in a small town in the river-delta and left Cairo to live in a cottage in the country on a tiny rivulet of the Nile that flowed past the door. The place was very old, but had been cleaned and washed with a white lime solution, and stone tiles had replaced the dirt floors. It was near Tanis where Tariq had a teaching post at a new college. Soon after they settled in the cottage, Bapset gave birth to his first child, a daughter he called Amina, a name that was honored in Islam. He was fascinated by the tiny one, his own precious child, and often sat up late to watch her as she slept and even held her at times until she fell asleep. He was smitten with the baby, and his heart was filled with joy whenever he looked upon her. Usually fathers paid little attention to daughters, reserving their devotion for sons, but Tariq had only his daughter, the beautiful child of his body and his heart. He could do nothing but love her without reservation, and in the process developed a deeper admiration for his wife as well. Their cottage was filled with the blessings of Allah.

One night as he returned home late from the college, his prophetic dream began in reality. He could see Bapset and Amina waiting for him as his heart thumped with the realization that he had been given the gift of clairvoyance and might become a seer who could look into the past and the future. He did not want that particular gift; it would set him too far apart from others if he ever told anyone about it. He had no idea what was actually in store for him.

Soon Tariq could no longer keep up with his visions. He wanted to record them for his own reference, but could never quite begin. He saw both the past and the future, and at times he couldn't differentiate between the two. He watched people visiting and working and playing and sinning from his vantage point as an all-seeing observer, and felt at times that he had somehow connected with the mind of Allah. It was both captivating and alarming. He saw the everyday life of the people, usually nothing spectacular, just the simple conversations and events that were common to all, but sometimes he looked beyond the mundane into situations that were not at all commonplace. Magnificent or deadly, dismal or exotic, he witnessed so much that he often lived in the world of his visions and had to pull himself back into his own life and pursuits. He managed, somehow, to teach effectively, but often wondered how long he could carry on.

Amina was a constant in what Tariq thought of as his chaotic existence, although she also changed and grew rapidly. He was aware of her as his own child as well as an ideal she represented; the new woman of a new age. He was her companion and friend and father; his intention was that she would have the best life he could offer. She was actually rather ordinary in most aspects, but blossomed as other female children never were given opportunity due to the devoted attentions of her father. It was at this point that Amun-Ra came to speak to him again.

Tariq walked to his school along a canal that joined two streams of the Nile, and one morning as he walked he caught up with an old man who leaned on a short walking stick as he stumbled along. Tariq greeted him politely.

"Good morning, Father. I hope you are well today."

"Never better," the man responded with a toss of his head. "I hope you are ready to talk to me again."

Tariq heard the voice and knew who was speaking. "My lord, I am honored."

"Walk with me now, and we can share some thoughts."

They walked slowly to accommodate the apparent age of his companion, although Tariq knew the old man could move much faster than anyone else if he chose to do it.

"I am concerned about your lack of motivation to write the things you see. You say you can do that, but so far you have done nothing."

"Do you want me to write it all down? That would be a big job."

"Not all, but the things you think might be important in the future. You can decide."

"I wouldn't know where to begin."

"You begin by beginning. It is really quite simple."

"It is said that the greatest books begin with the first word. Is that what you mean?"

"If that is what you think it is, then yes. You must start somewhere."

"I will do it, if that is required, but how will I find the time with my work and family?"

"Just a little time each day will be fine. You can work out a schedule."

"Why do you want me to do this?"

"For your good, certainly not for mine. I understand it all rather well. And for the help of those in the future who will read what you write. You are chosen for the task. Are you capable of doing it?"

"I'd like to think that I am. I'm a man of letters who is schooled in writing and thinking."

"Do not write the classical way. Use your heart, Tariq. Use your heart. It will be more useful for everyone."

"I might have some difficulty writing the way you seem to want."

"Do not be an ass! Let it flow from your pen. It will. I am sure of it. You have the right kind of mind for such a task, so do not keep asking these questions. You know very well what I mean. But you let your learning get in the way sometimes."

Tariq was silent.

"Come now, son. Why are you offended?"

"I'm not offended. I just don't understand very well."

"When you start, let go of yourself and follow your imagination."

"Are you planning to write through me?"

"No! Most emphatically, No! I have written nothing myself. Men have done it all in my place, and they have done a decent job. I coach them once in a while. That is all."

That night Tariq found time to begin his work after Amina was in bed. He set out the papyrus sheets and a stylus and a cup of ink, then stared at the blank sheet for a short time. An idea came, and he began to mark it down. The work expanded. Before an hour was up he had a few pages of neatly written words describing early events in the life of the city of Cairo, called al Qahira, the new capital of the Fatmid Empire in Egypt.

'The Fatmid Empire invaded the land of Egypt in the year 539 of the Islamic calendar, settling their capital in the new city of al Qahira, which they started to build that same year. The Fatmids originated in Tunisia, a country that lay to the west of the ancient land of Kmet, now called Egypt, after the native Berber population of Tunisia had converted to Islam. They were ruled at first from their original capital city of Mahdia, but as soon as the new city in Egypt was ready, the government for the entire empire was relocated; the caliph, al Muizz, being their leader in this entire project.

The ancient Berber people of Tunisia and Algeria were the basis for the empire, which was named 'Fatmid' after a daughter of the prophet named Fatima, or in the Arabic, Fatimiyyun. They walked into Egypt without serious battle and took the government by the force of their presence, wresting it from former invaders who held a loose power over the land. Islam rapidly became the major religion, although Hebrews,

Christians and followers of the old pharonic religion were accepted as equals by the Fatmids. It was a time of harmony and prosperity.

The Fatmids loved beauty, and arts flourished during their years. Architecture was a main focus; they had a new city to build, and it was constructed with the best that they could get, using quarried stones that they 'found' at various sites in the countryside; much of it had been part of older temples and structures. It is said that some of the new buildings were made of the limestone coverings of the pyramids, work forces 'mining' the stone as it was needed.

The most notable Fatmid buildings in Cairo were the university, al Azhar, and the mosque that was named for al Maqira, a great leader. Their designs were artful and encompassed the splendor of the east in their form. Interiors were decorated with Arabic calligraphy of Qaranic verse and scrolling designs that are common in eastern art, which purposefully makes no reference to any living creature.

Al Aziz, the vizier of the caliph, was surrounded by men he almost trusted to carry out the caliph's wishes for the empire, and he himself supervised much of the construction and other aspects of the new city. He usually rode a small donkey, much to the amusement of people who observed his movements. He was tall, and the donkey seemed too small for such a passenger. His long legs extended straight out on boards beyond the donkey's head, so the two made an engaging, comical appearance as they waddled through the construction sites. No one dared to laugh, of course.'

At this point Tariq stopped his work and went off to sleep, leaving the newly scripted papyrus on his table beneath a covering so it would remain undisturbed.

On his return after school the next day, however, he found that it had been tampered with. A short, rather cryptic note lay atop the few pages he had written. "Make it live," the note read. "Do not write only the facts; make it human. The end is better. The tall man on the little donkey is worth reading."

Tariq looked at the message, knowing its source, but never once considered that, except for the marks on the staff, it was the only known specimen of the writing of the creator god, Amun-Ra, or that it should be preserved as a relic for his temple. He smiled at the critique and started to rewrite his history.

Every writer has a style, and Tariq soon developed one. He wasn't unduly proud of what he did, but he knew that it was no longer the kind of history he had read as a schoolboy. He filled his works with descriptive thoughts and passages, most of which he had seen in his visions. They flowed easily, and he produced large numbers of pages every week. He was never sure that his writing was skillful, but Amun-Ra didn't make further critiques, so Tariq believed he was on the right track.

Most often he wrote about the common man of the Fatmid era which had ended only two centuries in the past. He watched the lives of the viziers and the caliphs with the same interest he had for the less lofty folk, and reported on what he observed with the same style. He could not write about everything, there was far too much, so he selected the events and the ceremonies - the simple suppers in a cottage or the lavish noon-time feasts of caliphs - from all the things he visualized. They were all fair game for his commentary, and he loved them all. They were like his own family, his children, he thought and observed, and eventually came to realize that he saw them in much the same way that Amun-Ra must see, and became increasingly unsure as to why he was given this 'special' vision. He wrote a short letter to Amun-Ra and left it among his other work. It was answered immediately.

"You have been given disambiguation, or second-sight as some call it, for a reason. There is a need for the world to know its history, and you will set an example for other historians who follow. Your style and descriptions are your own, but they please me, and I am content with the work you are doing. If you have further need, write to me again."

Tariq was thrilled with what he understood to be warm praise.

The historian tried to arrange the work into time periods or some other form to bring order from chaos, but the visions were too random for effective organization, so he discontinued any sort of time-orientation and wrote what he saw and learned day by day. At first there was no apparent structure to the flow of words and ideas, but after a time it started to take shape in some indefinable way, to flow from an unknown mind to his mind, and the subject of the material became its structural element. For over a year the images dealt with religious government and its often ruthless pursuits of citizens someone believed should come under controls from a pious force. Men who were guilty of crimes against religion, although that rarely happened, could be subjected to punishments that included fines, imprisonment, forced divorces from wives and loss of their children, or death. The children were then placed under the care of a brother or father or uncle who would attend to their bringing up as faithful Muslims of the 'right' sort. Those strictures tended to keep all the people faithful in their duties to Allah and toward each other. After watching scene after scene of the religious police taking action against individuals, Tariq wondered how the punishments meted out could possibly remedy the situation. It seemed to him that no one had any choices when it came to religious observance, and he also wondered why he had been subjected to such a barrage of that kind of scenario. He sent another note to Amun-Ra. In response, the god wrote:

"It is true that men have made the worship of god into a thing of duty rather than one of respect and loyalty. How can a man truly honor a god to whom he is forced to pay obeisance by other men? Properly acknowledging god is unlike any other matter. A man must do it from his own heart."

Tariq wrote that statement along with other comments as he weighed the nature of worship alongside human nature and found the best combination of natures to be a person who was indeed willing, even eager, to perform the acts that venerated god in his daily life. No one could do it for him, not even through threats and punishments. True worship of god came from within each man, not from any external source. God himself could not demand to be worshipped, he declared in his conclusion.

The next spate of visions seemed to relate to the qualities of 'neighborliness; the care and keeping of neighbors and friends, in addition to family. The images all pointed toward relationships of that kind, and sparked an interest in Tariq that he had never known: how could he relate to people he scarcely knew but had seen on the streets for years? He wondered why the great god was concerned about this aspect of human interaction, and sent another letter to ask that question.

The next afternoon, just after Tariq had returned from the school, Bapset came to him in agitation. "I was just looking out to the street through the mashrabiya screen, and I saw a stranger near the gate. Somehow he saw me there and asked for you!"

"Let me go to find out who he is," Tariq responded. "Don't be afraid, Bapset." He had a good idea who it was. The man was Amun-Ra. "I came to see you to answer your letter," he explained. "Let us talk inside."

"You are most welcome, my lord. My wife is a little frightened, so please allow me tell her that she should take Amina and go into her private room."

"Of course," the great god replied.

Tariq went into the house, then returned to the gate and brought Amun-Ra inside. They went immediately to the room where Tariq wrote. "Tell me, lord, what is your response to my question?"

"I will let you answer yourself, but it will take a few days to arrive at an answer. We can work on this together while we wait." He indicated the manuscript Tariq was currently writing.

There was a light tapping on the door and Tariq opened it narrowly. It was Bapset, well-hidden in the dark passageway. "Would you like some tea or coffee?" she asked. Tariq turned to Amun-Ra. "Would you?" he asked the same question.

"Yes, I would like some tea, thank you."

A little later the tapping was heard again, and Tariq opened the door to find the tea tray on the floor just outside. It contained honey cakes and a pot of strong, sweet tea. He brought it in, unsure as to how to proceed. As he poured, Amun-Ra reassured him. "You and Bapset are generous and hospitable, Tariq, and I am pleased."

The god returned to the cottage after a few days to talk about the history project and to take tea, and he returned once again, this time just as the evening meal was ready.

"Please come to the table to eat with me," Tariq invited.

"Thank you. I will, if Bapset and the child will be with us there."

"Bapset may not feel comfortable doing that," Tariq suggested. "She is an observant woman."

"I know that, but I insist. And I am sure I can make her feel comfortable."

"Yes, my lord," Tariq bowed to Amun-Ra and went to tell his wife that they would be having a guest for the evening meal, and that she and Amina should sit with the men to eat.

"If that is your command, husband," she said quietly. She had never heard of such a thing.

"I do not command, but ask you to do it as a favor."

"Should I wear the veil?"

"It's hard to eat wearing the veil. There is no need for it."

When Bapset brought in the lamb with lentils and some stewed greens, she was discreetly covered from head to toe, except for her face and hands. Amun-Ra and Tariq rose.

"This is, ah -"

"Amun-Ra," the god lowered his head in greeting. Bapset did the same. "I am Bapset," she told him. She thought his name sounded very odd - she had never heard it before. It certainly wasn't a common name for a man.

As they were eating, an activity Amun-Ra seemed to enjoy thoroughly, he spoke. "Have you found the answer yet, Tariq? To the last question you asked me?"

"I think I have," Tariq said with a question in his voice. He stopped and made lengthy eye contact with Amun-Ra, something he had never done previously. "It seems that I should treat all men the same, considering them all alike, and give equal attention and concern to everyone. Is that right?"

"In a way, yes. But it is easy to receive the great. What about a beggar you see along your path as you go to the college? Would you welcome him in the same way?"

"I should, shouldn't I?" Tariq smiled widely. "I did, too, if you will notice."

Bapset looked quickly from her husband to their guest. She knew something unusual was happening. 'Who is this man?' she almost spoke aloud.

"Did you really?" the god asked. Tariq gave no response. He looked at his daughter and Bapset with a bemused smile.

"Most men respond well when treated with dignity and respect," Amun-Ra said, "as do women. Let me tell you this; the day is coming when men and women will be completely equal."

Bapset gave a small gasp. She couldn't believe what he said.

"Do not be alarmed, my daughter. It will begin slowly, but it will happen."

"Is that my duty, then?" Tariq tried to ignore the remark about equality. He didn't understand what Amun-Ra was talking about.

"Not a duty only, and not yours alone," Amun-Ra went on smoothly. "You will not have a great many opportunities yourself, but all people, together, have very many. Everyone, men and women, ought to give the gift of a cordial welcome to anyone who is in need, according to their own resources. Each person lives in this world at a certain time, but their spirit of generosity will endure forever. Write it that way."

Bapset couldn't wait any longer to ask a pressing question. "Sir," she addressed Amun-Ra, "I perceive that you have known my husband for a long time. How did you come to meet?"

"I was along the wall of the khan in al Qahira, selling some things, when Tariq came looking for a fine jewel to buy for his wife. The one you have in your keeping, I believe."

She thought of the pearl and smiled. "And now you instruct him with his writing?"

"Yes, and I might add that he is doing a superb job."

Bapset gazed at Tariq for a moment, and then looked directly at Amun-Ra. "He told me that someone great had inspired him, and I believe that is true."

"You are very perceptive, my daughter," Amun-Ra responded.

The next fascination for Tariq was the sphinx; the great beast that sat in the sun century after century and millennium after millennium. No one had any idea about the age of the creature, but everyone was sure it had always been there, almost a pre-civilization work of stone, and they were honestly amazed at its survival that continued on into their world. Tariq saw it in its many forms, now time-worn and eroded, as well as its earlier state when it had just been redone with the mask of Khafra. He also saw the original lion that was carved from the rock by Pan and the people of Karnua. At first he did not know that the images of the great lion were one and the same as the sphinx, but began to guess after numerous pictures were juxtaposed against others. The most interesting aspect of all, however, was the face, supposedly of a pharaoh, with its nose intact. It caused him to wonder about the destruction of the nose and its consequent blighted appearance as it existed in his time. He didn't have to wonder long.

"It is an affront to Allah!" a man known as Sa'im was shouting to fellow worshippers at the mosque. "We cannot tolerate this act of disobedience and disrespect to Allah!" Tariq saw the scene as though it were happening at that moment.

Other men looked up from their own contemplations to discover who was doing the raucous shouting. Mosques were usually a quiet place where men could talk softly or even doze.

"We must shame the infidel and bring him down!" Sa'im continued in preacher style. "A true Muslim would never bring offerings to this creature!"

Sa'im al Dahr, a pious man with three grown sons, was exhorting his brothers to stay away from the false god, Hor-em-akhet, and to bring glory to Allah at the same time. He wanted to tear the idol down completely, but finding that it was made of the bed-rock caused him to reconsider. At least, he reasoned, something could be done about the head, the human visage that was forbidden by Allah, and he was eager to be the one to do it. Most of the men in the mosque, conversely, had little or absolutely no interest in destroying the ancient statue. It had been there for so long that it was like the sand of the desert or the river to them, a part of the landscape, and there was no reason for it to be disturbed.

Sa'im was insistent. There was no remedy but to destroy the head at least. The depiction of a human head sitting atop the body of a lion was surely the most offensive sight that Allah might ever look upon. It defied the creation. Beasts and men were not joined in the natural world. It had to be demolished in some way. After failing to arouse a furor in various mosques, he demanded that his three sons go with him to the beast and begin its systematic destruction.

The Great Sphinx sat mostly buried in the sand. His head rose above the drift that nearly touched his chin. The ridge along his back was bare, but all the rest of his shape had to be imagined. The winds had whipped the sand into drifts during recent years, and no one had been concerned enough to dig him out. That was a good thing for Sa'im al Dahr. He waded up the sandy edge, along with his sons, climbed up to the shoulder of the beast, and looked it over thoroughly. Sa'im decided to begin with the face of the creature, so he took his bearings and determined that the nose should go first. His youngest son was given the task of climbing across the head and standing on the top so he could lower rope ladders for the others to climb in order to get at the offensive feature. They carried out the plan well, and soon one of the men was swinging on a rope bridge suspended from the top, anchored to a jagged part of the headdress that protruded out to the sides of the ageless face. Sa'im al Dahr had brought two long and heavy wooden beams, carved to a sharp point on one end. He climbed one of the ladders and inserted one beam into the right nostril of the stone pharaoh. He held the beam in place as his oldest son, the strongest by far, used a heavy maul to strike upward from the swinging bridge. He struck several blows, each deflected by the hard stone, until, at last, one mighty blow sent a quiver through the beam and the limestone sheared off and fell with a thud into the sand, narrowly missing the man who had struck the blow. Sa'im al Dahr lost his balance and slid down the sand, landing hard against the mighty creature. When he looked up his heart was thrilled to see that they had succeeded in removing the entire nose. It had severed at a fissure in the rock, and was now in several pieces, lying near his feet. He offered a loud shout, "Allah Akbar!" and felt a surge of religious zeal pour through his entire body. It was at that moment that the local authorities arrived.

"Yes, that is the story of Sa'im al Dahr," Amun-Ra told Tariq two days later. That is how it happened. You have done well."

"I followed what the staff showed me, that's all."

"I watched it at the time," Amun-Ra responded. "Hor-em-akhet was originally mine, you know, dedicated to me."

"I didn't know that. Did it offend you to have Sa'im chop off the nose?"

"Not at all, my son. No, it did not bother me. He was not the first. That dirty little pharaoh, Khafra, was the one who destroyed the lion and made an abomination. Not Sa'im. But fate had plans for him, anyway. After he chopped off Khafra's nose, which I thought made a rather better statue of it, the authorities put Sa'im on trial for vandalism."

"What happened to him then? I didn't see any of that."

"He was hanged. His sons were unpunished because they were doing the damage in obedience to their father. The court found that commendable. People do some surprising things. At times I am amazed."

Chapter Eleven

1798 A D

The once mighty sphinx, now seriously eroded and nearly drowned by the Saharan sands, watched across the Nile toward the Moqattam Hills in the east, eyes fixed on the sunrise, noseless countenance facing the next event in his timeless journey. Deep clefts and furrows on his sides marked the centuries of water and wind, but his head held strong against the eroding power of the elements, having surrendered only to the pharaoh who changed the lion into his own likeness, and then in much later times to a man with a sharply pointed wooden beam and a heavy mallet.

The stone beast didn't seem to notice the furor that tumbled across the plateau above his left shoulder. The war between the Mameluks and the French invaders under Napoleon was winding down. The French were winning, but the sphinx did not turn his head, nor did he regard the invaders in any way. It was, after all, only another invasion. He was accustomed to such trials. Egypt had not had peace for so many centuries that he could hardly recall a time when the sun rose on a nation that was intact, content with self-rule, and not locked in an offensive against any foreign power. That was indeed long ago.

The French soldiers had not expected to win a battle with the Mameluks. They, except for General Napoleon, were terribly conflicted as they marched forward to fight the incredible force of fierce eastern men in turbans and robes; men who bore razor-sharp sabers and lances along with a brace of pistols, the latest weaponry in their arsenal. Napoleon, as calmly as though he were riding through the desert for sport, commanded that his men form hollow squares, shields outward, and withstand the enemy by doing just that, standing in place as the Mameluks swirled around them on horseback while archers from within the squares picked off the riders one by one. It turned into carnage. The Mameluks roared forward, unwilling to retreat, and were slaughtered as they attempted to break the squares. The masters of Egypt, themselves invaders in ages past, fell in great numbers while the French were able to maintain their positions with much lesser loss. Finally, as the sun was setting, the Mameluks gave way, and those that could still ride turned suddenly and swept away across the sands, leaving the new invaders with nothing but the falling night and a dread that the enemy might regroup and return. That was not the case. The Mameluks knew they had lost and left the French undisturbed after their sudden departure. The night was empty, dark, and troubled as the weary Frenchmen tried to find a resting place between the gigantic pyramids and the stony sphinx. At dawn the next morning the army moved on toward the capital city, al Qahira, and entered its gates without opposition. Napoleon had succeeded in subduing the might of the terrible Mameluk warriors.

The Napoleonic forces had landed at the port of Alexandria just ahead of the British who finally arrived in time to sail among the mostly empty French ships and sink all but a few, stranding the French army in Egypt. Most of the equipment the ships carried was lost, and a considerable number of seamen died attempting to defend the ships. Napoleon's library was gone, as well as all the munitions that had been stored in the flagship. It was a bad start for an invasion, especially when the British ships blockaded the harbor and no vessels were allowed to enter or leave.

The expedition was not only about fighting, however. The French had come with a large number of scholars and men of science who proposed, following the orders of the great General Napoleon, to study all things Egyptian and to learn from its ancient wisdom. Additionally, they hoped to accrue some of the wealth of that rich and fertile land for Napoleon and France. They wanted as much of that as they could possibly collect according to the unwritten rules of engagement in battle: whoever comes out the winner claims the prize.

The scholars and artists received the greatest advantages of the military campaign. Some of them went to work planning a new style of government for Egypt, while others set out toward various monuments and physical features of the land to collect specimens and take measurements as well as sketch and write reports about what they found. They were a zealous group, not at all like the soldiers, although they were housed and fed along with the army, and were soon in communication with Egyptians of all levels who would attempt a conversation with such infidels, as they were considered by the entire populace. Even the Mameluks, who had been overlords for nearly a millennium, were considered brothers within the Islamic faith.

Antoine Laplet, a twenty-year-old sketch artist from the countryside near Paris was in the first party to visit the pyramids after the battle. The reek of dead Mameluks filled the air. The French had given time for the collection of the bodies, but their brothers had not done so nearly two days after the battle ended. The scholars were intent on their discoveries and did not pay much attention to the stench. They were amazed at the ageless things they saw.

"Bring your sketch pad here," Georges Damiers called to Antoine. "Get a look at this!" He was clinging to a gigantic block of granite about fifteen yards above the ground. "There's something carved into this one."

Georges and Antoine had met three years before, at a new school for scientific studies in Paris, and had been friends since that time. They were closely associated in school, often in the same classes, and decided together to apply for the expedition. Both were chosen, and both felt the honor keenly.

Antoine worked his way up; clambering on the unyielding stone while hanging onto the pad and pencils wasn't easy. "What did they call these?" He tried to recall a name for the figures cut into the rock. "They told us in the classes on the ship. I can't remember."

"Hieroglyphics, that's what they call them. Their method of writing in those ancient times."

"Looks like birds and eyes and wavy lines."

"Those are the glyphs."

"Well, I'll get it all down. Easy to copy. Just lines." He took his place on the edge of the next toe-hold and leaned across the stone to copy the marks. He stayed in the spot long enough to get a careful replica and then relaxed as he stepped onto a larger surface of the pyramid-scape. "It was a stretch but it came out pretty well." He held up the notebook for Georges to see. "Does it look right?"

"Yes, they're the same. Let's go on up now. I want to see the sights from the tip-top."

"You go on. I think I'll stay here or go down a little. I don't like high places."

"Suit yourself. I think I could fly! I'll be back down after a while. No sense leaving until I've tried to climb to the top."

Antoine started down. He was too far above the ground already. The pyramid seemed to rock slowly back and forth. It wasn't a good sign. He moved across the face of the stone wall, not able to look down without feeling a sickening sensation, but unable to go on up as well. "I'm not good at this, never have been," he told himself.

As he worked his way carefully along the face of the wall he suddenly came to an opening, a cave or so it seemed, that stared at him from its dark passage. He felt a ripple of dread but was also intrigued as he stared into the darkness beyond, but the sun couldn't penetrate the blackness within. Where did it lead? He sat down on a rocky shelf beside the door and attempted to see inside. He was about to give up when he saw a light, wavering and flickering in the distant gloom of the passage, and heard voices. French voices. They were talking about a burial somewhere inside, and their echoing words were amplified by the corridor.

"It's there. Didn't you see it?"

"Well, no. I was looking at the walls. It's so dark I couldn't see much of anything."

"It looks like a huge stone bathtub, sitting over on the side opposite the entrance. And there's a lid for the thing beside it on the floor."

"Spooky. Do you think anyone's inside?"

"I have no idea, but it's a mausoleum for sure. Must be for one of the old kings. On the ship they told us that they're buried inside these things."

"Not anymore. They said they've all been stolen, and all their treasure, too."

"Why would anyone want to steal a body even if it's a king's?"

"Probably he's covered in gold. That would do it."

"Gold, yes, it would."

There was a pause in the voices. The figures of three men were barely visible in the torchlight. They were bent almost in half due to the low ceiling of the walkway, waddling like ducks as they panted and climbed up the steep ramp.

"Heavy going here."

"Sure is."

They were hardly able to talk by that time.

Antoine waited, watching the light move forward. Just before they got to the opening he called to them, "What's down there?"
One of the men raised his head enough to see Antoine in the light of the opening. "Who's that?" he asked.

"Antoine Laplet. I'm a sketcher. Who are you?"

"Pierre Arget, and these are Pierre Janot and Pierre Mariette. We're army." The man gasped out the introductions.

"Three Pierres! Well, anyway, you're looking good for the battle you just fought in."

"Well, we're cooks, you see. We're the best, too." He grinned broadly. "Maybe you've eaten our food?" Camp cooks stayed out of the fighting, and if they were any good they were much revered by the soldiers.

"I don't know. I eat with the third, if that's who you cook for."

"No. We're the fifth and sixth."

"So, what did you find down there?" The cooks had all emerged from the tunnel and thrown themselves on the rocks to rest, stretching out their backs and legs.

"You want to go down?" Pierre Arget asked.

"Maybe."

"Well, I'm not going back any time soon, but some other fellows that want to go down are coming in a little while. Maybe you can go with them."

"It's lots of work getting in and back out," another Pierre spoke breathlessly.

"But worth it. No one's been there for hundreds of years, I guess," the third Pierre offered. Antoine was impressed.

The truth was that local groups of young men and boys (many people called them gangs) went inside the pyramids whenever they wanted to go, and that practice extended in a long line all the way back to the earliest tomb robbers. They were the ones who routed out the animals and snakes and claimed the tombs for exploration and profit, if any could be found. They were always searching for other openings deep within that could lead them to unbelievable treasure hoards, and they were fearless.

Antoine let his anticipation wane as he considered the difficulties of the passage, and followed the shaky Pierres down the side wall and onto the flat stone pavers that surrounded the colossus. He looked up but couldn't see anything of Georges, who was toiling his way to the top, not yet even close to his goal.

Georges met a number of men on his way aloft, some going up and some down. Those who had accomplished the pinnacle told him it was worth the trip, so he continued to climb over the out-sized granite blocks, slowly and cautiously, filled with a sense of accomplishment the higher he went. It was worth it, he decided after he reached the summit at last. Several other Frenchmen were there, resting and looking across to the city and the great river-way within its green sward, peering back with guarded glances at the battlefield strewn with horses and men who had met their final defeat on the sand. It was a lonely place to lie in death, and jackals prowled at night.

General Napoleon laid the groundwork for a new French-style government in Egypt. He wanted to bring both the intellectual enlightenment the French were currently discovering as well as a more democratic kind of government to the country, but needed the help of the *divan*, the legislative body under the Mameluks, to convince people to accept French rule. He also wanted his forces to convert to Islam, but the men refused when they discovered they couldn't have wine and women freely, and they could never again eat pork. The divan was uncooperative as well. The Egyptians had no desire to become a part of a government run by infidels, as they considered the French, and boldly stated the fact. Napoleon altered his plans to accommodate the circumstances and moved forward in other ways with the subjection of the people, who hid their rancor well. Egypt was accustomed to handling invaders with enormous egos.

Antoine had a long wait to get inside a pyramid. He was kept busy as he copied the glyphs and stele and other works of art the scholars located, but a free day came at last. The tombs were never guarded, and all the entrances to the giants were open and gaping. He chose Khafra, the one that still had some of its limestone overlay. He felt a certain affinity toward that tomb without any logical reason, and especially liked its association with the great sphinx that crouched just down the slope in its own cleft among the rocky outcroppings along the side of the plateau.

The day of descent finally came. It was already hot in the early morning, so Antoine sought the dark entry tunnel with pleasant hopes of coolness, only to discover that the deeper it delved, the hotter it became. The ceiling was lower than he had thought; he had to stoop half over to get through, and that soon became a most uncomfortable position. The backs of Antoine's legs and his knees, especially, suffered as he descended. At the end of the long passage it turned and opened into the vast space known as the burial chamber and he could stand again. He went in with three Frenchmen who had already been down once. They carried torches inside, but the flames hardly made a difference in the gloom. They walked around the perimeter of the place, and Antoine took a lingering look at the stone sarcophagus that lay opposite the entrance. It was a little taller than his head so he couldn't see into its depth; the heavy lid was placed at a rakish angle on the stone floor beside the massive casket. It was made of the same stone as the walls, but the sarcophagus was polished. It gleamed as it reflected the light. There was also a sound, like a far-off drum keeping a steady beat, which seemed to be coming from inside the casket.

"What is that thud?" Antoine asked.

"There's no thud I can hear. What do you think it is?"

"It's probably your own breathing," another told him.

"Or your heart. Are you afraid of all this?"

"Definitely not," Antoine said with a stiff voice. He told himself that they couldn't intimidate him, but he still heard the rhythmic drumming as it gradually grew louder. It was almost certainly coming from the coffin.

"Give me a hand up," he asked the closest man. "I want to look inside."

Antoine placed his right foot into his colleague's two strong hands and was lifted high enough to peer into the depth of the box. He saw a faint light flashing from the far corner, struggled to lift himself over the edge, and jumped to the bottom, a place he imagined he had no right to be. A glowing stick in the corner pulsed with light and sound, but when he picked it up the thing suddenly went silent and dark. The floor inside the coffin was considerably higher than the floor outside; it was easier to reach the top, and he pulled himself up until he was sitting on the thin edge, carrying his prize. Antoine jumped from the coffin onto the stony floor.

"What's that?" a voice from the surrounding darkness asked.

"I don't know. I thought I saw it glowing but it isn't."

"Was that what you heard?"

"I don't know that either." He wanted to keep the stick for himself so he didn't give it too much importance.

"Come on, then. Let's take a look around."

He wandered along with the others, holding firmly to the staff, while they explored the chamber. It was an empty space, they concluded, except for the huge coffin, unless there was a secret opening somewhere that no one had found. They paced next to the walls, tapping them with broken bits of rock as they went, but all sides sounded the same. After they studied the chamber for nearly an hour they labored back up the passage together and out into the sunshine, Antoine bearing his trophy. No one else wanted to touch it. He took it to his barracks and slid it beneath the thin blanket that topped his cot.

The battlefield had been cleared of the dead at last. The French rounded up some Mameluks and commanded them to bury the men in a pit of sand a short way out into the western desert, and to burn the dead horses at the site. They built a huge fire in the middle of the field, and the decaying horses along with other refuse and paraphernalia of battle were pulled onto the flames with long ropes, where they were devoured. The air near the pyramids soon

204

became bearable again. The Mameluks who were forced to do the work were angry, but took their servitude quietly – at the time.

Two days after Antoine explored the burial chamber he missed his friend Georges Damiers. He had not seen him for more than a day and the head of his division hadn't seen him, either. Antoine was concerned, so the next morning when Georges failed to appear he took responsibility for finding him. The army official was absently making lists of supplies when Antoine appeared at his tent and reported the man missing.

"Oh, he'll show up soon. Probably found a floozy and is off somewhere with her. He's not the kind to stay away long." The military didn't have much concern for the scientists and artists who had been assigned to them.

"You are correct, sir. He wouldn't stay away so long. I think something has happened to him. He may be sick or injured somewhere. Can you send your men to look for him?"

The division commander was annoyed. "If you want to look, then do it yourself," was his curt reply.

"I will take that as permission and go now," Antoine responded quickly and turned away from the tent flap. He needed help, so he sought the men who had gone with him inside Khafra's pyramid.

"Do you know Georges Damiers?" he asked the man named Francois.

"He's your friend. I know that. Why?"

"I haven't seen him for the past two days. Usually I see him every day. I think I need to look for him."

"Ask the director. He should send out a search party."

"I talked to him and he put me off. Told me to do it myself."

"Do you think he wants to be rescued if he's happy wherever he is?"

"I don't think he'd leave without telling anyone. That's all. And he isn't out with women. He would have told me that."

"A man of noble character," Francois joked, but seeing that the joke didn't go well with Antoine, he pulled himself up taller and announced; "I'll go with you to look for him. I think I can get Philippe to come along. Will the three of us be enough?"

"It's a start," Antoine replied.

They looked for Georges everywhere around the camp until that day ended in dark. They called for him around the pyramids and down to the sphinx, out to the edge of the Sahara and along the side of the river valley, but no one had seen him and there was no response to their calls. Antoine was deeply concerned that night, so the next morning he added the three Pierres to the hunt. They placed their cooking responsibilities onto their assistants –without the knowledge of superiors – and left as soon as they could after dawn. Two men went down each of the pyramids, but no one was there. Antoine was near despair when Francois offered a suggestion. "You say he liked to go to the top? Let's go up and look around." It seemed logical, so they went, Antoine climbing with Pierre Arget. They labored up the long, steep sides of the titans, two men on each, to have a look around. It was Pierre who saw him, almost halfway down the side of Khufu, sprawled across the edge of a huge stone. Antoine looked down, dizzy at the sight, but when he saw the body he believed to be that of his friend he lost his fear and got down to the place as fast as he could. It was Georges, dead from a bullet through his skull. A large pistol like the ones the Mameluks used was lying on another stone block just below. The wind, rising to meet the oncoming sunset, whistled softly around the corners of the mammoth stones.

A military inquest, held two days after Georges was found, decided that his death was caused by an unknown person, probably an angry Mameluk. Georges had also been robbed; there was absolutely nothing in his pockets. The case was dismissed as unsolvable. Antoine was exasperated by the ease with which the division commander made his decision, "as though he wanted to get it over with so he could go to lunch," he told the men who had searched for the victim. It seemed that death was such a common event that it didn't need to be regarded seriously.

That night Antoine had a vivid dream. He saw a boy, not more than fifteen, standing on a stone in the side of a pyramid. Antoine himself was climbing down toward the boy who pulled a long-handled pistol from under his gallabeya and took aim. The dream ended, and Antoine sat up on his cot shouting words he couldn't understand. The men in the barracks were awakened by his shouts.

"Another screamer," one of them complained. "Shut up and let me sleep!"

"He misses his woman," someone else said, and Antoine jumped off his cot to grab the man but others sensibly intervened. Quiet was restored before a fight could start. "Time enough to fight during the day," someone growled. "Shut up now."

"I saw it," a shaky Antoine told Pierre the next morning. "I saw the guy who killed Georges. It was like I was Georges and saw everything."

"Well, you couldn't have seen it," Pierre explained. "You dreamed it, and dreams can seem real. My mother used to have terrible nightmares and her screams shook the house."

"It wasn't like that. It was life. Real life."

"I'm sorry Antoine. I know it's hard to lose a close friend."

Antoine was silent. No one would be able to understand what had happened, but he was sure it was more than a dream.

The scholars continued their work. The pyramids were measured and it was discovered that their orientation was exactly aligned to the four points of the compass. Each was based on a perfect square, and the tallest measured 146.5 meters. It was, by all accounts, the tallest building in the world, and had been for over three thousand years. The engineers who did the calculations were amazed. How could such an early people have developed the skills it took to build these things? Some of them believed that the ancients had mathematical proficiency which had been lost in the ensuing tides of time. It was the only logical explanation for the things they were learning. A new respect for Egyptians emerged from their findings.

A week later Antoine was working on Khafra. Someone had found marks on a stone in the base on the eastern side and he was copying the lines. The sphinx was over his left shoulder, sitting inside the enclosure Pan had made so long before. No one was nearby; certainly there were no scientists on that side of the monolith. Antoine was thinking of Georges and the boy who had shot him when he heard a new, disembodied voice speak close to his ear.

"Antoine Laplet, I will speak to you now."

Startled, Antoine looked around but there was nothing but sand stretching down the slope. He continued his copywork, thinking that he hadn't really heard anything. Maybe it was like the dream, he told himself.

"Antoine Laplet, I am here but you cannot see me." The voice was not threatening.

"Who is it? Why are you playing a trick on me?"

"It is no trick. I need to speak to you."

"Who are you?" Antoine asked tightly.

"There is no need to fear me. I will not harm you. And I am not a ghost or a demon. I am Amun-Ra."

"Who?"

"Amun-Ra, the creator. Do you know my name?"

"Yes, I know it. You're a mythical god."

"Do I sound like a myth?"

"No. Why do you speak to me?"

"You have my staff. You found it in the pyramid and carried it away with you."

"You can have it back. I'll go get it."

He heard a kind of laugh. "No, I don't want it back. I mean for you to have it."

Antoine turned to face the voice. "What do you want?"

"That is better. I need to speak to you. Alone. Come to the statue down there – the one you call the sphinx – tonight when the moon is rising. I will meet you then and you will see me."

"Why do you want to meet me?"

"I have chosen you. Do not fear. No harm will come to you, and perhaps much good will come of it. Be there at the rising of the moon."

There was a silence, almost a vacuum, for a moment. Antoine knew that he was alone again. He turned to the inscription again and made a hasty copy of the remaining lines. He would go, yes, he would go to meet the voice, but he was both skeptical and fearful despite Amun-Ra's assurance.

Antoine took the staff and waited at the sphinx at an early hour, long before the moon rose. He stood between the great forelegs of the lion-body, looking out toward the east, and then climbed carefully to the top of the left shoulder and watched the light change until it was dark and the full moon lit the eastern sky. He should be coming soon, the watcher thought, climbing down from his perch to await the creator-god outside the enclosing legs of the sphinx. He heard a sound, like a large beast panting, and saw a movement in the dark. Amun-Ra, in the form of a lion, appeared above him on the shoulder where he had been waiting. Antoine felt a pang of sudden panic. The beast could fall upon him with its great claws and teeth, but his fear was replaced with the lion's voice.

"I am Amun-Ra as the elder people thought I should look. I do not. I have no form, so I must use one to make an appearance. I have no plans to attack you."

Antoine was speechless. He looked with suspicion at the lion. Its eyes were aflame. Suddenly, the creature stood beside him.

"Hear what I say, Antoine Laplet. You have seen rightly. Georges Damier died at the hand of the boy you saw. That boy, and even Georges, is not important to us now. You are important, and you will help to usher in a new age."

Antoine was astonished, but found his voice. "How? I have no influence at all."

"You will. Have you met Napoleon?"

"No."

"You will. You will also have an impact on what happens in Egypt and the world as a whole."

"I told you I'm not important. General Napoleon will not see me. He's not concerned with someone he doesn't know."

"He will see you, and after that will be rather concerned about you, too. I have a message for him, but I may deliver it myself. I will tell you in a matter of weeks."

"What will I say to him when we meet?"

"You will know when the time is right, and you will say whatever is needed at that time. He will do as you tell him."

Once again Antoine was taken off guard. "Are you sure? He's the one who tells everybody else."

"I am quite sure. He will do as you say. At least the most important things."

Antoine wanted to ask a lot of questions, but didn't because Amun-Ra seemed too intense. "Here I am," he thought, "talking to this lion as though it's perfectly normal. What's happening to me?"

"The situation is this," Amun-Ra answered thoughtfully. "The British will try to take Egypt from the French, but will not do so yet. Napoleon has some ideas as to how he can prevail, but you must watch him for me. I will not meet with him yet."

"Then he will not listen to me. He has no reason to."

"When the time comes, he will listen to you. And he will take action as you tell him he should, because it will be what I tell him to do. You will simply watch and remind him. Keep the staff with you at all times. I will speak to you through it."

Antoine carried the staff with him everywhere. Some of the men suggested, mockingly, that it was a replacement for Georges, but others who were more sympathetic thought it was more an extension of his friend. Antoine heard reports of the comments but didn't respond. The truth was far more difficult to explain.

A group of scholars and scientists went to al Minya, south of al Qahira, to evaluate some ancient sites. Antoine went with them. He spent his days sketching tomb art and bits of ruined stone that bore inscriptions, but no one knew what the artifacts said. There was no one in Egypt to translate the writing, and no French scholar had yet broken the code of the ancient language. Then the Rosetta stone was uncovered far to the north, and the inscriptions took on a new importance. The stone contained information written in three different languages; Hieroglyphics, the earliest written language of Kmet, Demotic, a later language derived from the first, and ancient Greek scripts. Through it the scholars were able to translate the oldest forms because some of them could read the Greek. The Rosetta stone became the key to understanding everything from the Egyptian past.

Antoine didn't copy directly from the stone, but made replicas of one of the original copies so there were enough to pass around for all the scholars at al Minya. As a result they spread enlightenment from the past into their own world, and soon everybody who had a language background could translate the markings they found in such profusion. It was a remarkable event that carried the understanding of Egypt and its predecessors forward with one mighty stride.

Al Minya was another matter. The work there was often tedious and hot. Most of the men took evening recreation at one of the coffee shops that sat along the main thoroughfare of the town, if either 'coffee shop' or 'main thoroughfare' could describe such places. Al Minya was a dump, simply put, and no one wanted to stay very long. It was too far from al Qahira to get there easily, and the town all but disappeared at nightfall. The mosque was the only thing that looked half decent, and local men converged there for socialization, except for the few who went to one of the two coffee houses; both only open spaces filled with sand and dirt, without walls or roof. There were a few dirty tables and tiny stools for seating. The coffee and tea were prepared at a longer table in the back, and an open fire behind it served as a cooking spot. These two shops usually had very little business in the evening. Despite the lack of interest and stimulation there, the French soldiers and scholars began to frequent both the coffee houses, and their support gave new heart to the owners. They took on extra help to accommodate the crowds and soon the places became common meeting grounds for restless young Frenchmen. The three Pierre's had remained at the camp near the pyramids, but Antoine and Francois had become closer friends during the time they spent in the backwater of al Minya, and went for coffee every night. As Amun-Ra had told him, Antoine carried the staff everywhere, and began to feel secure with it in his hand. The two men talked with their French friends, and played cards or sang, but al Minya was about as far as anyone could get from the boulevards of Paris.

It was on an evening in an unnamed coffee house (neither of them had a name) that Antoine's world took another turn. He came face to face with the boy he had seen shoot Georges. The fiend, as Antoine thought of him, brought the hot little cups of coffee to their rickety table, and as he placed them there Antoine saw his face and was frozen for a terrible moment. He could not move and hardly breathe, yet he heard a thought that formed in his mind.

"Yes, it is the boy. Don't stare at him. When you leave, tell Francois that you will go to the camp later. Follow this boy instead. He will lead you to truth." Antoine was torn with frustration and anger. "Why," he shouted out, and all the men heard him. The boy was startled. "Do not use your voice. Talk to me with your thoughts," Amun-Ra said quietly.

It took discipline, but Antoine turned his thoughts inward and asked again, "Why?"

"The boy does not know that you saw him with Georges. He will leave soon and will lead you to a place that will explain. Wait and you will understand."

"What's wrong, Antoine? I can't tell you why if I don't know what you mean." Francois was bemused. "It's just déjà vu," Antoine told him. "I thought I saw Georges over there."

They drank their coffee and Francois chatted a little with some of the others. Antoine was extraordinarily quiet. Francois abruptly decided to go back to camp. "I have an early start tomorrow. We're going to Amarna. There are some old tombs somebody found and we have to measure everything." His group spent their time calculating the differences between their new measurements and the old cubits.

"I'll stay a little longer. Another sketcher told me he'd be coming tonight and I want to talk to him." Antoine told the surveyor.

"Don't be caught out here alone," Francois reminded him. Every scholar knew it was dangerous to travel alone anywhere in the country.

"I'll find somebody to go back with," Antoine assured him. "I'll see you when you get back from Amarna."

The crowd gradually thinned out. Antoine watched the boy as he prepared to leave, then walked slowly away from the coffee house and waited close to the path in the dark until the boy crossed in front of him, headed down toward the river. Antoine waited for what he thought was long enough, then ambled onto the path, apparently without purpose. The boy passed some hovels along the way, eventually turning into a roofless shanty close to the water. Everything was dark for a short time until a small light suddenly sprang up above the walls.

Antoine moved across the sand quietly until he stood at the back of the hut and waited. He heard nothing and was perplexed until the sound of steps along the path reached him and he heard the front door open and a gruff voice spoke to the boy in Arabic.

"Oh no! How will I know what they're saying?" Antoine was perplexed.

"Listen!" It was the voice of Amun-Ra, and immediately the language became intelligible.

"What have you got to drink?" the gruff voice demanded.

"Only coffee or tea. Nothing stronger. Sorry." the boy answered.

"Mmph!" was the only response.

"Do you want to call attention to me? It would if I got strong drink."

"Shut your mouth."

There was silence for a while and the sounds of water boiling and glasses clunking on a table were the only sounds.

"Do you have anything to report?" the gruff voice asked.

"Not much. I don't understand French that well."

"You're the only one who understands it at all! You need to listen better. Talk to them, you little fool."

"They're a crude bunch. I don't want to talk to any of them."

"There are lots of scientists in the mix. Talk to them."

"They don't have the information we need. I've tried. They're all full of the greatness of the old ones."

"We're almost ready. I've got to go back tomorrow. Nobody can decide when to strike. Keep your ears open. And eyes. Don't let us down or you know what'll happen! Your new contact will be Ashmer. Tomorrow night."

"How soon do you think it'll be?"

"Tomorrow night. I just told you."

"No, I mean our offensive."

211

"Soon. The men are restless. They want to taste Frenchy blood. They've got plans for those damned squares!"

"Wipe out the infidels!"

"We'll get our own back. The horsemen will ride harder next time."

The slurps of tea started. The drinks were cool enough.

"I'll go in the morning. Ashmer tomorrow night. Listen! You said you could understand French. You'd better prove it!"

"I said a little. Not everything."

"Just listen." He hissed the words. A moment later the door opened.

Antoine dropped low to the ground and watched in the dimness until the man was far enough down the path and then followed behind.

Early the next morning Antoine made his report to the military command. It was dubiously received. The sketcher felt that the information couldn't have been very important because much of the time he was before the assistant commander was spent going over the rules against traveling alone, especially at night.

"And what is that thing you have with you?" the assistant to the commander wanted to know. "You carry it all the time, or so I'm told. Do you need help getting around?"

"No, sir," Antoine said respectfully. "It's only a talisman which I like to keep nearby."

"You are superstitious then?"

"I guess you could say that I am, sir," Antoine agreed good naturedly.

"There's no place in this army for superstitious men."

"You will pardon me, sir, and I don't mean to be disrespectful, but I' m not in the army."

"Ah, yes. Too bad. I'd have that thing out of your hands in no time if you were. Now get out of here."

As he left the tent Antoine heard a distinct laugh. It sounded like that of Amun-Ra, but he was not to be seen. "He is a pompous ass, son, in your vernacular. Take no heed," the voice said.

"I never do," Antoine answered. "Will he give my report to anyone?"

"I am sure that he will not," Amun-Ra answered. "And he will be sorry."

Francois and Antoine went back to the coffee house for several evenings and the sketcher watched the boy as he served drinks and paused to chat with the military men. He seemed to seek out those of higher rank, and talked and laughed in guttural French with ease and hideous charm. Antoine listened but did not hear any military information offered, so he settled back to watch from a distance. He also kept an eye out for the man called Ashmer, and found him before long. He was a scrawny man with piercing eyes and a swift hand. He'd be good in a sword fight, Antoine thought. I wouldn't want to meet him without help close by. He also noticed that the boy seemed to stay away from the man, and watched Ashmer from behind with wary eyes. He's a threat, the sketcher decided. They were a good match for each other. He hated the boy who shot Georges.

Things came to a head abruptly one night soon after. Francois and Antoine were walking back to camp when they were jumped by two men. Their attackers came from behind a ruined wall and a sword flashed in the dim light. Antoine shouted and pounded the staff on the earth while Francois swung at the man, but before any contact was made a bright flash startled them all. There was a roar like thunder and the sword flew from Ashmer's hand. The boy with him turned to flee but was stopped by a large animal that pounced upon him and held him firmly to the ground as he shrieked in the agony of fear. The animal, a lion with flaming eyes, roared and snarled. Francois fell to the ground in panic, but Antoine stood tall and watchful. He knew this lion. They heard the voice of Amun-Ra speaking to the boy.

"Go from this place and never return. If you are not gone before the moon is high I will come to you and strike you down. I know your deeds, and you are an evil wretch. Go!"

He stepped away from the boy who ran down to the water in terror and jumped into a boat. There were no oars. He ran frantically from boat to boat until he found a pair, launched the craft into the main current and feverishly paddled away.

Ashmer, on the other hand, had stabbed himself deeply in the groin with a knife he carried in his waist band and was profusely bleeding into the sand. He could not escape the lion, who stooped over his form to study him for a moment. "You will be dead soon," the lion told him. "What do you want to say to me? You know who I am."

Ashmer refused to speak. The lion turned away.

Francois was still in shock and afraid of the beast as it came to him. "Francois, you are a decent man. Do not fear me. I am a friend of your friend Antoine. He carries my staff, which I gave him." The lion stepped aside from the path and walked away across the sand. A bewildered Francois stared at Antoine. "You have powerful friends," he said weakly.

Within a week Antoine and Francois returned to the camp at the Gaza plateau. There was still work to be done and the cadre of scholars at the pyramids needed help. It was a time of uneasiness because the dreaded plague had reached Egypt again. This time it was mostly the pneumonic variety; soldiers, officers, and scientific scholars were all dropping from the terrible disease. Not everyone who came down with the disease died, but those who did not recovered slowly and were unable to work for a long time after the fever left them. All the young men who returned from al Minya were concerned about their own chances of avoiding contagion. It seemed likely that they would eventually encounter the plague, so they faced each day with the hope of surviving until the following morning. It was all anyone could do.

Work on the pyramids and sphinx was almost stopped. No one had any desire to continue such mundane tasks in the threatening situation. Going out to measure or sketch seemed paltry, but they drove themselves along almost every day, and produced the best work they could in those circumstances. Antoine reacted differently. He seemed driven by the need to excel; this was his hour to shine. He worked doubly hard at sketching and assisted the others with measurements and whatever kind of work was needed. He readily went everywhere and took no heed of the dangers of the plague that hung around in silence, considering who to infect each new day. He behaved as though he was impervious to the threat.

On a hot morning a few days after his return from al Minya he was working with Francois between the extended forelegs of the sphinx, taking precise dimensions of the height of each part of the long legs, when he saw the boy from the coffee house on the path that moved along beside the great beast. Antoine signaled to Francois to be quiet and they followed their quarry at a distance.

At last they saw a chance for apprehending the boy. He was obviously headed for the French camp headquarters. They knew a shortcut between the tents and some shacks that had been there for years, so they cut through, waited as the boy approached, and jumped him from behind a shed. He hardly resisted, looking around furtively as they held him in place.

"We want to talk to you. We won't hurt you if you answer our questions." Antoine spoke slowly, carefully using simple words. His anger was mounting but he held it in check. "Tell me what you know about the Mameluk advance or you could face the lion again."

The boy was silent.

"Tell me!" Antoine commanded, holding the staff up.
"Nothing to tell." The boy was subdued but insolent. "The disease has ruined our army. We can't fight anymore."

"Is that really true?"

"Yes, you should know. You probably know everything we do."

"He still fears the lion," Antoine muttered to Francois..

"You have to come with us," he declared to the boy. "If you do the lion won't harm you. If not, then I can't say what will happen." The boy raised his hands above his head without a word and waited for them to take him away. They went to the command tent.

"The commander died yesterday," a youthful aide-de-camp told them, "and his assistant is sick, too. I don't know how long we'll have to wait for a replacement, if anyone is still living to take command."

"Is General Napoleon in al Qahira?"

"I was told this morning that he was there. He might have gone somewhere else by now. Lots of men have died in al Qahira."

"We'll go there, anyway. I have to take the prisoner to him." Antoine spoke with resolve. He hoped it was the right time to meet Napoleon.

They left the command tent and set out to walk to the river, which was about three miles distant, but a passing supply wagon picked them up and delivered them next to the quay that was used by their troops. The boy sat glumly in the wagon as they plodded slowly along. "Now we have to find a boat and row across," Antoine said. "I watched you when you escaped from al Minya," he told him. "You seem to be an expert on the water. You will row us across."

They had to hire a boat with a pilot in the end. There were no empty boasts available. It took them over the river and into a canal which washed through the city to a point near the Ezbekiya Gardens. Napoleon's palace, which had belonged to a Mameluk sultan defeated in the battle at the pyramids, came into view just past the gardens, now a sandy, nearly empty space where green lawns and trees once supplied the area residents with a cool, beautiful oasis. The French headquarters, the former stronghold of Sultan el-Elfi Bey, loomed on the far side of the wasted land. There was no noticeable sign of the plague, but there weren't many guards in the area. The three were stopped by two nervous young soldiers as soon as they were out of the boat, and their papers checked. Neither paid the least attention to the boy who produced no identification. Antoine guessed that they thought he was a servant.

Several fierce-looking Mameluks were lounging near the fort and questioned them again as they approached. This time Antoine had to vouch for the boy, who told them in a guttural voice that his name was Ahdahm, and the guards let them pass. There were more French soldiers at the entrance to the building, but they asked few questions and seemed concerned only about themselves. One sat on the ground a distance from the others, coughing unpleasantly. There was no further problem with admission.

Francois wondered if Antoine had lost his senses. He led them up to the entrance of the palace and opened the door. They passed down a lengthy hall and met a single soldier at the base of a staircase. He told them that General Napoleon was on the next level, and led them up the steps that were decorated in oriental style with something like hieroglyphs and pyramids worked into the metal balustrades. Halfway down another hall they turned aside into a large chamber with couches and tables and lamps, all framed on beautiful carpets obviously made of silk; a richly appointed reception room where they were invited to stand as they waited for the general himself. It was unnerving for all but Antoine, who possessed a sense of peace that seemed impossible under the circumstances. They waited. After about twenty minutes, a door at the end of the room opened and the imposing figure of Roustam, Napoleon's Mameluk bodyguard, entered, followed by General Napoleon and two other men who remained unnamed during the interview.

They all bowed, even Ahdahm, and faced the general. He sat in a low chair and gazed at each of them for an intimidating moment, then indicated the boy.

"What is your name and your purpose?" Napoleon asked. One of the men behind him was taking notes.

The boy mumbled barely audibly, "Ahdahm."

"Your purpose?"

There was no answer. Napoleon didn't seem to notice and looked questioningly at Francois.

"I am Francois Beauchant, a friend of Antoine Laplet."

The general seemed to scowl. "And you, then, are Antoine Laplet?"

"I am, sir," he responded with a sure voice.

"You two are in the expedition?" he gestured toward the Frenchmen.

"Yes, we are sir. I am a sketch artist and Francois does measurement and surveying."

Napoleon's eyes turned to Ahdahm again. "You are the spy, then." He did not ask, he stated.

Ahdahm did not respond.

"Answer," Napoleon commanded.

"A spy. Yes."

"They tell me that your army is nearly all sick or dead now. Am I right?"

"We will never accept the French!"

"That isn't an answer. Tell me what you know about your army. Are they mostly dead now?"

"From the great disease. But we will gain more men and fight again!"

"A pity if you do. There's really no need for fighting. France is here to stay."

"We will fight you! We have ruled here for centuries!"

"And your people invaded Egypt to rule it. We didn't come to rule, but to spread the age of enlightenment. I don't suppose you agree, but then, you are a spy. No one would expect you to."

Ahdahm swore in Arabic.

Napoleon stood as if to pronounce sentence. "Anyway, you are responsible for the death of at least one of the scholars. You will be properly punished for that. It would go better if you told me everything you know about the plans of your army. But of course, you are too young to get much of that kind of information offered to you."

"We will drive you out!" Ahdahm insisted in a cold voice. "We don't want infidels here!"

216

"Nor do we. Take him out," Napoleon waved to his guards. They hustled a defeated Ahdahm out the door. Napoleon sat down again. The others remained on their feet.

Napoleon turned to Antoine. "What are you holding there?" he asked with renewed interest.

"A staff, sir. It was a gift to me, and I value it very much."

"I have met Amun-Ra. He told me that the staff is his."

"It is, but he lets me keep it for him."

"What does it do?" he asked. "How do you use it?"

"It's hard to explain. It gives me ideas and tells me things sometimes." Antoine didn't like to talk about the staff.

"It's a powerful tool, I know that. Much more powerful than you are telling me."

Antoine inclined his head. "I don't yet know its true power, sir."

"I will take it for a test." Napoleon held out his hand, and Antoine relinquished the staff to him.

The lion suddenly sprang up beside Napoleon. "As I said earlier, the staff is not for you," he said with a growling voice. "Give it back to Antoine."

Napoleon didn't speak, but slowly handed the staff to Antoine who accepted it with a smile.

Amun-Ra continued. "The staff is mine to give or withhold. I do not speak to everyone through it, and I will never use it to speak to you. You are fortunate I meet with you at all. I do not like the company of men who are self-important."

The men behind the general protested, but they could do nothing. Amun-Ra was beyond the power of any man, even General Napoleon.

"There are a few more things we need to say together," the lion continued, "but I want only Antoine and Francois to remain with us. The rest of you should leave."

Napoleon gestured for the men to leave. The lion spoke to the general again. "I will go soon and never return. Hear my words! Go to France, for that is the place where you will be enabled, not here in this land. Go as soon as you can find ship. I will be watching your departure!"

Napoleon was obviously startled by the demand. "I don't plan to leave Egypt until my campaign is over."

"Your campaign is ended. You will go. Do not delay unless you want to test my patience. Further, you are to take Antoine Laplet with you. He has the staff."

"We will be in France," Napoleon stated. "What good will that staff do me there?"

"I am not limited to this land. Do you think distance would make me less potent than I am here? And I remind you that the staff is not for your use."

Napoleon looked stricken.

"And take Francois as well. I do not think he needs to remain here. There will be great destruction in this city."

"I do respectfully protest. I care about the city and will do everything I can to keep it from destruction."

"You are vain and deceitful, Napoleon, and I do not want or need to linger with you. I would leave you here if it were not for the suffering you would cause by remaining. Do as I say!" He turned to Antoine. "This general is blinded by ambition. He will not be happy until he has subjected much of the world to terrible battles and death. I will let him make his own foolish choices except for this one. He is not to return to this land. If he tries I will know. It will not be safe to be near him in that event."

"I will do my best to help in this matter, if the general will listen to what I tell him." Antoine could hardly believe he was saying such a thing. "But please tell me if the Mameluks are gathering to strike at the French. I'd like to know."

"The Mameluk power in this land is over. They will make feeble attempts, but the plague and the French army will keep them from taking control again. This city is not safe. There will still be suffering here, for all people. I only wish it would not be so." Much of the flame in his eyes died away.

At last he turned to Francois, who was watching wide-eyed as the scene unfolded. "Antoine will always be your friend," Amun-Ra told him. "He is trustworthy and will help you when life is difficult, and I know that you will be there for him as well."

Napoleon slumped in an agony of conflict and rage. He was not used to being ignored or slandered.

"I will go now. Be at peace," Amun-Ra directed his final comment to the scholars, and melted into the far wall.

Napoleon turned immediately to the two minions. "Get my guards in here and then go as far as you can from me! Never let me see you again!"

Antoine placed the staff between himself and the general and spoke boldly. "That is not the plan, as you well know. We will go with you to France, and I will make sure that you go. You have no power over Amun-Ra."

Napoleon recoiled visibly. Then he spoke again, more cautiously and carefully, but still with a cold, resentful tone. "I will contact your senior officer and let you know as soon as a ship is ready. We will sail from here at the next opportunity."

"I must hold you to this promise. Be sure you fulfill it," Antoine replied.

"What I have told you I will do," Napoleon answered flatly. He turned and walked through the door he had entered.

Francois and Antoine left the palace and the garden. They walked back to the river leisurely. Francois watched his friend with cautious regard, but by the time they reached the water they were laughing about some of the events in that room, and Antoine seemed to return to his former self. They took a small craft that was idle on the shore and slowly, laboriously rowed to the other side.

Chapter Twelve

1922 A D

The game of senet was progressing slowly. Hessie tossed the sticks and earned a four. She clapped her hands gleefully, made her move, and handed the little sticks to Moon. He shrugged and smiled. She was winning, but it made no difference. He threw the sticks with abandon.

They were sitting at a marble table in a large garden, actually a huge garden with no boundaries to be seen. Limitless green lawns filled with multi-colored flower beds and perfect trees rolled along toward the horizon backed by hills and wonderfully craggy snow-capped mountains. And water was everywhere; streams and ponds and fountains, a central feature of this land of bliss and harmony. It was a place of pure delight and uninterrupted time. Or was it a dream? They could not be sure.

It was, as they had always hoped, their final resting place where their kas had come to live on with the gods of the universe forever. A place of purity and love, but also a place of interest and excitement, if such things could be called by those names. There were endless activities they could enjoy, new ones all the time, people they could visit, and always, always, the presence of the Great God Amun-Ra to fill their hearts with tales of wonder and exultation. It was the life of perfection they had been promised while they lived in Thebes; another life that was anything but perfect, until they died years apart and found each other again in this timeless wonderland. They had no idea that a small crack was developing in their paradise.

Howard Carter arrived in Egypt in 1891, a seventeen year old with unusual artistic skills that were called upon to draw artifacts taken from Beni Hasan, an ancient cemetery near Al Minya. He stayed. His work at major excavations led to his appointment, in 1899, as the first Chief Inspector of the Egyptian Antiquities Service. He worked primarily in Thebes then, but was known all over the land. A young man of promise, he had the new, exciting world of Egyptology at his feet. That was often a literal position. He loved to dig and work in the sand and dirt. Howard was going somewhere, everyone knew, and he continued to climb for a few years. Then set-backs came into the picture, but he still dreamed the dreams of fame and fortune that drove so many men and, in the newly liberated environment, women, to Egypt for 'the dig.'

Howard went to work for George Herbert, better known as Lord Carnarvon, in 1907, and they partnered at various digs from that time, but it wasn't until 1922 that the world at large knew Carter's name and his fame became so great - the proverbial flash-in-the-pan - that most people in the knowledgeable world had heard of him within two months of his discovery of a wonderful tomb, that of Pharaoh Tutankhamun, in November of 1922. He was at once a great hero who provided enlightenment to Egyptologists, and the nemesis of Pharaoh Tutankhamun, known as 'the boy king,' who was only nine when he ascended the throne and died a short ten years later. It was Carter who nearly destroyed the idyllic afterlife of Hessie and Moon.

Hussein, a man of short stature and a strong back, carried water for several digs in the valley where many of the ancient kings had been buried. He wore a yoke that stretched from shoulder to shoulder, and heavy water buckets hung on both sides. He used a common gourd, cut in half and dried, to dispense the drinks, which thirsty men used to pour water into their mouths. The gourd was attached to his yoke by a length of cord. His equipment was simple, but he was indispensable to the dig. Hussein scaled the hillsides without spilling a drop. Even though the buckets were covered they were prone to sloshing water out during a steep descent, but Hussein knew the tricks for preserving it for the men who dug the trenches and moved the sands away with careful hands. Carter insisted on hand work whenever a fragment or a larger artifact was discovered.

On a day in early November in the auspicious year of 1922, Hussein worked his way carefully across an open space near a new dig, the drinking gourd swinging from its yoke on a frayed cord. His buckets were full, and he was careful. He turned away from the path a few steps to pause and lean against a pile of rubble to catch his breath before climbing to the next group of workers when the cord caught on something and snapped. The gourd rolled across the ground and sank into a small hole among the gravelly stones on the surface. Hussein took off the heavy water buckets and pulled the yoke from his shoulders to use it to rescue the drinking vessel. He wouldn't put his arm down the hole; the clever cobra of Egypt, the asp, was a master of hiding from the heat of the sun in such a cleft. He had seen too many of them slithering out of that kind of place to take the chance. He prodded and poked with the end of the yoke until the dry, sandy earth gave way and made a much larger hole. He stared into it, locating the gourd a little further below, and began prying with the yoke it bring it out, causing much more of the earth to give way. He could still see his objective on a level space just below and made one more attempt. The whole area caved in. The waterman jumped back to avoid falling into the hole himself. The gourd was still visible, lying on a smooth, flat surface that was coated with chunks of gravelly dust. As Hussein leaned down to retrieve his prize he noticed a sharp edge near the gourd, another even place with an edge just below, and then another and another, until he realized he had found an unknown staircase lying just beneath the top of the seemingly solid terrain.

"Sayyid Carter!" he called loudly. "Sayyid Carter! Heyna! Heyna!"

Howard Carter, who was in the midst of digging a trench on a hillside only a hundred yards away, heard the cry with its clear message of excitement and hurried to the spot. That cry soon became one of the defining moments of Carter's life and one of the greatest in the history of Egypt and archaeology and the world. The steps led to the small but nearly intact tomb of an unknown pharaoh, Tutankhamun, who had lived and ruled more than three millennia in the past.

Moon sipped his wine from a silver goblet as he sat watching the play of light in the trees and on the ponds nearby. Everything was still, no wind, no sound except for the plashing water as it fell from a lovely natural basin not far away, and he was satisfied. Almost. Something had come to his attention that was slightly troubling, but he brushed it away as well as he could. He wouldn't tell Hessie. There was no reason for her to be disturbed. At the moment she was napping in the small grove across the lawn. He could see her there, dark hair loose and falling round her shoulders, and his love for her felt a moment of intensity as he gazed. She was more than she had ever been to him, and as he often did, he thought of the first time he knew that he loved her. Just after their wedding, when she was so sweet and solicitous to his concerns and longings. That had never changed, and he was amazed. Time didn't exist as it once had, but he understood that it was ages ago that they had married. "Still the same after all that," he thought. His afterlife was far better than he had ever expected it would be.

Still the small shadow troubled him. He had dreams recently, dreams that someone was ripping his house down and he could do nothing about it. Of course, they had no house in their new life. They lived in nature, sleeping when they wanted to, but having no physical need to sleep. The bed was in the grove, and they were always untroubled there. Sleep was probably a comfort from the past, but he believed that someday they would both forget that habit and simply do other things with their limitless time. Was it truly limitless? He didn't know nor care. It was enough for the present to live as they did.

Carter refilled the steps after he was sure that they led to an entrance and posted guards along with strong threats, a thing all Egyptologists had learned to do. He sent a telegram to Lord Carnarvon and asked him to come immediately. All was excitement for both men about the find, and the lord responded that he would arrive on the twenty-sixth day of August. As yet Carter had no clear idea of what lay ahead. If it were a big tomb it could take months to get into all of the rooms. He didn't think it was big. It lay somewhat sandwiched next to the tomb of Ramses IX which had been prepared years later, one of the reasons the entrance he had found remained hidden for so long. There were plenty of others close at hand as well; Tutankhamun, although that name was still a mystery to him, seemed to lie at a crossroads of the ancient site, and the tomb would have been noticed by thieves at a much earlier time if it hadn't been up against so many others. "It must be small," he told himself. "I only hope it hasn't been seriously plundered."

When the lord arrived, Carter was prepared. He had completed the dig to the point where a sealed door that opened into the passage waited for the lord and his lady to arrive in Thebes. His intuition told him that this could be a major find, his first important discovery in the valley, and he was in a state of nerves when the lord finally appeared and they could get on with the business of opening the door. On the twenty-eighth day of November, Carter and his benefactor, along with Lady Carnarvon, looked into the first room for the first time. The tiny opening the archaeologist made in the door revealed gleams of gold, lots of gold, and Carter knew that at last his vision and hard work had paid off lavishly. It didn't take him long to get into all the other chambers, and they were all filled with fantastic treasures. It was when the tomb was entirely opened that Amun-Ra entered the scene.

"You have nothing to fear, Moon," Amun-Ra told him, using his familiar name. "Carter has opened your enclosure, but you have made it safely through time to this place, and there is no reason to be troubled."

Moon wasn't sure, which Amun-Ra credited to human nature, but took the word of the great god. "I have no idea what's happening there. I'd like to know, of course, but if it isn't needed, then I won't think about it anymore."

"Yes, it is better that way." Amun-Ra, in his familiar lion guise, crouched along the edge of the lawn.

"I wonder what they'll do with all the things I collected?" Hessie asked. "I hope they'll just leave them in place. How long has it all been there, anyway?"

"Since you have asked, I will tell you. It is over three thousand years by your measure since you directed the items to go into the tomb."

Moon gasped. "Three thousand! I thought maybe a hundred! Are all my things still there? Or have they gone to dust?"

"Everything is still intact. The dryness of your enclosure assured that. They seem to think it will go into a museum," Amun-Ra answered. "That is a place where they keep an assortment of things from the past and people come to see them."

"But why would they want to?" Hessie questioned. "All the people in the palace use the same kind of things every day, except for the special burial furnishings." She had little thought that peasants would ever have an interest in such objects.

"Conditions are very different now, Hessie, and people are different as well." Amun-Ra didn't mention that there was no more 'palace.'

"How?" She asked, her wide eyes curious.
"It is hard to explain. They have 'progressed,' as they call it, and they have made so many new devices that you would not recognize the place."

"Is it possible to go there? I have no desire except to see that Moon's possessions are properly cared for. That means a lot to me."

"You have the power to go, but I do not think it a good idea."

"Can you tell me why?"

"Not directly, but it could cause you to become unhappy with the way matters are now. In Thebes, I mean, not here."

"Well, then, I don't think I need to see it. Thank you for helping us understand." She bowed from the waist as was her custom, and the lion moved slowly away.

"You need to forget all that now," he said. "Rest your mind. All will be well."

But neither Moon nor Hessie was completely satisfied. The words of Amun-Ra continued to play in their thoughts. "You have the power to go - - -"

Carter's invasion of the tomb continued steadily. As he opened each new door he found wondrous pieces in every room; things that Tutankhamun had used daily, or at least frequently, and in the burial chamber the wall paintings told parts of the story of his life. He, along with Hessie, was prominent in all of them. There were no beautifully lined, repetitious miniatures extending from the entrance through all the passages as some tombs contained, but there had been little time for works of art. The ceilings were barren of the wonderful star-fields that had been done for previous kings, and there were few depictions of the gods. Not even a reference was made to the ceremony for Tutankhamun's heart as Anubis weighed it in the balance, one of the focal events in the afterlife. But these omissions didn't indicate a lack of respect. Time, which pressed so tenaciously on everything associated with life on the earth, had almost run out, and Hessie had not had enough of that particular commodity to do all the things she had longed to do for her beloved Moon. It was fortunate that she would never see the tomb again, nor be able to recall the sparse wall decorations of the rooms that would accompany the pharaoh on his voyage into eternity.

All the objects that could be stuffed into the spaces were there, however. She had tried to account for all his needs as his earth-life continued into the afterlife. She had done well, and she knew it. The glittering that Carter and the lord and lady saw through the peep-hole was a tribute to Hessie as well as Moon. She was consumed with the project of furnishing the tomb, and went to the limit the space would bear. All the small statuary, the vases and golden ornaments as well as the larger panels of gold had been included to provide the lushest possible environment for the king. He should lack nothing, she determined. The ointments and perfumes and some of the other, more easily disposable items had been stolen soon after Tutankhamun was buried, but they were only a tiny portion of the riches within those chambers.

Carter went through the whole and catalogued them with meticulous care. He alone seemed to understand the importance of the find during the first few weeks following the opening, and he alone was responsible for the disruption of the life that Pharaoh Tutankhamun was enjoying in the hereafter.

"Your things," Amun-Ra told them, "are in the grove over there. Go and change into them, and we will transfer soon."

Hessie and Moon changed quickly and returned to the lawn wearing the robes that they found lying across the bed. Hessie wore heavy sandals, but Moon was barefoot. Amun-Ra looked them over. He was now changed himself, into the woman with flaming eyes who had spoken the ominous words so long before: "Beware the carter." His eyes held very little flame this time.

"I don't know what to do with this," Hessie held up a long hood. "Am I supposed to wear it?"

"Yes, it goes over your head."

"Won't it be too hot?"

"All women wear such things in Kmet now," the god told her. "It is their current fashion." He didn't think it necessary to offer any further explanation. "It is the cool season, so you should not be overly warm."

Hessie pulled the strange thing over her head. Only her face remained visible. "Is this right?" she asked.

"Yes. Now I will put this one on and we can go." Amun-Ra settled a long caftan over his robes, and his eyes grew even dimmer. "We are ready."

Moon wore much the same kind of clothing he had used for a disguise on the night they had escaped to the festival of Hor-em-akhet, except that his robe was longer. At the last moment Amun-Ra produced some worn sandals. "You need these. There are sharp bits of stone we will have to walk upon." Moon slid them onto his feet.

They were instantly in the Valley of the Kings. Hessie gave a gasping cry, but Moon couldn't make a sound. The people pressed around them; strange looking men in tattered gallabeyas which swept the ground, a few women far behind the surge of men, covered in long, flowing black except for their eyes, and some other people were of such outlandish appearance that Hessie and Moon had no reference for them. Women, obviously women, but with strange dresses of bright colors and patterns, shoes that were totally unfit for walking on the landscape of the valley, and strange things on their heads that seemed more decorative than protective, hats of various patterns and styles with all kinds of decorations pinned to their tops; wide brims and small brims and no brims at all, a statement of fashion Hessie had never before seen or thought of.

Conveyances, which chugged about spouting clouds of smoky fumes, were noisy and yet amusing; their bodies were made of some kind of formed metal, Moon realized, but for what purpose were the little doors with their short silver handles and transparent tops? Surely it would be better for the carriages to remain open to allow easier passage for entering and leaving? He couldn't understand why people should have gone to this extent to ensure a private journey. There were strange-looking fixtures that seemed to provide light as well.

He looked around the area and saw unfamiliar tools for cutting stone. Men using those tools were working on the site located up the hill beyond his former 'house.' It was all unreal, confusing, foul smelling, and ugly. "Thebes is ruined," he thought. "How could they have done this?" It was a totally different place from what he held in his memory.

A tall man came along with a man and woman who were dressed in what must have been the finery of the times. They walked along the narrow gravel path, and then paused at the top of the newly discovered stairway. Bright lights flared as many men and a few women held black boxes up, flashed dazzling beams toward the three dignitaries, and then stepped back into the front of the crowd as the man Amun-Ra identified as Carter spoke in the strangest language they had ever heard. He sounded guttural, but there were some unaccented sounds as well, and some that were lilting to the ear. Not at all like their native Kmetian tongue.

Amun-Ra passed the words along in translation. "He is telling them that the contents of the tomb will be brought out today. Everything is marked and ready for the Egyptian Museum to receive the collection, as he calls it."

Hessie started to move forward. Amun-Ra made no attempt to prevent her. Moon followed, and the three stepped along the path slowly, working their way ahead until they came to the place where Hessie had stopped to watch the furnishings as they were taken into the tomb ages ago. She would see them all again as they came out, carried past the crowd to be placed into wagons that waited in the rear, which would take everything to the museum. It was a simple move, as transfers go, but one filled with trepidation for the pharaoh and his wife.

One by one they came forth, the large pieces along with the miniatures, and Hessie examined every one of them with her eyes. They were little damaged, some were even in the same condition as they had gone into the tomb, and most were only slightly different. The patina of years was upon them, but how could it have been otherwise? They were all lovely things, she saw as they were carried past, and still delighted the eyes of the crowd as they came along, carried by many different hands, but there were no priests there to venerate them as they entered a secular time in their existence.

Moon felt as if his house were collapsing, and his legs were hardly strong enough to keep him up for the length of time it took to remove everything, and for Hessie to be satisfied. There was one great concern he bore, but he carried it silently. What would happen when his sarcophagus and mummy were carried forth from their long vigil in the tomb? He could not even guess. Amun-Ra had assured him that he was safe in the afterlife, but how could he be sure? So much was dependent upon that single moment. Moon waited.

The parade of furnishings came to a halt after four hours. Hessie concluded that everything had been removed, but the crowd waited expectantly and there was no word. Finally, Carter himself appeared from the depths of the burial chamber, covered with the dust and sand of the centuries, and spoke to the waiting assembly. "Lord Carnarvon and I have discussed this for a few days, and have made a decision, along with the Egyptian Department of Antiquities, that the remains of the Pharaoh Tutankhamun should stay on in their place within his tomb. We do not wish to desecrate his rest there, and when the tomb is opened for public viewing, you may see his wonderful golden mask and the great stone sarcophagus that holds his mummy, although his mummy will not be open for public display. That is the conclusion of this amazing day." Carter seemed stunned at having completed the transfer so easily.

Hessie watched Moon during the announcement, and he seemed to sag but did not fall when Carter declared that they would not remove his earthly remains from the crypt. Amun-Ra extended an arm for support, and Moon recovered soon after. He had been desperately worried regarding his fate, Hessie knew, but wouldn't say a word to her about it.

The crowd dispersed slowly, leisurely, as though a great entertainment had ended and left them reluctant to find their way home. Hessie and Moon and Amun-Ra waited silently, gazing toward the tomb until the guards approached to say that the area would soon close. They turned away then, hesitantly, and walked up a small slope until they were whisked back to their eternal garden where Amun-Ra stalked around as a lion.

It was soon after their return that Hessie accepted an invitation to a visit with many of the ancients of Kmet. Moon begged off; he wasn't ready yet to talk about his experience in the valley, and did not want to be questioned by people who refused to go back and look for themselves. For him it was an issue of proper behavior, and he also had no intention of becoming an expert on Kmet as it stood in this new time of the early twentieth century, something that a few people believed he should be after the visit. His eternal house was disturbed, but he himself had not been, and that was enough for common knowledge.

"The general was there," Hessie told him on her return. "He asked about you."

"Eb? I suppose he wanted to gloat. He wasn't left intact, either, you know." Eb was the nickname for Horemheb.

"No, he wanted to tell you something. He's seen Lord Carnarvon."

"Where?"

"Here. He died very recently in Thebes. In a hospital there."

"A hospital? What's that?"

"A place where they treat sick people."

"So he got sick and died. Everybody does that."

"Yes, and now he wants to meet you. Thinks that would be a closure to his life, I guess."

"I don't want to meet him. I've seen him and didn't really like what I saw. He tried to ruin me, too."

"No. He wanted to save you. Carter was the one who wanted the ruin. No, not really. He had no idea what he was doing."

"I don't want to see any of them yet."

"You can't hide forever, Moon. Get over it. You're still here, and that's all that matters."

Moon didn't respond. Other things mattered, too, he thought. But Hessie wanted to go out more and see lots of people. He was just about sick of people. Especially after Thebes. He had no reason to meet anybody for a while.

"You really need to see him, Moon. He has some things to talk over with you."

No, he didn't want to see anybody. Not yet. Wait a while. A good, long while.

"What things?" he asked.

Before Moon had much time to think, Eb came across the wide lawn, looking happily satisfied with himself over something. Moon greeted him halfway.

"Hello Eb. It's good to see you again."

"Are you sure about that?" Eb responded. "You've been hiding here, I take it."

"Well, yes, in a way. But I can never do it for long. Hessie pushes me out soon enough."

"Good for her. Did she tell you the news?"

"About Carnarvon?"

Eb nodded.

"Yes. She says he wants to see me."

"Yes, he does. That's why I'm here. He asked me to come tell you, and he wants to meet you more than anyone has wanted anything for a long time."

"I wonder why?" was all Moon could say.

"He thinks you caused his death."

"What?" Moon was mystified.

"Yes, he thinks you cursed him for taking your tomb apart!" Eb smiled. "Did you?"

"Not that I know of."

"He says everybody in Luxor – that's the new name for Thebes - is scared of you and that Carter fears every shadow. They're calling Carnarvon's death 'The Curse of The Pharaoh's Mummy.'"

Moon smiled, then he tried to choke back a laugh but couldn't. Then he guffawed loudly and ended up sinking to his knees on the lawn, laughing until tears flowed. Eb laughed with him. Laughter is said to have healing powers, and in those moments Moon was freed from the resentments he had felt toward both Carter and Carnarvon, as well as the host of people who surrounded him in the valley near his tomb, and even his suspicions of Amun-Ra. He had never enjoyed a long laugh so much in all his years, and he felt renewed after, even though his coughing and wheezing took a while to stop. Hessie had come out of the grove and watched as the two men were struggling for breath. No one was happier than she, although she didn't laugh nearly so well as her Moon. They came toward her, walking with staggering steps as the wonders of laughter enfolded them again and again, and she was content at last.

Not many hours could have passed, although no one measured hours there, before the three looked up and saw a man slowly working his way across the sloping lawn. He paused and looked at them, then waved, and came on to the grassy path that led to the marble topped table where they were enjoying a cheerful lunch. Moon rose to meet him.

"I'm Carnarvon," the visitor said, bowing. "And you must be the Pharaoh Tutankhamun. I am so glad to meet you at last."

The pharaoh inclined his head toward the visitor in response. "Hello, George," he said. "There's no need to bow. We're all the same here. Let me shake your hand. I'm Moon."

Chapter Thirteen

2012 A D

The old man got off the bus at the Sphinx Coffee House and headed down the slope toward the ancient lion. He moved slowly, according to his age, using the primordial staff in his hand as a prop. The wall that surrounded the sphinx was not new but had been added only a century before, and there was no longer the open access to the beast the ancients had enjoyed. He wanted to leap over the wall and touch the great forelegs and the flank of the creature, but that was something he could no longer do physically, even if he defied the rules. Now visitors had only a 'look but don't touch' encounter; an enforced, impersonal meeting with the gigantic statue since the middle of the twentieth century. Hor-em-akhet himself did not like it, as the old man knew, but was unable to convince the human powers who protected his decaying body. They wanted him to remain with them forever, if they could only gain sufficient controls over men and weather to accomplish their goal. The old man shrugged visibly and leaned against the outer wall.

The staff had not spoken for decades, not since Omar, the old man, had first taken possession of it, but he had no doubts about the power that it wielded. Amun-Ra might be silent, but there was a brooding watchfulness that he felt as he carried the staff with him, and at times it glowed or vibrated just a little in his hand. That was enough, and Omar was satisfied.

The old man lived in Giza, down near the magnificent Nile, in a small room in a house owned by Mrs. Nabila. It wasn't a perfect house in ideal condition, but she kept it clean and even did his laundry once a week, keeping all his clothing, including his suit and ties, in good order. He always looked spruce, and he was grateful. He did not pay her directly; the government sent her a check once or twice a year (he didn't know the frequency of the payments) and he had lived there for over twenty years. Both he and Mrs. Nabila were old now, but she had her younger daughters who also lived in the house to help her, so the work was not too much. His small room was not connected directly to the house, but in what had once been a shed in the back. For that reason Mrs. Nabila was able to allow him to live there without concern. It would be impossible for him to share a space within the same walls where a widow dwelt. He smiled at the thought. Sometimes people were bound by such silly rules.

Now he was visiting his old friend, the sphinx, and it was time to concentrate on his purpose and his message. He had come to say good-bye. It would not be a sad parting, but one of mutual consent, and his friend could do nothing but agree. They had known each other for so long, from Omar's perspective, that there was a strong attachment, but the sphinx was accustomed to losing his friends and did not take it too seriously. Although they would see each other no longer, they would always stay in communication. The sphinx was well acquainted with many people who had gone before, and there would always be more movement across the undefined time-lines in the future. The old man adjusted his skull cap and concentrated on the deeply furrowed body of the lion that waited before him on the sandy rock.

Their final parting was gentle. There was no need for intense emotion, and they let each other go with pleasant memories of the past and the surety of the future. Hor-em-akhet remained, eyes straight ahead on the distant horizon over the Mukottam Hills, watchful with no trace of sorrow, as resilient as ever. Omar shifted his gaze toward the pointed pyramid in the background at the very last moment; it was pointing out his pathway, he thought, toward the trail that Amun-Ra walked in the sky-fields, and Omar would soon be privileged to take that way, to cross the great river from the earth to the sky and meet, at last, the reality of the great god and the world that he had made for the hereafter. It was a soothing realization. He turned, almost without looking at Hor-em-akhet, and walked up the long slope past the Sphinx Coffee House to the place where he would board the bus. He waited on a bench with his back toward the sphinx. His good-byes were over.

Omar attended the mosque every day. He enjoyed the prayers. He felt at home among his friends and neighbors as they bowed in obedience to Qaranic law and asked Allah for blessings and benefits and that they might be found worthy. He had no conflict with Islam even though he kept his god-shelf active in his little room, and brought daily offerings to Amun-Ra. He thought of his spiritual life as extended beyond either religion; capturing the best of both, making them into one. Had there been conflict he would have come down on the side of the ancient one, Amun-Ra, but there was no conflict within his mind or spirit, and he was at home with the understanding he had developed over a long life. Now he would see it through to the end.

He rode away from the Giza Plateau and changed buses at the busy stop in central Giza, then went out to the Island of Zamalek and got off the bus near his favorite café; one that sat on the very brink of the great river and served him nearly every day. He had no money, but there he had no need to pay. He had been having tea, as he liked to call his meal, at that shop every day for at least twenty years, and had never paid. He was considered a holy man for some reason which was beyond his grasp, and the café owner asked him for his blessing whenever he saw him at the shop. Omar smiled at the memory. They always placed him at the best table available, where he enjoyed the sounds of the water and the distant drone of traffic as it moved along the Corniche on the other bank. The western side of the river (its eastern flow was on the opposite verge of the island about a half-mile distant) was the stronger of the two, and it swept along toward the north with rapid splashes and swirls. The water was lovely and hypnotic to watch, and the old man spent at least an hour a day there, communicating in joy and wonder with the river. In many ways the water was as important to him as the great god and the sphinx. He often laughed at the wild tales it told with its distinct voice and antic behavior.

"The old man's here," one of the waiters told the cook. "What do you have for him today?"

"It's a lamb kebab, and some taamiyya. He likes both."

"I'll tell him."

The waiter met Omar at the gate. "Masaa' il-kheer!" he said in welcome. "Izzayyak?"

"Masaa' il-kheer," Omar responded. "Il hamdulillaa."

After the greetings the young man led him to a table against the green fence that bordered the water. It was a tall fence with iron spikes set at intervals, and was essential because the river tumbled along within a few inches on the other side. "We have a delicious lamb kebab today, and some taamiyya," he said to the old man. "And would you like tea or coffee?"

"Tea, please," Omar answered quickly.

There were only a few patrons at the restaurant at that hour. It was much too early for dinner and a little late for lunch, but Omar liked coming at that time. It was quiet, and he could concentrate on the voice of the water and understand its stories much easier then. He placed the staff against the fence and contemplated the water, an activity which never disappointed.

When the waiter brought his tea he sipped from the tiny glass, appreciating the strong, sweet drink; feeling both warmed and energized from its fragrance and flavor. "Tea is a thing of beauty," he repeated to himself for at least the hundredth time that year. His appreciation at times knew no bounds. As he waited for the food his ear caught a conversation at a neighboring table.

"But what will you do when that happens?" a man was saying. "Where can you go if you don't knuckle under and do what he wants you to do?"

"I don't know," the other man responded, "but I'm not going to give up my right to live the way I choose. He can force me out, and I may have to live with friends here and there, but I'm not going to stop protesting. None of us are."

The old man smiled. A young radical, or so they were called. Oh, how he wished that someone would call him an 'old radical!' But he hadn't the power to do what the young were doing. He no longer had the strength. He looked at the two; they were boys, mere boys, he thought, but they had the fire to overcome anything and to change the world. Inside himself he cheered them on.

His food came, along with some flat bread, and he tasted it with thanksgiving. The lamb was delicious, as the waiter had said, and he chewed cautiously as he continued his mental ruminations. He had said good-bye, at last, but what could it mean? He had thought it would mean his transition to another place or another life, however that could be interpreted. He wasn't sure, but things didn't seem to have reached that point yet, and he had no strong desire to be done with this life, anyway. He was old, perhaps, but he wasn't sure he wanted to go on anytime soon.

The river drew his attention. He watched it surging along the bank, foaming in swirls against some roots that extended into the water. It was green, but a putrid grey-green, polluted and smelly, especially in the city, and he thought of the past when the water was clean and fresh.

Nile Blue, as it was known. But not now. Not for over a hundred years. And most of the fish had died. Those that remained were dangerous, although some people still ate them. 'Mercurial' water. He smiled at the reference word. A double entendre. It was a suitable description.

He still loved the river. It had become dangerous through no fault of its own, and did not love the things that people had done to make it so. He touched his staff to speak to the water, but his hand started shaking. "What is this?" he asked himself the question. He wanted to stand; his feet and legs refused to move. He struggled for a few seconds. Why was his body making a rebellion? Then he knew. It was its final rebellion, so he relaxed in his chair and smelled the lovely aroma of the lamb and the taamiyya, willing it to fill his nose and his mind with the perception of a good meal even though he could no longer eat. He sat breathing it in for what seemed to be several minutes. Then a sensation of strange new proportions took him, and he became dizzy along with a great desire to sleep. He moved the plate out of the way with his right hand and slowly, tenderly, placed his head on the table where the plate had been. The café seemed to be rising and falling as though he were in the water, bobbing up and down, and he closed his eyes. The motion soon mellowed out and became much more pleasant.

The young men at the table nearby looked at him with curiosity. One waved his arm for a waiter and pointed to the old man. The waiter came quickly when he noticed that the man had his head on the table, and he touched his shoulder.

"Sir, sir, - - Do you need some help, sir?"

Omar made a small sound, an attempt at speech, but it was unsuccessful. He gave it up.

The waiter returned to the kitchen, and came back with another man who looked at the old man carefully, examined him with his eyes but without touching him. "I don't think he's conscious," he said. "Check his pulse." The waiter felt the wrist which dangled toward the floor. Then he felt the old man's neck. There was no sense of heartbeat.

"Should we call an ambulance?" he asked.

"It seems like we should."

The second man, who was the manager, went into his tiny office to make the call while the two young men and the waiter watched Omar intently for a sign of movement. There was none.

Omar was swimming. He had joined with the great tide of the river and was gradually moving away with very little effort on his part. The water was pleasant and smooth - and clean. He smelled and felt its purity and allowed his body to relax and float; there was little else to do. A great kadg came from nowhere and nudged him. There have been no crocodiles in this water for over a century, he thought. It did not seem unfriendly, nor did it seem to want him for a meal, but swam companionably along beside him, rising and falling in the soft, silky water. Omar wondered at this, but did not become alarmed. The kadg was joined by others. He found himself in the midst of a great school of the creatures as they made their way down the river together. A guard of kadg, he said to himself. Who could have guessed! He didn't recall having heard the name 'kadg' before. No matter. Were the old stories true? Had the priests of the

234

limitless past offered sacrifice to these kadg? Maybe he was to become one. No, he felt sure. Nothing like that.

The river flowed on, smooth and glossy, and he floated, gently bobbing on the top of the water as if it held him in its power. He saw his staff, his prehistoric staff, glide past. He wanted to reach out for it, but knew it was no longer his. It was headed for a new bearer, a new life. His diligence was ended. The thought gave him nothing but relief. He had grown tired over the years.

His mind drifted in much the same way that his body floated in the cool water for a time, until he looked ahead and saw an island. It was only a small island, surrounded by the enclosing water, but it shimmered with its own light, or so it seemed. As he was washed along toward it, the kadg drifted off to either side and his feet found the sand of a small beach. He rose, wet from the water, and walked up the strand until he reached a grassy field and saw the tree. It towered above the island and the river, glowing in the light of mid-afternoon, its green leaves translucent in the sun. He thought he recognized the tree although he knew he had never seen it before. It was the only tree on the island.

A lion whose entire body glowed stepped out from behind the tree. Omar had never seen the lion either, but he knew him. He bowed quickly, and then stood up straight to make sure he didn't miss anything.

"Hello Omar," the lion said. "I hope you have had a pleasurable journey."

Made in the USA
Columbia, SC
27 April 2023